All the
Seas
of the
World

# All the
# Seas
## of the
# World

## Gayla Reid

A Novel

Stoddart

Copyright © 2001 by Gayla Reid

All rights reserved. No part of this publication may be reproduced or transmitted in any form or by any means, electronic or mechanical, including photocopying, recording, or any information storage and retrieval system, without permission in writing from the publisher.

Published in 2001 by Stoddart Publishing Co. Limited
895 Don Mills Road, 400-2 Park Centre, Toronto, Canada M3C 1W3
180 Varick Street, 9th Floor, New York, New York 10014

*Distributed by*:
General Distribution Services Ltd.
325 Humber College Blvd., Toronto, Ontario M9W 7C3
Tel. (416) 213-1919    Fax (416) 213-1917
Email cservice@genpub.com

05 04 03 02 01 1 2 3 4 5

**Canadian Cataloguing in Publication Data**

Reid, Gayla
All the seas of the world

ISBN 0-7737-3280-2

I. Title.

PS8585.E5A84 2001    C813'.54    C00-932874-2
PR9199.3.R44A84 2001

An excerpt from this novel appeared in slightly different form in *Meanjin*, volume 57, number 3, 1998.

Jacket design: Angel Guerra
Text design: Tannice Goddard

THE CANADA COUNCIL | LE CONSEIL DES ARTS
FOR THE ARTS | DU CANADA
SINCE 1957 | DEPUIS 1957

*We acknowledge for their financial support of our
publishing program the Canada Council, the Ontario Arts
Council, and the Government of Canada through the
Book Publishing Industry Development Program (BPIDP).*

Printed and bound in Canada

*For Barry*

*All the seas of the world
tumbled about her heart.*

— JAMES JOYCE, "EVELINE," *DUBLINERS*

*I*t was Martín who suggested it.

"Is there a way up to the roof?"

"I think so," Deirdre said. "There's a ladder that goes up past the kitchen windows."

They are home because of the curfew.

Out there, somewhere, is the *whump whump* of mortar fire, followed by the exploding screech of rockets.

The fire escape is thin as a spider. Deirdre has seen Ong Ba using it. An old man, Ong Ba tends the garden. She hasn't thought about what he does on the roof. Cleans out the eaves probably, checks the tiles.

Up they go, Deirdre and Martín, one by one, in case the ladder can't take their combined weight. They look out towards Cholon, where the sky is bright with orange flares and, from time to time, red tracers.

On a flat part of the roof, they sit down carefully on the tiles.

Martín says, "*Venid a ver la sangre por las calles.*"

Deirdre looks over at him, to be told:

"Come and see the blood in the streets."

She listens to Martín saying this: the Spanish words, then the English. There is something in Martín's voice that in recent months she had chosen to shut out.

I am talking about a form of seduction.

⁓

All the time Deirdre was in Vietnam, I was a teacher at a secondary school in a small town on the north coast of New South Wales.

The school was a few blocks away from the sand dunes, the bright surf. I stood in the classroom, and outside, those few blocks away, limitless lines of breakers thundered in from South America. The sun shone brilliantly.

In the morning the boys came to school already dazzled from hours of surfing before breakfast. At lunchtime they cycled down to check the waves. As soon as school was out they would be back in the water: not scholars but "boardies." That was what they were, what they wanted to be.

In the classroom, they listened to me with restraint. The sea was on their left, my right. I noticed how often they looked out that way; their heads were full of the ocean.

There were no stones on their beach, only densely packed fine white sand. To walk upon it was like walking into heaven.

At the beach on most days, a young man stood at the edge of the waves. For hours, he cast a pretend fishing line into the surf. Cast it, then reeled it in. He had a real plastic bucket into which he dropped his imaginary fish.

I was interested in him because he reminded me of Deirdre's mother.

During the day he would move up and down the beach, checking the wind and waves, selecting the best place to fish. I watched him gather up his gear, his fishing line and bucket.

"I wonder why he does that?" I said to my husband. "Whatever has happened to make him so obsessed?"

Our house, the house of my marriage, was small and white and wooden. From the laundry, you could see the ocean, the line of breakers. Our backyard was at the edge of a paperbark swamp, out of which large black cockatoos rose up and cried out.

A place of utter beauty. A place in which I was beginning to realize that my marriage was a failure. Sometimes I managed to forget. Then I remembered again and was filled with a sick disbelief.

Other people's marriages fall apart, I told myself. Other people's.

I'd come home from school and there it would be, waiting for me. Like a lifesaver, like a rope thrown out into the water: an airmail letter, from Vietnam, from Deirdre.

*Dear Bernie*, she wrote.

My name is Bernadette Behan. I know heaps of Lourdes jokes: the miracles of water.

I was a completely inexperienced teacher. Sometimes in the classroom I said things simply to amuse myself. I did not yet realize that this is fatal, that what is needed is a voice that indicates by its own certainty where something stops and something else begins.

We were earnest, Deirdre and I.

When I received a letter from Deirdre, when I wrote to her, I sought out a spot I had claimed for myself on the headland, a private nest high in a rocky outcrop surrounded on three sides by the Pacific. Above was the southern sky, blue with its own distances. Between these two immensities, our exchanges took place.

That's how earnest.

Immediately before this story opens, Deirdre was in love with an Australian soldier, and then he was killed.

After that, she left Vung Tau and went back to Saigon.

We are at the end of 1967.

It is just before Tet, before Martín.

1

*H*e went down a tunnel and disappeared.

His name was Ron Ryan and he was with the First Battalion, Royal Australian Regiment.

They blew the tunnel but they never found him. Not a whiff, not a whisker.

She left Vung Tau, an old colonial resort with its beaches, with its ramshackle Grand Hotel on the esplanade, open to smooth easterly breezes coming in off the South China Sea. Vung Tau was close to the Australian lines, and it was alive with Australian soldiers coming in, getting drunk, getting laid, carousing and grumbling and going away again.

She'd taken a room in Vung Tau to be near Ron. In his dry speech she'd heard the geography of home, which left so much silent, open.

When she returned to Saigon she moved into a place down by the river, the Royale. It was where the British journalists went, those who were too cheap or too adventurous for the Majestic. The Royale was a dump.

Before Ron vanished, she'd been sending home pieces on the wire service, she'd been filing regularly. There had been at that time much talk of an expanded role for the Australian troops, of moving them out of Phuoc Tuy province into other areas of the war. Everyone knew the Americans had parked the Aussies in Phuoc Tuy because they believed the area to be insignificant — one of their many miscalculations.

All this was her material, and there had been stories for the taking. But after Ron, she no longer made inquiries. She stopped working.

Being with Ron had made plain that this was no business of hers, that nothing she could write would ever be honest, would ever make sense of the war, either to herself or to others.

She was afraid she had lost her grip on the truth.

When they could postpone it no longer, when it came time for Ron to push off — his phrase — he would take a shower. She would get out his shirt, which during his brief time with her had been washed and ironed by an expert, a Vietnamese.

She'd press her nose into the cotton, listening to the noise of the shower. As long as she could hear the water running, it was still happening, he was still with her. In the freshness of the cotton, she searched for and found his smell.

He finished; he turned off the taps. It was beginning to be over.

She listened to him stepping out of the shower. Sometimes he hummed a tune at this point, but mostly not.

When he started getting dressed, putting on his clothes, she would insist on buttoning his shirt for him. Ron would adjust it, moving away from her a little. Taking his body away from her, back to the war.

But now she could not remember how Ron's shirt had felt in her fingers. When she buttoned it up for him, before he moved away from her, before he left her. She could not recall the exact texture of the cotton, laundered and pressed.

There had been no such thing as ordinary time, dull in-between time. Every time was the last time, that was the whole point.

So how could she have forgotten?

Because she was not working she was going broke.

The Corsican who ran the Royale divined something of her situation. He gave her one of the cheapest rooms, at the back, overlooking the rear courtyard.

One morning at breakfast she was seated near the wrought-iron grille that separated the dining room from the staff area and she overheard the Corsican murmuring to the Vietnamese cook.

"The Australian girl," he said in French, "the poor little Australian girl. She has lost a friend of the heart."

Covertly, both cook and Corsican sent her tender glances.

The cook had problems of his own. His children — or at least the children for whom he was now permanently responsible — roamed the staff area behind the iron grille. His entire village, it seemed, had come to live in the back courtyard of the hotel.

She waits until the rain has stopped, in mid-afternoon. Then she walks up to the Caravelle, along the crowded street, which is dense with the basic smell of Saigon: rotting garbage, exhaust, and something else, a smell like wet cardboard; above that, and mixing it with it, jasmine and gardenia, a surprising, uneasy sweetness.

The road itself seethes with old taxis, cyclos, motorcycles, bicycles, minibuses with Lambretta engines, large army trucks, smaller fruit-and-vegetable trucks, police jeeps in bottle-green and white. A few large American cars. All of them propelled by the honking of horns and the ringing of bicycle bells.

Deirdre walks along the footpath, dodging the Honda scooters that bump up in front of her at intersections. She walks beside the street stalls, which are selling cigarettes, American chewing gum, Vietnamese sweets, and — strangely, it seems to her — ampoules of sterilized water. On the walls are signs in Vietnamese, in red and white. They are government signs, and they are saying something about the war, she doesn't know what.

She picks her way around the rolls of barbed wire (to be pulled across the street at curfew), moving with the crowd: women carrying shoulder-poles with baskets at either end; slim young ARVN in their green-and-brown uniforms, laughing in groups or looking bored; children just let out of school, who in their sandals run down the shallow steps and burst out into the street behind a blaze of bougainvillea.

Often you see two girls on one bicycle.

*Just like us as kids*, she wrote. *I thought of you doubling me.*

Back in Kelly's Creek, I'd had a bicycle and she had not. I would stand and pedal and she would sit on the seat behind me, her legs dangling. We got about the countryside, Deirdre and I.

Sometimes I'd let her pedal, and I would swing my legs in the rush of air.

The letters she wrote to me described her room and the courtyard. She did not mention the death of Ron Ryan. She told me how she and Ron and Johnno went about as a threesome, seeking out the bars along the beachfront, ending up at the Grand. Coming back to Deirdre's hotel room, playing cards and drinking Fosters until Johnno said he reckoned he'd better leave them to it. All of them saying goodnight in a casual way that denied what each of them knew. Which was that Johnno would have taken Ron's place (gladly, gladly).

It was unintentional and unacted upon and nobody was to blame.

Would she have wanted Johnno? If it hadn't been for Ron? Johnno, who wouldn't look her in the eyes, who glanced over her shoulder, then swiftly down at her breasts.

Ron was coming down to Vungers. With Johnno. Couldn't he leave Johnno back at the Dat for once? She'd heard of blokes who took their mates along on the honeymoon. Great time had by all.

With her record player blaring, Deirdre took a shower, then slipped into her newest miniskirt, the one she'd had specially made out of real linen that smelled so good. She pushed her sunglasses up on her hair like a flyer, an aviatrix.

Easy to summon up the music: Vivaldi, thumping briskly away.

I see her, stepping out into the steaming late afternoon, slender, gold and green.

Shining hair. Her freckled face sunburned. (She really should be wearing a hat.)

Emerald green linen shift, to go with her eyes.

Slim long legs that emerge at mid-thigh.

Young.

Christ, *young.*

Deirdre walks through the streets with Ron on one side and Johnno on the other, making for the beach — the beach was the focal point, the destination to be reached — and knows she is desired.

Together they gave her this, Ron and Johnno. The one who had her and the other who didn't.

There was more to it than that. More than being desired.

In those early days in Vietnam, when she was first down in Vungers, she'd wake at daybreak, and as the room righted itself she'd realize where she was and be unable to believe her good fortune. She'd actually made it; she wasn't going to be stuck out in Woop Woop reporting on Pastures Protection Board meetings. Not now.

She was here, and she was sending stories home by Telex, out across the South China Sea.

And she wasn't even a C-grade journalist yet, just someone with an honours degree in history who knew a bloke who knew a bloke who toiled in the Australian embassy offices, in a corner suite of the Caravelle, right in the heart of Saigon.

It was far out, as the Americans said. It was too freaking much.

Deirdre paid attention to the banter that flowed easily between Johnno and Ron. They had a ritual of complaints, celebrated over cold beer. On such occasions they spoke with one voice.

"You know what happened at Bien Hoa, don't you?" Ron would say, addressing Deirdre simply as a formality, to get things going.

As regular army, they'd been in Bien Hoa with the First Battalion, Johnno and Ron. They'd had to work with the Yanks, who, to be quite frank, couldn't go two rounds with a revolving door.

Within three hundred feet of the Airborne perimeter at Bien Hoa, the Aussie patrol had come across a permanent VC camp.

"Out in the bush they hear a monkey fart and call in gunships to flatten the joint. Thousands of dollars up in smoke. Puff! Matter of minutes."

"Scares the monkey shitless but . . ."

"Wastage on an epic scale, mate. Bloody Roman Empire."

"Decline and fall of."

The narrative at this point reached a familiar resting place. Ron shook his head; Johnno sighed; they emptied their glasses.

"Things looked up when the pollies down in Canberra —"

"Those idle mongrels."

"— finally extracted the digit and gave the go-ahead for our own lines at the Dat."

They moved on to another of their themes: the superiority of the Australian lines.

"The tents, mate."

The Aussie tents were on wooden platforms up out of the wet, but naturally those Yanks preferred to flail about in the mud.

"Mob of show ponies, waited on hand and foot. Fancy having the nogs in to do the lot." Vietnamese did not work at the Australian lines; the army maintained the place themselves.

"Clueless Yank bastard doesn't even have the gumption to roll down his shirt sleeves when it gets dark."

"Blind Freddy'd know better than that."

"Begging every passing mozzie to do the honours. Down on his knees, begging them please."

Deirdre's two uncles had come back from the jungles of New Guinea with malaria. They'd be fine one day, and the next groggy and sweating, swimming in fever. Once malaria got into your system, it was there to stay.

"He's got that Hoover Dam tucked away behind his ears, I reckon. Secret weapon of the Pentagon."

"Spectacular no-hoper."

She stopped listening.

What she wanted was what she wasn't meant to hear. She came quietly back from the toilet, stood behind a bamboo screen, eavesdropped.

They'd skinned the fucking zipperhead cunts, shipped them right back to Uncle Ho.

She sat down in a hurry.

"What's been keeping you?" Ron asked, his face tightening.

She didn't answer. Put her middle finger into a drop of beer on the table, played with it, made a shape.

*Fucking zipperhead cunts.* Cunts: what kind of a word was that? (A fist in the face, but furtive, nobody looking.)

"Couldn't expect those dumb pricks to know sweet F.A. about the jungle, now, could you? Don't have a square yard of their own jungle over there, do they, mate?"

"A menace to themselves, not to mention their gallant allies."

"With friends like that . . ."

"Don't even know when to keep their big mouths shut."

"Lacking in rudimentary nous. I'd call that rudimentary, mate, wouldn't you?"

"Rudimentary, my dear chap."

"Hear them all the way to Hanoi. Talking and smoking and tuning in their little transistor radio to the hit parade."

"Phoning home to mother."

"Sticking out like a dog's balls."

"Victor Charles's never laid eyes on a bigger bunch of drongoes in his entire life."

"Sits up there like Jacky, snug in his hidey-hole."

"Charley sits up like Jacky?" queried Deirdre, to keep herself amused.

"Mate," Ron said to her, looking pained. "Mate."

Eventually Johnno would piss off and she'd have Ron all to herself. But she didn't mind the wait, not all that much. She felt happy, drinking with them in the open bar by the beach, waiting for the sea breezes and watching the sun go down.

They were gorgeous to look at: strong and tan and whole and handsome. And as they got more and more beer into them, they'd falter in their repartee and begin to look at her with a startled, hungry appreciation.

One Saturday morning Ron didn't come down from the Dat.

She sat, listening for his footfall on the stairs, for the solid promise of his step.

Saturday, midday. It was her waiting that was the problem, she decided. She forced herself to leave the room and went out on the street, because by the time she got back he'd be there, sitting by the window, demanding where the hell she'd been. Or she'd be walking along and he'd call out, "Deir, yoo hoo, Deir."

Saturday afternoon. Something was wrong, he should have come by now. If he couldn't come he would have sent someone.

Saturday night. Steps, not his, lighter. Coming slowly up the stairs.

Johnno, squinting at her like a nervous stranger.

Ron was having a spot of bother.

"A spot of bother?"

Johnno looked down, away.

At the funny farm, as it turned out. Not for long, mind you. Nothing to go getting herself upset about.

"Where's this funny farm?"

"At Bien Hoa," Johnno replied, seeking relief in contempt. "Bien Bloody Hoa."

What had Ron done?

"We were out on patrol. In the Long Hais." That was all Johnno was going to give. She was aware of the tightly guarded spaces underneath the words.

Deirdre went to visit Ron. They were keeping him in a prefab in a dreary corner of the main base medical quarters.

They could do better than this, she thought, for men who were having such problems. You'd think they could come up with a colonial villa, stone walls and tiled floors and cool, vine-covered verandahs. Why they hadn't sent Ron to the regiment's own field hospital in Vung Tau she didn't know. Inside her head she could hear Ron fooling around, hear him, much too clearly, saying they didn't have a rubber room big enough.

When Ron came to meet her on the stifling porch, he was wearing only his boots, long khaki socks, and a pair of American boxer shorts.

Deirdre and Ron sat on steel chairs, facing each other, holding hands. Perhaps the strange baggy underpants were the coolest thing he could find. Or maybe he'd lost his clothes in a card game. That'd be more like it.

She was going to make a joke about it when he began an urgent, talkative whispering. "You shouldn't worry yourself," he said. "No need to get all upset. Plans are well in hand."

"What plans?" she asked, noticing the weariness around his eyes.

"For the boat, of course," he confided. His Adam's apple bobbed. Inside the boxer shorts, he was becoming hugely erect.

"Which boat are we talking about?"

"Only the finest materials. The bones of a bird." He took his hand away from hers, made a smooth shape in the air.

"You're making a boat out of bird bones?"

"Bones, hollow inside. Light and tough. Waterproof, a snap to steer. That's the ticket."

"Who are you taking with you? Who's in your band of happy rowers?"

He sat with his hands joined, legs apart, considering. "Johnno," he said. "I couldn't leave without Johnno."

"Just you and Johnno?"

"Lofty and the Ferret," he said. Two names she recognized. "Snow and Tiger Lyons too, I reckon."

"What about me?" she asked, unable to resist. "Am I coming too?"

Now he was busy lighting a cigarette, couldn't be hurried.

"Of course, sunshine," he said, exhaling. He relaxed, looked pleased with himself. "I thought you already knew that."

"Where are we taking the boat?"

"Where the hell do you think?"

From one of his socks he pulled a small, sweat-stained Spirax binder, flipped it open, handed it to her.

"See here," he whispered. "They're after us."

He showed her a drawing, in ballpoint pen, of what looked like an egg with a halo above it. It couldn't be an egg; there were faces inside. It hung in the sky in front of some hills. It had long bright red legs all around it, so that it walked upon the earth.

He said, "Pretty good likeness, I reckon."

So childish, it was embarrassing. What was she doing hanging around with a man who drew like this?

"Who are they?" she asked, pointing to the faces in the egg.

"From Hell." He pointed to the sky.

"No, Ron. Heaven's up that way. Hell's down below. Good Catholic boy like you, you know the layout."

"That's what they say. It's just a furphy." An idle rumour.

"Let me get this straight. You're building the boat to get away from these creatures that are coming down from Hell."

"Ssshh," he said. "They might hear you."

He grinned and reached for her hand again. This time he took it and placed it on his penis. Held it there.

"Is there somewhere we can go?" Deirdre asked.

The trick cyclist turned out to be a woman. Good skin, very thick red hair cut extremely short.

*I bet they call her Spike*, Deirdre decided.

A rapid, authoritative voice and what sounded like President Kennedy's accent. Although it had begun to rain — it was pouring down in tropical buckets — the shrink had no trouble competing with the din on the roof.

"In what capacity are you visiting Sergeant Ronald Ryan?" she asked, surveying Deirdre.

Which way was she going to get more out of her?

"Professional," Deirdre answered, and she saw Spike brighten. She'd made the right guess. Good.

"A routine case of traumatic neurosis," Spike said briskly, "combat stress. You get it in every army and every war invents a new term for it. Initially he didn't talk at all, even though the physical injuries he sustained were minor. When I first examined him he was tremulous."

Deirdre almost liked her for "tremulous." (The young wallaby caught in the car lights, unable to move. Stop the car, turn off the lights, wait. Wait until the little thing gets up the nerve to vanish into the bush, leaving the road empty. Not until it's quite sure you've gone over the crest, leaving the night to settle again, not until then will the wild thumping in its chest recede.)

"A borderline case. Under observation and responding well. He'll be back with his unit in no time."

"What do you make of that drawing of his?"

Spike threw back her head and hooted with laughter.

"Oh," she said, recovering, "sorry if I startled you. But you don't usually see something so straightforward. It's a gunship, quite literally. From a nearby mountain he saw gunships. In a firefight, you understand. Steady fire from the ground, AK-57s, tracer rounds, and from the gunship itself, three General Electric mini-Gatling guns."

What exactly were mini-Gatling guns? The shrink seemed to know, even right down to the supplier's name.

"We're talking thousands of rounds a minute here. You'd have so much firepower reaching the ground that it would look solid, exactly like legs reaching down."

*Christ, even the shrink rejoices in matériel. No doubt her boyfriend's been and seen. We're talking a little pillow talk about firepower here.*

"It's interesting," the shrink went on. Now she was sitting back in her chair, warmed up, thoroughly entertaining herself. "The Australian command does not favour diagnoses of character or behaviour disorder. Many in the regiment have been professional

16

soldiers for fifteen years or more. They've seen service in Korea and Malaya."

*Gee, thanks for the history lesson.*

"The striving for perfection is noticeable throughout the whole regiment; individuals very much need to believe that they're the best, the most dedicated, the most experienced jungle fighters."

*She's cooking up a paper on this, you can bet your sweet life on it.*

"Precisely because the regiment's presence is insignificant overall, the unit ends up fighting a private war. No way they can affect the outcome, and this makes their participation purely symbolic. Hence the need to reduce it to personal terms, to bring it down to a single unit versus the enemy."

With this verdict, the shrink treated Deirdre to a big smile. Perfect, even teeth. Pearly white.

Ron refused to discuss it. Deirdre was not to ask, that was understood. It was as if it had never happened.

But later, when she was living in the room at the Royale, she thought about Ron and his lightweight boat of hollow bones.

Sergeant Ron Ryan, whose presence was insignificant overall and purely symbolic. Who strove for perfection. Whose number had come up one afternoon in the rubber.

During this period her letters came thick and fast. She described so much that what I have — what I am drawing upon now — is like a photograph, reassuring in the authority of its detail. (Those letters contrast sharply with the vague, staccato notes she was later to send me.)

The room at the Royale, she wrote, had rusty green shutters on the windows. There was a fan, with its electrical wires tied in place with a bit of string. You could close the shutters and run the fan, but it was noisy and stirred up the dirt in the corners of the room.

She had a wooden bed, a table, a chair, and a big double wardrobe. Above the bed, a discoloured yellow canopy of mosquito netting, complete with holes.

In some other era the room had been painted cream. The outside wall now had quirky brown stains where rain had leaked from the roof. There were lizards, insects, and cockroaches. In the shower stall at the end of the hall, spiders held command of the drains.

None of these creatures bothered her; they reminded her of home.

The lizards were plump, putty-coloured, soundless.

In the mornings, after breakfast and before she goes out, Deirdre sits at the window and watches the people in the back courtyard: the women in patched black pants and old blue or white cotton shirts held together with safety pins. The old men stationary on their haunches. The young children running around with shirts but no bottoms, with red stains of mercurochrome over grazes. They live in a series of sheds along the courtyard wall.

A tap over a cement drain is the centre of domestic activity. The tap, which drips constantly, is used for all washing. Around it, the women squat or sit on low wooden stools, chopping vegetables or fish with a sharp knife.

A small boy, pulling on a bit of string, is dragging a younger child in a big saucepan through the mud near the tap. At first Deirdre assumes that it's just a game, but then she sees that the toddler has damaged legs and does not, in fact, toddle.

By the back wall, amid carts and boxes and a wire hutch where the chooks are kept at night, grow a few scraggy hibiscus bushes. On those bushes, washing is hung out to dry.

By day the chooks have the run of the yard, where they search for food, often climbing on the shed roofs.

One of the boys (is he eight or even twelve years old? — hard to say, he looks so young) is mending a bicycle inner tube. Gently, he places it in a basin of water. The old men on their haunches advise and spit.

Once in a while all activity in the courtyard comes to an excited halt. There is much talking and gathering around. Even the chooks stop scratching and stick their necks out. The cook's son has arrived on a motorized trishaw.

She avoided, if at all possible, being there in the early evening. The yellow light of the kerosene lamps and the smell of braziers — the bitter smell of the fire, followed by the sharp smells of cooking — set up an aching inside her.

It was a small village out there in the courtyard. Families, living together, caring for one another, having rows, getting by somehow.

In these evenings she would write to me about how, at Vung Tau, she had been happier than anyone had a right to be.

*Whoever said anything about rights?* I'd chide in my letter to her by return post. *We're not talking about rights here, surely; we're talking about gifts.*

Happy with Ron. Johnno standing to one side, wanting her too.

She wrote to me about how she longed for the rhythm of waiting, the rhythm of Vung Tau. Waiting for Ron to come down from Nui Dat, counting the days off on the calendar, arranging her hair in front of the mirror, doing her nails, putting on clean sheets, standing by the long French windows for a smell of the sea. Afterwards, in the utter emptiness of the room, beginning — beginning within the space of a few hours — to wait again. Surely that, too, had been a kind of happiness?

At the Caravelle in Saigon, Deirdre sits in a high white banquette in the Jules and Jim, drinking a *citron pressé*. She stares at the strips of brown paper on the windows. She's smoking Capstans, slowly, one cigarette after another. She is waiting for the evening to come round.

To pass the time, she's daydreaming about articles she knows she'll never write. One about how the Aussies see General West-moreland. The top Yank general is all tight-jawed spicky-span, creases in his trousers, stripes and gongs hanging off his ironed shirt. Now get up close, take a good look into those eyes behind their camouflage of eyebrows. Nobody home.

To round the article out, she'd include the elaborate jokey plans the Aussie pilots had to bomb Westmoreland's Saigon HQ. Maybe she'd send that one home to the *Quadrant* hawks. Another piece, this for the *Women's Weekly* and the brave wives, about the steam-and-cream parlours, ten bucks a job.

Ron had a wife. He was the kind of man, solid and decisive in his truths, who could never forget he had a wife.

Could never let you forget, either.

Deirdre lights up one more Capstan, orders another *citron pressé*, drinks to all those women whose men were taken, married. If you were the bloody wife, by now you'd have a nice big pile of condolences from the parish priest, from the rellies, from the nuns at the kiddies' school, from the tennis club. A hand-signed letter from your MP, pricey stationery even though a little late. Everyone busy praying for the new widow.

Enough to make you throw up.

About men, she develops her own generalizations and preju-dices. She won't ever go with an Australian. Not after Ron. She's afraid she will bring them bad luck. But she sits in the Jules and Jim and talks with every Aussie soldier she can find. Leans forward, asking questions.

Without a word being said, by some kind of bush telegraph, she knows that they know she's lost one of them, she's off limits.

She stays right away from the civil engineers, those who are building the airfields, the roads, the bridges, making a mint. These men are older, thicker, Americans mostly. They booze in a deliberate way that has a mean, focused energy to it.

She also stays away from the journalists, British and American. The British journos drink themselves into a stupor so that the sex won't have to count one way or the other. And they understand too much about her. They know she has lost someone, an Australian soldier. What is she doing living at the Royale, and in one of the back rooms? The Americans aren't sure if she's a real journalist or not. If she is, she's competition. If she isn't, she's a bit flaky, isn't she? Whose chick is she, exactly? If she doesn't belong to anyone, why hasn't she gone home?

She prefers the youthful Americans, the soldiers. Likes their anxious, polite faces. They are grateful, say please and thank you before they pass out.

By seven o'clock she's found herself an American soldier for the night. She recommends a good French restaurant, the Guillaume Tell. Suggests he order the crepes Suzette (seems about his speed).

His name is Philip, he tells her, one "l." Comes from South Bend, Indiana.

She is amused by the way Americans recite the town and state as if you were about to dash off a letter. He begins to tell her about himself, but she takes his wrist and says, no, no, she doesn't want to know.

Uneasily, he laughs. Then he drinks a great deal of Algerian wine and feels much better.

In a good mood, they go down to the Majestic in a trishaw, to dance and drink on the sixth floor. She can tell that he doesn't enjoy the Vietnamese singing. It's too high and fast for him, too nasal and sweet. He's much happier when they dance to rock 'n' roll music from the States.

He sings along, they both do. *We've gotta get out of this place, if it's the last thing we ever do.*

At the end of the evening the band plays "Moon River." He

holds her close and she watches him look over her shoulder to the windows, out to the Mekong. There are searchlights on the far shore.

Over there, the war is going on.

She reaches down and touches him, briefly, right on the dance floor. She hears his indrawn breath, he's shocked a little, he's a polite boy, he isn't used to this.

He likes it, oh yes, he likes it.

They find a room somewhere, quickly now, before curfew. He wants to stop to buy her a ceramic elephant at a street stall, but she doesn't let him.

She does not take him back to the room at the Royale; she takes nobody there.

In the hotel room he rents for the night, she brings out of her bag a squat candle, which she puts by the bed, and she switches off all the lights. He is nonplussed by this, but definitely turned on. (Maybe she's some kind of weird pro? No problem, he's got tons of money.)

Her tongue moves down his belly and she takes him into her mouth. Listens for his little groans of pleasure. These are the moments she loves best, when the man — it doesn't matter who he is, it's supposed to but sometimes it doesn't — becomes solemn and tender, finally permitting himself to admit to his enormous longing: he wants to be caressed, petted, comforted, now, more, more. His lips tighten, he calls her his baby; she licks his ears, her tongue poking and probing. Willingly, he giggles. He sighs, whispers, reaches for her. She pushes him back down to stroke, in turn, the insides of his upper arms which, despite the sun, despite the war, despite the fact that he is a soldier, are so soft and pale you can see their vulnerable network of veins.

*Fuck me*, he pleads. *Please fuck me.*

She gets on top and watches his face, flushed and earnestly full of sex. She moves upon him until she sees his gaze turn inward, so that she, too, is alone.

Afterwards, he lies with his head between her breasts. This is a dangerous time. This is when they start to cry. To avoid such things, she has him roll on his tummy and gives him a back rub. He goes off to sleep. Sweetly, like a baby.

In the morning it's different.

He's had a shower and a shave. He sits in front of her, in his white underpants, putting on his socks. Everything about him, in the middle of a war, is extremely clean and tidy.

"Tell me about your parents," she demands. "What are your parents like?"

He looks as if he were trying to swallow a stone.

When it's morning in Vietnam, it's evening in the United States. Mom is in the scrubbed kitchen, making a pumpkin pie. Dad sits in his easy chair in front of the TV, which is flickering in shades of grey. He is watching the news about Vietnam, where their son is. Their son, Philip Wayne. Why oh why does Mom have to bang around during the news?

Mom and Dad, South Bend, Indiana.

It is simply not credible: them there and him here.

Deirdre feels something hard inside herself, something hungry, being fed.

He's more relaxed when she asks him what he does.

"Cobras," he answers. This means that he does something on helicopter gunships, which bristle with machine guns, rockets, grenades. A helicopter gunship was what Ron had drawn, the faces behind the cone-shaped perspex, the firepower reaching down, thousands of rounds per minute.

He says it again: "Cobras." Holds the word solidly. He will be relieved to get back.

"What do you do on the Cobras?" she persists.

"I'm a gunner."

"Of course," she says. "What else would one do on a gunship."

He considers this to be a question.

"You could fly the thing," he suggests.

"Quite."

He smiles at her, politely.

In a matter of hours, she thinks, he will be back on the job: escort reconnaissance, or some other bland, deceitful term.

They go down to breakfast under the banyan tree.

She orders the small, sharp strawberries that yesterday were flown down from Dalat. The taste fills the back of her throat.

He does not ask if he can see her next time, and she does not see him on the streets again.


She goes back to her room and the courtyard.

Beside the sheds there is an even smaller shed, used for storage. One morning there are women in and out of that shed on a regular basis, lifting iron bedsteads.

A young man rides into the courtyard and they help him load an ancient bed frame onto the bike. So that he can balance it, it has to be tied to him, then to the back of his bike. He rides off, careful and stiff.

They improve upon it. One short bamboo pole is tied to the handlebars, sticking out to one side, for steering. Another bamboo pole is tied to the bike itself, sticking up, to balance the load. With this, he can take five or six bed frames at a time.

*They could carry the entire world on a bicycle*, she wrote me.

The next day there is a bright blue plastic bucket by the shed door, and in the evening, inside the shed, sporadic bursts of laughter.

*I now have twenty-six Australian dollars left*, she wrote.

She did not write about coming home.

Instead, she described the way they cooked, in that courtyard. How they twisted the chook's neck, slit its throat, watched the blood drain. Legs, feet, head, and neck went into the water for boiling.

They boiled and ate the coagulated blood as well.

*Nothing is wasted here.*

She added: *I have begun smoking Vietnamese cigarettes. They are menthol, made from American tobacco, and come in packs of fifty. In piastres they cost the equivalent of twenty Australian cents.*

In the lounge of the Royale there is a bookcase full of discarded English books the journos read on the long trip out from London: thrillers by Ian Fleming and Hammond Innes, *Catch 22*, and five copies of *Homage to Catalonia*.

She takes a copy of *Homage to Catalonia* up to her room, where she puts it on the table, next to her talcum powder. In the late mornings she opens the pages of this book.

POUM. To rhyme with room. Under the intense Spanish sky, the tall Englishman breathes deeply, looks around. He's in love, this gangly articulate lad with blue eyes and big ears. In love with a dream, a serious, generous, capacious dream.

He discovers he has come too late.

He writes so well. Just looking at the words is soothing; he's so clear and real. If she could look at such words for the rest of her life, she tells herself, she might be truly happy.

Sometimes, when she is reading Orwell, she reaches down and touches herself, makes herself come. After that, if she is ready, she might think about Ron.

She is sitting in the train station at North Sydney, on one of those massive, sturdy wooden benches designed to withstand generations of schoolchildren. This is an underground station. On the far wall, trickles of water are seeping down the soft sandstone cliffs. The city-bound train is about to arrive; there is a sour rush of air. She knows that when the train stops, when the doors open, he will be there.

She will have to look at him.

Or Ron is coming up the stairs at Town Hall station. Near Woolworth's. He's wearing his army uniform, starched and pressed as if he's going on parade. This time she is invisible above the dense crowds on George Street. The people on the street make way for Ron, smiling at the handsome, manly soldier.

Ron glances up and recognizes her, then looks away, briefly embarrassed. He's relieved she's the one who's dead.

Ron went down into the tunnel and never came back.

When they blew the tunnel, later, they found Lofty with his throat cut. They never found Ron.

They got leave on Sundays, the Aussie soldiers at Nui Dat. In the morning they came down by bus to Vung Tau and spent their time hurriedly having sex and drinking, then roaming along the water-front, still thirsty for something — a fight would have to do.

By mid-afternoon they had to be on the bus again, going back to their lines in the rubber plantation.

Deirdre and Ron stood at the window of her room, looking out. She was wearing her happi-coat, the new kimono he'd bought her with the white chrysanthemums on it. They'd been in bed most of the morning. He didn't have to be back until Tuesday. Heaps of time yet. Together they watched them, the youngsters doing their 365 days. They moved in groups along the street, down to the beach, shouting, kicking at things, throwing their arms around one another with nervy, uncertain bravado. (Ron was older, more

26

experienced; he'd been in the regular army for ages.)

They turned away from the window, went back to bed. And this time she was transformed into one of those female figures at the prow of a boat, a boat that glowed with the whiteness of bones. It was sailing away in full wind, crossing the line of the equator, making for the edge of the world, racing with fine, flying energy over and down to their own country.

And they came at last to some deserted island off the north coast of Queensland. Just the two of them there, at peace. No Johnno.

She would remember how, just before she'd fallen down upon him, washed up on that quiet beach, Ron had removed his hands from her body, perturbed by her vehemence.

"You always kick up such a racket," he'd grumbled. "Calling out my name. Do you know you do that?"

In Saigon she could save money by eating at the street stalls. If she skipped breakfast and had noodle soup mid-morning, she could get through until nighttime, when she could usually count on having somebody buy her dinner.

It was at a street stall that she met Sandy.

She already knew him slightly. His name was Sanderson, and his hair was thin and fair. Most of the time he wore a floppy white hat, as if about to play a game of cricket.

He was tall and he stooped a little, overwhelmed by his height. She wondered if this stoop had become more pronounced since his arrival in Vietnam and decided that it had.

Sandy was a Kiwi who had become a Saigon regular. He had his own flat because, it was rumoured, he was having an affair with the wife of a high-ranking U.S. intelligence officer.

They sat at a small wooden table on the street. Sandy took off his hat, rode back in his chair, and leaned his head against the trunk of the tree.

The women at the stall appeared hugely amused to have two big white customers at the same time. Deirdre had soup. Sandy had a rice dish with buffalo meat, with lots of *nuoc mam*, fish sauce. Sandy attempted to order in Vietnamese (much laughter).

He knew she was in the back room at the Royale; he knew she wasn't working any longer.

"I can see there are no secrets in Saigon," she said.

"I think perhaps there are," he replied, but gently, without a trace of argument.

She noticed how soft his hair looked against the tough, fluted bark of the tamarind. He wore it long, as everyone was beginning to; over the last year, hair had emerged as a virtue.

"What are you doing these days?"

"Nothing much," she replied.

"Do you ever think," he said neutrally, "of packing it in?"

"I don't want to go home," she answered promptly. "I can't," she added, more weakly.

"No," he said, as if they shared some understanding. "No, of course not."

She was silent.

"Coffee?" he asked. "Coffee should always be followed by a glass of Chinese." There was already a pot of Chinese tea on the table, and two glasses.

Deirdre nodded.

The woman who was preparing coffee took the water from a tap on the street and began to boil it on a primus.

While they were watching the primus, a bus with chicken wire on the windows went by, slow and close. It was carrying American soldiers. She could tell from their faces that they were just arriving. They gawped at her and Sandy.

She felt proud to be out there on the street, on the side of knowing.

She looked over at Sandy, and her face must have shown something of her thoughts, because he stretched his legs and laughed and took her hand for a moment.

Their coffee arrived. Sandy lifted up the small cup and drank carefully, like some large animal.

"More light for the end of the tunnel," he said, gesturing with his head towards the bus, which was now stopped at a checkpoint at the end of the block.

They sat at the table, drinking and sweating, and Sandy talked about how he'd been here more than twelve months. "I love it," he admitted. Then he talked at length about how some people were meant to live in the tropics. "You can be born somewhere completely different, but you know it as soon as you step off the plane. It's a homecoming, a recognition of sorts."

Sandy patted his long, thin hair with his hands and put his hat back on. Deirdre wondered if she looked as totally out of place, here on this street, as he did.

Before coming to Saigon Sandy had been in all the other big journo places: Algeria, Indonesia, Israel.

"Which place do you like the best?" she asked. "After here."

"Indonesia," he replied immediately. He rattled on about some mountains in Java he was particularly keen on, how they were a profound and ancient green.

Without any transition at all he began to talk about his arrival in Vietnam.

"The first day I got off the plane, by the time I saw the goats nibbling at the grass on the road just outside Tan Son Nhut, I knew I'd come home."

The coffee was making him loquacious. His face was going bright pink in the heat. *I'll tell him about Ron*, Deirdre thought. *Because I bet he knows already.*

Before Ron goes down the tunnel he takes off his watch.

It's forty minutes since Lofty went down. He hasn't come back up. Ron's in charge, claims he's the one who should go find Lofty.

Ron and his mates are in a small group, in their sweat-drenched uniforms, out there in the midday heat. They'd just come out into the rubber. Behind them, dense jungle, a solid, dark wall. They are speaking softly, aware of their words falling into the listening silence.

Ron's mates are advising against it. He's too big, it's a dumb idea. The Ferret wants to go instead. Him and Lofty, they're the ones who sniff out the tunnels.

She can see Ron insisting. He's the sergeant.

He takes off his watch and gives it to the Ferret.

Someone sends the watch home later. To his wife.


They began to meet regularly, Sandy and Deirdre, at one of the street stalls. They would have lunch together and talk. She found him easy to talk to.

After about four weeks of this he asked her if she'd move in with him.

"Come and stay with me in perfect safety," he offered. It was partly a joke; this was what the local advertisements always said: at this bar/hotel, you can drink/stay in perfect safety.

She looked down at the wooden table, at the cheap little pot of Chinese tea.

"Are you going to say yes?" he wanted to know.

She did not ask about the wife of the high-ranking U.S. intelligence officer.

"Say you'll say yes," he urged.

She had five Australian dollars left.

"Yes," she said, "Yes, I'll say yes."

She became Sandy's girl.

Sandy had a place behind the main market. "Definitely not the high-rent district," he explained happily.

His flat was on the top floor. On the ground floor were French teachers whom he didn't know.

"Ong Ba takes care of the garden. Ba Tu does the house."

He led her up the dark stairs and unlocked the door.

There was a huge brown sofa in the living room. They both sat down on it. Sandy produced a cigar box from under a cushion, fished out some dope, rolled a joint, and offered it to her. This surprised her; he was not one of those journos who loudly discussed the virtues of local dope, boasting that it blew their minds.

"Long enough for Charles de Gaulle," Sandy said, patting the sofa. It was covered with that material that predates vinyl, like oilcloth but not shiny. "Special beds had to be made for his visits to the outposts of empire."

Royal-blue tiles on the floor. The usual French windows, minuscule balconies.

In front, a small apron of a garden was tucked between the house and a cement fence topped with a single strand of barbed wire. The barbed wire had to be purely symbolic, she decided.

"Ong Ba waters the garden at sunset," Sandy said with enthusiasm. "You can lie here in the dark and the smell of frangipani fills the room."

Sandy came from the South Island of New Zealand. The mainland, he called it.

There were old wooden fans and a wheezing air-conditioner ripped off from U.S. Aid. Sandy pointed out the logo: two clasped hands, originally one brown and one white. Now both hands were painted navy blue.

Shutters, also navy blue, to keep out the light.

In one corner of the living room he'd rigged up a hammock, made out of pale-blue nylon. A VC hammock, somebody's souvenir.

On the table was a big vase of fresh peonies.

"Picked them up this morning on Nguyen Hue," Sandy said. "In honour of your coming, Deir."

On the walls, were old photographs of Vietnamese men. Dignified, remote, and confident in ceremonial robes, they regarded the camera with mild interest.

"They give the room a sense of peace, I think," Sandy said. "From Cochin China," he added.

"Did they come with the place?"

"No. They're mine . . . But Madame must be eager to inspect her quarters."

He opened the door to the bedroom. It was a square room, with a massive wardrobe that cut the space in two. On the back of the wardrobe he'd pinned up an Indian bedspread, to cover the bare wood.

There were double beds on either side of the wardrobe. On the far side, a row of windows. Beneath the windows, a desk and a bookshelf. A portable record player balanced precariously. On the desk, books were lying open, their pages curling in the humidity. Intimidatingly good books: Balzac, Conrad. Then a Len Deighton. On the wall was a weather-stained map of the French administrative districts: Cochin in the south, Annam in central Vietnam, Tonkin in the north.

She wasn't sure what to do.

"Here you are," he said kindly, and he pointed to the other bed, beside the back of the wardrobe. This side had a lowboy with a small oval mirror on top. It also had a bedside table and a reading lamp.

"Milady is to have the guest room," he explained. Obviously this was it.

She looked around. Why had he brought her here? What was going on, exactly?

"A lot of this stuff is quite old," he said, indicating the furniture.

"Cochin China," he said again.

She nodded. He liked having the phrase, *Cochin China*, in his mouth, you could tell.

"Is it okay?"

"It's fine, fine." Her best reassuring voice.

She sat down on the bed and wondered what she'd let herself in for.


In the afternoons he often went out and did not reappear until just before curfew.

Sometimes when he came in he went straight to bed. At other times he sat on the sofa by the open window, smoking a joint and drinking "33" beer. Kept the lights off because of the insects.

They did not discuss politics. Instead, they talked in an idle way about their lives back home. About their parents, where they went to school, what books they'd read at university.

In April 1941 Sandy's father had been captured at El Fetei, a few miles out in the desert near Derna. For the rest of the Second World War he'd been a POW in Italy.

"What I took from him — in that subterranean current that passes for communication between Kiwi father and son — is that the most signficant event in either private or public life is the arrival of food: tinned meats, tinned stews, puddings, chocolate, jam, and if you're really lucky, sweets."

Deirdre was immensely interested in this because her own father had been in the desert. "He got sand in his brains," she said.

"He never spoke about the desert," Sandy went on. "But it lived with us, deep in the domestic substrate. Then at school I was educated by men who'd come home with reason to be wary of causes. The flags of war hung in the chapel, gathering dust."

Sandy had got a first-class degree in history at Christchurch before doing a PPE at Oxford.

"I spent my time at Christchurch lying on the bed and reading *The Outsider*."

"I bet you read a great deal more than that."

"I only took the PPE because I liked the way it sounded. *Pee pee eee*. A train on its way to the lavatory. Philosophy, politics, and economics. And the greatest of these, the only of these, philosophy. Stuff the economics, that dismal science, big fat yawns all round."

Back home from Oxford he'd applied for the dip corp. To his surprise and annoyance he was turned down. Took up journalism instead.

"Stuff the politics, too," he added, stretching his long legs and standing up. "As a matter of fact, just for the record, I've finally lost all interest in politics, signed off, over and out."

She would have liked to ask him what had been the final straw with politics, but was afraid of being intrusive. Why, how, and where?

"Over the years," Sandy added, vaguely. His answer to the unasked questions. A pre-emptive strike.

Sandy was a man of emphatic projects.

"What?" he cried. "You haven't seen the ice factory?" Or, "You mean you haven't walked along Hung Vuong Street?" This was the street that went right into the centre of Cholon.

And Deirdre would climb out of the VC hammock, in which she was rereading *Homage to Catalonia*, while he pulled the cover over his Olivetti.

Off they would go, towards the river to the ice factory, or out towards Cholon, threading their way among the beggars, the blind ones, the lepers, and the mangy dogs. They did their best to dodge the children with their chatter (*you number one, you number ten, chop chop, you cheap charley* — on and on it went).

Sandy would have his nose in the air, identifying the smells that drifted above the standard stench. "Ginger, anise," he would say, pleased with himself. "Chilies frying in oil."

He was delighted with himself, being in places foreigners did not go.

For breakfast, he made a soup of noodles, vegetables, and slim pieces of beef. Chopping fresh mint leaves and hot red peppers, he explained that it was what the Vietnamese had for breakfast at this time of year. He instructed her to add a slice of lemon.

Sandy's journalism was devoted to explaining Vietnamese food, culture, and religion to New Zealanders.

*I think he must be a terrible journo,* she told me in her letter. *There's something completely distracted about him.*

His working space was a scrubbed wooden table in the corner of the front room. There, with his hunt-and-peck typing, he produced overlong pieces for *The Listener* back home. As he typed, and she lay in the hammock, he shouted out pieces of information to her.

He was writing about the Cao Dai sect. Deirdre wondered if the Waikato farmer, coming in from the milking, putting his feet up for a cuppa and a good breakfast read, would wish to familiarize himself with the intricacies of Cao Dai.

They go daily to market.

"Every day everything must be completely fresh," Sandy pronounces. "First, coffee. Then purchases with the discerning shopper, *moi.*"

In his cricket hat he strides down to the market, pushing through the crowds around the double row of stalls out front. Once inside, he heads for the fish section, pausing first to roll up his pants, because the fish and eels are kept alive in wooden crates covered with ice that melts and runs over the cement floor.

He begins negotiations in what, judging by the mirth among the women squatting barefoot among the fish, must be deplorable

Vietnamese. His voice becomes tremendously eager. Because the women laugh, he laughs too, and looks about, like a child expecting and relishing praise for an act of daring.

Deirdre, shut out of this exchange, walks away. She looks up at the huge signs urging her to buy Grundig, Philips, Vespas, and wonders what she's doing there. Absorbed in the ritual of serious bartering, Sandy does not notice her go.

The successful end comes. The knife flashes and the fish's head flies off. Sandy and the women laugh in triumph at the decisive act.

Sandy stuffs the fish in his maroon Qantas bag. Looks around for Deirdre. She sees him doing that and walks back to him.

"No need to look so grim," he says. "Veggies next."

Today, Sandy buys Vietnamese spinach, ginger, and garlic.

They stop for mangoes, spread out on a plastic sheet, with Sandy asking to buy in Vietnamese.

"Should I get some starfruit, too? Durian? Stinky enough to be yummy."

"Don't bother."

Flushed with achievement and sloshing water from his sandals, Sandy is finally ready to investigate the food stalls. Roast locust on banana leaf.

"Fabulous," he declares, and crunches it on down.

They step out together, Sandy and Deirdre, into the Saigon nights. Nights like bad dope: edgy, full of treacherous diversions. The military police drive about in their jeeps. A South Vietnamese, a black American, a white American. In some of the jeeps, Aussie provos.

A prostitute in hot pants, a wig, false eyelashes, and bright-red lipstick is bargaining with an American soldier, her voice full of tenuous authority. She moves impatiently on high heels while the soldier stares. A Vietnamese boy on a Honda, sensing hesitation, comes over and briskly makes another offer: his sister (she's sitting on the back of his bike, wearing oversized sunglasses although the night is by now thick tropical dark).

The soldier's uniform has been recently pressed by a Vietnamese. Beneath all those smart creases, the soldier sweats. He's been brought up to understand that his life is an open book, one clean white page every day. Here, he is not so sure.

He looks at the hot pants, and wills himself in the role.

The Honda boy and sister in sunglasses move off. There are more American soldiers with money in their pockets. When curfew approaches, the boy will be down by the river, buying a thin piece of dried fish.

His sister will be busy, and who knows what she might bring home?

Overripe, warm Saigon nights. They stay with Deirdre: she will speak of them often; they hold her with the strength of a disturbing dream.

When they are out on these streets at night, when they are sitting in restaurants or bars, Sandy takes Deirdre's hand, walks arm in arm with her. They look like lovers.

She realizes they are meant to.

They are on the roof of the Rex, drinking with a group of journos. The journos are British, and they all know Sandy. Tonight is somebody's last night; it's always somebody's last night.

At the far end, near the long oak bar, a group of Vietnamese boys are getting ready to sing. Their shirts have waves of ruffles running down the front. Around their tiny waists they are wearing broad crimson cummerbunds.

Sandy puts his arm along the back of Deirdre's chair. Drops his hand onto her shoulder. She feels, when he is doing this, a mixture of loyalty and shared deceit. Both attractive emotions.

She is sitting in an uncomfortable wrought-iron chair; the name of the hotel, "Rex," is fashioned into its back, she can feel it pressing into her. She wonders if it will leave a mark on her.

The band starts to sing. *You can't hurry love, no, you just have to wait.*

She leans her head into Sandy's shoulder.

If she can do this with good grace, if she can pull it off, she is convinced that one evening he will come to her bed. She will know then that he wanted her all along. He wanted her, after all.

They will wake up in the morning with the change that sex brings between friends.


This is how it is in the months leading up to Tet: Sandy and Deirdre going shopping together, walking out like lovers in the Saigon night. At home, they eat and gossip and loaf about; they are domestic and discontent.

*It's only a matter of time*, Deirdre tells herself.

She becomes more sociable. Renews friendships she had before Ron was killed. Goes down to Vung Tau to see some Aussie nurses. They assume Sandy is her new boyfriend. Everyone assumes that now.

In the north, in the Democratic Republic of Vietnam, General Vo Nguyen Giap is busy planning the winter-spring uprising. Dressed in civilian clothing, his troops are slipping into southern cities. There are an unusual number of funerals: heavy coffins lowered into the damp earth, filled with guns.

Sandy goes to Da Nang.

He gets up when it's still dark, in time to catch a morning flight. He usually stays overnight at the press centre there, then takes another flight the next morning, so he can get out to a unit on a supply helicopter. Comes back four or five days later, with complaints of delays.

One afternoon when Sandy is up at Da Nang, Deirdre is walking along Petrusky Street to the bus station. She passes the buses, looking at the wooden boards listing their destinations and departure times.

The street is full of makeshift, open-fronted cafés. She walks among the crowds, street vendors, children selling food for the journey. Some boys are tying Honda motorbikes and bicycles to the top of a bus, nipping out of the windows and up onto the roof. On top of another bus, two boys are asleep in a hammock.

Deirdre is going to the bus station to collect a parcel for the nurses in Vung Tau. She has to get this parcel off one bus and onto another. She will pay one of the boys a few piastres to take care of it.

As she is walking along Petrusky Street, she sees Sandy in his ridiculous cricket hat. He is greeting a man. A Vietnamese man. This man is getting off the bus from Ben Tre. Tall for a Vietnamese. He looks like a businessman, politely confident, self-assured.

Sandy embraces him, and they both laugh.

They go and sit down at a table at a café. The man orders something.

Sandy, facing the Vietnamese man, puts both his hands on the table. As Deirdre watches, he turns them over and offers them.

Sandy's hands, palms up, are on the table.

The man leans forward.

Two days later, Sandy comes home.

"How was the flight from Da Nang?"

"All right. Had to wait, but not to worry. I took myself off to the museum."

There's an impressive museum in Da Nang, of the Cham people. The Cham were a tenth-century mob who went thundering about Vietnam taking on the Chinese and having, if the massive stone statues are to be believed, enormously important sex lives. Sandy's a big fan of the Cham.

"Did you get out to a unit anywhere?"

"Oh, it was quite useless," he says, briefly, cutting her off.

"Where did you go, exactly?"

"Just out from Dong Ha. Nothing special." Then he adds: "Turns out all they were doing was playing silly buggers in the bush." He carries this off quite well. His face is tired and convincing. She feels triumph and dismay, all mixed up.

She is going to stay overnight in Vung Tau with the nurses. On Saturday, at lunchtime, she walks down to the bus station. There are delays. Something has gone wrong. On the road to Vung Tau nothing is moving (a mine, perhaps, or a bridge blown up). After three hours of waiting she decides to abandon her plans. She could get a local train, but it goes only as far as Bien Hoa.

She walks home.

And there they are in the living room, Sandy and the Vietnamese man.

On the table she can see the remains of Sandy's best pudding: a mixture of coconut and bananas and arrowroot. They have been having a meal together. Now they are drinking Bac-Xi-Dai, the lethal local whisky.

This time Sandy isn't as clever. "What went wrong *now*?" he asks, as if things were always going wrong, with her.

Deirdre immediately escapes into that part of the bedroom designated as hers. Shuts the door.

She lies on the bed and thinks of the local boys at Café Pagode. They have high cheekbones that are so fine they look hollow. They sip their Cokes, these slender young boys. Their faces are delicate as lavender. They lift up their heavy, thick, black hair and shake it.

Who are they flirting with? Are they aware they are flirting?

She hears Sandy and the Vietnamese man going out.

Wife of a high-ranking U.S. intelligence officer, my foot.

It is night. She is on a bridge, one of those small cement bridges the French left all over Vietnam, with lookout towers on either side, surrounded by bunkers.

She's the one in charge. The bridge is under her command.

In the middle of the bridge is a powerful spotlight. It's sweeping up and down the river, exposing everything.

Tet is coming.

Sandy brings home little pink cardboard boxes tied up with string. Inside are sweet rice cakes. He chatters on about what's needed: the firecrackers, the blossoms, the incense.

From her hammock, Deirdre listens.

"We don't need any crackers," she says. Every night, for almost a week, there have been fireworks going off in the streets.

Sandy gets up on a chair to hang a Tet message on a strip of red paper in the middle of the room. It's in Vietnamese, but the letters are written in a style that makes them look Chinese.

For Tet, Sandy has saved the Christmas cake his mother sent him.

"Your mother wouldn't approve," Deirdre says. "That cake was meant to celebrate the arrival of baby Jesus."

"Mum'd have a cow," Sandy agrees, unconcerned.

At midnight, he promises her, he'll make a special soup, sour and sweet at the same time. "But right now," Sandy says, "a little refreshment, no?" From beneath the de Gaulle couch, he's pulled out the cigar box he keeps his dope in. He's rolling two joints.

"Stir yourself, Deir," Sandy urges. "Blossoms to arrange."

Deirdre climbs out of the hammock and goes off to look for

vases. Sandy's got a flair for occasion, she has to admit. It reminds her of the big feast days at boarding school — for a few hours, everything is transformed.

She rinses the vases, turns on the radio. The Armed Forces Network is playing "Downtown."

She and Sandy sing along. They are smoking a joint each.

"One each, in honour of Tet," says Sandy. "Very grand."

After that, the radio has a report of fighting around Da Nang. Hearing the name Da Nang makes her feel cold. Da Nang is where Sandy doesn't go. He goes downtown instead. To the bus station.

He can always go. Downtown.

She wonders if that Vietnamese man gave Sandy the strips of red paper. She decides not to ask what they say. Probably just "Happy New Year" or "Happy Year of the Monkey."

"The ancestors come back; they're welcomed on New Year's Eve," Sandy says.

"Whose ancestors? Not yours or mine, surely. Ours are stumbling about in some northern fog."

Sandy insists on singing stupid songs.

"*Cool, clear water*," he sings.

"*I do hope that doggie's for sale, arf arf.*"

"They're talking about people who live in the same place, generation after generation," Deirdre goes on. "Those are the ancestors who can find their families. They know where to look."

He has something planned, she decides. With the Vietnamese man, the tall, confident, Vietnamese businessman. Together, secretly, those two are plotting something special.

What porky-pie is he cooking up to tell her about that?

⌒

This is the afternoon, the eve of Tet, that Martín arrives from London.

Martín. The things about him that were entirely his own — his full name, what his soul knew — are not mine to speak of.

Martín was an Anglo-Argentine. Before she met him, Deirdre hadn't known there were such things.

"A mate of mine is coming in," Sandy said.

This mate of his, Martín, was currently a stringer for one of the London papers. They'd met in Indonesia.

In an old heap some journo had left behind, they'd driven into the green depths of Java. Lounging about on hillside terraces, waited upon like demigods, they'd begun to argue. They did not disagree that the return of the Dutch to Indonesia and French to Indochina after the Second World War had been hubris, bad habits dying hard. The issue wasn't one of substance. It was that Martín had sympathies, was partisan, engaged.

I imagine Martín's plane landing at Tan Son Nhut, an airport ceaselessly busy with commercial flights, with fighters, bombers, reconnaissance aircraft, and ammunition trucks. I set him against the background of sandbag barricades and revetments for the bombers. Then I imagine stepping into the picture to turn him back.

Typical footage of the Vietnam war: a reporter is standing in front of Saigon traffic. He's a white male, of course, in a white shirt, with short hair, wearing Buddy Holly glasses. Whenever I see one of the old Renault taxis sliding by behind him, I know Martín is inside. I watch him being driven along Cong Ly to the flat, driving towards Deirdre.

This is where I step into the picture, to conjure up a different ending.

What would Martín like? Paris? London?

He ignores me, sticks his head out the window to sniff (the taxi isn't air-conditioned). "No way you're taking this afternoon from me," he says. "Her cream cotton blouse, sleeveless. The open neck, the beginning."

We both realize she will love him. Her heart will tighten around him, holding him in.

"After that," he says, "you already know what I want. I want to die in yesterday. *I want to die out of sight of the sea.*"

## 2

At Sandy's flat behind the market, at two in the afternoon, there was a knock on the door.

Deirdre saw immediately that he was a man used to travelling. She could tell by the way he put his bags down in the corner, neatly stacked. That corner was all he was claiming; in the morning he might be out the door, gone.

A fairly large man (not as tall as Sandy) but controlled, drawn in, compact, as if by an act of will.

"The first visitor at Tet is of enormous importance," Sandy said, holding Martín's arm.

"It's not Tet yet," Deirdre said.

"Almost, almost," said Sandy.

"The first visitor at Tet should be a man of virtue, a happy man," Sandy went on. "He determines the path of the future."

Martín laughed. "I stand before you, sir," he said and gave a little bow. He straightened up and added, "A man of virtue, *che*." He hugged Sandy, and they both laughed.

He did not say he was a happy man.

Sandy pointed out the hammock. "Courtesy of the NLF."

"NLF," repeated Martín, and he touched the thin blue nylon, held it in his hands. By the way he said *NLF*, you could tell he was pleased with the hammock. He said *NLF* the way Sandy said *Cochin China*.

"What do you bet it came down the Ho Chi Minh Trail?" Martín said, his hands still on the hammock.

"Almost certainly," Sandy agreed.

The men sat on the long couch and talked. They had their backs to the bright light so they were almost in silhouette. Sandy the tall one, Martín thicker, denser. Probably he, too, was used to being in the tropics. He'd be familiar with the smells, the disarray, the overwhelming feeling that life was crowded, abundant, messy, vital. He'd be used to being the stolid, conspicuous European in the middle of all that. Except he wasn't a European, he was from the southern hemisphere. Like Sandy, like her.

Sandy and Martín worked their way through the repertoire of journalists' themes.

The quagmire was a pile.

That light at the end of the tunnel? Turns out it was a Soviet mortar round.

Martín took off his shoes and socks, put on sandals, flexed his toes luxuriously.

Deirdre wondered what he made of the room: the blossoms, the red strips of New Year's greetings, the tiled floor, the French windows, the dark, serious photographs from the old days, from Cochin China.

She watched Martín lean back on the sofa, turn to face Sandy to give him an answer. She'd have to remember to pronounce his name properly. It wasn't Martin, it was *Marteen*. Well out of his teens. How old was he, anyway?

They talked about the muddy fiasco up in the DMZ, the demilitarized zone between north and south. About ignorant American faith in air mobility. About the leaders, Pham Van Dong and Uncle Ho, how they were both sons of Confucian scholars, intellectuals. How Ho as a young man had heard an American president at Versailles pledge support for the dreams of small countries. How General Giap's wife had perished in a French prison.

Then — as everyone did — they talked about Dien Bien Phu and *la guerre salé*, the Dirty War.

So they'd been mates in Indonesia. Good mates? *Really* good mates? How did one tell?

(You couldn't bloody tell. You had to find out the hard way.)

Martín had the usual disparaging opinions about the new government, Thieu and Ky. He was familiar with the others, too. Already he knew the name of the chief of the Saigon police force, General Loan.

Deirdre, noting this, was surprised.

Martín spoke not of the VC, but more precisely of the NLF-PLAF, the National Liberation Front–People's Liberation Armed Forces.

You could tell he was a man who took himself seriously.

Within half an hour Sandy, too, was off on some riff about the Front pyramid, with its village base. Whatever that was, exactly.

It was quite obvious what Sandy was doing. If Martín was going to be serious and political, Sandy was going to be, too. Sandy, who ignored the war, who wrote about culture and talked about food, who went to the market and sang silly songs.

It was a betrayal. (Another one.)

What would Martín make of their sleeping arrangements? She

didn't want anyone to know what wasn't going on.

She went into the kitchen and began slicing mangoes, sprinkling them with lime juice. Normally she lay in her hammock and watched through the kitchen door as Sandy assembled tasty things, no effort at all.

There was enough food for days. Sandy said that's what you did at Tet: you got in food for at least the first four days.

They drank "33" beer and shared a joint. Outside, a light rain had begun to fall.

After smoking a few more joints they went out and had a massive meal at one of Sandy's favourite restaurants, where the cooks all came from Hue. "Hue has the best food in the country," Sandy explained. He was talking to Martín, not to her.

They walked about the teeming streets — no curfew tonight, because of Tet — enjoying the surge of excitement, the sound of fireworks, the excess of so many flowers for sale, the feeling of celebration, of suspension, of reprieve.

Sandy said that there were quite a few police around, considering that it was the holiday.

They came back to the flat, and Martín, worn out from the time change, went to sleep, fully clothed, on the sofa.

Towards morning, Deirdre was woken by the sounds of explosions. Martín and Sandy were already awake, looking out the living-room windows.

Over towards Cholon there was a repeated, almost constant sound: a whine, followed by a deep thumping.

Flares and tracers in the sky.

But it was closer, too, behind them.

"They've got some great fireworks," Deirdre said, sleepily.

"No, listen," said Martín. "Some *boludo*'s shooting his balls off."

"An arsehole," supplied Sandy, for Deirdre's benefit. "To be more precise, some bloke with delusions as to the dimension of his balls."

"Sounds like artillery fire," Martín added.

Down towards the river? Closer than that?

"What the fuck," said Sandy, in his high, most excited voice (the one he used for speaking Vietnamese). "That sounds like downtown."

Sandy and Martín opened the French windows and stood there, alert and agitated, pointing things out to one another. Their talk was of mortars, anti-tank rockets, bazookas. They used the technical terms: AK rifles, RPGs.

"Their mortars are accurate but their rockets are not," Sandy told Martín.

*This is how it's going to be*, she thought. *Boys together, yapping about matériel.*

She went back to bed.


At six in the morning the phone rang. Surely someone from London, confused about Saigon time. But there was Martín in the doorway, crossing the room, walking towards Sandy's bed on the other side of the wardrobe.

(What must he think? He's seen it now, how they don't sleep together, Sandy and her.)

The city was under attack. They had stormed the U.S. embassy and the presidential palace.

It was clear that Martín thought Sandy was going to leap out of bed, put his clothes on, and run out with him into the extraordinary morning; he stood at the end of Sandy's bed, expecting that to happen.

So that was exactly what Sandy did.

The reports, on their return, were outlandish.

"It's not just Da Nang, not just here," said Sandy.

"No," said Martín, swinging his arms in excitement. "It's an offensive right throughout the South. Coordinated, fierce," he added, and he clenched his fists, punched them together.

"Long Binh — of all places," said Sandy, unable to get it all out. "Bien Hoa!"

"It's being shelled," supplied Martín.

"No mate, they're *inside* the base at Bien Hoa."

"Holy shit," breathed Deirdre. Bien Hoa had a gigunda U.S. base. Big, bigger, biggest: Mr. Muscle, U.S.A.

They were in all the other cities, too. Cities, towns, villages. They were everywhere.

"The whole bloody country," Sandy said, tense. He threw himself full length on the couch.

It was completely and utterly staggering.

Last night, Martín elaborated, they'd gone after U.S. Army billets throughout the city. They'd attacked the Navy headquarters down by the river. Now they were at the airport, *on the runway*. They were at the radio station, they were holed up in a half-built hotel opposite the presidential palace, they were at the race course.

What on earth were they doing at the race course? Deirdre wondered.

U.S. troops, in armoured personnel carriers, were ringing the city. The NLF had gone right into the U.S. embassy, a commando raid.

"Right inside," Martín repeated.

"A monumental cock-up," said Sandy.

"That means nothing is safe," marvelled Martín, vindicated somehow.

There had to be inaccuracies, exaggerations, in all this. There *had* to be.

"From now on nothing is sacred. Nothing," Martín went on. "Absolutely nothing."

Martín is walking up and down the room like an overwrought animal. A tiger. Deirdre can feel the energy exploding out of his body and she knows, without thinking, that he could harm himself in some way.

"Take it easy, mate," she says to him.

As these words are coming out her mouth she's aware that her tone is more intimate than anything that's passed between them so far, that she's crossing some kind of boundary. He is, just for one moment, jolted out of his agitation. Stops pacing. He looks at her, and his eyes have a startled, open seriousness.

But then he's off again. This is the journalist's dream: here he is, Martín, in precisely the right place at the right time.

"Jesus Christ Almighty!" he says.

With an extended curfew, the city shut down and waited for the worst.

At the end of the first long day of Tet they were sitting in the flat, Sandy and Martín and Deirdre. They stared at one another in fatigue and disbelief.

Sandy was no longer energized by what he'd seen in the streets. Like a schoolboy on his best behaviour, he sat tidy and upright on the sofa, holding a book in both hands.

"When you hear a gun, reach for your culture," Sandy said. This fell flat; it was obvious that he hadn't been able to read a single word.

There were bodies lying out there in the streets, dead.

Even Martín was looking anxious; it was beginning to sink in.

A phrase formed in Deirdre's mind: *the balloon's gone up*. She wasn't sure if it was from the First or Second World War. The bloody balloon had gone up, and she was stuck here with these two. Right in the middle of it.

Sandy — towering, enthusiastic, loping Sandy. The balloon had gone up and she would have to rely on Sandy, who stood out like long, white thumb. At least he spoke some Vietnamese.

They could hear constant small-arms fire. It sounded as if it was coming from the end of their street. Or maybe from the market.

Something heavier exploded, and then there was silence.

To cheer themselves up, Sandy and Martín dusted off an old routine. Hans and Fritz, the Katzenjammer Kids, have left their tropical island and have just arrived in Saigon with the Captain. Martín, playing the twins, asks Sandy, the Captain, to explain what's going on.

"Chust von moment, der Captain. Vot iss going on Zaigon?"

"Yankees here fighting for zee free vorld. Yankees iss free pipple!"

"Vietnamese vish to be free vorld, free pipple?"

"Zee Yankees vill zet zem free. Zee don't let enyt'ink stop zem!"

"Dots vot Vietnamese vont?"

"You're getting on my nerves," said Deirdre.

As the Captain, Sandy explains the domino theory to Martín. If the north wins, if Vietnam falls to the Communists, the rest of the region would follow.

"Zot? Und zee dominoes invade New Zilland?"

Their talk moved to Indonesia.

Sandy said, "We'd go round in that huge tank of a Yank car someone was fool enough to leave with you. Windshield wipers doing double duty and that crappy little fan on top of the dashboard creaking back and forth."

"Smoking *kreteks*."

"It got us out to that weird little drive-in they had in the hills. *Hamlet* in Dutch. All we saw was Act One before it came on to rain. The dead king his father closed the place down. You said we never quite figure out how we feel about the ghost. Are tempted to think it would solve everything if we did."

"The witnesses are full of it while the rest wonder what the fuss is about."

"Pity about the deluge. Larry'd laid on a lovely lot of film noir clanking about."

"We had some good times in that car, didn't we? They knew how to build cars in the Fifties, they've lost their nerve since. What else did we see? Didn't we see *The Robe*?"

"Christ, yes. *The Robe*. Richard Burton and his slave Demetrius both being noble in Cinemascope: the Modern Miracle You See Without Glasses! Amazing, those Fifties flicks we grew up on. You in Argentina, me in New Zealand. The same screen in the same dark. Tea at The George before going back to school."

"All those single beds. Who did they think they were fooling?"

Martín, with his dark brown eyes, thick brown hair, lots of it. A conventionally attractive square jaw; healthy skin, clean-shaven. A quiet, respectable face, the kind of face that in any western country could disappear nicely. (But in Saigon?)

I believe this was the last time she saw him clearly. By the end of the month she had fallen in love with him, and I doubt if she could have described him with any accuracy.

Sandy goes out alone. Especially in the morning, when the Vietnamese are not under curfew, Sandy plunges into the streets.

Comes back at two o'clock and sits, morose, at the kitchen table. Then he goes out again, coming back at five. Lies on the sofa, drinking, refusing to talk.

Martín takes Deirdre to look at the U.S. embassy. The American flag has been raised again and there isn't much to see, apart from the four-foot hole in the fence. It's the number-one media event, the biggest story of the war.

"The NLF commandos were sprawled there, by the flower tubs," Martín says, pointing.

They are big, white, modern tubs with small trees in them.

Martín has been here earlier.

"They've taken the bodies away," Martín says. "Progress is being made," he adds in an ironic voice. It is the phrase that the American general was using repeatedly in the weeks before Tet.

Martín's stories for the London paper focus on the military victory, the psychological victory. Martín explains how, for the NLF, "coordination between the military struggle and the political struggle is a law of revolutionary struggle."

Deirdre knows what his sub-editor will do with that. Three uses of the word "struggle" in the one sentence.

Sandy's absences mean that Deirdre and Martín are together in the flat. He sits at the kitchen table and she makes a meal for them both, something simple.

Martín is the kind of man who eats without thinking, his mind elsewhere.

He tells her which districts are "red," meaning unsafe. He tells her the flower truck story: the NLF slipped into the cities in trucks that were bringing flowers for Tet.

He tells her, "In Cholon, people are fleeing, their clothes alight."

A strange sentence. Could such things be true?

He has a such thick, energetic body. What would he look like naked?

"Cholon is under constant attack from American rocket fire," he goes on. "Residential areas have been totally destroyed." This rather formal phrase, she realizes, he already sees in print, in his head.

Martín takes her to a hotel still under construction, directly opposite the presidential palace, where some National Liberation Front sappers are holed up. From the shelter of the acacia trees on the footpath, she can hear the sound of intermittent rifle fire.

While they are standing there, beneath the acacias, Martín talks to her about his younger brother.

His brother was a student at the University of Buenos Aires. It was a time of a right-wing crackdown. "Miniskirts were 'subversive,'" Martín says. "Wearing miniskirts, going to nightclubs, working with the poor."

There was a protest at the university. The police arrived, and Martín's brother was kicked down three flights of stairs. His kidneys were weakened — permanently, as it turned out. From a blow across the face, he lost the sight in his right eye. This happened two years ago. The Night of the Long Sticks, Martín calls it.

It feels strange to be standing beneath the acacias on a street in Saigon, listening to rifle fire, and hearing about miniskirts and Martín's brother and the police halfway round the world.

"Those sappers are surrounded," Martín says, looking up. "They know it. It's only a matter of time."

The sappers are going to die. Does belief make it any easier? Are they true believers, or did they just have the bad luck to end up there?

Martín assumes that her interest, like his, is complete. He does not appear to find it absurd that she is still here: an Australian woman, a journo without work, a hanger-on.

With Martín, she begins to take notes.

She begins to think of writing about the war again.

They go around the city in a battered Citroën some friends at Reuters have lent him. They see rice and pork being distributed at relief centres.

"It's completely chaotic," Martín says.

The homeless — and there are many — crowd into the grounds of pagodas, schools, churches. "If someone went missing, it would be impossible to find them," Martín says.

"But that would be terrible."

Back in the flat Deirdre and Martín tell Sandy what they have both seen, breaking in on each other's sentences.

One morning she asks Martín, "Where's Sandy? Where does he get to these days?"

"He's out looking for Tran. He's not at the photography studio."

In this way she learns the name of Sandy's Vietnamese man. His name, and what he does for living.

On the walls of the studio, on the dark wooden walls, gathering dust, would be pictures, old pictures, from Cochin China.

Sandy cannot find him.

At Tet, Tran disappeared.

As soon as the curfew is relaxed Martín goes up to Hue, where the fighting is. Sandy spends most of his days out on the streets, searching.

Deirdre is left alone in the flat. She listens to the news on the Armed Forces Radio and wonders how much they are leaving out.

In Hue, the South Vietnamese and the U.S. are fighting not the ragtag Viet Cong but General Giap's NVA, the North Vietnamese army.

(When Martín insists that the more accurate term is PAVN, the People's Army of Viet Nam, Sandy shrugs and says, "Mate, go on, go ahead and disappear up your own behind if you want, be my guest.")

Combat in Hue is most intense in the older, walled part of the city called the Citadel. Initially the reports focus on the ancient capital's lush lotus pools, elegant buildings, and imperial treasures, with some debate about how old the moated palace is. As the fighting goes on the reportage changes in tone; it becomes direct and naturalistic: North Vietnamese, their bodies blackened by decay, sprawl in the doorways.

Deirdre tears out a picture of Hue from a magazine and sticks it on the fridge, to think about Martín and stare at the names: the Perfume River, the Palace of Peace.

When Sandy is not out looking for Tran, he lies on his bed and listens to records. Deirdre, on the other side of the room, behind the barrier of the massive wardrobe, hears for the first time Monteverdi's *Orfeo*: *Tu se' morta, se' morta, mia vita.* Sandy plays it over and over. This simple vocal line, with its small organ and lute, speaks of the intense privacy of loss, even when cried out loud for the whole world to hear.

Sandy and Deirdre talk: vague, desultory conversation, in which nothing is explicitly acknowledged.

"No luck today?" she asks.

"No. No luck."

"Perhaps tomorrow."

"You never know," she adds after a while, the words fatuous in her own ears.

She hugs him, feels his indifference.

At the end of the battle for Hue, the Citadel was in total ruins. For over twenty days in unusually cold February weather, the fighting was from street to street, house to house. The gardens of those houses became impromptu graveyards. Occasionally there was time to leave a name on a grave. Picking their way among the bodies, among the shattered, burned-out homes, were the homeless, thousands of them.

The story went round that in the Citadel, the NVA, near starving, lived off the algae in the palace moat. Another story went round that the NVA had massacred huge numbers of people and buried them in shallow mass graves outside the city.

That's what Deirdre heard.

What Deirdre knew about Hue was this:

When Martín came back, he arrived mid-morning. (Sandy had gone down to the Delta.)

Martín stepped into the room, looked over at Deirdre. Put down his bags, closed the door, crossed the room, stood in front of her, and waited. Seeing him standing there like that, she knew immediately what she was going to do.

He held on to her with unrestrained insistence. Held on to her like a man whose arms reach up for one more chance. Held on like a man who was drowning.

# 3

When I receive the letter, I drive over to Sandy's. He comes to the door, winces as a plane roars overhead. He lives on a flight path from Mascot.

"Am I imagining things or does the earth move?"

"Afternoon commuter flight," he replies. "Get those business-persons home in time for tea."

"You know they leave a trail of toxic shit in their fumes."

"All the better for jogging."

From the top floor you can see Sydney Harbour. At night in the summer, Sandy says, the harbour floats in the air; the Southern Cross hangs upside down in the water.

It's a terrace house, with a marvellous dank little garden out back.

Despite his profession, Sandy is in no way a voyeur of evil. I believe he knows little of self-magnification, of the belief that you walk as a giant, heroic on a vast stage. He's still a working journo, writing to please himself rather than anyone else. His thin, fair hair is long gone; people think his nickname comes solely from his surname, Sanderson. While he remains lean and enthusiastic, today's children have made him seem less tall.

He reads the letter. It's very brief, more of a note.

"I can't think," I say. "I'm all jumbled up."

He puts the letter down on the kitchen table and looks at me.

"Drinks. Drinks on a tray. In the garden."

We sit back in his garden chairs, surrounded by vines. Beyond his garden, up the hill in a public park, a jacaranda is blooming next to a flame tree. Years ago, I think, somebody planted them together. It was quite deliberate.

Me and Deirdre.

Deirdre and Sandy.

Sandy and Martín.

Martín and Deirdre.

Although not given by temperament to disclosure, Sandy has told me much. I have worked away at it, ferreting it out of him, assembling it piece by piece, so that by now I have heard all he can remember of the first weeks that Deirdre and Martín spent together. He's told me about their sleepwalkers' movements, their careless meals, about their constant need to touch, to reaffirm each other's miraculous presence.

After Martín came back from Hue, Sandy has told me, Martín and Deirdre stayed in the bedroom.

"I left them to it. Took up residence on the de Gaulle couch.

"It was the first time I ever saw Martín ignore his work. They'd sleep late, go out for boozy lunches, and it'd be almost four by the time they got back. They'd immediately disappear into the bedroom again to smoke Gauloises and drink vodka, of all things.

Martín got records from somewhere — Bix Beiderbecke and Cream, he did have fairly eclectic tastes. He must have borrowed them; I know he didn't travel with them. In the bedroom it would be Paris circa 1959; then, a half hour later, London 1966, Ginger Baker on drums. No wonder Martín forgot completely where he was.

"This was after Tet, and I don't know if you remember, but by May of that year there was another round of fighting. It was meant to be their second offensive. Little Tet, we called it. I don't think Martín filed a single story during the whole of Little Tet.

"Martín was a talkative lover, I could hear him. I remember thinking that that'd be a turn-up for Deirdre, she'd be used to the strong, silent type. Not that there's anything wrong with quiet men full of purpose. You can send me over one of those any time you like.

"Finally the door would open and Martín would wander out in his bare feet and sit at the kitchen table drinking a glass of Coke. He had a threadbare T-shirt he'd got from some Yank back in Indo. Notre Dame, it said. Fightin' Irish. He sat at the table like a man on drugs. I'd tease him about his crappy T-shirt being insufficient breeding plumage. He'd laugh, embarrassed and pleased. You could have said anything to him, he wouldn't have noticed, he was past caring. Blissed out of his mind, as the parlance of the day had it."

"What about Deirdre? Was she blissed out of her mind too?"

"Oh, Deirdre would stay in the bedroom, writing madly away in her diary, getting some of it down. Nothing wrong with that either. I'd rather be a dirty diarist than a journo any day. Sweet heavens, the luxury of having something real to say, however transparent."

"She wrote to me that she never wanted to leave."

"But it was portable, wasn't it? Indolent afternoons snugged in beside your lover are on tap anywhere in the world as long as you're together. The farthest reaches of the Orinoco would have been just fine by Deirdre. It was Martín who made the move. In June he wangled something in London. The whole idea was to get over to Paris; he'd lived in Paris, his French was pretty good. As you know, 1968 was a happening year. Martín had it right up there with 1789, 1848. Overly optimistic, I'd say.

"When they were leaving Saigon I decided to pull up stakes, too, head out with them. If it hadn't been for Martín's leaving, I suspect I would have stayed. I would have hung on until the helicopters fell into the sea.

"I don't think leaving mattered to them, not all that much. Not the way it did to me. But they were kind to me, or tried to be. We packed up together, singing, '*And we'll all go together / To pick wild mountain thyme / All among the purple heather*.' Took us all of one hour to finish the job. I left most of the stuff there. Pots and pans. The pictures on the wall.

"I shut the door, turned the key in the lock. Deirdre and Martín looked in one another's faces and toddled off down the stairs, oblivious as clams, intent on their own story."

↬

The orchard stands behind a small farmhouse in the Tigre delta where a very young Martín went, on holidays, to stay with his maternal aunts. (The uncles, distant leathery men, were turning the place into a market garden.)

It is an old-fashioned orchard of quinces, peaches, and cherries.

To show her how it was, Martín divides Deirdre's body into the different sections of the orchard. He runs his hands over her, the farmer testing for ripeness. Then brings his right eye down to each of hers in turn, closer, closer. Vision is blurred into breathing.

"I wonder what's going on in there?" he asks. "Do you suppose I'll ever know?"

"You already do," she replies.

"Listen," he commands. "In the marshlands, when you're silent and listen, all you can hear is the flutter of butterflies."

As a child he called these butterflies Vanessas, Martín remembers. That was their name.

"Red Vanessas."

"Like Vanessa Redgrave in *Blow Up*," Deirdre says, helpfully.

"Yes," he says. "Yes, you clever girl. Vanessa in *Blow Up*. Vanessa and her daring darling breasts."

At the bottom of the orchard, he claims, are the marshes of heaven.

"This is where, at the end of the hot afternoon, tiger comes for a visit, to lie on his splendid bed of passion flowers."

He explores the marshes, seeking out their shy places.

"Tiger likes to stretch right out in the marshlands, to make himself into a yard of silky beast. Above his head bright red butterflies gather. The Tigre tiger's completely worn out by now. Can you feel him, all exhausted?"

"Oh yes," says Deirdre. "I feel him."

⌐

"Occasionally in Saigon," Sandy says, "they'd snap out of their amorous stupor and ask me about Tran, how the search was going. They were bursting with an urgent generosity. Lovers full of goodwill. Wanting to hug you as well as each other. A distinct pain in the arse."

"Must have driven you barmy."

"Oh, I wanted to smash the furniture. But it was wonderful, too. I'd never seen Martín in that state before. He'd come undone."

"When did they get over the non-stop mooning?"

"Sometime after we left Saigon. After Paris, I'd say. They came back from France at the end of the summer in an altogether sterner mood. Started going to anti-war meetings. Shared belief can be exceptionally erotic, or so I'm told."

"And you settled down in London?"

"It was a strange time. Only a few months before it'd been me in a goofy condition. Me and Tran. I kept dreaming that he'd come back to my flat in Saigon, walk up the stairs, and it'd all be still there, in place, waiting for him. I'd left a note in my desk, so he'd know exactly how to get hold of me."

Sandy has, over time, let me come to know about him and Tran. The personal, vulnerable details. How, not meaning to, he had fallen in love with Tran; how at Tet, Tran had vanished.

Tran grew up in Kien Hoa province not far from Ben Tre. (Tran's father was a doctor who supported the Viet Minh.) After the Geneva Accords, Tran's elder brother went north. A lot of the young men from the Delta went north at that time. It was supposed to be just for two years at the most, but they didn't come back.

"Why didn't they come home? What happened to them?"

"They were drafted, I think. One way or another."

"Didn't they get leave? Or if not leave, there must have been letters," I insist. "Surely there would have been letters."

"I'm not sure they had reliable postal service across the DMZ. Not so you'd notice."

I am always making these assumptions — the naive assumptions of peace.

Tran told Sandy how his elder brother would sing songs at village meetings. Traditional themes, but with updated verses and an inspiring message. Young Tran admired his big brother and his important, busy life — going from village to village, holding meetings, getting people excited and determined. Tran wanted to be like his brother in every possible way.

"We used to speak French," Sandy says. "We made love in French."

"Of course," I say. I know he's talking about Tran now, not

about the elder brother.

"I don't know what happened to him," Sandy says.

"Yes."

"I went down to the Delta after Tet. I went looking for him, bumbling idiot that I was."

"You did what you could."

"You should have seen those cities in the Delta after Tet. Amazing, it truly was."

"Yes." (These replies are no more than background murmur.)

"Who was he, anyway?" Sandy asks. "I often wonder if Tran was his real name."

I make a soft noise in my throat.

"Tran used to come back to that story, the one about his elder brother going north and not returning. Do you know what he said?"

"What did he say?" I prompt.

"Tran said, 'It's the not knowing that doesn't go away.'"

We leave Sandy's and drive down to the beach, to take the cliff walk from Bondi to Bronte.

We walk up the path, and Sandy looks bony and gaunt. As for me, I've thickened into middle age: Jack Sprat and the Missus. We find the bench that is our halfway mark and sit on it, looking out to sea.

Together we reread the letter.

Sandy's had mail too. Last week he received a note from an old journo dying in London. "When I look back over my life," this man wrote, "I find the whole thing to have been a bit of a balls-up."

"Martín would have liked that," I say.

Sandy is the one person I talk to about Martín.

I have learned not to speak to others of Martín. I wish not to trespass, not to become an imposter.

I have not always been as cautious. When I was younger, more of a party-goer, I'd toss back four or five glasses of bubbly and my speech would become persuasive to my own ears. I would begin to hold forth; I would presume to proffer revelations.

One evening I was in someone's garden, at a party in Sydney, and I began to speak of Martín to a man I found attractive. He cut me short, this handsome man. I saw the world in black and white, he declared. I was drawing a medieval cartoon, completely lacking in moral ambiguity. He strode off, leaving me alone in the garden to puzzle over the phrase "medieval cartoon."

He had humiliated me — it's the humiliation that keeps the moment fresh and lively.

There were poinsettias in the garden. I looked at them and thought they must have been brought in especially for the party, what a fuss to go to. Then I realized that they were growing there; it was early winter and they were naturally in bloom.

"He knew him, you know," Sandy goes on.

"Who did?" I ask, confused. "Who knew whom?"

"The guy I've just been telling you about. The one who says it's been a bit of a balls-up. Martín and I knew him in Indonesia."

"Ah, the year of living dangerously."

"Too bad it wasn't just the one year."

"Were there really tons of young Mel Gibsons running about?"

"They rained from the heavens, but one had to be the essence of discretion. Don't forget, it was B.E. or thereabouts."

Before Everything. The year before Saigon. Before the seas of the world ran in their veins.

Joggers puff by our bench, urged on by exultant dogs. Then the evening crowd arrives, coming from Bronte to Bondi for the restaurants. Up towards the Heads, a mob of cumulus clouds has gathered, changing the water from Pacific blue to thick vermilion. Over at Waverley the sun continues to shine and the rows of graves are saturated with late-afternoon light.

He was right, the handsome man in the garden of poinsettias. He was on to me, he'd picked up on it, the tendency I have to become lofty, to elevate myself by accusing others with a safe, self-promoting passion. Perhaps it was a vice of my generation, especially when young.

But in saying that I romanticize, I generalize. Really I am speaking only of myself and Deirdre and Martín. Not Sandy. Sandy isn't like that, never was. Sandy is, as he says, a true non-believer. Pity the country that needs heroes, Sandy says. And I don't think of Martín and Sandy as being of my generation. They were older; they were at university in the Fifties.

Out here on the sandstone cliffs, we're sitting on the bench and we're still talking. The moment comes when we have to decide whether this was just an afternoon visit or if we're going to go back to Sandy's to talk all night as well. About me and Deirdre, how we grew up in the bush.

"Nobody grows up in the bush any more," says Sandy. "You're an anachronism in your own time."

"Looks who's talking."

"But you might as well go on, I suppose. Having come thus far."

⌒

The novel I had been writing in my head for the past twenty-five years was a portrait of provincial life in the place Deirdre and I came from, Kelly's Creek. This novel tried to capture something of the wildness of our small town in the early Fifties. It was a village, a hamlet, although these terms were never used. Kelly's Creek was a place where people who had mental illnesses never thought of going to a doctor; where nuns routinely beat children, especially those who were unhappy; where there was not a single washbasin at the primary school and yellow jaundice was common enough.

In short, I was writing a severe socio-cultural portrait, critical ethnography, in the voice of someone who, although shy, believes herself to be absolutely in the right.

It was a story that did not approach the mystery of the long, clear days, their unquestioned, leisurely accumulation. A story that shied away from the disjunction between the time before and the time after.

It was the kind of story that would have interested Deirdre in the years immediately following Saigon, that she herself might have written before she was married.

I have discarded all of it.

I am no longer concerned with the belated arrival of school milk in our final year at Our Lady of Sorrows, Kelly's Creek. What stays with me now is the way the school milk sits sweating under the pepper tree before lunch. How, inside those empty bottles at the end of the day, flies move slowly, intently.

What stays with me is the tilt of the tableland: towards its eastern rim, green tongues of cedar and coachwood reach down the gorges to the coast; in the west, stringybark ridges stand sharp against an enormous sky.

This is what abides: the place from which we are about to set out, the beginning that is never left behind.


Deirdre's parents, the Hogans, ran the Kelly's Creek general store. Of the two of them, I always felt I knew the father better. We were both children of Kelly's Creek.

Deirdre's mother was a foreigner.

There were two things we all knew about Deirdre's mother, Dorcas. She was from Britain, which meant she was a whingeing Pom. And she was a nutter. As my father put it, Deirdre's mother had a roo loose in the top paddock.

Most of the time Deirdre's mother worked in the store like a normal person. Then one day you would see her out front, watching the shadows on the footpath. With great deliberation, she would be jumping from the shadows into the sunshine and back again.

Hogan's store had a corrugated iron awning above the footpath. It was the only awning on the street until you got to the pub on the corner. So the footpath immediately in front of the store was in shade while the footpath on either side was in bright sunlight.

Having jumped for several hours from shade to sunlight beneath *The Billy Tea* (white on faded blue), Deirdre's mother would move to the other side, *Peter's Ice Cream: the Health Food of a Nation.*

Next time you were in town you would see Deirdre's mother sitting behind the counter again, swishing her perfumed hankie and complaining about the weather. As if nothing had happened.

She always gave the right change.

Deirdre's uncles, her father's two brothers, worked as shearers. When they weren't off shearing they lounged around the house, which was built onto the back of the store. They lay on the dilapidated couch on the back verandah, listening to the races at Randwick or the dogs at Dapto. Sometimes they sat on the steps of the store, waiting for opening time at the pub. (Not when Deirdre's mother was doing her jumping bit.)

The uncles were capable of anything. They had been heard to say, "Gunna take a leak," when there were people right there in the store. If they didn't like something they'd say, "Let's pull the chain on that," then laugh, because Kelly's Creek had outhouses.

"Uncouth," my mother said, of the uncles. "Boors."

"Thank heavens she won that bursary," my mother said, of Deirdre.

My mother got Deirdre's clothes ready for boarding school. Deirdre's mother was having one of her turns so it was my mother who sewed in all of Deirdre Hogan's little tags, her name in red on a strip of white tape.

But it was no surprise she got the bursary: she was brainy. She read something once and she knew it. She had to watch her step, though. Didn't want the other kids saying she was stuck-up.

I'm flying the night-mail from Toulouse to the coast of Africa. I'm alone in the cockpit, conversing with the stars. From a great way off, I hear the nun calling out my name, Bernadette Behan:

"For what were the Phoenicians famous?"

"What is quinine used for?"

"How did the Little Flower become a saint?"

I am not convinced that I need to know these things.

Deirdre, seated beside me, provides the answers. She has taught herself to talk without moving her lips; the words in her throat become the ones I speak.

"It's nothing," she says. "I just remember everything."

I come to depend upon her memory.

The Royals are one of Deirdre's serious interests, because she is half English herself.

Princess Elizabeth is at Treetops when the telephone rings. The King has died in his sleep.

Deirdre is Princess Elizabeth lying in bed with extra pillows. She's sleeping in because she was up late the night before, watching the elephants come to their salt lick.

I get stuck being the servant because I'm a bit shorter than she is, and I'm dark — black hair, dark eyes. Black Irish, my mother says.

I have to knock on the door. "Telephone, Your Royal Highness."

After that, we are no longer the future queen and her attendant but our adult selves on safari, deciding what we want to do first. I want to find the lions, she wants the zebras.

We are going to see them all.

In the lounge room at my place we get out the piano rolls. Our favourite is "Now is the Hour." One day we will be getting on the boat at Circular Quay, it will be our turn.

The band plays "Now is the Hour" as the P&O liner pulls away from the quay. P&O means they have pay toilets, ha ha. Which one of us would be going and which one would be standing on the dock, hanging onto the streamer, hanging on and on until it finally broke?

We dance about the room, complicated eurythmics we make up on the spot, with grand bows at the end.

"*I will dream of you,*" I promise Deirdre, waving my arms around, "*if you will dream of me.*"

Deirdre and I listened from her back verandah.

When the Queen stepped ashore at Farm Cove, she was wearing a chiffon frock painted with wheat-ears and wattle.

The uncles were listening too, worse luck.

As the *Gothic* came through the Heads, it was escorted by countless small craft. "Bursting with pride" and "amid thunderous applause" were phrases favoured by the ABC.

"Here they come now, the RAAF fighters, flying in tight formation, a beautiful sight. We're hearing the twenty-one-gun salute from the Duntroon cadets, what a proud moment it must be for them. What a wonderfully bright, shining morning this historic summer's day is for the first reigning monarch to ever set foot, yes, now she has one foot, now she has two feet, Her Majesty Queen Elizabeth has *both feet* on Australian soil!"

"Pig Iron Bob must think he's died and gone to heaven," said one of the uncles, referring to the prime minister.

"What does she do with all her old clothes?" the other uncle demanded. "Wonder if she gives them to the Salvos?"

They're away.

"Mustn't let the hoi polloi get their hands on them, no siree. Up the royal incinerator at Buck Palace."

"How about the one at bloody Glarms?"

"Or Sandringham. Christmas message at Sandringham. 'My corgis and I . . .'"

The uncles made you feel guilty, for listening.

"They keep their own royal worms, mate. To spin the you-know-what. Her Royal Highness makes beds for the corgis out of it, I kid you not."

"She wouldn't want to do it herself, though, now would she? Bet HRH gets her ladies-in-waiting to make beds for the corgis out of it."

The uncles went on and on, pitting themselves against the thunderous applause.


Deirdre's mother couldn't even make chocolate crackles. Chocolate crackles, as everyone knew, were just rice bubbles, copha, cocoa, and sugar. You mixed them up, you didn't even have to stick them in the oven.

Deirdre's mother had her sweater done up on the wrong buttons. She slumped in front of the copha before she even got it into the saucepan to melt. She sighed. Sat down at the table and stared. You could hardly call her a mother at all.

I was used to my mother and grandmother flashing about with bright cake pans. The two of them busily sifting, stirring. Cakes, my mother said, might be life's one totally reliable pleasure. My grandmother pushed the bowl across the table, with batter left in it for me to clean out with my fingers.

But Deirdre's mother completely dropped her bundle. Took one piece of her lank hair and twisted it around her fingers.

"I think I'll have a lie-down," she said, finally.

At Sunday Mass, there was Deirdre's mother, all dolled up, gloves on, clean curled hair, walking up the aisle, my mother said, as if it were Westminster Abbey.

"All that rain back in England made her soft in the head," my mother told my father as we drove home.

How my own mother got to act so sure of herself, I didn't know. It was precarious, though. Everyone understood that Deirdre's mother couldn't cope — the cat was well and truly out of the bag about what went on at the Hogans. But hadn't I'd seen my own mother trying to summon up her practical self when she was going to town, when she was speaking on the phone, when people came to visit? At home on our property, Ardara, she was quite capable of wandering about with an open, broken look on her face, humming a thin tune for herself alone.

"Get a hold of yourself, Alice," my father would urge. "Get a hold of yourself." He used my mother's name only when he was cranky with her.

In the Hogan household, hugger-mugger was to be expected. In my own, normal life could easily falter and had to be safeguarded.

Deirdre's father, Jack Hogan, did odd jobs.

Stonemason, for one. In an unobtrusive shed down by the park, Jack cut the headstones for the graveyard on the hill, where the local dead lay in quiet astonishment. This was in the modern Fifties, when even brief phrases — *Gone to Glory*; *Asleep in the Bosom of Abraham* — were considered too fulsome. *Beloved Wife/Husband of*; *Rest in Peace*: those were the choices offered by Jack when called upon. It was a small joke in the pub that Jack, who didn't have much to say for himself, who leaned silently on the bar for hours, would have the last word on them all in the end.

Jack also built chimneys for anyone smart enough to ask. Guaranteed to last while the house itself fell about its ears. Jack's grandfather had been a brickie back in Ireland; it was in the genes.

And once in a while, Jack worked in the store.

Kids poured in for musk sticks, licorice steps, sherbet, bullseyes — and were sobered when they saw the tall man waiting behind the counter. It was Jack's hesitant politeness, not his sweaty singlet, that took the skylarking out of them. (Deirdre and I would be sitting at the back table, drinking Passiona, superior.)

When he sold a grown-up baling wire or an inner tube, he'd turn to the shelf behind him and, in a vague way, pull something down — a tin of sardines, baked beans, condensed milk — and push it across the counter.

"Doan worry mate," he'd say, when the customer began a murmur of protest. "She'll be right."

Under her breath, into the soft drink, Deirdre would imitate her mother's voice: "But Jack, these are *paying* customers."

"Doan worry about it, mate," Jack would urge, and he, not the customer, would be the supplicant.

Jack's mother and father once ran the general store. An old woman in black, Deirdre's grandmother lived in a permanently darkened room behind the shop. The only time you saw her was when Deirdre's mother was having one of her turns. Then she might emerge and sit behind the counter. Outside, Deirdre's mother jumped into the sunlight and back again. Inside, the shrivelled grandmother cast an ancient smell over the store.

It wasn't good for business. Not that there was any competition, in Kelly's Creek.

Deirdre's father had been in a POW camp during the war and had gone silent. Sat in the pub and drank. Jack Hogan was, my father said, a sober drunk.

Sometimes Jack's eyes went blurry on him. He'd look out at

paddocks that heaved and shifted like the ocean. The doctor put it down to the grog, but Jack knew it was the desert.

My father reckoned Jack Hogan came home from the desert with too much sand in his brains. My father said this in a matter-of-fact way, as if it were self-evident and completely unremarkable.

Jack had some scrubby acres of his own down by Maguire's place where he ran a few sheep. The rest was left to the roos. Jack was even known to leave gates *open* so roos could get through.

Perhaps Deirdre's father was most himself when, crouched behind some rocks, he looked up and saw a young grey roo, the scout, holding himself erect, breastbone quivering, disconcertingly recognizable. At such times Deirdre's father would sketch at high speed, his own breath trembling.

One year Deirdre's mother made the mistake of sending Jack Hogan's sketches to the local show, where they won prizes. (*Kids' stuff, poofter stuff.*)

What saved Deirdre's father from disrepute was his skill at cricket. An opening bat, he cast the other side into early despair. Later, he would shuffle onto the field as the humble batsman ready to give the bowling a bit of a go. Then he'd send down balls that changed character in mid-flight and floated onto the bails in a climax of deception.

Deirdre's father could be counted upon to lead Kelly's Creek to the district's A-grade finals. It was not to be sneezed at.

Deirdre's father took care of the cricket pitch in the park by the river. Watered it, rolled it. He strapped himself into the harness as if he were a horse and strained up and down with the big roller. Then he'd get the little roller out to do the finishing touches.

So that the pitch wouldn't be invisible in a sea of long grass, Jack took his scythe to the paspalum. He worked in a navy singlet, and his arms were the colour of bark. He moved his right arm in a broad arc and the grass went *swish* pause *swish*.

The rabbits made themselves scarce quick smart.

Sweaty, fulfilled, Deirdre's father would go down to the pub and sit on the hotel verandah with his mates, Saturday's cricketers.

And he wasn't stuck-up, either. Not like some people.

In her good periods, when she wasn't having one of her turns, Dorcas was shameless, vocal, full of criticisms.

Deirdre's mother had imagined that she'd be joining the landed gentry.

"Dorcas thought she was coming out here to sit on her tuffet and sew a fine seam," my mother would say, then laugh, full of hard knowledge.

In the lounge room behind the Kelly's Creek general store, there was a photograph of Deirdre's father and mother licking ice creams in front of a cart that said "Ices." Deirdre's father was exceedingly thin and wore his slouch hat. It looked as though the sun was about to go down, but no, the sun was always like that in England.

Dorcas had brought with her her own mother's language, from the Fens. We unwittingly picked it up, used it, and thought of it as normal local speech. Old people were said to be "mozing" by the fire — part dozing, part musing. "Puttering" was used in its ordinary sense, but in Kelly's Creek it could also mean mumbled grumbling. Everyone did a bit of that about Dorcas, the wife Jack Hogan had got himself saddled with in the war.

Jack Hogan had been a prisoner in Africa. In 1944, he'd been sent to England to hang about until they brought him home. While he was waiting for the boat, he'd gone to the country to visit his POW mate, Bert, who was a good bloke even though he was a Pom. Dorcas was the bloke's sister.

Jack got Dorcas up the duff and there was no turning back.

In Kelly's Creek, people knew Jack'd had a rough spin.

Bert's cottage — it was on the coast in Suffolk — was tiny, built of stones people took from the beach.

"Price is right," Jack said to Bert, of the stones.

Bert laughed, and Jack relaxed, a little.

Bert said that when it came to the churches, flint was the stuff round here. Jack remembered there'd been an Age of Flint, hadn't there? Bert agreed there had, a long time ago.

"In like flint," Jack said, and Bert laughed a second time.

Bert's home was as poky as a rabbit warren. You'd have to be a bloody little ferret to fit in. When Jack walked through the front door he had to stoop. His voice flooded the room, threatening the rafters. He felt like Jack and the Beanstalk, only he was the beanstalk.

Bert's mother cooked the tea and passed remarks about hollow legs.

It wasn't the same as it had been in the camp. Living with his mother, Bert had gone skittish about such simple things as going down to the boozer.

After a night of impressive rain, he and Bert walked along a path through fields that shone with water. (Water came cheap here, it was small change, beer money.) They emerged on what had to be the main street.

Shops looked out at rolls of barbed wire on the beach. A black Scottie went after a kid on a bike. It was the kid he wanted to bite, not the bike. The sea smell was like steel wool: cold, but at the same time a bit rotten. It was difficult to get a handle on.

"There's a whole town buried out there," Bert said. "Houses, churches, shops, everything."

"Garn," Jack said, "pull the other one."

"You can hear the bells of the churches tolling. When the wind is right."

The sea was brown where the small waves curled, and farther

out a chilly grey. Not much of an ocean, Jack reckoned.

He'd wanted to get out of London. He'd thought it would be bigger out here, but it wasn't. Not much, anyhow. The sky was a fair bit wider, especially near the sea. But it was low, weighed down by clouds.

The whole country was too bloody small.

Jack closed his eyes and wished he were back in Africa, in some stinking trench. The sky in Africa was huge and starched and stretched out to dry.

Bert's sister Dorcas came home on her first leave, silly with excitement because she was finally inside a uniform, a perky little Wren. She was that easy to tease.

"One sheet per woman per day perhaps," he said to her.

"Oh Jack," she said, and she giggled as if she would choke.

After the desert, Jack couldn't keep a hold on things the way he used to. Sometimes he'd be sitting in a pub with a beer in his hand and he wouldn't be able to remember how he'd got there, what had happened earlier in the day, the day before. He could remember back home, no problem. He could get a grip on bits here and there.

He could remember being on a great boat in the ocean.

Was that coming or going?

They were playing cards.

Weren't they?

At these times Jack went still inside himself and waited.

He felt his largeness, his arms, his legs, drawing Dorcas in. She was like an animal stunned by the light. He just had to lift his little finger and there she'd be, going all soft and limp on him. He hadn't done anything yet, but he was full of the certain knowledge that what he might do would be what she wanted.

He wasn't sure he wanted it himself. She wasn't the kind of girl you could slip your hands up and that would be that. She took herself too seriously.

They went for a picnic — her and him and Bert. It was all arranged. Bert dived off along another path, so it was just her and him. Some beer and bread, one hard-boiled egg, and a blanket.

She was so white and pale, with her dark blonde bush and her thighs that were surprisingly big and her firm pink wet business. It was hard to put that all together with her head, her neck, her hands — the parts of her anyone could look at. The stuck-up parts.

He pushed her down into the bracken and cried out like an animal that had been injured. And she, having nothing with which to compare it, imagined that this was how things were done.

She dug her fingernails into his back and tried to hang on until it appeared to be over. She was worried about the skirt on loan from her best friend Gladys. She hoped he wouldn't tear the skirt.

But it was worth it for the power it gave her.

Over Mum, for one.

Coming into the house Dorcas now felt as if she, too, had to stoop. She looked at her mother knitting by the fire and felt a surge of wildness. She was going to be able to tell Gladys, who was such a great big flirt. She would say to Gladys, "You're not the only one, you know. Not the only one."

The mother noticed. Shrank. Went hard and closed. Took it out on the saucepans in the freezing kitchen.

Jack, having given this much, was keen to be off. He climbed on the train and was glad to be on his way. Bert had gone shy on him. It wasn't the smartest thing in the world, to do your best mate's little sister.

Dorcas went back to her camp. She lay in the bunk above Gladys's and listened as the night-bombers went out over saltmarsh and shingle. When they had gone, she listened to the wind. She imagined the owls skimming over the fields, silent and accurate; the bright-eyed mice beneath the bracken, trembling. The part of her that knew the worst would surely happen was ready to welcome it.

*Gayla Reid*

Inside, the little thing was already doing its clever tricks, multiplying and dividing at the same time. There wasn't anything anyone, not even her mother, could do about it.

She sat down and wrote the letter: *Dear Jack*.

Something else: Deirdre's family was poor.

Other people were getting their Holdens but the Hogans still bumped around in an ancient Dodge. (You cranked it up; it had running boards and a rumble seat that wouldn't open.) Dorcas turned sheets and made skirts out of tablecloths. Out back she grew spuds, but she refused to put in pumpkin. Everyone else in Kelly's Creek grew pumpkin and ate it daily. "Horse food," pronounced Deirdre's mother.

Jack had to go down to the pub to get a proper feed.

Dorcas ran chooks and sold the eggs in the store, enthusing over their brown shells and deep-orange yolks. "You'd think she'd laid them herself," my mother would say.

When Deirdre won her bursary to the Angeline convent, there was a chook raffle at the pub and a whip-round to come up with the cash for the school uniform (maroon tunic, three beige blouses, sweater, blazer, overcoat, sports dress, gym pants, velour hat winter, panama hat summer, gloves, shoes, sandshoes).

Then the brothers, the shearers, had a win on the Dapto dogs.

It was touch and go, for all that.

At the age of seven Deirdre and I teach ourselves to swim in the river.

We watch the boys under the bridge and see what they do. Then we go up the river to a place called Sandy Gully and teach ourselves.

We ride over; I'm in front on Old Waler (you say that like *Whaler*), holding the reins, with my feet in the stirrups. Deirdre's in back, hanging on. (It's the same way we ride the bike out from

80

town, doubling.) Deirdre is afraid of harmless Old Waler, unnerved by his probing lower lip, his wide, enthusiastic tongue. Old Waler loves to come to the river with us, to doze beneath the spindly she-oaks. Resting a hindleg, he drifts off.

From the water, we look up at the folded hills with their blue eucalyptus haze. We lift up our eyes to the highest peak, Black Joey, and beyond that, the Moonbi ranges. *Look at the moon, boy*, Dad reckoned, but Mum got cross and said it didn't mean that at all. Mum's family had been on Ardara for over a hundred years.

"So what?" says Deirdre, when I remind her of this. "I'm fourth-generation Australian too, you know."

I lie back and shut my eyes, floating.

"On Dad's side," she goes on. "Dad's lot's been here for ages. His grandfather came out in the gold rush."

"I'm Spanish way back," I tell her. "Sailors got shipwrecked on the Irish coast after the Spanish Armada. The locals nursed them back to health." When my mother talks about me being Black Irish her face goes deliberately vague, as if she's hiding something. Is there something wrong with being descended from the Spanish? But soon her face brightens and she strokes my hair. Black as a raven's wing, she says, admiringly. Black as a raven's wing.

The clean muddy smell of river on sunburned granite is up our noses and down our ears and in our throats. Dragonflies skim the water, flashes of light. My dog Trix leaps up to get at them. She misses, sinks back down, snapping her mouth shut just before she hits the water.

We sit on stones in our puddles, feeling the warmth on our bums and picking each other's leeches off. We marvel at our shrivelled hands and feet.

"What if you drowned?" I say. "You'd turn completely blue."

"Then you'd swell up." She puffs out her cheeks.

We push each other into the water and shriek.

Above the river, above the she-oaks, above the rocks, high in the air, hangs the gummy smoke of bushfires.

The rocks are massive granite boulders, absolute, beyond time. The gums, too, are huge and assert themselves. There are places where we know we must talk in whispers. Old Waler and Trix sense it first — their heads, ears, and necks go down. Humbly, the four of us negotiate our way home through places where the air is thick with power. It is easy to imagine being crushed, obliterated, simply taken out of existence.

Our fathers know about these things. We see it on their faces when they come in from the bush.

Being daughters, we also move in another world.

For afternoon tea on my eighth birthday my mother allows us to use the best china. We put out the butter dish, the sugar bowl, and the cream-coloured milk jug. The milk jug has a small band of orange berries around its base. Those berries are repeated near the top of the jug, just below the spout. Around the rim of the jug and the base of the jug — around all the extremities — is a thin, undiminished band of gold.

Afternoon tea is laid out on that part of the verandah which is, at this time of the year, dense with Virginia creeper. (My mother puts the bathwater on it.)

Deirdre sits down on one side of the table and I sit down on the other, as if these were our accustomed places. There is nobody to ruin everything by saying, "Let's pull the chain on that."

The shape of our lives is as civilized as the milk jug, as the butter dish, the sugar bowl.

It's my birthday but she gets to be the Queen.

I'm the Prince.

I don't even like the bloke.

Later that same year I woke up with legs that wouldn't work: polio. For the next eleven months, I was away in hospital. During that time, Deirdre faded. She sent me letters, she came to visit, but it was not the same. I was the one who was ill; she was the one whose life went on.

Deirdre arrived on Sundays with my parents, who were absorbed, as I was, in the daunting event that had seized my life. Sometimes the visiting adults would congregate at one end of the verandah and gossip of daily things: the weather, cricket, wool prices. No doubt when they were out of our sight, they talked more frankly about us, our chances.

On that first Sunday, Deirdre came over to my bed and sat on it, quite confidently making herself at home, swinging her healthy legs. Then she reached into her pocket and took out a small white cloth bag that contained our jacks. (Until recently it had contained our marbles, which now rolled around in my dressing-table drawer, ignored.) Jacks was the current craze. I was good at jacks. I could do Charley over the water, Charley over the sea. I could throw up one jack, two jacks, and scoop up four, even five, while those were in the air. The trick was to make the throw slow and high, and then not get rushed. We made our own jacks: I got the sheep knuckles from my father; my mother dyed them red and green. Deirdre wasn't quite as good as me but together we were a tough pair, the ones to beat. We took all before us, including teams of earnest boys. (As their luck receded, the boys would grow anxious. They would begin breathing in a laboured way as if they were running in a race that required a great deal of exertion.)

As soon as the adults had gone, Deirdre tumbled the jacks out in front of her. Her hands and wrists were narrow, delicate, mobile. She was planning on a game; it was the natural thing to do.

The jacks, green and red, lay on the cream counterpane. Then it dawned on her what was wrong with this plan. I could not move my arms much, and I certainly could not manipulate my hands; my tenure as jacks champion of the world had ended overnight.

I saw her realize this. A flush grew up her neck, flooded into her face and overwhelmed her.

I had put her in the wrong. It was my fault.

I felt I was watching her through a screen, a scrim.

I saw her white hands take the jacks away, slip them into the cloth bag, return the bag to her pocket. I saw her tuck her auburn hair behind her ears, a nervous gesture.

Neither of us knew what to say after that. In terrible silence, we waited for the adults to return and take over.

Deirdre came again. She came, on and off, throughout the entire eleven months I was in hospital. But she had lost faith in her ability to do or say the right thing, and her conversation was prepared, rehearsed.

I was sent home, and in time I recovered.

Resuming our friendship, we carried on as if nothing had happened. We went down to the river again, Deirdre and I, and played among the rocks, skylarking and shrieking and pushing water into one another's faces. It was as if my time in the hospital had been a bizarre interpolation, a series of completely unreal events having no connection with anything we did or knew in the ordinary world.

By that time, the game of jacks had disappeared. Hopscotch was king, and I was not a contender.


We read the children's books that Deirdre's mother has sent by ship from England. Their pages have a peculiar smell. Deirdre says it reminds her of the smell on the boat when, at the age of one and a half, she was brought to Australia. She claims to be able to recall that journey, the storm three days out of Colombo, then the healing drench of the moon.

"How can you remember that? It isn't possible."

Dorcas was able to obtain passage on the *Empire Clyde*, one of a clutch of English wives of already repatriated Australian soldiers.

"Some govvie Pooh-Bar took pity on them," my mother said. "With all that food rationing they couldn't possibly give their kiddies a good foundation."

As for me, I was born in boring old Kelly's Creek. The bush nurse came. Nobody at home was willing to talk about this important event, neither my mother nor my grandmother. (I didn't even consider asking my father.)

In one of these English books, a girl goes on holiday with her family to the beach. There's an illustration. They are all sitting with their backs to a fence that goes right down the beach into the water. Grandmother is wearing a long black dress.

We wonder what a fence is doing there, on the beach.

Because she was born in England, Deirdre's the expert.

"To stop erosion," she says. We both know about erosion, all the best topsoil washed away down the gully.

We study the picture again. "Sand erosion, Bernie," she says, more confidently.

"Look at the beach," I demand. "Take a good look. It's all stones."

"Stone erosion," she says stubbornly.

She has to be the one to know.


One day, on our way back from the river, I take her up to a place the family calls the Lookout and teach her how to co-ee properly. Deirdre's voice rings out into the smoky blue depths of the hills, one echo rippling into another.

When we get back to my place, something's up. Dad's horse is already in the home paddock even though there are good hours of daylight left.

My brother is waiting in the yard to greet us. "You're gunna get it," he says, excited.

"I haven't been doing anything wrong." What on earth is he on about?

"Not much you haven't."

My father and mother are in the lounge room and want to see both of us immediately. We go in, puzzled and much afraid.

My father looks immensely grave.

"I was down at O'Brien's Flat," he says. "And I heard you two co-eeing. I believed somebody was hurt."

"We didn't know it would carry like that," I say, trying to defend myself. (Because haven't I co-eed myself, up on the Lookout? And nobody has heard a thing.)

"Your father came right home," my mother says. "But I told him you girls were just fooling around."

How did she know that?

"I thought I'd have to send out a search party," my father says.

We have trespassed. We have interrupted my father's work.

"Never, *ever*, let me hear you do that again," my father continues. "Do you two girls understand me?" My father has one of those famous Easter Island faces, immobile now in its sternest pose.

"Bernadette should know better," my mother declares. "I'm ashamed of her." She's talking to my father about me as if I weren't there.

With that, we are allowed to slip away in disgrace.

A few weeks later when things have died down, I decide it's safe to bring it up.

"How did you know we weren't in trouble?" I asked my mother. "Up at the Lookout?"

"I could hear it. You don't listen just for the words. Words are only part of it."

Deirdre and I declare that we will get married to each other. We're both going to be brides, in a ceremony to be held down by the river.

Planning a wedding, we find, requires attention to detail.

I decide I can risk borrowing one lace tablecloth from my mother's collection in the linen press. Taking turns, we wrap ourselves in it and stick it into the top of our swimsuits, so we can have bare shoulders like film stars. Veils are easy, we have our first-communion veils.

We hold the dress rehearsal in my bedroom. I find an old pair of my mother's shoes, toe-peepers. She's taller than I am, but not by much. When I'm in the toe-peepers we're the same height.

"What about a priest?" asks Deirdre. "Don't you think we ought to have a priest?"

"We can stand in front of Old Waler," I say. "I'll take the missal and say Old Waler's words for him."

"We don't need the missal," says Deirdre. She doesn't want me making the decisions. "I'll write the wedding vows myself."

On the day of the wedding we set off on Old Waler. The outfit is wrapped up with our towels and swimsuits. Deirdre has brought the wedding feast: soft drinks and biscuits from the shop.

We have to take turns. First I'm the priest (standing in front of Old Waler) and she's the bride. Then I'm the bride and she's the priest.

"Do you vow to love Bernadette Veronica Behan as long as ye both shall live and then go to Heaven with her forever?" I ask Deirdre, playing the role of the priest and reading from her script.

"I vow," she whispers through the veil. She lurches in my mother's high heels.

"A vow is a solemn promise made before God," I read. "A vow is impossible to break."

When Deirdre's mother is having a good spell, I go to town and stay with Deirdre overnight. There's an old double bed in one of the spare rooms that can be moved out onto the verandah on hot nights. It's probably used by the shearers when they're home. I don't want to think about that, I have to put it out of my mind.

Deirdre's father rigs up the mosquito net. It's dark green, a jungle mozzie net. (The shearers were in New Guinea and the Islands, like my father. It was only Deirdre's father who was in the desert getting sand in his brains.) The net has two smells. The first layer is familiar: dust. Below that is something dense and rank, attractive and repulsive at the same time. That's the jungle.

"Mosquito! mosquito!" Deirdre and I shout as loudly as we can. If you repeat any word long enough it begins to turn into magic, but *mosquito* is special. *Mosquito* is sleek, *mosquito* flies, it dives and pulls out at the last minute. *Mosquito* triumphs.

"You're in the jungle now," says Deirdre's father.

"Stop your yelling, you two," Deirdre's mother says, coming out onto the verandah.

Deirdre's mother insists on tucking the mozzie net in under the mattress all the way around. She's terrified of anything that moves in the grass. Couldn't tell a skink from a tiger snake.

Deirdre's father asks, "What if they have to go?"

Deirdre's mother frowns.

"They'll have to slither out," her father continues. "Slither out and in like little snakes, I reckon."

Deirdre's mother gives a small, ladylike shriek.

Satisfied, Jack goes inside.

We've been reading an English book about a girl whose bed lifts off at night. It takes her across the town and into the countryside. All night long she is riding about the sky. That's what we're going to do. After the pub down the road has closed and Pegleg Muldoon has rolled the last of the kegs out (*stump clinker clinker stump* — it could be me with a leg like that), when the dogs are bored with barking, off we go.

Deirdre and I look down at the cricket pitch in the park beside the river. This is the pitch that Deirdre's father rolls. (There's a blue streetlight down there. Insects are competing to drown themselves in it.) We leave the park to follow the river out into the bush, where it's totally dark. We're high above the gum trees and granite boulders. The mosquito net billows out behind us like a splendid long wedding veil.

"*Mosquito, mosquito,*" we chant.

We're looking down at the river, snaking its way to Sandy Gully. We're out over the paddocks, smelling the dry grass. We're at least fifty, maybe ninety feet up. We're very wide awake.

"Aloft at last," I say, importantly.

"If only we could fly like this forever," says Deirdre. "And never go to school again."


Before we went off to the Angelines, Deirdre and I attended Our Lady of Sorrows, the Catholic primary school in Kelly's Creek, run by aggro nuns and aptly named. The nuns, who were Joeys — St. Joseph nuns — appeared fully happy only when they had their skirts hitched up and were charging across the playground teaching the boys to play rugby league: the tough, rural version, heaps of kicking and biting.

One of the nuns, Sister Basil, was gentler. Older, slower, thicker. Oblivious to the ructions at the back of the class. She couldn't be bothered. After a while those kids back there would quieten, too. They would settle down and listen, because she told stories. She read from a book called *Come Rack, Come Rope* about dungeon, fire, and sword, about Irish scholar-saints and English perfidy. They even stole our saints, she'd tell us. All those Protestant saints were ours first.

She was Irish, old Baso. On the one journey of her life, the trip out to Australia, she'd made a stop and visited Lourdes for a fortnight.

Every day she went to the grotto, which was where Our Lady had appeared to Bernadette, a simple peasant girl. At the grotto, Baso said, you didn't notice the passage of time. You could be there for three hours and it seemed like three seconds. There were processions every day — people on crutches, in wheelchairs, you name it. No, they weren't all cured; sometimes it wasn't God's will for them to be cured. But from those who weren't cured, from those in particular, came a calm air of healing grace.

She'd been in the waters.

When Baso got to the story of the waters, the mood of the classroom became engaged, alert.

This is the way you go into the waters: first, you enter a large room in which there are canvas partitions. A nun comes in and together you say an act of contrition. You slip into a simple calico sheet: put your arms in and gather it around the waist with a tie. The nun takes you to the water and you squat down on your haunches, shivering. Just when you're so icy cold you think you're going to die, the nun pulls you back so that the water comes up around your neck. She holds you tight and doesn't let your head go under. Then the nun turns you around and that's when you get out of the water and put your clothes back on. (All the while you're saying Hail Marys.)

On the way home from school, Deirdre and I considered this.

Had Baso taken off her habit before she put on the calico sheet? Had she taken off the rest of the stuff they wear?

It certainly sounded as if she'd taken everything off. Because hadn't she said, you put your clothes back on?

She squatted down in the water. On her haunches.

Wouldn't the sheet cling to you?

When you got out of the waters there was no need to dry yourself because you were immediately warm.

There was, Baso said, no need of towels at Lourdes.

Sister Basil was also a master of the standard repertoire. From her we learned about Catherine on the wheel; Lucy with her eyes plucked out; Agnes with her breasts chopped off; John boiled in oil; Lawrence politely being fried: "Please turn me over and do the other side."

Deirdre's favourite story was about Saint George, the patron saint of England and a Catholic, not C of E at all. Saint George was tied to a wheel full of spikes, which, when turned round and round, made his body one mass of wounds. Because he didn't die, more tortures were in store for him. A heavy stone was rolled over him, but still he would not yield. At last he was put to death by the sword.

These were not distant matters, not at all. The war was raging right now between Satan and Christ, old Baso said. It was the war between the Commos and us Catholics. We were in the blue army, they were in the red. The blue was the cloak of the Blessed Virgin.

Satan, old Baso explained, was busy in China. At that minute, he was sticking chopsticks into the ears of Catholics, sticking them right through their heads. The chopstick would go in your left ear and come out the right. We must prepare ourselves for the torture that was coming. Because the Reds were going to get round to us, they were coming down to Australia, it was only a matter of a few years at the most. We must start preparing, now, for the day when we would have to give our lives for the faith of our fathers. We should begin immediately, taking baths that were hotter and hotter all the time — or colder and colder, like Lourdes.

We were important, each one of us, even those lumpy wild boys at the back of the class. God was incredibly interested in us. Satan was just as keen. We had immortal souls and the battle for them was intense.

As Sister Basil tells these stories, I see our school from a height, as if we were in our flying bed.

Our Lady of Sorrows sits in a paddock on the shoulder of a hill. Around it, gums and birds and dust and sheep. Above, a sky that goes straight up to eternity. It is a mighty stage, and upon it Our Lady of Sorrows stands out quite clearly.

I am visible; so is Deirdre. God has us in his sights. The choices we make, what we do, will count. Nothing could ever be more important than that.

On the largest stage of all, in the battle between good and evil, we are protagonists. We matter.

I see Deirdre taking it all in.

I see her eyes: wide and bright.

# 4

Some years ago I watched a TV show in which two young Russian men were leaving their village to go into the army as conscripts. With their families, having a send-off party, they were expansive, noisy, proud of themselves. But by the time they approached the barracks, they were sticking together for protection, their faces raw.

I did not immediately realize why these images unsettled me.

Deirdre and I went off to the convent for the first time at the age of eleven, to St. Angela's College in Armidale. Our trunks contained our new school uniforms, complete with the name tags my mother had sewn in. They also contained mysterious packages of Moddess, each package carefully wrapped in brown paper to prevent identification, for use should the need arise.

Before my father drove us up to Armidale for the start of the school year, we put on our uniforms. They hung heavy and slightly too large. We looked at each other, two strangers about to embark upon a journey. We were in awe of our new blazers with their elaborate pocket crests of maroon and beige. A cross upon a shield, and the school motto across the top. *Serviam*: I will serve.

"That all cost a pretty penny," said my mother. "Not that you can expect the nuns to know the value of money."

The convent was for us large and dark and quirky, with corridors that could not be trusted to take you out the way you went in.

We were confronted by girls who sniggered in a complex range of tones that constituted a language in itself. These girls knew exactly when to stop.

A nun, bearing down at high speed. "Girls, after lunch I expect to see everyone in Sacred Heart for the rosary. May I remind you, girls, that no girl is permitted to go up to St. Charles Borremeo in the afternoons."

"Yes, Sister Dominic." "No, Sister Dominic." (*Old bag.*)

Deirdre and I looked at one another and acknowledged that we had much to learn: the tone, the tenor, the significance of the unsaid.

Up at six, to Mass, to breakfast, back to Borremeo to make one's bed, to chapel for morning prayers, to class. We were soon swept up in the implacable routine.

Even when you thought you knew what they were talking about you were wrong: lunch turned out to be two pieces of bread and fish paste at eleven o'clock in the morning and three o'clock in the afternoon.

Soon it was our own lives that were alien to us, rather than this.

There are compensations, we discover. Latin grammar, for one.

A dark-blue book with gold lettering on the front shows us how to decline a noun. The first noun is *agricola*, a farmer. We feel confident with *agricola*, we know about farmers.

"See how a noun changes depending on what's happening?" Deirdre says. "Nominative, vocative, accusative."

Other nouns follow: table, lord, war, master, slave, consul (that one's easy). Ships defend the harbour. Titus gives darts to the citizens. Go far enough down this road, Deirdre believes, and you will end up somewhere grand and stimulating. (We're in a posh taxi gliding down a cobblestone street in Europe. It is evening and we're off to the theatre, we are grown-ups.)

We learn to conjugate the verb "to love."

"They have so many kinds of past tenses," says Deirdre, her voice full of willing respect. "Do you think they have more pasts than we do?"

"Wouldn't be surprised," I say, "seeing they're all dead."

Deirdre puts her nose into her grammar book, snuffs with pleasure at the smooth, thick pages.


We avoid mention of our parents whenever possible. I'm safe enough. My parents have the property, Ardara, and a property can mean anything from a massive pastoral company to a bit of useless scrub. Deirdre has to say her parents run the Kelly's Creek general store, which is a whole lot more dicey. The real details of Deirdre's life — her crazy mother, her crude uncles — are secrets we both know we need to keep.

The nuns collude in this. Although they read our letters from home before we do, they never refer to our other world. It does not exist. We have appeared from nowhere at the age of eleven and now we are theirs, for life.

During the holidays it is strange being back where we came from. The general store, with its dingy confusion, cannot compare with the sparse, polished surfaces of the convent.

When I ride my bike into Kelly's Creek, to Hogan's store, Jack is out back in his sweaty navy singlet, mending a meat-safe with a bit of wire. One of the uncles, home from shearing, snores on the verandah beside a row of empty beer bottles. Dead marines, the uncles call them.

Although we would never admit this to the nuns, we miss the convent. We miss the elegant ambition of the chapel, its polished parquet floor of West Australian jarrah, its Romanesque arches, its altar of Siena marble, its elegant stained-glass windows from Germany.

All of that.

By our third year at the convent we will have begun to take such luxuries for granted and pity our younger selves for having been so impressionable.

Home for the holidays, we collect soft drinks from the store and ride my bike back out to the property. Then we climb on Old Waler and go down to the river at Sandy Gully. We take off our swimsuits — there is nobody around. We compare breasts.

We are both too small.

Deirdre wades into the water and pretends she's a ballerina, effortlessly tall on tiptoe. I dive and force myself to open my eyes. I want to see Deirdre's legs, long and white and thin, moving in the sunny water.

We go down between the rocks to find the rushing water, to feel the pressure of it on our bums, between our thighs.

It occurs to me that the nuns wouldn't approve of what we're doing.

With the water moving through our legs, we stare at the sky. Carefully, we plan our own trip by boat. We're going to England, of course. France. Italy. We're going to have deck chairs on a great ocean liner, with blankets to keep us warm and magnificent books to read.

I do not remember us ever mentioning Indochina or Argentina, although in our greed we might have.

At primary school, we learned by heart all the ports of call from England to Australia. Southampton, Marseilles, Aden, Karachi, Colombo, and the rest. Then Fremantle, and around the Bight, stopping at Hobart in the apple season.

"In Aden," Deirdre tells me, "you have to be careful not to get lost in the market. You could be kidnapped. They come up behind you with chloroform on a handkerchief. Next thing you know you wake up and you're in a harem."

"How could I possibly get lost? I'd be with you."

She grabs me from behind, pretends to be sticking a chloroformed handkerchief over my mouth. I put up a terrific fight.

"How many countries do you think we'll have seen by the time we're twenty?" Deirdre asks, panting. She's finally got me pinned down in a rock pool, a slave in her harem.

"I don't know," I say, happily. "About one hundred and fifty? How many countries are there, anyway?"

We can feel the water, moving over the stones and between our toes.

"I bet there's at least three hundred and sixty-five," she asserts. "One for every day of the year."

"Bet we'll have seen the lot by the time we're thirty."

"We'll be old by then, Bernie. Imagine that."


In mid-winter we have our school retreat, three whole days of prayer and no talking. A Passionist father comes. He doesn't stand up to deliver his sermons in the chapel. A desk is brought in for him, and he sits behind it in a large oak chair.

As we file into our places in the chapel, Deirdre and I communicate in our language of gestures.

From me, a lift of the shoulders and a point of the chin: strange to see a desk and chair at the front of the chapel.

From her, a drop of the mouth: yes, almost blasphemous.

We should have a special devotion to the Immaculate Heart of Mary, this old Passionist says. We should wear the brown scapula at all times and make the Five First Saturdays without fail.

Here we go.

"In 1917, which is not all that long ago despite what you young ones may think," he tells us, "Our Lady appeared to three simple peasant children at Fatima. Lucia, Francisco, and Jacinta were out watching their sheep."

I look at Deirdre, lift my eyebrows. We've considered this before. It's odd, we've agreed, the way people in Europe stand about watching their sheep. If you had to watch all the sheep on Ardara, you'd never sleep. *While shepherds washed their socks by night.* Although that wasn't Europe, that was the Middle East.

"When they told their parents that Our Lady had come to save the Church from apostasy and countless souls from damnation, the three children got into a lot of trouble. They weren't allowed to go to the pasture any more. So Our Lady told them she would send a sign to show everyone they were telling the truth.

"One afternoon in October a large crowd gathered at the pasture. They were waiting for her sign. Many in the crowd jeered. An eyewitness — a medical doctor, a highly professional man — noticed a cloud of smoke gather around the three children, then rise into the air.

"The sun began to dim, and the crowd fell silent. There wasn't any fog. It had been raining earlier in the day but it was by now a perfectly fine afternoon.

"Then the sun started to dance." With this, the priest gets up and begins to waltz, stiffly, in front of the desk. "Our Lady had commanded the sun to dance."

Deirdre rapidly crosses and uncrosses her eyes: the old boy's really getting carried away, wouldn't you say?

Lowering his voice to a confessional murmur, the priest continues: "The horizon turned a strange, sickly purple. People saw their skin become the colour of old linen."

The priest picks at the loose folds of his own hand, holds the hand up. We glance down at our own smooth skin.

"The sun," — he thumps the desk and begins to advance upon the front pew, shouting — "the sun turned blood red and was racing towards them. It was going to crush them!"

The kids in the front duck. One of them dives for the protection of the first pew, sends it crashing into the parquet floor. There's a moment of intermission while a team of nuns dart out from their prayer stalls at the side of the chapel and quickly heave the heavy pew back into place. A few prefects stand about ineffectually.

Now the priest is ready for the climax: the three messages Our Lady gave the children. First, the vision of souls falling into Hell. Second, the prophecy of the Second World War and the rise of Communism. "Lucia revealed these first two secrets in 1941, and it goes without saying that they have been absolutely accurate.

"Now," says the Passionist, his voice dropping once more to a whisper. "What about the third message?"

In the silence of the chapel, we wait.

"As I've told you, two of the three children, Francisco and Jacinta, died in the odour of sanctity only a few years after Our Lady commanded the sun to dance. The eldest, Lucia, became a Carmelite nun. In 1943, Lucia fell gravely ill. The Cardinal was worried she might die. He asked her to write down what Our Lady had said in case it was lost to the world forever.

"Every time Lucia picked up a pen, something prevented her from writing. Was it God or Satan who was stopping her?

"Lucia prayed for a sign.

"In January of 1944, on a freezing winter's day, Our Lady and the Christ Child appeared to her and Our Lady confirmed that yes, she did want the message written down.

"All along, you see, Satan had been the one preventing Lucia from writing."

The Passionist lowers his voice still further. We're leaning forward, trying to hear him.

"Lucia wrote and sealed the letter from Our Lady, foretelling all that would happen in our century. Lucia indicated that it should be read by 1960 at the latest.

"It is known that this sealed letter is twenty-five lines long — the Cardinal held it up to the light, just to check that it was in its envelope.

"The letter, I am happy to tell you, is now safe in the Vatican. The Holy Father himself keeps it in a locked wooden chest in his own private study."

Deirdre and I find each other's eyes, which have become shy.

We want it to be true.

We want to believe that a letter direct from Heaven is waiting to be read. A letter, stern and estactic, that will explain everything.


It is a Saturday afternoon, September holidays. We've been roaming about Kelly's Creek on my bicycle and now we're on Cemetery Hill, hidden in deep paspalum, waiting for a funeral to arrive. The burial is going to be in the Protestant part of the cemetery, and it's a Methodist or Baptist funeral — something like that — because the minister looks like a headmaster in an English boys' school book.

Catholics aren't allowed to attend Protestant ceremonies, but out here, in the cemetery paddock, we decide it's okay. We're at least fifty yards away, we're not attending, we're not taking part, we're just looking, thank you.

Before we rode up here, we were down at the sports grounds to see who won the toss for the first match of the season (Kelly's Creek). Deirdre's father put on the pads and strode out to the pitch he'd rolled before lunch. When we left on the bike, Jack Hogan was at the crease, patting bits of ground into place with his bat while the visiting team prepared to fight a losing battle.

We know who's being buried, of course. The stationmaster. From down Cessnock way, my mother said. Lived all by himself in the railway cottage, went about collarless unless dressed in his NSWGR uniform. Grew geraniums in tractor tires at the station. He'd invite children to weigh themselves on the large scale for wool bales at the end of the platform. Slowly, he would count out the solid round weights, exclaiming in admiration as more were needed. "Can you beat that?" he'd ask. "Can you beat that?" And we would be proud of ourselves, impressed at the marvel of our growth.

He was a man completely alone, but today, for the funeral, people have turned up on the train. A dry voice inside me, my mother's, speculates that a special railway pass would have been made available to mourners.

So they gather at the grave, the minister in his drab togs, the crowd recently arrived by train. They glance around at the unfamiliar cemetery. Restless in their Sunday best, they are unnerved by the racketing currawongs that have gathered in the stringybarks by the fence. These sleeky black birds are interested in the coffin. With its shining wood and sparkling silver handles, it gleams in the sun: just the kind of thing to attract their gold-button eyes.

In the front row at the graveside are two women. They must be sisters, they may even be twins, they look so much alike. Both expecting. A dusty spring westerly blows, and their concealing smocks are pushed against their bodies. From our nest of grass we see the two smocked bellies protrude over the grave.

Deirdre points. With both hands, she makes a huge round gesture over her body; she looks to me to take it up. This gesture we find absolutely hilarious, and the need to repeat it, over and over, is completely beyond our control. We double over in our mirth, straighten up and make it again: that shape, that round, massive shape, right out in the open.

"They've been doing the Lambeth Walk," Deirdre gasps out.

Lambeth is some place in London. It has an Anglican archbishop who gets in the Sunday papers, saying perilous things about birth control.

"*Doing the Lambeth Walk! Hoy!*" On the *Hoy!* we jerk our bellies out.

We keep this up through the prayers, through the lowering of the coffin, through the hugs and pats of shoulders, the first turning away.

Some of the family members look up at the trees, searching for strange, tableland parrots.

Now the service has definitely come to an end. The two pregnant women have their backs to us and are making for a black Austin. They seem to be together, but not with anybody else in particular.

"I wonder where the hubbies are?" says Deirdre.

"Down the colliery in Cessnock. Miners have to work around the clock," I say.

"Cessnock knock, who's there?" she tries, but we let it slide.

Worn out, we lie back in the grass, picking off pieces to chew and watching the high, dry clouds that sit in the sky, month after month.

The mob of currawongs decides to push off.

"Today we're here," says Deirdre, looking up at the sky. "This time next week we'll be back at school."

From the sports grounds we hear a small round of clapping. "What do you bet Dad's hitting sixes," she adds.

With those words, I feel a surge of content rising, not only inside me but also inside Deirdre. We are winning, the two of us. Not at the cricket, not at anything domestic or mundane, but at something intangible and potent. We are winning, right here in the spring afternoon, with the stationmaster in his shining coffin and Deirdre's father down at the sports grounds batting away like Don Bradman. My own father applauding.

After the last of the funeral crowd has left, the bloke who digs the graves — a good mate of Deirdre's father, a spin bowler — gets out of his ute, where he's been sitting and waiting, smoking a cigarette. He comes over and fills in the new grave, rapidly, with his spade. He has on his cricket whites. As soon as the pile of dirt is in, he bangs the mound with the back of the spade, then gets down on his knees and briefly tucks the old boy in, his bare hands patting at the red soil. That done, he tosses the spade in the back of the truck and dusts a bit of soil from his trousers, which are by now brown around the knees. There's a pale pink stain on his pants as well, near the crotch. That's where he rubs the cricket ball up and down before he throws it.

He opens the ute door and turns, looks back briefly. Then he jumps in and revs the engine. As he drives down the road, switching gears, there's the clatter of the spade bumping about.

It's large and quiet, up here on the warm hill.

We walk over to inspect the fresh earth.


At school, we develop a finely honed hierarchy of the things that count.

Holidays become vastly important. (Girls more fortunate than ourselves, those who live down at the coast, are free to go to the beach; they lie on towels and look at the Woodlawn boys.) Running a distant second are outings. These are the times we leave the convent for an event: Anzac Day, St. Patrick's Day, the Sydney Symphony Orchestra on tour. Third in importance are the short trips we make away from the convent: after school we may go in pairs to the dentist or doctor. Fourth are visits by others to the convent. Somebody comes to speak to us: priests, usually. (Once, a wildly public-spirited chap from the uni came for a lecture series on everyday life in ancient Rome.) Last is the regimen of small privileges we look forward to.

One of these privileges, inaugurated late in our third year, is permission to wear mantillas to Benediction in the convent chapel on Saturday evening. We buy our mantillas the day before the beginning of term. The woman in the store lifts them out of their box: small lace veils imported from Italy, with scalloped edges, the elegance of piety.

There are two kinds. One is crowded with neat rows of roses — we know exactly which girls will go for that one. The other is a tangle of leaves, which we judge to be vastly more tasteful.

As we get out our mantillas for Benediction there's a shivery feeling, pleasure let loose in the air.

The only mirror in the entire convent is at the end of the hallway that leads to the chapel. Its sole purpose, we are told, is to ensure that girls are respectable before entering the house of God. We're not supposed to linger in front of this mirror, but whenever the coast is clear, we do, we do. In the flattering gloom — no lights at this end of the hallway — we study ourselves in our fresh white mantillas.

In the mirror, Deirdre looks over at me, gives a wide, open-mouthed smile: we look stunning, the pair of us, don't you think? Her fair hair is framed with foaming lace.

An important man comes to town, all the way from London. He's talking to us, the convent school girls, and the sixth-class kids from the local primary school. The boys from the Brothers aren't coming. We're not told why.

We're marched in a crocodile down to the Police Boys' club to hear the visiting Englishman. I'm puzzled that he isn't speaking in the parish hall, but this is much better. It's quite a long walk from the convent and we can look over people's fences, see the washing hanging on the line, hear the chooks boasting about eggs they've laid. Some yards even have ducks. There are babies in prams, women chopping wood, a man delivering fresh bread from a van.

"He used to have a horse but his mother died," some day girl says.

The van smells utterly delicious. We walk past it as slowly as we can. The nuns aren't talented cooks, corners are cut, and none of us has enough to eat. Being permanently somewhat hungry is a fact of life, like unheated dormitories and chilblains

"Doesn't fresh bread make you want to swoon?" Deirdre says. "Yum yum, gimme some."

Once he had been a Communist, this visiting man. He used to edit the newspaper the Commos have in Britain, the *Daily Worker*. Now he's a Catholic. He's a convert.

The Police Boys' club is a Nissan hut made out of corrugated iron, adrift in high tough paspalum. After the cropped lawns of the convent, it's good to see real grass again.

Inside the hut we sit in rows, sweating into our school uniforms. I'm also bleeding into my pad, I can feel the warm wetness.

At one end of the hut there's a boxing ring on a raised platform. This is a strange and interesting thing. Smells different. A punching bag, too, hanging by a rope from the roof. I'd like to be able to get up and take a good look round, climb into the ring, put my fist into the bag, feel its resistance.

"I wonder what you have to do to become a police boy," Deirdre says.

"I don't know. Steal milk bottles, maybe. Get into fights."

"They get into fights in here," she points out. "Proper ones."

I imagine being a boy, up in the boxing ring. I'm bouncing around on the balls of my feet, in little red satin shorts. Making deft, quick jabs. (I don't have my period.)

Now Deirdre is staring up at the corrugated iron roof. She says to me out of the corner of her mouth, "You could get a trapeze going up there."

We follow the circus, or rather, Deirdre follows the trapeze artists. *Artistes*. Back home, Deirdre has a picture of one of the trapeze artistes stuck on her bedroom wall: La Frankie. In a startling golden bikini, La Frankie is up there in the spotlight, grabbing hold of the flimsy swing and flying out across the top of the tent.

One night last winter, La Frankie, performing without the safety net, fell. Injured, she would not fly again. Her real name was Frances Janet Duncan, the *Women's Weekly* reported. Not the kind of name that goes with risking one's neck.

Wirth's Circus came to Araluen during the next school holidays. (Araluen, on the Armidale road, was big enough to warrant a circus; Kelly's Creek wasn't.) My father agreed to drive Deirdre and me. As we came over the hill into town, we could see the fairy lights swooping between the two big poles of the enormous tent. My father dropped us off, after we'd promised to rendezvous with him before the show. We were left free to roam around, inspecting the guy ropes and smelling the canvas, the crushed dry grass.

At the back of the big top was a lane of caravans where the circus people lived. A dwarf in overalls came out and hung up some clothes on a low washing line. There was a strong smell of onions frying.

Set apart from both the caravans and the big top was a smaller row of tents, lit only with kero lamps. Here on display were deformed animals, which we decided probably had more appeal to people who lived in cities. We peeked in and saw a sturdy, two-headed calf, each head munching peaceably away.

The tents beyond these had no open flaps, only mysterious signs: "Gents! Double Your Pleasure with the Siamese Twins," "Meet Mabel and Her Tempting Tresses." We stood outside these tents and heard the murmur of men in from the silent paddocks.

We knew not to mention these tents to my father. They were something to be thought about, to be discussed in whispers later.

During the circus act itself, disconsolate golden bears from Malaya sat on stools and then had to get up and dance. It was a relief when the horses arrived — fine palominos with girls kneeling on them (I could do that myself, I told Deirdre, except Mum and Dad would never let me) — followed by the dapper little pugs who jumped, bored and businesslike, through burning hoops.

We were, both of us, waiting for the final act: the trapeze. Celestina and the Flying Dutchman, they were called, the new Wirth's Circus trapeze artistes. The show had gone on.

La Frankie's successor, Celestina, slipped off her shoes, dipped her feet in what we decided was chalk, and climbed lightly onto the platform. In her blue and silver two-piece costume, she snaked up a thin column at the platform's edge. Up she went, alone in the spotlight, up and up, to the tedious insistence of drums.

The foolish music stopped, the lights were dimmed.

Just the one spotlight, high, high in the tent, where Celestina, in silence, folded herself in two and then did a handstand at the top of the column, isolated, sparkling in the heavens.

Then it was back down to the platform for swinging and catching with the Flying Dutchman. Another climax was on its way, and once again, the drums were quiet. The Flying Dutchman, his arms and legs wrapped around the swings, dangled Celestina from a rope in his mouth. The rope went around her waist and there was a device on it that enabled her to spin. Suspended in the Flying Dutchman's jaws, she spun in the air while the net below was removed. I felt a thinning inside myself. How could Celestina be so foolish as to let the net be taken away? What if he let her go, what if his jaws couldn't hold her any longer?

I found I couldn't forget them: Celestina suspended from the man's jaws, La Frankie flying through the air. Lying in my dormitory bed, I'd conjure up La Frankie in her golden outfit, Celestina in silver and blue. I would do this, deliberately, to torment myself. I always had to have them both. I had to have them both at once, and I had to slip back and forth, from one to the other, more and more quickly until shame began to blossom inside me, growing more attractive as I pushed myself on, through the flying, through the spinning, to the fall, the fall.

There lies La Frankie, a damaged lump in the sawdust. Celestina is dangling and there is no safety net below.

I have not told Deirdre any of this.

Now, in the Police Boys' shed, the man from England is droning on. He tells us about the Commos and what he once believed. He doesn't go on about Satan the way Sister Baso used to. He talks about trade unions instead. Incredibly boring.

"I bet the police boys could rig something up," Deirdre whispers. "Some ropes, a ladder, a platform, a net. We could wear our swimsuits. Put some sparkles on them. Maybe we could get bikinis." The nuns disapprove of bikinis, which provide occasions of sin.

"I wouldn't want to be a trapeze artiste full-time," I tell her. As I say this I'm aware of being dishonest, of holding something back. You can lie by what you leave out as well as by what you put in. "Maybe as a sideline when we're travelling round the world," I concede.

"It would be better than working as a chambermaid. Guess what we'd be emptying."

"Not these days."

"Well, you'd be cleaning bathrooms, same thing. Making beds."

"Maybe we could go hop-picking," I say. We'd seen a short at the flicks about hop-picking in the south of England. Everyone stayed up late and sat around a bonfire, singing.

She is not to be diverted. "We'll have to change our names."

Of course, but who would we be? Odette and Claudine? How about Violette, after the spy Violette Szabo, who parachuted into France? They caught her, and she was terribly brave. As she was being killed there was a shot of huge cumulus clouds and we heard her saying, "Death will be but a pause / and the rest of my years in the long green grass / will be yours and yours and yours." It was wonderful, Deirdre and I exclaimed, sighing, it was so *sad*. (And there was nobody, nobody, to warn us that this could become a treacherous pleasure.)

"How about Violette?" I suggest. "In purple and gold."

"Which one of us would that be?" she whispers back.

Sister Perpetua has decided to glare at us.

The man from England is talking about a rich young woman who lives in London, which actually might be pretty interesting.

She falls in love with a married man, a non-Catholic. He's going on a trip to the south of France, this married man, and he asks the rich young woman to come with him. Against her mother's advice and the laws of the Church, she agrees.

They fly from London to Paris, where they stop for lunch. (Breakfast in London, lunch in Paris!) There is a dreadful storm. The pilot says they shouldn't go on, but the married man insists. On their way to the south of France they run into a dark curtain of thunder. The plane breaks in two and the rich young woman falls to earth.

Her mother refuses to attend the funeral.

"And do you know what her mother said about the plane crash?" He's got my attention now.

"She said it was God pointing His finger and saying No!" He presents this punchline as though it is some wonderful truth he is tremendously pleased to be able to share.

"We'd fly through the air with the greatest of ease," says Deirdre, still looking up.

"Now I want you to tell me," the man goes on, "what you can learn from this story."

In the corrugated iron dome of the Police Boys' club, there is a hot, stubborn silence. Seems nobody wants to learn anything.

We continue to stare like stunned mullets.

"Think for a moment," the man urges, his voice becoming uncertain.

The nuns realize that they need to rescue him. They go into action, looking around for the senior girls in the Sodality. Deirdre and I are not Sodality girls, nor do we expect to be chosen as such. (You have to wait until the nuns decide you're holy enough. Don't hold your breath.)

"Thou shalt not commit adultery," says a Sodality girl timidly. Anyone could have got that.

"Always make a good confession before starting out on a journey," pipes up another, more firmly.

That's a bit better. Practical, like pack a toothbrush.

He's quite pleased with these two answers, this Englishman, but he's having trouble keeping things going. Maybe English kids are keener. Bet they don't have to sit around in some sweltering shed.

"Avoid occasions of sin," offers a kid from the primary school, brave and nervous and going all red.

That bright spark will go far, I think.

You can see the man's relieved when it's over.

On our way home, in the crocodile, Deirdre has other suggestions.

"Never fly in lousy weather." A few of us laugh, and Deirdre brightens with pleasure.

"Avoid having a nasty mother." This is more like it. Bolder now, she has another go.

"If you can't be good, don't go any farther than Paris."

Giggling begins to spread along the crocodile as the lines are repeated.

The nuns, who've been patrolling from the rear, move alongside.

That evening, during study period, I'm doing maths and I'm thinking about our outing: the bread van, the grass around the Police
Boys' club, the cozy feel of oozing blood (I've just changed my pad),
the boxing ring and punching bag, me and Deirdre changing our
names and becoming trapeze artistes, the man going on about the
Commos.

And God saying No!

I don't want to think about God pointing his finger and saying
No!

I'm watching Deirdre at the next desk, doing her Latin home-
work. (Later, we'll swap.) I raise my desk lid and pretend to be looking for something in my desk.

"About that plane crash," I whisper to her. "Do you really think
it was God saying No!?"

She looks up from what she's doing, raises her desk lid too. "It
wouldn't be fair, would it?" she says. "He'd have to kill the others on
board as well. The pilot, he'd have to kill the pilot just to get at her."

"Maybe he decided to have the innocent ones sent directly to
Heaven. Maybe she was the only one who died."

"But why would God be more interested in her than in the rest?"

"Because she was rich?" I suggest.

She fell through the air with the greatest of ease.

The idea is becoming more far-fetched as we talk. I'm feeling
calmer. You can't have God going around crashing planes. You just
can't. Not if He's the good shepherd.

I've seen baby lambs, limp as wet socks, gone. I've cradled them
while my father coaxed the life back into their bodies. Watched
their eyes blink and their pink mouths open, getting ready to
complain again. Held the warm milk bottle and felt them wriggle,
determined to get at it.

Deirdre says, "It wasn't God, it was the weather."

We both want to be convinced of this.

"It was the thunderstorm," Deirdre says later, when we've put on our slippers and are making our way up to the dormitory. "The thunderstorm," she repeats, deliberately making her voice sound confident.

I realize that I am lucky to have her here, beside me.

In our fourth year we're put in different dormitories. I'm in St. Lucy's, she's in St. Scholastica's.

I lie in St. Lucy's consumed with a new and terrible emotion. I watch for the bird-like swoop of light on the ceiling when, out there in the world, a car stops and makes its turn.

It gives me no pleasure at all.

What is she doing down in St. Scholastica's? Is she sitting on someone else's bed? Are they sharing hand cream?

Someone else is a girl from Sydney. Her father is a barrister with chambers in Elizabeth Street.

Distance grows up rapidly between Deirdre and myself. (It's like the time I was in hospital.) She no longer waits for me outside the classroom. We do not pass notes. We do not exchange glances full of shared, superior judgments. In the space where these glances once were, I see only her averted head. (Coward.)

Chambers in Elizabeth Street. Chamber pot in Elizabeth Street.

There are now, as never before, gestures of impatience between us, and a need to disagree, to argue, to prove wrong. If she has one opinion, I adopt another.

I watch her in a different way.

We are in the refectory and she is carrying a jug of water to her table. I see her holding the jug away from her, and acknowledge that she is too fastidious, too tidy. Like her mother (prissy, barmy).

I watch the way she sits down and brings the glass up to her mouth. Afraid of her own lips. Who would want to have that stupid skin of hers that peels and can't take the heat. Gives her away, betrays her by blushing.

I develop a new daydream which I linger over whenever I have moments to myself: at Mass, at morning assembly, at tennis lessons, during the rosary.

I am going about my business and someone — a younger student, just a messenger — runs to me.

"Deirdre is crying her eyes out. She needs you to come. She says it has to be *you*. You must come, she says you *must*."

I wither the messenger with an indifferent gaze. Go back to my book.

"Bernie," the girl gasps, "how can you be so *cold*?" Because I am refusing. I won't come running simply because she calls for me.

Then for the best bit: the messenger twists in disbelief as it dawns on her. I don't care whether she takes any message back. It's all the same to me.

So much for the fantasy.

The truth is that whenever I know I am about to see Deirdre I feel a tension in my stomach, in my chest, around my heart. The first time I feel it each day is when we go to put on our shoes before morning Mass.

That particular tension will stay with me as an adult. When I wait for the train or the plane that is to bring Deirdre to me, or when I'm on the train or plane going to her, the minutes immediately before I see her will always be tense, a mixture of anxiety, mild nausea, and vertigo. I will be afraid, convinced that something will go wrong at the last minute. The plane or train will arrive, and she won't be on it. Or I'll arrive, and she won't be waiting for me.

I'll be scanning the crowd for her face and she won't be there.

It's a winter twilight, early evening. We are in the schoolyard.

The convent is on the side of a hill. We can look out and see the town in the hollow below. There is smoke in the air; most homes still have wood-burning stoves. In the fading light the smoke sits above the town, a tender grey gauze.

We are watching this, a group of young girls, sixteen years old.

Someone suggests that we rub faces to see how they feel.

I put my cheek against the next girl's and the soft warmth is astonishing. When it's my turn to put my cheek against Deirdre's, it's completely different; there is a connection here, fierce and quick and demanding. I feel it pounding through me. I am convinced she feels it too.

That's why I turn away from her.

I realize that soon she will dump the barrister's daughter. She'll have to, she will have no choice.

A few nights after this, we are cleaning our shoes by the boot press on the verandah. After that we'll go up to the dormitory in slippers: I to St. Lucy's, she to St. Scholastica's.

I don't let myself check to see where the lawyer's daughter is.

I watch the way Deirdre slides the polish around her shoe, feeding the leather. She knows I'm looking.

There is a weak incandescent light above us, a single bulb.

She breathes over the worn, pliable leather. Buffs it to a high shine. Breathes on it again. Gets out a chamois rag and goes for the perfect finish.

Then she looks directly at me and gives me a shrug, an admission.

At the end of the year the class puts on *The Merchant of Venice* — the nuns are wildly enthusiastic about theatrical performances of every kind. The lawyer's daughter and Deirdre both want to be Portia. Neither will give way.

Deirdre gets the part.

After that, they no longer walk together. The barrister's daughter immediately acquires a new best friend, a girl with cow eyes who's been simply dying for an opportunity to bow and scrape.

Then my own luck changes. Shylock comes down with chicken pox and is whisked away home. I am the replacement.

"If you prick us, do we not bleed? If you tickle us, do we not laugh? If you poison us, do we not die?" With these words I plead with Deirdre in the school play, on the last night of term, in a public auditorium, in front of the entire world including my parents, my grandmother, and Aunt Hazel.

"We're the only ones who understand the first thing about *The Merchant*," Deirdre tells me, at the end of the evening. Euphoric, we hug one another, our faces heavy with real greasepaint. (Wherever did the nuns get that?)

We clean up, collect our luggage, and the nuns have to let us go for the Christmas holidays.

Deirdre and I sit in the backseat as my father drives fast down the tableland highway.

I have her back, I know it.

The night pours in, the dry smell of sunburned grass. The moon with its direct, enormous gaze.

Deirdre leans over to whisper in my ear. "Mosquito!"

"Mosquito!" I reply.

We are powerful and vast, we are flying out together over the bush, above the stringybark, the manna, and the white ribbon gum.

Ahead lies everything.

One afternoon in our final year at St. Angela's, Sister Perpetua sends for Deirdre after dinner, which is the midday meal. Perpetua's in charge of the senior girls but she isn't nosy, she isn't particularly interested. For that we rather like her. And for the fact that, despite the demanding convent routine, Perpetua seems able to keep herself amused. We've seen her skimming along with a sly, inward smile on her face.

Perpetua gives Deirdre the news that she has found in a letter from my mother and in an unprecedented note from Deirdre's father. Deirdre's mother has been taken away, to Morisset. It's down near Gosford somewhere.

Put in the mental home. Locked up.

The nut house at Morisset. The loony bin.

"For her own good" — my mother.

"Hoping for the best" — Deirdre's father.

Deirdre emerges from Perpetua's office to tell me this just before the bell goes for afternoon classes. All through the afternoon I am desperate to know more. Conversation is out of the question: the topic is too risky. (Nobody knows about her nutter mother except me, none of the other girls.) After class we take our two slices of bread and fish paste and hurry off behind the hedge at the back of the science block.

My mother's letter reveals more than her father's note.

Dorcas was found cowering behind the chook run at Maguire's. Discovered by Maguire in the evening when he went to put the cows up. She'd been out delivering groceries — an innovative move designed to coax people to stay with Hogan's general store and not drive into Araluen to the brand-new Woolworth's.

She'd waded into Maguire's dam. There was no water in the dam, just dry mud. There's a drought on, we've had no rain for five years.

Dorcas was muddy and raving. The sky was after her, she informed Maguire. The sky pushed her face down in the mud in order to drown her. It threaded pieces of string through her head, to tie her into the mud, into the ground.

These facts are there in my mother's letter, in handwriting that moves like a neat bird, always a little above the line.

Deirdre and I walk between the hedge and the science block, back and forth, back and forth, like nuns. Anyone who saw us would think we were praying together.

I hear our feet on the gravel.

I notice the hairs on Deirdre's arms. She has her sleeves rolled up, as do I. (This is not officially allowed.) I can see a spot of ink on her blouse, not quite hidden by her tie. I hear how she is breathing.

What takes me by surprise is how aware I become of my own arms, the small hairs sitting there, completely ineffectual. (What are they supposed to protect us from?) I am conscious of my blouse, sitting over my petticoat over my bra over my breasts over my heart over my lungs, which do not seem to be getting enough air.

We pass my mother's letter to each other, taking turns to examine the curves and dots that make up the sentences, that bring the news.

Her father's brief, carefully printed message Deirdre cannot bring herself to read. Although she has one of those faces that blush easily, this news has drained her of colour. It's true, I decide: people do go pale. They blanch. (Despite the crisis, I savour "blanch.")

"What can I do?" asks Deirdre. "Tell me what I can do."

I am young enough to believe that because I love her, I can save her.


Off we march to Sister Perpetua's. She looks up, startled. Not a trace of her smile this time.

I outline our demands. We have to make some telephone calls.

Girls do not make telephone calls. On rare occasions, such as a death in the family, a phone call might be received. Consideration would be given as to whether the girl should be called from class; usually it would be decided that a message should suffice. The news would be given, prayers offered.

"We have to know what's going on," Deirdre says, keeping her voice steady. I am appalled at our daring. Impressed, as well.

"We have to know more," Deirdre insists.

"And who do you think will be able to tell you that?" asks Perpetua, in an affable, rational way.

This throws Deirdre off. As for me, I've become a useless great lump with nothing to say for myself.

"Your father?" asks Perpetua, pushing her advantage.

Her father. Jack Hogan.

Deirdre knows how her father will stand in the lounge room behind the general store, reluctantly holding the telephone to his ear, heavy with his own silence.

Perpetua starts in on me.

"Do you wish to speak to your mother on the telephone, Bernadette? Here in my office? Is that what you want, Bernadette?"

I've been thinking about my mother. When Maguire found Deirdre's mother behind the chook house, what would have happened next? Whom would he have called? And who would have got in touch with the authorities, gone to town and packed Deirdre's mother's things? My mother's the one who dobbed Deirdre's mother in. My own mother was acting the bossy-boots.

I could hear my mother putting on her practical voice, a sliver of doubt piercing through.

Dorcas thought the sky was threading *string* through her head.

Who was threading string? my father asks.

The sky was, my mother replies, edging towards exasperation. Dorcas said the *sky* was out to drown her.

My mother pauses, hoping for some sign of disbelief. My father returns to his newspaper.

"They can't lock her away," I protest, gathering my strength to take on Sister Perpetua (behind her, even more daunting, stands my mother). "They can't haul her off just like that. They can't put her into an asylum and throw away the key."

"No reference was made to the throwing away of keys," says Perpetua, still being ever so reasonable. "Not that I noticed," she adds, permitting herself a little victory smile.

"They can't," I repeat. "They can't."

"In a few weeks' time you'll be going home for the school holidays," says Perpetua. Having scored her point, she's turned away from me. For Deirdre, she is putting on a tone of sweet comfort.

"Perhaps you'll be able to go to see your mother then. Meanwhile, what we must do is pray for her. For her speedy recovery. We must all remember her in our prayers."

I do not recall either Deirdre or I petitioning Heaven for her mother's recovery. I don't think either of us offered up special rosaries, masses, novenas, the busy rituals of grace and favour.

The world of prayer never did "take" with us, as it did with other girls, who regularly sent up requests for packages of biscuits from home or for a fine day for the swimming carnival. We believed in the risen Christ, walking in white in the garden on Sunday morning, we believed in the life of the world to come. But we did not involve ourselves in the incidental traffic between Heaven and earth, we were unable to find it plausible. My explanation for this, which is immediately inadequate, points to the country of our childhood: the distance of its sky, the clear, empty air.

Deirdre would not see her mother those holidays, or the next. From time to time letters from Dorcas arrive, full of unconvincing cheer. She is, she claims, learning to play carpet bowls.

Deirdre's mother does not come home until near the end of the year, when we are busy studying for our final exams. To be able to afford uni, Deirdre needs a scholarship. I'm aiming for one too. We're both getting up at five in the morning. There are not enough hours in the day, and much of our time is interrupted by prayer.

My mother announces that she's going to bring Deirdre's mother on the next visiting Sunday. I tell her that this will upset Deirdre and distract me at a time when neither of us can afford it. My mother goes ahead as planned and arrives with the whole female contingent: Deirdre's mother, my grandmother, even Aunt Hazel.

Deirdre's mother gets out of the car and looks around like a new girl. I am certain she doesn't recognize where she is.

Deirdre steps forward.

Her mother offers her cheek to be kissed.

In the long Sunday afternoon, precious hours away from our books, Deirdre's mother sits at a picnic table in the park and tears at the cold chicken my mother has brought. She doesn't ask how our studies are going or reassure Deirdre in any way. Her eyes are busy, closely watching my mother for more food. "Yes please, I would like a second helping, thank you very much," she says. On best behaviour.

"It will take a little while," my mother murmurs to Deirdre. Dorcas has gone off to the toilet.

Having eaten at enormous length, Dorcas turns to emphatic, bright conversation.

"When I was staying down near Gosford," she announces airily, "the nurses were absolutely marvellous — as I'm always telling Alice, aren't I, dear? English girls they were, the best. Some of the New Zealand girls were quite good too, you know. We had a super time together, we were all in stitches. There were times I thought I'd die laughing."

We watch them drive away, safe again behind the convent gates. "There goes nothing," says Deirdre.

To cheer her up, I sing some lines from "The Purple People Eater" under my breath at Benediction, during the *Tantum Ergo*. "*I like short shorts,*" I chant.

It works; Deirdre begins to giggle.

"You're as bad as my mother," she says afterwards. "I thought I'd die laughing."

We sit for the leaving certificate and, to our relief, do well. A Commonwealth scholarship for Deirdre, a teachers' college scholarship for me. We are both going to uni.

Back in Kelly's Creek, Deirdre's mother undertakes a spring cleaning that impresses even my mother. Dorcas collects and tears and burns. Jack Hogan's favourite chair is relegated to the verandah. Dorcas washes, she paints, she cleans and shines. Gets potted plants, puts them on the kitchen windowsill. Decals on the fridge. Air freshener in the outhouse.

"Well, I'll be buggered," Jack admits, down at the pub.

⌒

At university we discover the library, we go to our first foreign flicks. On Sunday mornings we sit in Deirdre's room, drinking instant coffee, eating oranges, and reading poetry to each other.

We hunt for anything in books that refers to us, to our own country. We find a footnote in *The Waste Land*. It turns out that Mrs. Porter and her daughter probably washed their feet in soda water in Sydney. There, in the most famous poem of the century, a reference to us. We are flattered.

In our third year, to entertain ourselves during the slack period at the beginning of second term, we begin collaborating on a novel. We understand that writing novels together is something women can do in Australia. At the convent we read a book by Barnard Eldershaw, who turned out to be two women, Marjorie and Flora.

We keep a list of words we simply must have: plangent (definitely), numinous, detritus (essential for gum trees and love affairs), refulgent, exigent (anything with an "x" is super), delitescent.

Our novel is about two nuns. The younger nun is in love with the parish priest. The older nun is a wacko. We consider this to be pretty wild stuff; it is 1964.

We haven't decided what to call our nuns yet. Naming is powerful, a treat worth saving up.

At night God tosses the older nun out of bed, commands her to walk barefoot on the frosty ground until she is worthy of him. She worries terribly that it isn't God throwing her out of bed, it's the Devil in disguise.

"Devil with a black soutane on," says Deirdre.

The younger nun is in the grip of her impossible love. Takes it out on the kids.

"All of those children who made mistakes in their catechism come out to the front right now," she says in a crisp, strong voice, getting out the cane.

She loses her nerve, runs into the storeroom, weeps.

If only the priest would look at her, if only he would see.

Instead he leans down and says in Latin, "May the Body of Christ preserve you unto life everlasting," and moves indifferently on. He never looks, not even once. Why doesn't he? If he did, surely he would recognize her soul reaching out to him, yearning.

Then it's back to the classroom and on with the forlorn brutality. This time she doesn't falter. The cane, in its descent, stuns the air.

But we are restless, we hunger for something more romantic than this. We want a few light touches.

I decide to have the younger nun taking down sheets from the clothesline. The priest is watching her. He's standing outside a shed in the convent yard; his eyes have locked onto her. The sheets fill with wind, billow out, press against her body, surround her in white. She keeps on with the task, aware that by the time she's taken the last sheet from the line, they will be face to face.

I have stolen the ingredients from a French film we saw on Saturday night in the Student Union.

Deirdre asks, "What on earth would the priest be doing standing about in the convent laundry yard?"

"Search me. Maybe he lost his puppy. A sweet young spaniel called Bosco, his solitary companion. In the lonely presbytery he kneels and strokes Bosco's ears. *Bosco*, he croons. Bos*co*."

"Why Bosco? Where did that come from?"

"Just popped into my brain. First thought, best thought."

"Riveting, Bern. Riveting."

Deirdre wants the younger nun and the priest to be in a boat, rescuing families from the rising waters of a flash flood. In their struggles with the floodwater — which is running cold and dangerously fast — the nun's veil comes off, snagged by a tree branch. Her fair hair, released from the veil, cascades onto her shoulders.

"It glows into words," Deirdre says, getting overly ambitious.

"Nuns have cropped hair," I point out. "Dull, from never being in the sun. And what about her headgear? Does she still have that white box thing hanging off her forehead?"

"Well, how's this?" says Deirdre, changing her tack. "The older nun gets up in the middle of the night, commanded by God to walk in the frost. The path leads directly across to the presbytery, to the priest's bed."

"Not bad. Then what?"

"When the younger nun finds out, she too goes crazy."

"Let's call the younger one Madeline. Sister Madeline."

"Then we could have Mad go mad," Deirdre says, considering.

"That would be perfect, wouldn't it?"

For research, Deirdre goes out into the frosty night, takes her shoes off, to feel the cold against her feet. I read and reread *Daughters of the Late Colonel* and plan what to say about the moon.

I look out my window and there she is, a pale figure among gums. Deirdre has become a ghost.

We never finish this story. Deirdre gets a boyfriend instead. The mere sight of him, she reports, gives her a case of violent crumble legs.

"I think I'm in lust," she boasts. Throws herself upon my bed with a stagy, self-satisfied sigh.

"Don't you think you'd better tell me about it?" My voice has gone thin.

She tells me about him, more than I want to know.

His real name is Ian and he's English. Early in the Second World War, his father went down on a British ship, the *Hood*. His mother took up with a Polish RAF officer, whom she married and who later deserted her. In the Fifties, mother and young Ian emigrated to Sydney on an assisted passage (ten-pound Poms). Ian, growing up in the inner-west suburb of Burwood, affected what he thought might be a Polish accent and said *tak*, *nie*, and *do widzenia* as often as possible.

I stand in the common room and watch Deirdre go off with him. *Do-vee-dzeh-nyah* yourself, I say, looking at his departing back. Good*bye*.

She has her arms around his chest and her hair has gone wild.

He's changed his first name to Jan, pronounced *Yarn*. Wears a leather jacket and is careful to keep his face cloudy, as if attending to grudges.

"What are you rebelling against?" Deirdre asks him.

"What have you got?" he replies. One of their dumb routines.

"He's a joke," I tell her. "Can't make up his mind whether he's Biggles or Marlon Brando."

I wait for the sound of his motorbike.

"Biggles Brandowski at three o'clock," I call to her through the wall.

"Roger," Deirdre calls back, humouring me.

He is older, he is finishing his master's. He does not live at the uni, he has a flat in town. When you live in a flat, he tells us, you stay up all night and for breakfast you have vodka on your cornflakes. Should you desire cornflakes.

"What kind of boy, a pommy immigrant in Burwood, would want to pose as Polish?" I ask Deirdre.

She claims she does not find his choice in the least surprising.

"It's all well and good to go round making up stories," I say, "but he's supposed to be mature."

I did not know that he would turn into a journalist on the Sydney paper where Deirdre would get a job. I did not know she would move in with him, live with him. I did not know he had a friend at our embassy in South Vietnam, who would in time put in a word on Deirdre's behalf, grease the wheels.

In short, I did not know what he would lead to. If I had, I would have taken him more seriously.

On Saturday nights there are parties. Jan invites Deirdre and she invites me. These booze-ups take place at Jan's flat, which he shares with two other men, also graduate students. At the end of the evening Deirdre and I get a lift back to the university and sneak into the residence, giggling loudly about the need to be quiet.

"I don't give these parties," Jan is at pains to point out. "They take place where I live."

The front room has been tidied, more or less, and on the makeshift bookshelves are saucepans filled with potato chips. In the kitchen, guests arrive with hessian sacks filled with bottles of beer.

On one side of the front room, Jan and his best mate toss about matters of substance while drinking vodka with red wine chasers. Their voices compete; they solemnly score points. Because she's Jan's girl, Deirdre sits with them. They are talking about Jean-Paul Sartre. The air fills with dense clouds from their Soubranies. Jan and his mate don't dance, dancing being beneath them.

I'm on the other side of the room, in another decade, a different sensibility. On the small record player, an LP is playing. This is the era of the Beatles' first LPs, and better yet, the wicked Stones.

There are always many more men than women at these events, especially after the pubs close. It's easy to be asked to dance, all you have to do is stand about in the front room.

The kitchen, where the beer drinkers gather, is best avoided. There is never any food, only men drinking and shouting at ever-increasing volume. At the beginning of the evening they are bois-terous and determined; later, they become earnest with emotions that have floated to the surface, confusing them. That's when they stumble into the front room to dance. (At one of these parties, in just such a way, I met and danced with the young man who was to become my first husband.)

This evening, the one I'm remembering, I'm dancing to the Stones. *Can't get no. No no no.*

I can see Deirdre looking over at me. I've been drinking beer, and the walls are no longer stable, they are moving upwards, everything is moving upwards, especially if I close my eyes. My body feels light and right, wonderfully right.

Jan and his mate are discussing Sartre's famous falling out with Camus.

Now Deirdre sits up and takes an interest. She leans forward.

"Sartre's right," Deirdre says boldly, "nobody lives outside his-tory, we're in it already, right up to our necks."

"Here, here, old girl," says Jan's mate. Then he looks anxious.

A long, flat silence. Over on my side of the room, the record ends; a new one is put on. Again, music, dancing.

On the other side of the room, no one says a single word.

"Nature calls," Jan finally drawls. "I believe I shall have to look into the matter."

Jan's mate laughs, much relieved. They leave the room together.

Deirdre comes over to me, puts her hand on my shoulder. Slips in front of the beer drinker who's been dancing with me. He backs off, nonplussed.

"Let's dance," she says, brisk and angry.

"Trouble in Soubranieland?"

"Don't you start."

"How come he didn't stub out his cigarette before stalking off? Surely that was called for. A slow, significant grind."

"Who gives a stuff, anyway. I most certainly don't."

We dance about the room, waving our arms wildly. She's wearing a silvery shift and pale lipstick.

"*I will dream of you,*" we sing too loudly, "*if you will dream of me.*"

Tonight we are going to dance forever.

"Those dames are pissed," I hear somebody say.

⌒

A week after this party, Jack Hogan suffered a massive heart attack. Cardiac infarction.

He'd been sitting in the pub on Saturday afternoon, a schooner in his hand, listening to the footy finals on the bar radio because the brand-new telly had packed it in.

As a decisive goal was scored, Jack Hogan fell to the floor, spilling his beer. (To the cheers of the crowd, he lay there with the light from the window falling over him in purple and yellow lozenges, the beginnings of the letter "B" in reverse along the edges of his sweater. The "A" and the "R" swam backwards across the wet tiles.)

In characteristic silence, making no complaint, Deirdre's father slipped away.

Jack Hogan was buried in the cemetery paddock above Kelly's Creek. The priest's cassock looked oddly out of place in the tall grass — in recent months Jack had been letting the mowing go. The priest's words were out of place, too. They certainly didn't fit Jack Hogan; they would have found no home in his own sparse speech. Those who stood by the grave, those who had loved Jack Hogan, knew they would have done better to listen to the wind, which tossed the trees about then swept down to the sports grounds.

After the wake at the pub, Deirdre, in ruins, claimed that the silence of her father was the silence of God Himself.

"Infarction," she repeated, stumbling over the word. "Sounds like a mistake, a mispronunciation."

She wanted him back, she told me, in a crumpled little girl's voice. Oh, how she wanted him back.

I returned to university with no way of knowing how different things might have been if Jack Hogan had been given the good luck to grow old.

I am convinced that if he had lived, Deirdre would not have been able to stay away. For her father, for gentle, laconic Jack Hogan, she would have come home.


We both did honours: Deirdre studied history, I took English.

Modern Europe was her period, and she was writing a thesis on the Soviet defence of Leningrad during the Second World War. An unusual and daring thing for her to be doing, studying Commos.

We wondered if the Angelines had found out about this, and decided they probably had. Before we'd left school, they'd warned us that some of the professors, particularly in the History department, were Communists. You could tell who they were, the nuns said, because they wore bright-red ties on Mayday — a particularly insulting piece of godlessness, May being the month of Our Lady.

We concluded that the nuns must have heard about Deirdre's thesis from the university chaplain. Early in the year, he'd approached Deirdre and spoken obliquely about the perils of contemporary heresy. (He was in no peril himself, being a pale, otherworldly man, seriously in love with sacred music — which led to endless student jokes about organ playing, which he must have found terribly tedious.) He had no stomach for debate, this chaplain. What he was doing at the university, on the barricades of secularism, nobody knew.

As he must have figured out right away, his words to Deirdre only compounded her determination. It was well known that the famous visiting professor from England would be given the best students. Deirdre meant to have him as her thesis supervisor, and she did.

It was also well known that Deirdre would get first-class honours, maybe even the university medal. Sure enough, she sparkled, she shone. The famous professor was heard to say that working with her was like throwing fish to a seal.

My own thesis was in Middle English. I wasn't up to anything daring, I was writing about the Harrowing of Hell. Christ descends into Hell to negotiate with Satan. He wants to get some people out, those who were stranded there when the gates of Heaven slammed shut at the Fall.

In our last year at university Deirdre lost her faith. This shorthand phrase — suggesting a mislaid library book — in no way captures this sad and subtle process which, in hindsight, feels much like the decay of a long-term marriage.

Where did the break come? Was there a particular hour or moment when you knew, decisively, that it was now over, gone? (*Snap* went the consecrated host, as the priest broke it at Communion. You couldn't see it, his back was turned, he was hunched over the altar in sacred intimacy. But if you were close enough and paying attention, you could hear it. *Snap*.)

Deirdre, who was at last spending whole nights with Jan, debated with me in a worried voice. She claimed she was being driven away for the obvious and completely unoriginal reason: the Church had emerged as a martinet. It waved the rule book, stamped its foot, promised punishment.

We sensed that further losses might be involved, ones that we could not yet foresee. We consulted the texts we had — Stephen Dedalus, refusing to make his Easter duty, upsetting his mother so, but unafraid to make a mistake, even perhaps a lifelong one.

"Look at this," Deirdre said. "He has doubts that he does not wish to overcome."

"Is that how you feel?"

"Getting there, Bern. Getting to Stephen's 'I will not serve that in which I no longer believe.' So much for the old school motto."

"It was said once before," I reminded her. "And you know what happened to him. Given the boot. Hurled headlong. With hideous ruin and combustion down."

"Yeah, yeah."

It was a decision I could feel myself approaching as well.

What impressed us was that God didn't seem to have much to do with any of this. He remained utterly distant throughout: no comment. We began to suspect that what we called God might have had more to do with rocks and earth and stones than with the strictures Deirdre was bravely, nervously, preparing to cast off.

And somewhere underneath all this, below the anxious chatter about the thou-shalt-nots, was a single truth: Jack Hogan was gone.

Jack Hogan was buried in the cemetery on the hill above Kelly's Creek sports grounds, and nothing was about to bring him back.

It is eleven o'clock in the evening, our time for a glass of port. Tawny port, that's our favourite. We tell each other we can taste the oak.

She's lying on her bed in her dressing gown and green socks.

Deirdre keeps her port in a glass decanter, for those hours of the afternoon when men are allowed in the women's residence. For her Polish hero on a motorbike.

"In that summer they didn't push on to Moscow. They turned south instead, to the endless wheatfields. That's what did them in. They found they had to stay the winter."

She waves a green foot to one side: Moscow. She waves it to the other side: the south, with all that wheat.

"Some went north, too, as a matter of fact. History is terribly complicated. The more you find out, the more complex it becomes."

I pour the port, give her a glass. I had bought her the decanter and three port glasses for her last birthday. I'd got them second-hand, and the glasses were round and small and old. It was a set from the Twenties, perhaps earlier. The remains of someone's wedding present, I decided.

"The Germans pushed on into the Soviet Union, and the farther they got, the farther they had to go. They became disconsolate. "

I massage her feet through her green socks.

We finish one drink. That's our ration. Then we each lick out the inside of the little glasses, savouring the sugary taste.

"The people of Leningrad were living on sawdust," she says.

She speaks of how the people of the besieged city resisted, and her eyes carry the strangeness of what is happening to her. Brought up believing that these people were to be feared (godless atheistic Communists), she is finding that they are laying claims upon her, that her sympathies are now emphatically with them. It is a disturbing shift in texture. Neither of us knows what to make of it.

"They ate the crows on Lake Ladoga," she says, puzzling.

"You don't have crows *on* lakes. It would have to be the crows around Lake Ladoga."

She pins a magazine picture above her desk. A young soldier stands in a ruined Leningrad street. He's buying a ticket from an old woman who sits at a table out under the sky, surrounded by rubble. Beside the woman, pasted onto a bombed-out wall, is a big advertisement, all in type, for the premiere of a symphony. (It's Cyrillic, of course. The caption explains what it says.)

In the midst of ruin, the soldier will hear music.

I walk into Deirdre's room one evening and she's standing on tiptoe in her green socks, staring at this picture, as if the black-and-white dots could yield greater understanding. She turns to me, frowns, and asks, "Have you ever heard that music? I *have* to get hold of it."

Many times as she sits at her desk, half daydreaming, half studying, Deirdre examines the young soldier, the old woman, the destruction in the street.

I think the image might have formed a template in her heart.

⤚

When I get married Deirdre is my maid of honour. She takes a few days off from the paper and comes up from Sydney.

My mother and Deirdre's mother, Dorcas, have worked together with my grandmother on what they call the gorgeous outfits: white for the bride, lilac for the maid of honour.

Dorcas now sews and cooks all year round, like a real mother, a real wife. (During her stay at Morisset, Dorcas discovered medication.)

On the morning of the wedding, I go into Deirdre's to get dressed. That way I can walk to the church and not get all crushed.

This is the only time we have together, without everyone else poking their noses in. We are in her old bedroom, lying on her bed and speedily downing a bottle of champagne.

Deirdre's mother puts *My Fair Lady* on the gramophone. I hear both our mothers and my Aunt Hazel singing along.

"*And get me to the church/Get me to the church/For Gawd's sake get me to the church on time.*"

They are dancing about in the kitchen, sipping sherry and arranging trays. Their high heels click on the lino.

Deirdre thinks that the man I'm marrying is a bit of drip. So staunch, so loyal, so dependable. But these are good qualities, surely?

The maddening thing is that, after a few hours with Deirdre, I begin to think that when you get right down to it, he *is* a bit of bore.

Then I see him again and my knees go weak. Violent crumble legs.

Good job I'm going to be living four hundred miles away from her, I tell myself.

"You'll have to come and visit," I say. "We'll have long walks on the beach, I promise."

My new husband and I are going to teach on the north coast. We have rented a house by the sea.

"I'd love to, Bernie."

Today, I am relieved to note, Deirdre's not in a critical mood, not at all.

"You can see the ocean from the laundry. We'll be able to lie in bed and listen to the breakers."

"I think that's marvellous," Deirdre says. "That's absolutely marvellous." She thumps the pillowcase by way of applause.

Deirdre lives in sin with Jan in an inner-city Sydney suburb. "Groaning to God from Darlinghurst," she claims.

Today she's in extremely good spirits. I decide that I can tell her everything.

Everything is this one momentous fact: we have already slept together. Have been sleeping together, "Since last November," I claim proudly.

"Thank Christ. Now we can both walk up the aisle with our heads held high."

"Eat your heart out, Father Doherty."

"Seriously, though, what do you make of it?" She props herself on her elbow and looks at me. It is time for real conversation.

Deirdre's wedding presents: The first was a pottery serving bowl, orange inside, cross-hatched bright lime and royal blue on the outside, the latest Sixties colours. Meant for the marriage but in fact more for me, the cook-to-be. The second, the more important of the two, she produced from her case with grave reverence. All the way from America, a record made of red vinyl. *Red* vinyl! Ginsberg's "Howl."

In the early years of my marriage, I would play this record on our portable record player when my husband was out of the house (. . . *who let themselves be fucked in the ass by saintly motor- cyclists*, made him blink, rapidly). I'd stare at the red vinyl going round and think of Deirdre, hearing and seeing this for the first time at some journo party in Sydney and deciding that it was so astounding she had to get it for me.

She was determined, you see. The world was out there (up there, over there). We were going to reach out and get our hands on it.

The mothers are at the door, in bouncy little pillbox hats.

"You girls'd better get cracking," my mother says. "We've got to get you to the church on time."

Before we leave the house we toast each other.

"Better to marry than to burn," says Deirdre, and we clink glasses.

Then she says it: "If all goes well, I expect I'll be off to Vietnam later in the year. I think I might just be able to wangle it."

"My God. Why didn't you tell me?"

Already we are being ushered out of the house.

As I walk up the aisle, I see him. In a smart new dark suit, he is standing at the front of church, standing up before God and the world to tell them all that it is my body he plans to worship with his own. *Going to Vietnam*, I say to myself, looking down. One white silk-covered shoe is moving up the aisle, then another. Deirdre is going to Vietnam. Whatever am I going to do with these shoes after today, they're totally useless. I hope I don't sweat too much during the reception at the pub. My dress will be dripping. *Going to Vietnam*. There will be the telegrams, the dirty ones, the ones that don't get read out but are passed from hand to hand. Read by the bridegroom to the bride, while the others look on. I bet one of the telegrams will say, "Nothing could be finer than to be in your vagina in the morning." As he's reading it, I'll hear the guffawing and the snorting around us. I will blush, I know I will. His mates will jab at each other and call for more drinks, more drinks. Then what do you bet one of them will begin to sing, "You do the hokey-pokey and your knees bend, knees bend, and that's what it's all about"?

When we approach the altar Deirdre is beside me, we're almost touching. She looks great; she holds herself so well. She could be walking up the aisle in Westminster Abbey.

My lover turns to glance at us in our gorgeous outfits, white and lilac. He swallows. Runs his finger around his collar in a helpless male gesture. Pulls himself together, stops fidgeting, turns to face the priest.

He'll be glad when this whole thing's over and we can rip off our clothes and lie down in the dunes. Sand in your vagina, whatever could be finer?

First, we have to get through the nuptial Mass.

"Break a leg," whispers Deirdre, as I slide in beside him.

Already I know that he has his own opinions about me. About my family. About Deirdre Hogan.

Two years later she is in Saigon and it is the eve of Tet.

During my honeymoon something happens. Not to me — I am absorbed in intense physical happiness, barely able to walk — but to a family in Glenelg, in South Australia.

Three children catch the bus to the beach.

This is what children did in those times — they went out fearlessly, alone. In cities and towns, doors were left unlocked, children slept out in the backyard at night, and nobody gave it a thought. It was the way we lived.

But this time, in the Adelaide seaside suburb, the three children, all under the age of ten, do not come home for lunch. They don't come home for tea.

No phone calls, no ransom demands.

A woman claims she saw the children with a surfie who was wearing blue swimming trunks. A surfie meant practically any young male with blond hair. The police developed an Identikit image of the surfie. He looked wiry and ordinary.

The children's father and mother offer their home as a reward for information. It includes, the father says, a small bar and a TV set. "I will walk barefoot for my kids," he declares.

In the period of blasting heat that lasts throughout the first months of my marriage, I am irrationally interested in this story. The parents contact a man in Europe with psychic powers. They send him an aerial picture of the beach suburb. The children, he writes back, are dead. They have been killed in some kind of cave-in near the beach.

Somebody gets the money together to bring this clairvoyant to Adelaide. He walks about the beach suburb, concentrating.

Finally he gives instructions to dig.

"Their voices are strongest here," he says.

They dig, and find nothing.

## 5

It is the northern summer, 1973, and I have left the marriage that once so dazzled me with pleasure. (This is not my story but Deirdre's, and it is not about how we are in love and love vanishes. On the contrary, in this story, love is what remains, love is what is left.)

I have deserted my husband in the house by the sea. I found that I did possess the necessary courage, the cruelty. The irrevocable words have all been said, dropping heavily.

Now I am going to London for three months. Then, in September, I'm off to Canada as an exchange teacher.

Before the plane lands I line up for the toilet to brush my hair. (I have abandoned make-up.) I feel the anxious nausea I always get before I see Deirdre after an absence. Soon it will be all right, I say to the mirror. Already they are telling us to sit down, to fasten our seatbelts. Soon I will see her face to face.

Deirdre is in London with Martín. They are living with Sandy.

Deirdre is teaching English as a second language; Martín works for a news agency and is based partly in London, partly in Mexico City.

"He's away too much," Deirdre complains.

At the end of the summer they are getting married. In the southern spring they will go together to Buenos Aires as husband and wife.

At this time I am convinced that there is a lot to be said against marriage. I, for one, have quite a lot to say against it.

"It'll all be quite painless," she says defensively, of the wedding. "No need to get all hot and bothered."

It is going to be an incidental affair in a registry office.

Nonetheless I am bringing off the plane with me serious presents from Kelly's Creek. A wedding cake, made with anxious excitement by her mother, mine supervising. It is wrapped and stitched in cloth.

"No way I'll be a matron of honour," I say. "Not even for you."

"Don't worry about it. You'll aways be my best woman."

Deirdre is standing in the crowd at Heathrow, holding car keys. "How clever we are," she says. "From one end of the world to the other, we can locate one another."

"Like birds. We do it on instinct."

"I reckon we're programmed, mate. A homing device buried deep in the spine."

It's good fortune that we walk backwards into the future, that present and past are all we see.

Immediately we drive to an anti-war meeting. A small organizing meeting. A dozen people — ten of them men — are sitting around a table. Outside, there's some kind of northern tree, full of broad summer leaves. By now I've been up two days in a row, but I pay attention to Deirdre as she makes her points. Her voice goes tight and the blood creeps up her neck into her face.

While the others are speaking I think about taking a shower, the luxury of warm water splashing over me, then lying down, stretching out. Talking to Deirdre, having her to myself.

The meeting turns on code words and rituals I do not understand. Many of the speakers, I surmise, are just discovering them themselves. Deirdre leans forward and says that opposition to the war has to be built among progressive elements in all sectors of society.

Progressive elements?

I wonder how much of what she says is Martín's. Some of it, I know, is already hers.

After that, she takes me to Sandy's place. She shows me the flat and the garden and for a few minutes she looks guarded.

"Do you like it?" she asks, awaiting judgment.

Good lord, she's anxious about me. She's afraid I won't like him. For it must be Martín she has in mind, I decide, not the flat. It's Sandy's flat, not hers, and it's tidily crammed with books in real bookshelves and paintings in proper frames. The home of someone older than us, richer, more settled.

"Don't be silly," I say. "It's great. I love it."

With that, she breathes out, relaxes.

I have promised to appreciate him.

"I'm not going to use his last name after we're married," Deirdre assures me. "Not on a daily basis. That would be going too far."

We move on, to home and families. I begin to talk to her about the husband I have left: his virtuous sorrow, my guilt.

She tells me about how restless she feels with Martín away so much of the time. "Soon," she says, "when we go down to B.A., we're going to get our own place. You'll have to come to visit."

It's true, I decide, time is a concertina. Years can be as nothing. We're kids again, and this is Kelly's Creek, this is boarding school, this is university.

We put our feet up; I massage hers. In this familiar way we get down to the good gossip, chewing on the details.

"Have you noticed," she says, "how talk about sex has changed? A few years ago you'd hear women our age say, 'I fucked my way round Europe, I fucked my way through South East Asia.' Then tot up the score."

"Give me half a chance," I say, "You forget I'm a recently unmarried woman."

"You wouldn't hear anyone talk like that now. But until a year or so ago it was commonplace."

"So what happened? *Click*?"

"I think so. And I've been trying to figure out how on earth I got from Jan — remember Jan? — to Ron."

"Men are not the signposts of our lives."

"Thank Christ for that."

"I always did wonder about Ron. What were you doing with a soldier in the regular army? Not even some poor bastard whose birthday came up in Tatt's lottery."

"I was terribly fond of him," she says. "But if you want to get me down on the couch, I suppose he reminded me of my father."

She cannot say the words, "my father," without tears coming into her eyes. We go silent for a bit. I caress her feet with the long pussycat strokes I know she enjoys.

"Stuck up the coast, I was always a few paces behind," I say. "Overnight it was no longer daring to have slept with your future husband before the wedding night."

"And you were so proud of yourself."

"It became open season."

"And boy, were those boys pleased to hear about that. The road to Saigon."

"You'll be embarrassed one day, Deir. You'll have have to hide your past from your innocent children."

"Children? Hold it right there. Whoever said anything about children?"

"I read somewhere it was like that in the early Twenties. The men came home from the war and for a while everyone went nuts. Danced all night and mucked up a treat. A few years later they were busy pretending none of it had happened."

"'Sorry to have to tell you this, son, but your mum was once a wanton woman.'"

"'No better than she should be.'"

Deirdre wriggles her toes in the air and we giggle.


A week later, Martín arrives from Mexico. He will be here, he assures Deirdre, for the rest of the summer.

In the chitchat about his arrival and mine, he realizes that I find him immensely attractive.

The first thing is — and this I do not underestimate, this alone would be enough — he's hers. But there is more. Beneath that unconscious chemistry men turn on automatically, he conveys a sense of genuine physical affability. Here is a man, I tell myself, who when alone would be at home in his body.

He has a manner that gives little away, but I can see that he knows he is being a success, and that this does not particularly surprise him.

In a courteous, mildly flirtatious voice he says, "This is wonderful."

I say, "Yes it is, isn't it?"


"Well, what do you think?" Deirdre demands. We are alone together and she is waiting for me to say something about him.

Best to focus on a head-and-shoulders shot.

A rather short neck. Fine, wide forehead. All that thick brown hair Deirdre has told me about.

"He could be on one of those old coins," I suggest.

"He could, couldn't he?" she agrees, eagerly. "A coin a farmer digs up near Hadrian's Wall."

"The farmer's wife rinses off the surface dirt, puts it on the sideboard, writes a letter."

"The specialist arrives, tippy-toeing up the mucky path in city shoes. Endures cups of tea. Picks the coin up and says, 'Yes, *that's* what he looked like.'"

"The Emperor Martín."

The first thing we all do together in London is go to the cricket: me and Deirdre and Martín and Sandy. We sit in the stands in that order, our chain of connection.

Sandy has packed cold chicken, potato salad, Alice B. Toklas brownies. We watch the cricket in a brownie-induced daze. The New Zealanders come back from a hopeless situation and doggedly, run after run after run, they recover.

Going to the cricket seems to me a natural thing to do; it takes me a while to appreciate that what we are actually doing is slumming with the bourgeoisie. Down among the Home Counties gentry, we are the only dope fiends in sight. With the superiority of someone stoned, Deirdre stretches out along three seats. She is wearing a long skirt she's made out of an old curtain from Oxfam.

Sandy does one of his riffs about cricket.

"After a day or so of cricket one enters into a deeper understanding of existence, realizing with the heart that nothing much happens in a single life span, only a small miracle once in a great while."

"It's all those strong young men in their whites," Deirdre says. "Gets Sandy going."

"Consider," Sandy goes on, ignoring her, "the repetitive flash of the ball, the solidity of the umpire standing like a bored vicar. Feel the calm, the soothing monotony, slow as bees. Then just when you've accepted that life is slipping by without moment, something marvellous happens. The bowler leaps into the air, shouting."

"It could equally be a nightmare," Martín observes. "Murder rather than a miracle."

"Geez," says Deirdre. "Call me the future Mrs. Pollyanna."

As the New Zealand batsmen toil up and down and the English bowlers fail to shift them, Sandy and Martín offer opinions, advice. "Forward leg glance," Martín says. "Fantastic. Right down the wicket-keeper's throat."

I didn't know they had cricket in Argentina. I say as much to Martín.

"No," he says. "We have revolution instead."

Sandy drives the VW home to London in the summery night. Sitting outside in the garden of a pub, after watching the New Zealanders slog their way to triumph, I hear for the first time about the return to Argentina of Perón.

Martín speaks about it. A month before, Perón came back. At the airport, where thousands came to greet him, there were ambushes and gruesome deaths as Perónist factions fought it out.

Sandy says of the Perónists: "They're a party of both the left and the right."

Was that another one of his riffs?

Martín stands, holds up his arms for attention. "Ladies and gentlemen," he calls. He gives a low, theatrical bow and begins to use the emphatic gestures of mime. With his right hand he puts a gun made of fingers to his head. With his left he pretends to hang himself with an imaginary tie. Then he falls backwards into a flower bed, playing dead.

Martín is quite a shy man. After that performance he looks

embarrassed, as if asking himself, *Was that me, did I do that*?

I soon forgot about Perón.

I forgot because all the talk was now about Vietnam. I forgot because I was thinking about how Martín looked, lying there in a bed of flowers, eyes closed, pretending to be dead.

The flowers were anemones, with their bright, primary colours and black hearts.

Next morning when I come down to breakfast, Martín and Sandy are in full flight, debating Sandy's version of cricket: the quotidian enlivened, when you've given up hope, by the drama of a *howzat*. "Such moments," Sandy claims, "are time's consolations."

"Consolation prizes," counters Martín.

Deirdre looks up at me, pats the seat in the sunshine next to her. "Men's singles in progress. Quiet please."

Martín talks about a writer in Paris, a fellow Argentine. "Wrong side of forty. One day he goes into the *cafés-crème* of Saint-Germain-des-Prés and finds himself surrounded by boys in baggy sweaters busy reading Durrell, Beauvoir, Duras, Nabokov. Inside himself he's carrying around the whole body of surrealism — not that he's been doing much reading lately. Too busy looking at trees and pieces of string he's found on the ground. "

Martín's words are accompanied by a steady gesture of his hands, rather like dog-paddling.

"Surrounded by the next generation, the writer wonders, What are the boys talking about in my own country? And in his country the boys *do* talk, believe me. He realizes he can't guess any more. He's been gone too long.

"You know something? I understand *exactly* how he felt."

When he comes to this point of emphasis — *exactly* — Martín's hands stop their humble dog-padding and become demanding.

They reach out to scoop up the morning sunshine.

"You should find that reassuring," says Sandy. "You know how he felt, yet to him you'd be one of those young sprouts reading Durrell."

"Old enough to be untrustworthy, though," interrupts Deirdre, reaching over to stroke Martín's hair.

"Would you trust this doddering codger?" she asks me.

"No way José," I agree. "Way over thirty."

"Forty's the cut-off, not thirty," Martín claims. "From that time on, our true face is the one we have in the back of our heads."

"Martín's afraid that on his fortieth birthday he's going to wake up sans everything." Deirdre says fondly. "He'll be rabbiting on about the war in Vietnam and nobody will give him the time of day."

"No worries, mate," Sandy tells Martín. "We'll be right there with you, boring everyone's tits off."

⌐

Martín drove Sandy's VW, Deirdre at his side. They took me everywhere with them.

That summer I was in numerous flats of anti-war activists: bearded men with serious, moist mouths; women with soft, long skirts. More men than women, always. Everyone with streaming long hair and sharp, fervent opinions. Laundry was scattered about living rooms, posters hung askew, political magazines lay open on the floor. There was always dope but often the milk had run out.

I would read startling articles in *Ramparts*, the magazine from America, and play with the cats. Lots of cats, you could count on that. Often nobody would notice me. But sometimes there would be covert exchanges, with glances in my direction. Who is *she*? Is it safe to speak in front of her? Deirdre's nods would vouch for me, but if the mood grew uncertain, I'd get up, as if spontaneously and go out into the small, neglected garden.

Towards the end of the visit someone might put a record on, and a pure voice would sing of injustice and resistance. Listening to her, faces would soften, mine as well. I would feel myself quite capable of heroic love, of brave and selfless sacrifice. Then the house cynic would proclaim that such sweetness was possible only from the mouth of someone who had experienced justice every day of her life and had every reason to expect she would continue to do so.

It was a relief to go home to Sandy's flat, which he kept humming along, tidy and serene, where I felt I had a place, and where nobody seemed to notice that my own opinions were as insubstantial, as unmemorable, as air.

Martín puts his arm around Deirdre, holds her tight, sinks his face in her hair. His tongue finds the lobe of her ear.

"So soft," he says. "This kid's so squishy."

She looks out at me. Her eyes are full of delighted possession.

"I dream of Martín with the brown bear eyes," I say.

"What do you think?" he asks, holding her. "We both love her, don't we?"

"Show-off," Deirdre says, leaning back into him. "Show-off, skite."

"She's nice and squishy but she's strong, too. Mmm, I can really get my teeth into this girl." He bites her neck and makes slavering, growling noises.

He looks over and gives me his most handsome smile.

What was so tremendous, Deirdre says, was that the day he came back from Hue and put his arms around her, from that day forward, he acted as if the whole matter had been settled. He wanted her, he had her, that was that. They were in it.

He didn't court her, he bedded her immediately.

"It's old-fashioned to put those things in the passive," I point out.

"It was true for both of us," she says. "We didn't spend any time deciding, it was just there, a full-grown fact."

"What's wrong with that?"

"We didn't discuss things. We never sat down and said, this is what I expect, this is how I want us to be."

"Don't you think there's something dreadfully earnest about that? Spelling everything out, life as a flip chart?"

"He simply gets on with his life, and I'm supposed to fit into the cracks."

"You should just get on with *your* life, too."

"Well I do. Sort of."

"You're not the kind of woman who needs a man between herself and the world, to deflect it. Neither of us is."

"No we're not," she says, brightening. "And we got that way long before it became fashionable. Why do you think that is?"

I say that it might have something to do with our upbringing. From the age of seven, I was allowed to get up on a horse and ride off into the bush, unaccompanied. We were packed off to school and to university and nobody gave it a second thought, nobody worried that we might be lonely, living among strangers. We had at our core the knowledge that we continued to exist even when people weren't looking.

One hot afternoon, before we go to the market on Portobello Road, we decide to get drunk, like ladies, on Sandy's gin.

The temperature has reached the middle seventies, a heat wave for England. On the street you can smell tar and petrol fumes. Windows have been forced open wide.

"The locals are getting daring, casting off their cardies," says Deirdre.

"Dying of heat exhaustion," I add. We are egging each other on. "Putting on their socks and sandals."

We are in the garden, our legs, arms, and faces bare, greedy for some real sun.

"If it gets any hotter than this," says Deirdre in a low, conspiratorial voice, "they'll have to go all the way. Leave their socks off. Go about with *naked* feet."

"Shocking," I agree. "They'd have to be on drugs to do it."

Deirdre upends her glass, drinks it all down. "We ladies don't take drugs," she says, putting on a toff's accent. "It simply isn't done."

"But a little gin-and-It will do the trick. Even without the It."

"We'll do nicely with tonic, my deah."

After four gins I am flushed, I am buoyant, I brim with goodwill towards the shining, perfect afternoon. If I were home in the surf, I would be catching all the waves, riding them right into the beach.

Off to market we go, setting a steady course, acting sober.

At a stall Deirdre tries on an old hat with blue feathers and dangerous-looking hatpins.

"You've got to have it," I say.

"Hatpins are an offensive weapon. Just the thing for undercover work."

A young man is running the stall. "It's Victorian," he says. "A real bargain."

I hold up a mirror and Deirdre looks at herself, laughing. The young man says cheerful, insincere things.

"You should buy it," I tell her. "It'd be great for the wedding."

"I could wear the hat and do my hair up. A Victorian virgin." She giggles. "In a long skirt."

"It would be such a turn-on."

"I could flash my ankle."

The young man laughs.

She takes the hat off and shakes out her red-gold hair. "Sold to the Breck Girl," the young man announces pleasantly.

Tumbled in with some tacky Fifties costume jewellery I find an antique lipstick case made of hammered silver, with a small, single ruby on the lid. I fish it out from behind a string of fake pearls.

"Take a look at this," I say, handing it to her. "Isn't it fabulous?"

"It's terrific. But Bernie, what's it for?"

"You open it like so," I say, demonstrating. "You put your lippy in." Neither of us wears lipstick.

"Just the thing for your hash stash."

She waves the lipstick case in the air. The ruby flashes in its silver casing.

"It's *gorgeous*," she says. "Do you have any idea how gorgeous this is?"

In a hurry — because I can't afford it — I buy it for her.

"You'll never regret this," says the young man, pocketing the cash.

"A wedding gift," I say to Deirdre. "A ruby for milady."

"I'll keep it in my purse. It will go with me wherever I go."

She hugs me; we walk along together. "*Goodbye Ruby Tuesday*," we sing. "*Still I'm gonna miss you*."

She would keep it with her, in her purse. The lipstick case would be one of the things to find its way back to me, through Sandy.


The hot weather continues. Deirdre and I put on our swimsuits and step onto the roof, which has a flat ledge outside the bedrooms. We stretch out our towels, make hats from pieces of newspaper. Lie back, lift our legs in the air, and study them critically.

How long before her legs get a decent tan? Mine are much further along than Deirdre's because I'm having my second summer in a row and I tan easily. She doesn't shave, disapproves of me because I do.

"I have to," I say, sticking up for myself. "Esau was a smooth man; Deirdre ditto. Not so Bernadette."

We pat suntan lotion on our faces and arms. Then I take the

tube, squeeze out a little pile of white lotion, and rub my hand up and down her legs, feeling the long bones. Tibia, fibula, I say to myself. Which is which?

*Tibia, fibula*, the smoothness of Latin words.

While we work on our tans, Deirdre reads to me from her stack of Orwell. (Today, when I can bring myself to read him, his work carries the smell of the suntan lotion that Deirdre carefully wiped from her fingers before she touched the pages.)

"I like to think of him arriving in Barcelona," she says. "Such a tall man. Head and shoulders above the locals. But completely out of his depth."

She finds me bits she knows I'll like.

He's keen on toads, this tall, thin Englishman. Knows about heavy horses standing in high summer grass. Can capture the solid roundness of the earth, including the authentic details — what we eat, where we work, how we talk to ourselves as we're walking along.

Having coaxed me thus, Deirdre moves on.

Blair has the Fascist in his sights but cannot bring himself to fire because the bloke's pulling up his trousers as he runs.

A man, on his way to be hanged, steps around a puddle.

For such a long time, Winston is brave under torture. The thing that he clings to, that constitutes the sum of his dignity, is that not once in any of these terrible sessions does he betray his love for Julia. Then he is taken to Room 101. "Don't do this to me," he screams. "*Do it to Julia.*"

After Deirdre has read me this passage I go downstairs and get a rockmelon out of the fridge. Everyone calls them cantaloupe, everyone except Deirdre and me. I cut the rockmelon into pieces and take it up to the roof.

"Eat," I command. "Here, let me feed you."

I begin stuffing the pieces into her mouth, two at a time, two at a time. The juice runs down her mouth onto my hands.

We go to another anti-war meeting. This time it's a big do in a hall.

A basic routine of four speakers.

First, an American combat vet, gawky, unpolished. A speech to the heart with a strong Southern accent.

"I'm doing this for my buddy who died at Hue for no reason whatsoever." He sounds close to the edge.

Martín and Deirdre have a picture from Hue on their bedroom wall. In this picture an American marine stands at a bathroom window. It's a big, old-fashioned, wooden-frame window, with square panes. In the room you can see the claw-footed tub, with the basket hanging over for the soap. Beside the tub is an elaborate wooden chair. The light in the room is both bright and soft. It makes you want to lie in the tub and soap yourself and watch your breasts float in the perfumed water. You could look out the window, up at the sky. Trouble is, at the window stands the soldier in full combat gear, against the light, holding an automatic rifle.

I listen to the vet speaking, and I wonder if the soldier in that picture also died at Hue for no reason whatsoever.

It's difficult to know about the soldiers. Are you meant to feel sorry for them or be mad at them? But this crowd likes him, the exotic American Southerner; he's the prodigal son, and that makes it uncomplicated.

Deirdre speaks next. She's here to provide the background, the context, the history. Like a lawyer, she claims her territory one step at a time.

"In 1945 there are massive pro-independence demonstrations throughout Vietnam, and the Viet Minh takes power in Hanoi. Their leader, Ho Chi Minh, issues the Declaration of the Democratic Republic of Vietnam."

I am annoyed that they have given her the difficult bit, the dry, intellectual role. In an effort to pep things up a bit, she's using the present tense.

"In 1946, a general election gives Ho 98.4 percent of the vote. Despite this, the French, supported by the British, move to reconquer southern Vietnam."

By this time my mind has glazed over. I watch how she speaks. She's trying not to rock back and forth, reminding herself to stand still. She talks without notes, her voice clear and true; easily, it reaches out to the faithful at the back of the hall. This is the voice that carried across the hills when we were children. I feel a wash of pride in her fluency, her ability to organize facts in her head.

She traces the French fiasco up to Dien Bien Phu, the Geneva Conference, Diem's refusal to set a date for elections.

This crowd appreciates a bit of I-told-you-so. Deirdre recalls for them what Ho's premier said to a French journalist, as long ago as 1962: "Americans do not like long, inconclusive wars — and this is going to be a long, inconclusive war. Thus we are sure to win in the end." She's rewarded with a ripple of approval, murmurs, and some clapping down at the front. Encouraged, she repeats the date.

You'd have to be a keener not to find this heavy going. At times she reminds me of myself teaching back home, pushing ahead with the information while the kids scuff their feet and daydream about the surf.

The incidentals are what I pay attention to. "The elaborately planned defences of Dien Bien Phu," Deirdre says, "have a series of outposts named for the French general's girlfriends: Claudine, Beatrice, Elaine."

When she's finished there's a solid round of conscientious clapping.

The third speaker is Martín, and it's back to emotion. The crowd cheers up, awaiting horrors.

Martín takes his time. He's self-assured, at ease in a public setting. In a relaxed voice, Martín gradually gets graphic about the prisons, the tiger cages, conditions at Con Son prison, the torture devices supplied by the U.S., the massacre at My Lai. He's absolutely certain he's going to be believed, and that makes him convincing. He's a bit of priest, I think. What could be more sexy to a convent girl like Deirdre than a handsome, serious priest? To two convent girls. Looking for adventure, or whatever comes our way.

He does have dreadful clothes.

"I thought men from that part of the world were natty dressers," I told Deirdre.

"I didn't think you cared about things like that," she replied, getting pissed off.

"I don't give a stuff," I said, "I'm just observing."

When Martín's making an effort and dressing up, he puts on one of his grungy old soccer jerseys. Soccer's the national religion down there, Deirdre says. *Fútbol.* Today he's wearing the blue jersey with a garish yellow stripe around the middle. He favours this jersey, Deirdre tells me, because it belongs to the working-class team he roots for back in B.A.

Martín has the crowd with him. He's talking about the devastation in the Delta, after Tet. "It became necessary to destroy the village in order to save it," the U.S. major told the AP reporter, who told the world. They've heard this line before, but are ready to hear it again.

The meeting climaxes with a short speech from a Vietnamese woman who is, we are told, part of the Saigon opposition. She's definitely the highlight, even though she's hard to understand. The important thing is, she looks just right: delicate and fierce. She's fought to expel the French; she's fought in what she calls the American war; she's been inside those prisons Martín's just been describing.

Afterwards there's a gathering of the activists, with dope and wine and flirting and, above all, talk — a passionate, competitive mix of reportage and sparring. There are polite introductions to the woman from Vietnam, each person on his or her best behaviour, endeavouring to be lucid.

These parties go on for hours. I remind myself to go easy, to pace myself with the booze.

"Was I okay?" Deirdre asks me as soon as she can get me alone.

"You were fine. Cucumber sandwich at a garden party."

"Did I sound nervous?"

"No. You were totally on top of it."

"Thank Christ for that." She looks around for Martín.

We drive home at two in the morning. Toke up again and put on some records. I get bread and cheese out of the fridge. Martín and Deirdre dance in a lazy way while I sit and watch them.

Deirdre puts her feet on Martín's and he carries her like that, in a slow, floppy dance.

I wander over to them on the pretext of sharing the last of the joint; they put their arms around me and the three of us form a sleepy circle, humming something to the record player. (I remember the song, not that it matters. "Where Have All the Flowers Gone?" Pete Seeger, a cappella. I claim to be able to recall everything about that summer, including details that don't matter, the unimportant things Deirdre might have done, or I just think she did.)

I remember those particular minutes: the exhausted, companionable warmth of the three of us dancing together, barely moving.

Outside, the city has gone dead quiet.

We shuffle some more and finally run out of energy.

"Oh my oh my," Deirdre says, and pretends to collapse in my arms.

"Oh my ears and whiskers," I reply. "This is one tired speech-making girl."

"She surely is," says Martín. In a friendly way he takes her from me and begins to guide her upstairs.

"Night, pets," I say.

"Goodnight," "Goodnight," they chorus.

I hear them go into their bedroom and shut the door. Then I put the food away and go upstairs to my room, next to theirs.

Martín the untidy will be dropping his clothes on the floor. I lie on my bed and listen to their murmuring.

The susurrus of water, running over stones.

⌒

Two sets of people come to the flat: Sandy's lovers, and Martín's friends from back home.

One night Sandy surprises us all by coming home with the Southerner, the vet whose good buddy got killed at Hue for no reason at all. Although not invited to linger in Sandy's bedroom, the vet refuses to leave the flat. For several weeks he camps on the living-room couch. Calls out in his sleep, those cries that are muted whimpers for the listener but for the dreamer, deafening. When he finally heads off to Sweden we are all relieved.

"Whew," says Sandy, "I thought my people management skills had deserted me."

"Crowd control skills," says Martín.

Most of Sandy's young men come and go as planned. Graceful, slender men who appreciate the breakfast Sandy prepares.

When they've departed, Sandy gossips on the kitchen phone, getting the rundown on the night's activities elsewhere. "Don't tell me," he says admiringly. "You didn't. No, you didn't. Help me, Rhonda."

I tell myself I shouldn't be listening.

"If Sandy could arrange it," says Deirdre, "he'd reach out and feed all the beautiful young men of London, every last one of them."

"Sandy's got five Fs instead of four," says Martín. "Find 'em, feel 'em, fuck 'em, feed 'em, forget 'em."

"Must you?" says Deirdre to Martín.

"I think it's rather sweet," I say. "At least the middle bits."

"What else is there in life," says Martín, "when you get down to it? Food and sex. Birth, food, sex, sex, food, *kaput.*"

"I hate it when you go all philosophical on me," says Deirdre.

"These are the pleasures available," says Martín. "To tiny chameleons creeping across the vast, multicoloured carpet."

"You've hit the floor running," says Deirdre. "Give it a break, mate, it's only breakfast."

He puts his arms up, rests his head on his cupped hands. Swings on his chair. Prepares to enjoy himself.

It's another high summer's day, with the sun pouring into the kitchen, catching Martín's brown hair. On the breakfast table, the glass coffeepot swims in its own brightness.

"Sooner or later," Martín says, "you have to face the alternatives: go crazy, defenestrate, or seize the day and make a date for the movies."

He raises his arms in the air, plays "here is the church, here is the steeple, come inside and see all the people."

"Men love that word," Deirdre says to me. "It sounds so sexual they can't resist sticking it in at every opportunity."

"What we really go in for is fornication," Martín interrupts. "'The masses are fornicating, send in the Marines.'"

Sandy, still busy on the phone, calls over to us: "I rather like 'the grand panjandrum' myself. A weekend pyjama party that got deliciously out of hand."

"As it happens, we've already made our choice," Deirdre tells Martín. "You're taking us to the midnight show. Bernie's coming too."

Sandy gets off the phone, comes back to the table. "Little ones," he says, "you have *no* idea."

The phone rings again. More dirt for Sandy.

Martín abandons the kitchen before the cleaning up begins.

As she washes and I wipe, Deirdre tells me about Sandy's lover Tran, how he disappeared at Tet. Deirdre says that Tran, who ran a photographer's studio, was in fact with the People's Liberation Armed Forces and died in the Tet offensive.

Sandy had fallen in love with the enemy.

"Do you know that for certain?" I ask Deirdre. "About his being in the PLAF? Or is that just what you want to believe?"

Martín's friends come to the flat for impromptu, lengthy barbecues on the terrace. They smoke black tobacco and speak Spanish in the accents of Mexico, Uruguay, Argentina, Chile.

Two worker priests are due to arrive, on their way through to Paris and Rome. Sandy corners us in the kitchen and tells us about them. Worker priests, he assures us, wear black leather jackets and are exceptionally good with their hands.

"Think of it," enthuses Sandy. "All passion unspent."

"Bet you've never met a worker priest in your life," challenges Deirdre.

Sandy brushes that aside. "We should keep an open heart. To whatever the good Lord sends. Whomsoever."

The priests show up as promised. Not a leather jacket in sight.

Neither worker priest speaks much English. Sandy tries to imitate the soft, slurry sounds he hears in the visitors' Spanish. The priests begin to smile.

"It's all Greek," I say, "to my tin ear." We're in the kitchen, in the coziness of gossip. Sandy frowns, to indicate that I'm being tedious.

"I should have given them the benefit of my views on the Resurrection," says Sandy. The Resurrection, Sandy likes to claim, turned a fairly well-shaped tragedy into an also-ran dark comedy.

"You don't think they'd have fallen for that, do you? Smarty-pants claptrap."

At Martín's side, Deirdre listens carefully to the conversations in Spanish. She understands more than she can speak and is driven wild by the barriers of language. "The emotions are the same, the thoughts are the same," she says. "It's all so maddening."

I am relieved when Martín's guests speak English, which, out of courtesy, they often do.

In Martín's homeland, they were building popular power. It was a class alliance to confront imperialism and its allies. It was a fight against the monopolies — industrial, financial, and agricultural. In the name of liberation, they were going to redistribute the wealth. It was the serious struggle, *la lucha seria*.

I did not know then how dated these conversations would become, and that what would date them, in particular, was their optimism.

It is one of the barbecue evenings, and Deirdre and I are watching from her bedroom. Hers and Martín's. The bed is unmade, the sheets are tousled.

The men talk rapidly, their voices rising and rising again, their arms mobile. To me they seem immensely articulate, smart, urbane. The women, in their high heels and perfume and delicately feminine clothing, are making what must be clever interjections.

Martín looks up and waves for us to come down. As he does so, he becomes self-conscious. Clenches his fist in a jokey power-to-the-people salute. He even blushes a little.

Deirdre says, indulgent, "He can be totally self-assured in public, but when he knows people, and cares, he gets timid."

"Why do you think he's like that?"

"It must be his English schooling. The self-control, the public face. Underneath he's all luscious mush and soft beating heart. But it unnerves him to think it might be showing through."

We continue to look down at the gathering, admiring Martín and his party.

A man pours a glass of wine and passes it to a woman, who holds the glass up to the light.

One of these women, from Uruguay, is the wife of Martín's only brother, Paco. His little brother, the one who was beaten up when he was at university.

Paco's wife has shocked us both by speaking in a plummy, upper-class English accent. Turns out she went to some ultra-posh boarding school in Kent.

"Isabel, that's her name," says Deirdre.

"Queen of Spain," I say.

"Close but no coconut. Her family is one of the most powerful in Uruguay."

"What does that mean? Lots of land?"

"Land, bishops, generals. Generals in particular."

"Do you reckon she's madly in love with Paco?"

"Don't know. I gather she's estranged from her family."

"Estranged," I repeat. In the summer afternoon, this word carries a chill. I run my hands up and down my bare arms.

"She's been estranged from them for years. They wouldn't even know what country she was in." Then Deirdre says, lowering her voice, "I think she's involved with the ERP. Paco is, you know."

"The ERP?"

"The People's Revolutionary Army," she explains. "They're pretty heavy-duty."

"Bet Daddy's ever so thrilled."

"Daddy doesn't know. "

"Then what's the point? If Daddy doesn't know, how can he be horrified?"

"Strictly between you and me," Deirdre confides. "I believe she's in up to her eyeballs."

"Up to her mascara," I say. "But what kinds of things does she do exactly?"

"I couldn't say, " Deirdre replies. "Nobody says, not in so many words."

We both look down at Isabel, with her black hair, flawless skin, and expensive make-up. She's wearing a creamy blouse and royal-blue pants, both silk.

"You know something?" says Deirdre. "I wouldn't be surprised if she goes to those posh lingerie stores."

"Orders little items in coffee-coloured lace. Has *Modom* bring them to the dressing room."

We wear cotton panties and no bras, me and Deirdre. We have heard of shops where they measure your breasts and make bras personally to order, not just off a rack. They do it for the Queen. The senior lackey scuttles off to the Palace with a tape measure for the royal breasts.

"Isabel's got a law degree, too," says Deirdre.

"You'd think, if her parents are so rich and powerful, they'd try to find her. Hire a private dick or something."

"They're members of the intelligentsia," Deirdre explains, waving her hand to indicate the whole group below.

I consider this.

"Martín isn't intelligentsia," I say. "Martín's almost me, almost you." It's a line we both like from a jazz record Sandy often plays: *Almost me, almost you, almost blue.*

But he leads this other life, does Martín, in another language, another culture.

In my mind I replay a conversation I'd had the week before with a Scandinavian student in a pub down the road. I was trying to tell him what the Melbourne Cup meant, how, for a few minutes on a November Tuesday afternoon, the whole country stops, how nuns in hot, dusty country towns run a sweep with their pupils, how Reverend Mother at Our Lady of Sorrows knew the names of the winners, all the way down from some horse called Carbine, how, with her veil pressed to the radio, she urged her horse on with prayers to Saint Jude. Country towns are always hot and dusty, I added. It's a given, along with the harsh crying of birds.

Saying these things, I watched the student move his head back and forth, not agreeing, but trying to find a way to place this, to liken it to something in his own life. I could tell from his sober courtesy that he was having a hard time, that it was a long way from his hometown — wherever that was — a long way to Kelly's Creek.

What can I possibly hope to understand about Martín's country? I couldn't even convey the flavour of Cup Day.

Deirdre continues to look down at the gathering in the garden. Her face has gone vague. She reminds me of her father.

(Jack Hogan is pulling the roller up and down the pitch. He has harnessed himself like a draught horse and his chest is straining. At the edge of the field the grass has run riot. Time was when Jack would have gone after it with his great scythe.)

"How much have you told Martín," I ask her, "about home?"

Isabel comes to the flat. It's a muggy afternoon, a storm is on its way.

Deirdre and I, in old jeans and T-shirts, are sprawled on the living-room floor on cushions, making a mess of the Sunday papers.

Sandy answers the door and in pitty-pats Isabel, wearing high-heeled sandals in leather the colour of buttercups.

Deirdre and I sit up and try to make ourselves tidy. There is a sudden smell of powdery perfume.

"I've come to see Martín." Isabel is addressing Sandy.

Martín's been in Paris but is due back this evening. A few months ago, before I arrived, Deirdre had been in Paris herself. Some conference or other.

"He's not back yet," Deirdre says, making her claim. "His plane doesn't get in until eight."

Milady ignores this.

"He has something for me. It is of the utmost importance. I must see him," she insists to Sandy.

"He's not here," says Sandy. "I expect he'll be in later this evening."

Isabel narrows her lips in displeasure.

I inspect Isabel's pleated black-and-white skirt, her blouse of lace over polished cotton. Nobody dresses up like that. Nobody that we know. Not unless they're going to a wedding. Or a funeral.

"Cup of tea?" suggests Sandy.

"We're terribly *House & Garden* at number 7B," says Deirdre, under her breath.

"Yes, thank you, that would be lovely," Isabel replies graciously.

Deirdre and I escape to the kitchen to make it.

"It's good to be back below stairs again," I say. "Where we less-than-couth peasants belong."

"Be sure to leave by the tradesman's entrance."

I put on the kettle; she opens the big pantry cupboard.

"Me from the bogs of Ireland," I say, getting into it. "You from the bogs of Ireland and East Anglia."

Deirdre takes it up. "We know our lot in life. The bog sisters, at your service."

"Trouble is, soon you'll be her sister-in-law. She'll be yours."

"Blimey," says Deirdre, in Jack's voice.

"In a way," I say, "you'll be partners."

"No way. I'm not going to be her partner."

"You and Martín. Her and Paco. The husbands; the wives."

I'm rinsing the pot under the hot tap; she's arranging cheese and biscuits on a plate.

"Do you think this bikkie plate is up to scratch?"

"What are you marrying into, mate?"

"Don't ask me, Bern," she replies, going somber.

When Isabel leaves, Deirdre and I watch her hastening down the street, the clickety-clacking of her high-heeled sandals.

Rain is beginning to fall.

Soon it's a hard summer rain, most unusual for London. Sandy comes to the door and he stands beside us, looking out.

"It's a mini-monsoon," says Deirdre.

Right on cue, there's a massive clap of thunder.

"Just like Vietnam, mate," says Sandy. "Or the end of the world."

I look at Deirdre, and she looks back at me. I know exactly what she's thinking. Before Isabel can get to the train station, no matter how fast she runs, she's going to get soaked. Neither her fine clothes nor her sandals of buttercup leather will offer any protection whatsoever.

"Caught on her way to the station," Deirdre says in a fake-neutral reporter's voice.

Then Deirdre begins flapping her arms at the elbows and making chimp noises. I start it too, so we're doing it in unison.

"Girls, girls," says Sandy in mock reproach. "Behaviour."

It's after eleven when Martín arrives home.

Sandy, Deirdre, and I are loafing in front of the television: Elgar's cello concerto at the Festival Hall, followed by a long piece on beavers. The kits, snug in their lodge, stay dry beneath the water.

Deirdre's restless, first sitting tucked up on the sofa, then sticking her legs out on the footrest. Flinging her arms above her head. Stretching them out along the back of the sofa, where her fingers fret with the velvet piping.

"Quit it, Deir," orders Sandy, "you're pulling that thing to pieces."

As soon as we hear the key in the lock, Deirdre is down the hallway to open the door. Sandy switches off the TV and turns on the lamp. Still on the sofa, I watch them walk in: Deirdre and Martín.

"How was it?" Sandy asks.

"What a laugh, everybody cried," Martín replies. One of his tag phrases, some private joke.

As she stands beside him, Deirdre's eyes are soft, her skin seems brighter. When she looks up at Martín her whole face expands.

⌒

We sit in Sandy's garden and Deirdre tells me about Martín. She'd rather talk about Martín than anything else.

Martín has gone off again. For some reason that isn't clear to me, he's had to return to Paris. Deirdre is pissed off.

"He promised the whole summer. He came right out and promised."

"Tell me everything," I command. "I want to know everything about him, about you and him."

"I'm afraid," she admits. "What if he's going to be one of those men who are forever just passing through?"

"Keep your fingers crossed. Both hands."

"What do you think?" Deirdre persists, turning to face me. "Do you think we'll be happy together?"

"I do. I do." And saying this, I feel guilt pushing its way up. "Of *course* you'll be happy together," I say, more emphatically. "He adores you, you know. Anyone can see that."

There is something I've decided not to tell Deirdre, never, not ever. (I'm betting Martín won't tell either; what would be the point?)

Part of me is amazed that I can do this. The burden of deceit seems such an adult thing. It has forced me to realize that there are pieces of her life Deirdre might be keeping hidden from me, things that she and Martín might have decided it's best I don't know.

Earlier in the summer, a few weeks after we'd all been to watch the cricket match — and Martín had pretended to murder himself — Deirdre went to Birmingham overnight for an organizing meeting. At the breakfast table she announced that she was going to be billeted with some "gung-ho neophyte I.S.-ers." From this I gathered that these I.S. people were in some ways not quite sound. But with such groups, Deirdre explained, it was still possible "to forge a basis of unity."

I pictured Deirdre banging away at a horseshoe; not an altogether unpersuasive image.

The two of them were always bandying political acronyms around. I wondered what the initials I.S. stood for, but I knew that when I found out the name itself would mean nothing to me — like knowing the colour of the soccer jersey and where the team comes from, but not what the game is about.

Of course I couldn't stop myself. "What does I.S. stand for?" I asked.

We'd finished eating toast and marmalade. Martín had just made a second pot of coffee.

Deirdre said, "What does I.S. stand for? One wonders if they know that themselves."

"Inept socialists," Martín added, pouring coffee into Deirdre's mug and pretending to spill it.

And they were off: inane socialists, irritable socialists, impecunious (what else?) socialists, incoherent socialists.

"No," I said, feeling excluded. "Tell me."

"International Socialists," Deirdre answered, acknowledging that I wanted this game to end. "Trots."

"Trots" meant Trotskyists. I knew the term from Deirdre in her honours year, when she'd toiled through the history of the Russian revolution. In exile in Mexico, Trotsky'd had his skull smashed in with a pick-axe, often misidentified as an ice axe. Clearly a murder conceived in a cold country.

Trotsky had been out feeding his rabbits when a visitor walked up the driveway. On a day of steady, cloudless blue, the man had a raincoat draped over his arm. Trotsky left the rabbits and accompanied him to the study because he was not entirely a stranger, this visitor — in recent months he'd taken up with one of the secretaries and was often seen about the place.

Deirdre also told me how the official pictures had been altered, memory revised. Where Trotsky had once stood among the others in Red Square, giving and receiving approval, there was now an empty space. Proof: he had never been there.

I persisted. "For these I.S. people you're visiting, what does that mean, their being Trots?"

"They're engaged, they're committed," Deirdre answered. "It's just that they have these doctrinaire blind spots here and there."

"Doesn't sound like anyone I know."

Because of his work, Martín hasn't gone to Birmingham with her.

Sandy is off somewhere. On the prowl.

I make dinner, my best effort, with a salad and wine. I prepare it late, for when Martín gets in from work. I do not stop to ask myself why, for once, I've dressed carefully, why it is so important that he enjoy the meal, why we need, have to have, a second bottle.

Over the debris of the meal, we are drinking and toking up, passing the joint from his hand to mine. This goes on for a long time.

It is the dope, I tell myself, that has turned the silence thick, that has me watching, with such care, his fingers, his mouth.

How deliberate they have become, his fingers. He's rolling

another joint, his fingers guiding the dope. His mouth is confident; his lips smile.

Delicate as a cat, he licks the flimsy rolling paper.

I don't want to meet his eyes.

I can't. I tell myself, I can't.

I can't watch his mouth a second longer.

That's when his hand comes over and touches the side of my cheek.

He lifts my head. "Look at me, *che*. Look at me."

So the night I spent with Martín began predictably enough, with the usual rash amount of dope. It moved on into prolonged, somewhat self-conscious, ambitious sex (during which we were probably both in some degree of shock), and then, more soberly, into whispered conversations with touching and stroking that seemed to me to have all at once become permitted, or at least finally possible.

All the while I was doing this, I was aware of Deirdre in her meeting room in Birmingham, explaining, planning, making notes, letting the talkers have their say, then seeking agreement, reaching compromise, getting the wording right.

I imagined her after the meeting, after the socializing, in the home of the neophyte gung-ho I.S.-ers. A child's room is what I pictured, with animal posters on the wall (the child, for this special night, permitted the treat of the big bed).

How could I do such a thing?

An alphabet frieze of jungle animals. Toys casually tidied into a big box by the door. The light from the street — unlovely, industrial — coming through a gap in the curtains, making a chilly blue geometry on the floor.

The details are a distraction, nothing more.

I did it. I loved her and I did it.

I took Martín into me, enclosed him in my arms and found his chest, his belly, his buttocks, his penis, his toes. I felt his substantial legs press down on mine. Quite intentionally, I committed Martín's body to my body's memory.

He talked about classical music. Music, he said, was a paradise of double meanings. He was keen on Mahler; he liked the way Elgar fooled about with mathematics. He talked about codes. Did I know that on the night before Tet, Radio Hanoi broadcast a poem from Ho Chi Minh with the line "Forward! Total victory shall be ours!"? That was the signal, Martín said, that the offensive should begin. I said it didn't sound much like a poem to me, more like corny propaganda. Okay, he said, how about the message to the French resistance on the eve of D-Day: "The long sobs of the violins of autumn wound my heart with a monotonous languor." This, I told him, was overwritten, far too poetic.

He laughed and said it was from a famous French poem and that I was impossible to please. In this one respect.

Sometime during that night he told me how he'd been home in May when the military was kicked out and Héctor Cámpora elected to office. People opposed to the military dictatorship poured into the streets of Buenos Aires. The air was filled with the chant: *Se van, se van, y nunca volverán.* They're going, they're going, never to return.

At the formal event, Martín explained, hecklers prevented the band from the Navy Mechanics School from performing. Nixon's secretary of state, on his way to Government House, had his car blocked by demonstrators and had to scamper to the U.S. embassy for cover.

"It was crazy, crazy, all over town," Martín said. "Like being on a high and never coming down. Impossible not to be caught up in it."

I wondered if he found this night of ours to be crazy, crazy, and if he was caught up in it, too.

I managed to stop myself from asking.

I was coming down, I realized. Or starting to. I shouldn't have been there in bed with him. I should not.

I told him: "I feel like I'm on a high, being here with you." And having said that, I burst into noisy tears.

We slept little, woke early and subdued. It was obvious that this would not happen again. Already, I didn't want to think about it, I needed to blank it out.

As I dressed modestly and in haste, Martín spoke in a serious, composed way of what he had been talking about the night before: his return to Buenos Aires in May.

"Political prisoners were released all over — from Rawson, Villa Devoto, Ezeiza, Córdoba, Resistencia, Chaco, and Salta."

He said the names of the prisons with a conscious lucidity, as if he were a priest reciting a public prayer.

Among those released from prison was Martín's brother, Paco.

∽

Martín, as an Anglo-Argentine, grew up in a fading colonial world where he attended an English-speaking school with school houses named after English heroes, Nelson and Marlborough. (Some sense of decorum prevailed, Martín said, and they did not use the names Drake and Raleigh.) His father's family was English; his grandfather had worked on the railways. His paternal grandmother had on her living-room wall a dusty picture of the British Trade Fair of 1931 being opened by the Prince of Wales. She claimed to have been at a Buenos Aires party at which the Prince of Wales and his brother Prince George were both present. She had drunk champagne until dawn. Had the cork to prove it.

So many corks in so many households, Martín said. Those princes must have been royally pissed.

His mother was Italian, from Genoa.

Even blindfolded, Martín claimed, he could tell the difference between an English and an Italian home. Immediately he would know from the smell and the air pressure. It was, he said, a matter of furniture polish, social relations, and above all, the temperament of God.

Martín's earliest memory: his mother is calling to him, in Italian.

"My boy, my little boy," Mamá calls. She squats down and opens her arms as wide as she can. He runs to her and she scoops him up. He rides along on her capacious breasts.

Behind her, standing erect, his father watches.

His father, who went voluntarily to the Second World War and fought in the British Army, has returned. His father informs his mother that Martín is far too old for cuddling and carrying.

His father has been away for five years. Martín has no memory of him; he is no more than a picture on the piano; he is worse than irrelevant.

His father insists on mispronouncing his name. His father is, as the English say, a wet blanket.

Way back, his father's family had come from the same part of England as had Deirdre's mother. Well, almost. What had they been? Farmers? Traders? Martín doesn't know — his father's family went out to Argentina before the middle of the last century.

"They could well have met, you know," Deirdre says, seriously. "My mother's family, his father's family. On the road, at market."

"I don't think you've got a grip on what distances meant back then," I say. "And I don't expect your lot were taking the coach."

"You know my grandmother came from the Fens," she replies, getting annoyed. "When my uncle was a boy he used to go back up that way in the winters. He was a champion skater."

"Okay. So your family and Martín's went crashing about in the Fens together, did the odd spot of skating in the winter. Were they fleeing the Normans? Or was this earlier, when they were pals with Boadicea?"

"Have it your own way. Where was I?"

"Father just got back from the war. Less-than-enthusiastic reception from Ma and young Martín."

"Right," she says.

"Give me the goods on Martín," I urge. "Skip the rellies and get on with it."

After his father comes back, Martín watches his mother's expansive gestures, her confident adoration of him — her little boy, her most darling one — grow more tentative.

Together they wait for his father to go off to work. Martín stands at the doorway with his hand in his mother's, and, united, they watch until they're quite sure the father has disappeared. He works for a huge English meat-packing firm.

The father is going to Santa Rosa, an ordinary business trip. He might be obliged — he says this as if it were a threat — to be away for several weeks.

Martín gets into bed with his mother, lies snug against her tummy. She weeps.

"What am I going to do, my darling?" she whispers into his ear.

With his Hornby train set from England, Martín plans an accident for his father. He lays a matchstick body across the rails. When the train runs over it, it falls off the track and smashes.

His father comes home and finds out he's broken the train set. He beats Martín with his belt.

When Martín has given up hope, when his mother has begun to walk always on tiptoe, this happens: his father goes away on business and is gone for months.

His mother becomes happy again. She laughs, looking at herself in the mirror, twirling in front of it in her best skirt, revived like a flower after rain. Catching Martín up, covering him with triumphant kisses. Then going out and coming back even more excited, taking him into bed with her and holding him, breathing out long, delicious sighs. He rides on her legs and falls down into her warmth.

His mother gets out the best china and cutlery. They take turns looking at themselves in the back of the biggest spoon. His mother kneels in front of him and puts a rose in his buttonhole. A man comes to the house and eats and drinks with his mother. Before the meal he gives Martín a serious present. It's a strange round ball, large in a child's hand.

"See this," the man says, running his big fingers over the ball. "Sharkskin. Feel it."

The sharkskin is smooth and, at the same time, rough. It's scary, but Martín doesn't let on.

You opened the sharkskin ball by flipping back a little gold clip. Inside the ball was a globe. You could lift it out. On the lining of the ball were stars in a navy-blue sky. Not just a few stars spotted here and there, but a real map of the heavens: the Pleiades, Orion, and the Southern Cross, tiny and accurate.

"It's for you," the man says. "I give you the world and the stars of the heavens."

"That's lovely," his mother sighs. "So lovely." She hugs Martín and the visiting man, pushing them together. Martín's face is buried in the man's pungent trouser leg. He hangs on tight to his globe so it won't get damaged.

There is going to be cake for dessert.

Another setback. His father is coming home again.

His mother cleans the house and serves her husband steak over-done, the way he likes it.

Within a few months his mother is getting bigger, nervous but joyful, too. His father looks abashed, embarrassed, proud.

Mamá is having a baby.

He is going to have a little brother or sister. Martín is dismayed at first, but then he realizes that the baby will change everything. The baby will make his father go away forever.

And that is exactly what happens.

The baby is six months old, dark-eyed and lively. Christened with a string of names but called Paco by everyone.

Martín's father goes away to Rosario and does not come home when he said he would. Instead, he writes to Martín's mother that he has secured a job with the meat-packing firm back in England. He intends — "fully intends" the letter says — to take his new lady friend to England with him and "begin life anew."

Martín understands it is his own desire to be rid of him that has made his father go away to begin life anew. That, and baby Paco.

And now his mother sits in the living room, weeping with anger and, in time, a tentative courage. She clutches at baby Paco, who protests. She looks over at Martín and says, bravely, in English, "This time he's gone for good."

Martín goes to his room and opens his drawer. Takes out the sharkskin ball, holds the globe in his hand. He sits on his bed and stares at the round world, the stars of the heavens.

At the age of ten, Martín believes he carries inside him the power to make his father disappear.

The family lives in a comfortable middle-class suburb on the southern line. After the father's defection it is made clear by the father's family that while there will be money for Martín's education, there will be none for Paco's. No money for small, dark Paco, who is lively, sociable and — everybody now says quite openly — not at all like Papá.

His mother, who does not own the house or any part of it, takes them back to her own mother's in San Telmo. Martín still attends his English school, getting up early each morning to catch the train.

They live in his grandmother's house, which is full of dark panelling. Huge windows look out upon an unkempt courtyard.

Before his father left them and the invitations ceased, Martín regularly went on holidays to his paternal grandfather's *estancia*. These holidays were his idle fields of summer, where he discovered that perfection is everywhere around us: in the wings of insects, in the fanfare of pampa sunsets, in the shade of the singular trees.

In his adventures on the *estancia* he was accompanied by two adults, Wen and Dai. He never thought of Gwen and Dai Evans as servants. They were Argentine Welsh, but as a child Martín did not know of such communities, of those who had come to his country in search of its vast isolation. They were simply there; they were Wen and Dai, and they went with him everywhere, approving. When he gobbled up his two soft-boiled eggs and the baked apple with brown sugar on top, they exclaimed with pleasure.

After his bath Wen dried him, not in a towel, but in a white cloth of quilted cotton. Then she passed him over to Dai to be carried, still wrapped in soft cotton, to the open verandah, there to be rocked and sung to. Until he was fast asleep, they sat with him, one on either side of the bed.

The rail in the stockyard was slippery but Dai's strong arms were around him. He sat up and watched the gauchos in big hats and bigger boots doing things with the cattle. Both cattle and gauchos exuded a powerful, dangerous smell.

It's out on the pampa, with Wen and Dai, that Martín sees the ocean for the first time. He stands in the ditch behind the orchard and looks out. Beyond the mulberries, beyond the double rows of poplars on the driveway, there it is, the flat sea: yellow-brown dry grass with the darker rust of giant thistles threading through it.

He watches.

In the hot north wind, clear flames turn to silvery sheets of air.

The cattle wade belly-deep in shimmer.

This is the real ocean. Its brilliant floating expanses have nothing to do with the sluggish delta that his parents refer to as "the front." (But the front was where you went when you were having a war.)

Soon, when he is bigger, he is going to ride out into the dancing air, gallop until his horse is swimming.

When he's fifteen, Martín's mother finds a lump in her breast.

Grandmother, Mamá, Martín, and little Paco: they all kneel down together in the living room and pray. Of the four of them, Martín's the one in charge.

"My big little man," his mother says.

In church, under arches that fly up and away like prayers, Martín begins to talk seriously with God.

"What kind of deal do you have in mind?" God asks.

"There is not enough money," Martín says. "And Mamá has a lump in her breast."

God advises Martín to get a job.

So before dawn he gets up and goes to one of the big newspaper offices and climbs in the back of a delivery truck. For three hours, between four and seven in the morning, he's jumping in and out of the truck, dumping piles of newspapers on pavement. He watches the sun coming up and in winter feels the insistent wind from the river, bringing rain.

After work he goes directly to seven-thirty Mass. Comes out of church exhausted, light-headed from fasting for Communion, and walks all the way home. Parts of him float away and lodge in the tall sycamores.

He had wanted his father to go away, and he did. Now he prays for his mother to get better, and she does.

Martín attends the university and studies law. At night, he holds copy for the proofreaders on the newspaper. He is working and studying at the same time so that Paco, too, can attend the English school.

At university, Martín is drawn to the edges of a group that is active in the law union. Martín does not fit in with the rest of them; he's older, he has family responsibilities. He begins to read about Camilio Torres, the worker priest who plans to secure a bridge between Heaven and earth.

Martín finds out that poverty and injustice are what God is taking an interest in these days.

In this way he becomes conscious of the wealthy suburbs north of the city: their high, secure walls, their gardens. When he thinks about them he finds he feels shamed in some way, and filled with a restless doubt.

On the weekends he begins to work in the shantytowns, the *villas miserias*.

Martín at twenty-five: unworldly, inexperienced, a solemn young man. But already acquainted with the big bargains.

After his law degree, he is given a job on the paper as a reporter. When he at last overcomes his shyness with women, he finds what he had been expecting all along — he can lay his head on a woman's breasts and from there on everything becomes quite simple.

Women will be there, waiting behind the doors he opens, willing to give as much as he needs.

He comes back from Hue and finds Deirdre, waiting.

⤳

We are sitting on the terrace and dinner is over. The evening is gathering in the garden.

Dessert was Sandy's latest: thin buckwheat pancakes, lingonberry sauce, sour cream. Deirdre doesn't like the buckwheat, which she calls kasha. Says it tastes like river mud.

"Pass the sour creek," she says to me.

"Such wit," I say.

"Fine Russian fodder," says Martín. "That's why they won the war, you know. Kasha and garlic."

"You reckon they won the battle of the Kursk salient on kasha?" asks Deirdre, getting ready to take him on. (Her old territory, first-class honours.)

"Give me their stomachs, and their hearts and minds will toddle along behind," says Martín.

"That doesn't follow. You're shifting ground," she objects.

Sandy gets out the water-pipe and it goes from hand to hand. We're leaning back in our cushioned wicker chairs, stoned and talking. There's wine, but nobody's drinking; we were drinking earlier.

Sandy has put in a white garden: a border of sweet alyssum, white phlox, lilies, and untidy, vigorous masses of shasta daisies. And — his pride — heavily scented night-blooming nicotiana. He lectures me about his garden, about the names of his flowers. "The thing about gardening," Sandy says, "is never to overdo it."

Deirdre puts her feet into Martín's lap, and Martín begins to massage her feet.

"I see you've got him all trained up," I say.

"Yes, love," she says. "My standards are exceptionally high."

Martín speaks of armed propaganda, how crucial it has been in building popular power.

"I don't know what armed propaganda is," I say.

Armed propaganda, and massive popular support for it, led to the end of military dictatorship in Argentina.

"You have to tell me these things," I point out. "I need to know what you're talking about." And they do tell me, taking turns to provide the information.

Deirdre sits up straight because this is serious.

Martín says, "Blow up a Jockey Club, or the golf course buildings."

"Jockey Club?"

"Fancy country clubs," explains Deirdre. "Toffs only need apply."

"They go after buildings, not people," Martín says firmly. "Never target the police or army conscripts."

"They'll put up a sign," Deirdre adds, "to warn people off. *Danger: Dynamited Zone.*"

"Discourage foreign investments by blowing up beach houses," Martín continues. "Not the executives themselves, mind, just their houses."

"Fasten your seatbelts, ladies and gentleman," says Sandy. "I believe we've just commenced our descent into Looney Toon City."

"They might expropriate money from the bank or blow up a police station under construction," Deirdre says, ignoring Sandy. "Or take milk from a dairy and give it to the poor. Remove a load of lumber and deliver it to the slums, where people are living in packing cases."

"We're getting quite a list here," I say.

They're both more serious about this than I'd thought at first, with Martín's prank in the flower bed.

"And who's getting killed, exactly?" Sandy asks in a nasty voice.

"Militant actions are always symbolic," Martín says. "The message is the important thing."

"Pull the other one, mate," Sandy says.

Martín takes his glasses off and rubs his hand across his nose, as though talking about this wearies him.

*Sandy didn't start it*, I think. *You did.*

The urban guerrillas apparently had speed, style, élan, success. Their popular support snowballed.

"It's always symbolic," Martín repeats, gathering himself. "Bombs go off on important Perónist anniversaries, and everyone knows what they mean."

"But mate," Sandy says, "Juan Domingo Perón's a corrupt arsehole in overpriced pyjamas. A dithering, dangerous old nincompoop."

They look each other in the eyes, Sandy and Martín, tense. This is something they've had rows about before, you can tell.

"Before he was doddering, when he was just a corrupt arsehole — and you know this perfectly well, you were there, it was your own childhood — he was a man happy to call himself a tyrant." There's a petulant trembling in Sandy's voice.

Goodness. Sandy's dropping his bundle.

Martín's face darkens. "You'd know, I suppose. The gods of Olympus have such a splendid lending library." It is an attempt, not successful, at amiable sarcasm.

Sandy's almost in tears. "You and your bizarre bloody convoluted politics."

"In the fight against monopolies and all forms of dependency . . ." Martín's at it again. There's a speech on its way.

Sandy gets up, goes and stands directly behind Martín, puts his hands on Martín's shoulders. "Leave it right there, mate," he commands. "Just leave it, okay?"

Martín looks up aggressively, then lets his shoulders drop.

He doesn't go on.

For a few moments nobody says anything. Then I feel the irritation pass out of both of them. Martín exhales, a small groan. Leans back into Sandy, who is still standing behind him.

"I swear, you'll be the death of me," Sandy says.

Deirdre turns and pokes playfully at Sandy. "Blessed are the peacemakers," she says, "for they shall be called the children of God."

Then she takes Martín's hand to show whose side she's really on.

"I'm not sure He'll be ready for me, Deir," Sandy replies, beginning to clear away the dishes.

By now it's dark, and in the garden the nicotiana is open, white and perfumed. Sandy brings out port in a decanter. Dumps it down. "Better drink and be merry, treasures," he says and goes back inside.

Just the three of us in the garden.

Martín begins to talk about the right-wing death squads.

"What a downer," Deirdre says.

"Somebody pass the port," I say.

Deirdre's and Martín's fingers are tightly entwined. They look like people walking down the aisle together to a thumping wedding march.

When I go into the kitchen to help Sandy, Deirdre will put her feet back in Martín's lap and he will massage them, kiss them with slow precision. I imagine his tongue moving in the small, tender pockets between each toe. (Martín's tongue probes and licks. Deirdre's eyes close, her head falls back.)

They won't be walking down the aisle, it will be the registry office, with Sandy on one side and me on the other.

Sandy disapproves of these half-measures. "Might as well go all the way. Serious dress-up, some halfway decent organ music, flower girls strewing rose petals at your feet."

"You'd need rellies for all that," says Deirdre. "We've just got you and Bern."

They're doing this so Deirdre can emigrate, that's all. That's the only reason left to get married.

Still, there is the matter of celebration.

"Lunch at a Wimpy's after," Deirdre suggests.

"Heavy on the onions," Martín puts in.

"Jesus wept," says Sandy.

"If you're serious I'll go down to Sainsbury's and rip off a chook," Deirdre tells Sandy.

Sandy looks over at me and we exchange the knowing smiles of co-conspirators. We've been having private conferences about the feast he is planning. He's drawn me in to the point where I'm busy worrying about the logistics of what to get and when to serve it.

"No sweat," insists Deirdre, "all we need is tons of wine and dope."

"Wine and wassail," I say. "I want wassail as well. Whatever that is."

"By rights it should be an old nautical term," says Martín.

"No," says Deirdre. "A bunch of stoats and weasels getting drunk at the footy."

Sandy says, "Permit me to set the record straight. Dark brown ale, brown sugar, sherry, lemons. Nothing to it. Best in mid-winter, though."

"A little mulled ale goes a long way," I say.

"It would certainly fit with the spirit of the meal," Sandy advises, "but what we have here are the dog days of summer."

Sandy is hatching elaborate plans for a gigantic turkey with a goose cooked inside it. Lamb and pork sausage stuffing inside the goose. Served with Tudor pies: chard, chervil, cream, ground almonds, and dried currants soaked in hot milk.

"Tudor anything is a bit of worry," I say. "They weren't exactly big on happy marriages, were they?"

"We could go completely traditional," Sandy suggests. "Serve a swan instead of a turkey. A peacock?"

Sandy and I sit together at the kitchen table, studying his cookbooks.

"What's this bird-within-a-bird business anyway? Don't you think you're going a bit overboard?"

"Trust me, " Sandy says. "This lot will be a mob of serious meat-eaters."

At midnight we all go to see a film, a farce set in Victorian times. There is a tremendous mix-up about which coffin has the right body in it. Horses in exotic mourning plumage are plunging at cross purposes across the countryside.

Martín's hand creeps across to get beneath Deirdre's blouse. Then down between her thighs, most secretly.

I stare at the screen.

Going home in the early hours of the morning, Deirdre puts her arm in mine as well as in Martín's.

Deirdre gossips with me about what happens to Martín when he's with his friends who are *porteños* like himself. "Port-dwellers, from the port of Buenos Aires," Deirdre explains. Among the *porteños*, Martín speaks in rapid, slangy idioms, using the familiar *vos*. Together, they take delight in piling irony upon irony — all of it self-assured and irreverent, much of it gloomy, most of it sexual — then sharing it round like a plate of splendid truffles. "After a while," she says, "they become completely unintelligible to me. I can't follow a word of what's being said or implied. But I can see Martín's face, how relaxed he becomes. I know that going with him is the right thing to do. I know it will be for the best."

"Ruth volunteering for the alien corn," I say.

"Oh, stop it," she says. "Don't you believe me?"

"You're scared," I say. "I'm scared too."

"You'll be homesick," Deirdre agrees, when we discuss my upcoming trip to Canada. "They'll be speaking your language but it won't be your language, not quite."

Before I fly off to Canada, there is the do in the registry office, followed by the wedding feast at Sandy's.

Deirdre wears her blue hat, the one we bought at the market. She has her hair up. Standing slightly behind her, I can see tiny tendrils of auburn hair escaping. They fall lightly down the back of her neck.

Throughout the ceremony she shifts uneasily from one foot to another. She's wearing a pair of my shoes, and they are too small for her. At the last moment she decided her long skirt needed high heels because of the occasion. "I don't own anything that straight any more," she said.

"You'd better buy some the moment you hit B.A.," I told her, "if Isabel is anything to go by."

Martín wears a new shirt Deirdre has bought for him. Brand-new, in a shop, not second-hand at a market. A posh shirt with a designer label. It's a cornflower blue, well cut, with really elegant sleeves.

"What's this? Something new? Something blue?" I say. "Just as I suspected. You're secretly taking this wedding to heart."

Using nail scissors, Deirdre is carefully picking out the label.

"I don't want Martín to see what it is. He might think it's too bourgeois."

When he tries the shirt on, Martín laughs and twirls around with his arms out. "Some *bulodo* in his party dress," he says.

"*El Yanqui* off to the stock exchange," Sandy contributes.

The wedding takes place at twelve-thirty, lunchtime. As we walk into the registrar's office, the official is stuffing half-eaten fish and chips into a desk drawer. All through the ceremony, we can smell them.

When the official, in a crisp, bored voice, describes Deirdre and Martín's lifelong promises to one another, I get an attack of the hiccups.

"You're lowering the tone," Sandy hisses. "If 'twere possible."

All through the signing, the hiccups continue. And into the kisses and hugs afterwards, in the parking lot.

"Shall I throw you my bouquet?" asks Deirdre. "Maybe that would distract you." Sandy has picked white flowers for her from his garden.

"Hold the bouquet," I reply. "Unless Sandy's interested in catching it."

"Do you know what the world record for hiccups is?" asks Martín. "Eighty-three years."

"Somewhere in Latin America, no doubt," Sandy says. "The regions of excess."

"You wouldn't be slandering my people, would you?" asks Martín.

"I need carbon dioxide. It equalizes something."

"You want to breathe into a paper bag," Deirdre says. "Don't we have one in the car somewhere?"

Martín rummages in the front of the VW and comes up with a rumpled paper bag, grocery size. He opens it and begins to fit it over my head.

"Not over Bern's head, you silly darling," protests Deirdre. "Where have you been all your life?"

"I could go to the party as Ned Kelly," I suggest.

Deirdre takes the bag from him, scrunches it at the top, hands it to me. "Breathe into that," she commands.

We pile into the car: bride and groom in the back, Sandy driving, me beside him, breathing into the paper bag.

"That certainly was a piss-weak wedding," Sandy says. "But things are about to look up, I promise you."

I cannot remember the party well, being anxious in my role as Sandy's *sous-chef*. But it was elegant, that I do know, full of guests and easy laughter.

I helped Sandy whisk plates in and out, organize drinks. We served a massive trifle in a punch bowl.

Sandy posed for a picture with Martín. Each has an arm around the other's shoulder. With his spare hand, Martín raises a clenched fist, in solidarity. Sandy flaps an imaginary apron and declares,

"A dinner party is not a revolution."

There were photos of the bride and groom, too. Deirdre and Martín. Of course there were. I do not look at them.

Night comes, and on the terrace the festivities continue at full blast: waves of talk in Spanish and English, the sweet, thin smell of dope, the heavier smell of black tobacco, and behind it, the scent of the garden.

An air of contented fatigue gradually sets in. The event has been such an obvious success, the cooks can relax. People have begun to talk more quietly, in smaller groups. They pick at what remains of the food; some switch from booze to coffee or wander into the kitchen in search of water.

Martín, surrounded by friends on the sofa, has settled in for a prolonged debate.

"But it's his wedding night," I say. "Is he going to talk like this forever?"

"I suppose it's no big deal," Deirdre says. "It's not as though it's meant to be a major production."

"Off with her hymen!" says Sandy.

"Get off yourself," she says. Sandy is putting on his jacket and preparing to go out. He often goes off at this time of night and comes home at dawn.

"Let's get some pots and pans and bang them together," Deirdre suggests. "Isn't that what the guests are supposed to do?" She is drunk enough to be weepy. Also drunk enough to be open to distraction.

"Come upstairs," I suggest. "We can bash some books together instead."

We go upstairs to their room and gossip about the guests. We recite bits of her Portia to my Shylock. Then she gets out Neruda and finds the poem Martín quoted from at Tet, when they went up on the roof and looked over towards Cholon. In return I search for an epithalamium, a wedding poem, but can't find one that isn't a dead bore.

We discuss what to do with the wedding presents. For the first time in her life, Deirdre now owns domestic things: plates, knives and forks, glasses. (Until now she has been the beneficiary of Sandy's domestic skills.) And the best present, not surprisingly, has come from Sandy himself: a set of Lalique glasses, with naiads holding urns of water on their thin shoulders. In milky opalescence, the water falls down the glass.

Several years ago, Deirdre's mother sent her books, on the long sea voyage from Sydney to London. Now, those books are being packed for another voyage, this time down to Buenos Aires. Should she send the wedding presents with them, by sea?

"You should carry the really good bits with you on the plane. Take the brown pottery plates, the Finnish ones. And Sandy's glasses, of course."

I'll go out, I decide, and get her a bunch of tea towels at Oxfam. She can use them to wrap her carry-on luggage. Tea towels with old-fashioned flowers on them, the kind Sandy has in his garden.

Deirdre bounces off the bed and announces that she is going to read me something else.

I lay my head on the pillow and yawn.

"Just one more quote," she says.

"Don't give me any sermons."

"Not a sermon. My own anti-sermon, and don't you forget it, Bern."

She finds the passage she wants: "Where a government has come into power through some form of popular vote, fraudulent or not, and maintains at least an appearance of constitutional legality, the guerrilla outbreak cannot be promoted, since the possibilities of peaceful struggle have not yet been exhausted."

Deirdre reads this passage in a sincere, intoxicated voice. In response, I begin to grunt loudly and scratch myself under my armpits.

"Chimp outbreak over here, mate."

Years later, I would search for this quote in libraries and see for myself who wrote it: Che Guevara.

At the end of the night we roll off the bed and make it afresh with sheets that smell lightly of lavender. About six in the morning Martín comes up and they both go to bed.

All through the next day they are in there.

I walk about my room. On the other side of the wall, giggles and shouts, both muffled and abandoned.


The goodbyes have been said. I'm in the back of one of those roomy black London taxicabs.

"I can't believe you're leaving us," Deirdre said. "It's too improbable."

At the end of the street there is a detour. It reminds me of the signs: *Danger! Dynamited Area.*

The taxi driver is forced to double back. He drives down the lane behind Sandy's place to find a queue of drivers who've had the same idea. The cab comes to a halt outside the back entrance to Sandy's flat and garden.

I see her. She is standing on the terrace. Martín is standing behind her. He is wearing one of his soccer jerseys — this one a washed-out maroon. (The expensive wedding shirt would be lying on their bedroom floor.)

I am glad that on this day he's managed to be home. It that just happenstance or has he actually planned ahead?

She has her face in her hands. She is weeping.

Martín's voice comes into my mind. *What a laugh, everybody cried.*

For no particular reason I notice Martín's hair. Such thick brown hair. He has his arms around her, and he is rocking her from side to side. In an effort to cheer her, he puts his head down and nuzzles her neck.

This is the last time I see Martín. The last time I see them together.

## 6

At Christmas, 1975, I flew down from Vancouver to L.A. Deirdre came up from B.A. We joked about the acronyms.

What my mind wants to think about are the things that don't count. On the plane down from Vancouver they served small bottles of red and white California wine. The flight attendant brought them around in a basket lined with a checkered cloth.

I was full of the familiar warm anxiety: I was going to see Deirdre again.

Way thinner, wearing a grey woollen skirt that sat on the curve of her hips. Black turtleneck, hair pulled back.

"You look like a ballet dancer," I said. "You look terrific."

"The old homing device," she replied. "Works like a dream, doesn't it?"

"Not nearly often enough."

The room she'd rented was some dump in North Hollywood with toilets down the hall. We sat on our beds and talked about the news, which was of Deirdre's mother.

Soon after Deirdre had arrived in Buenos Aires, her mother, back home in Kelly's Creek, was pulling out onto the highway. A crisp frosty morning and she was on her way to the dentist up in Armidale.

Kelly's Creek is an eight-hour drive from Sydney in the south. Almost the same from Brisbane in the north. The suicide zone, they call it. Drivers on the highway are tired, especially those who have been on the road all night.

An elderly man in an equally ancient Prefect was dazzled by the bright winter sun. He did not realize that his car had crossed the road, and that he was travelling in the wrong lane.

Deirdre immediately got on the plane and flew home. (Crippled her savings.)

At the wake, Deirdre said, she felt angry. Angry at her mother for having been ill when she, Deirdre, was a child.

By the time Dorcas, steadied on medication, emerged as a pillar of the Country Women's Association — sponge cakes, fundraising, euchre parties — Deirdre had already left home.

What happens when we are young, Deirdre said, happens forever.

I told her about Vancouver, how all winter long clouds make landfall after their Pacific journey, and rain drips from the dark coniferous forest. "The locals like it," I reported. "They claim to find it restful."

Weird, we agreed. Too weird.

We discussed how in June, at the end of the school year, I was going home. Where was I going to live? Sydney, probably. I was thinking of chucking in the teaching but didn't know what else to do.

"You'll find something," she said. "No point in worrying about it until the time comes."

L.A., we discovered, had supermarkets that stayed open all night. After midnight we went out and bought milk and small chocolate doughnuts. Came back and talked some more. Catching up.

Some things I already knew from Deirdre's letters:

She and Martín were living in an apartment in the expensive, leafy area of Belgrano. A high-rise apartment with a tacky little wrought-iron balcony. Across the street was a tennis court. Martín and Deirdre had bought racquets; occasionally they went down and ineptly batted the ball around, laughing at their many mistakes.

Martín's uncle, who owned the apartment, was in a home for the aged. This was his father's brother, who, like Martín's father, had worked for the huge English meat-packing firm. As soon as he kicked the bucket, the uncle promised, the place would be all theirs.

"We're living off profits from the slaughterhouse," Deirdre had written. "The offal of empire."

She'd told me that, before they got the apartment, they'd stayed in San Telmo with Martín's mother and Paco.

Isabel, Paco's wife, had left him.

In the San Telmo apartment, Martín's mother did things with pasta; Deirdre didn't have to cook at all. She helped, chopping and rinsing.

They are in the kitchen, Deirdre and Martín's mother.

Deirdre stands at the counter, dicing tomatoes and wondering what she should say to make small talk.

"They're ready now," she says, of the tomatoes.

Martín's mother sweeps the tomatoes into the big pot, then stands by the kitchen window inspecting her legs. "How old do you think they are?"

Deirdre looks.

"Take a guess," Martín's mother encourages.

Martín's mother has shapely legs; her toes are painted a brave, frivolous scarlet. Martín has told her that his mother is in her mid-sixties, but probably she isn't supposed to know that.

"The legs are the last to go," Martín's mother says. "But the arms," she sighs. "Oh my dear, the arms."

Deirdre doesn't know what is expected.

"Feel," commands Martín's mother, and Deirdre touches the soft arms. (Is she supposed to feel the firm legs as well? Surely not.)

Martín's mother hugs her, taking her by surprise. Maybe it's going to be all right, Deirdre thinks.

"Go and see what Martín is doing," says his mother.

Relieved, Deirdre escapes into the living room. Martín is reading the newspaper he works on, the same one he delivered as a boy.

What is she supposed to do now? Return to the kitchen and report: Martín's got his feet up and his nose in the paper?

But Martín's mother is standing beside her. They are both looking at Martín, who keeps on reading. He must know they are there, must at least sense it. His hand comes out from behind the paper and picks up a chocolate from a bowl on the coffee table. The chocolates are wrapped in brightly coloured paper; his mother keeps a constant supply of them. Using one hand and his teeth, Martín unwraps the chocolate, his head still behind his newspaper. "Mmmm," he says.

His mother leans forward, lightly rearranges some hairs on his head.

"Mmmm." He continues the pretence of ignoring them, of not acknowledging the hand on his head.

When did they first do that together? Deirdre wonders. He would have been eight or so, the important little reader with his book, not to be interrupted.

Martín's mother looks over at Deirdre, full of indulgent

complicity. "Come," she says, "and I'll show you what my boy brings me."

The bathroom cabinet is crammed with lotions Martín has purchased in his many passages through duty-free. "Why don't you try some of this cream," offers Martín's mother.

Deirdre rubs the expensive cream on the back of her hand. It immediately disappears into her skin. "It's beautiful, Mamá," she says politely.

Martín has decided to come and see what they're up to. "What are you two muttering about?"

"He tries so hard to keep me young," his mother says, pulling Martín to her. Martín, playing along, looks dutifully reluctant.

"My big little man has made his Mamá happy, so happy. At last he's come home to her."

Over his mother's shoulder, Martín pulls a face at Deirdre, rolls his eyes.

They often make a foursome at the San Telmo apartment: Deirdre, Martín, Martín's mother, and Paco.

Paco is a short, ebullient man with an already balding head.

"Talks non-stop. Nowhere near as gorgeous as Martín," Deirdre has reported. "But then they had different fathers."

Paco, the younger brother, has a face certainly not ruined and perhaps even enhanced by his damaged eye, legacy of *la noche de los bastones largos*, the Night of the Long Sticks.

In our letters we speculated about what would have attracted the hoity-toity Isabel to the homely Paco. His political connections, we concluded.

"The three of them speak in English, for my sake," Deirdre wrote. "Except when Paco and Martín are talking about politics. Then they speed along in Spanish, shouting at high volume."

After they have eaten, Martín's mother goes into the kitchen and cleans up, urging Deirdre to relax.

Deirdre examines the room, seeking clues. She looks carefully at the polished dining-room table; at the doilies on the armchairs, to ward off sweaty heads; at the clutter of family photographs on the upright piano. She inspects the china cabinet with its unappealing lineup of heavily gold-rimmed cups and saucers. None of these individual details are so different from what you'd find in Kelly's Creek — not in the home behind the general store, granted, but in somewhat more affluent homes, such as my own parents' place. The house-proud motivation is the same, and the result only slightly more ornate, a bit heavier perhaps, more fusty. Yet the sum of it feels profoundly different. She is alien here in ways she doesn't know how to begin to describe. There are times — not only in her mother-in-law's living room but also in their own apartment in Belgrano — when the air around her becomes solid, dense as water, robbing her of breath.

She looks to Martín for reassurance. He is totally absorbed in disagreeing with Paco. She studies his face briefly, then looks away. (It is important not to become demanding.) Picks up a magazine and pretends to be reading it.

When she's finished in the kitchen, Martín's mother comes and settles in with a piece of elaborate crochet. While Martín and Paco argue, Martín's mother sends Deirdre, over her crochet, a series of domestic smiles. Political talk is men's business, these smiles say. Nothing to do with us. (At this point, Deirdre wrote, she had an image, ghastly in its clarity, of Martín's mother cooing over an infant, triumphant that Deirdre, too, had been reduced to nappy rash and chuck-up, while in the background, Martín, oblivious, continued to dispute with his brother about the factional infighting and the direction of the militancy.)

Martín's mother pushes the crochet hook in and out of the thin white silk.

*Sometimes by the end of the evening,* Deirdre wrote, *I get this feeling that none of them, not even Martín, believes I'm actually here, or that I'm in the least little bit real.*

From Buenos Aires Deirdre wrote me nothing that resembled the detailed descriptions she'd sent from Saigon.

"*In B.A.,*" she wrote, "*the boulevards are wide and flat.*" And, "*On a hot day we wait for the breeze to come up from the river.*" "*Here they wrap simple, ordinary things like soap in coloured paper.*" "*They have sugar with ham on toast.*"

Her sentences read like someone learning to write in English. In another time and place, I might have put this down to married happiness.

She did write that it was unnerving to find in Buenos Aires so many trees from home — gum trees, casuarinas — in formal parks with tiled paths and Spanish sounds dipping and sliding all around. She wrote: "I look at the trees and I ask them, what on earth are *you* doing here? There must be some mistake."

In recent months we'd been down to postcards.

Almost as soon as I saw her, I demanded to know why she wasn't writing to me the way she used to.

"I don't have a story I want to tell," she answered. "Or I have a story I don't want to tell."

In the nights I was with her in L.A., I found myself thinking about the months I'd spent in hospital as a child with polio. In our tacky North Hollywood room, I'd wake in the dark of early morning and images from that childhood time would flood in, unbidden and unwelcome. When I was an eight-, nine-year-old kid with polio, I was quite aware that it wasn't fair, that it was bad luck, and that "luck" was an inadequate word. Disturbed by these thoughts, I'd watch Deirdre sleeping, waiting for the sun to come up and for her to awaken. As soon as she spoke to me, I assured myself, I could begin again to forget.

"Sometimes I'm afraid you might be drifting away," I said. "We don't keep in touch the way we used to."

"How could you ever lose me?" she said, turning sleepily to face me.

"I don't know. I'm afraid, that's all. I almost lost you once before."

She looked blank.

"When we were little kids. When I was in hospital with polio."

She got out of her bed, came over, put her arms around me. "Look at me, mate," she ordered. "It's me in here. Deirdre."


On Christmas Day, fending off depression, we dressed up for our midday dinner. We talked about what we'd done at Christmas in Kelly's Creek: the excitement of midnight Mass, bulging pillow-cases next morning at the foot of the bed. In later years, a casuarina moping in its bucket of water held steady with bricks. On the radio, talk of bushfires; at the table, plum pudding with sixpences to jeopardize one's teeth.

"Christmas exiles," Deirdre called us. "Huddled together in a non-place. This is a non-place, isn't it? You could think you were here and actually be somewhere else. And vice versa."

"What is Martín doing today?" I asked.

"Beloved Mamá is gathering both her boys under her wing."

"You and me, mate," I said. "We'll make our own entertainment."

"Yes," she agreed. "Starting now, I declare this café the centre of the entire known world and the galaxies beyond the sun."

"This one beanery our everywhere."

In the paper I'd found a place that was putting on Christmas dinners for free: Dorothy's Beanery, a café made famous by a local artist who'd recreated both café and clientele, life-sized and stuffed, and put his piece in a museum. In their white overalls, his Bekins moving men sit motionless at the lunch counter, ordinary hungry ghosts.

So we went to Dorothy's Beanery that Christmas Day (Gay Liberation Front posters crowding the walls, superb food). We ate two free dinners each, poking the cranberry sauce to the side of the plate. Then we drove out to Santa Monica and stared at the unimpressive winter waves.

We watched the dogs, eager for sticks.

"Look at them, will you," she said. "All turned on and ready for fun. They don't know anything."

We walked along the beach and she said, "I've lost my nerve."

Deirdre was trying to get a job. Her best lead so far was the chance of stringing for the English-speaking newspaper, reporting on women's fashion.

"Fashion," she said, in disgust.

"It's just a job," I told her. "Not the rest of your life."

"I keep trying to get something, teaching English. I spend most of my time on the train, visiting rich women in the suburbs who turn out not to need an English tutor for their children after all."

She'd been writing, she said. At first a piece of journalism about the experience of being Australian in Argentina. An apolitical article focused on the visual.

In this article she claimed to find it easy to understand how the vast pampas sat unnervingly at the back of the urban port-dweller's consciousness; equally easy to understand was the history of colonial embarrassment about stepping out of official buildings onto unpaved roads — cigar in hand, polished leather shoes sinking into the mud. Of course, she found the latitude itself normal, familiar, and friendly. What was disturbing were the buildings themselves: their insistent, stuffy pretensions, their shuttered, self-conscious inwardness, their obeisance to corrupt hierarchies shipped over from the Old World. The piece ended — she claimed this to be inevitable rather than predictable — with a contrast between the *villas miserias* and La Recoleta, with its monuments to the wealthy dead, its extravagant, mendacious promises. The cemetery lies, she said, lies at the heart of the city.

Sandy showed the piece around a bit in London, but there were no takers. Probably just as well, I decided. Too much interior decoration, like the buildings she sought to describe.

There was more. In the long afternoons, after Martín had gone to work and Deirdre had nothing, absolutely nothing, to do, she'd begun to work on a children's book, and, much more tentatively, on a work of adult fiction. (When she told me this I felt a stir of regret — the last time she'd attempted fiction, we'd done it together, and now here she was, having a go all on her own.) *Scottie of the Antarctic* was a robust tale of rescue and reward: dog-biscuits, still fresh after fifty years. Her grown-up story was about a woman who was translating Chekhov into the Spanish of Argentina. The protagonist-translator knows neither language but works constantly from two sets of dictionaries, one at the left and one at the right side of her desk. She's adapting for the local context: Moscow becomes Paris. The translator got the job only because her husband's a theatre director. He's always away at the theatre, working on an upcoming production (a musical of *Madame Bovary*, with brief but sublime moments of tango). Problem is, bodies keep turning up in the theatre. In ever-increasing numbers they fall out of cupboards, they slump in the stalls. When sets need to be moved, problems arise. Cast and crew carry on as if this were entirely-commonplace.

"Where are you taking this?" I asked. "How's it going to end?"
She shrugged.

"I get so lonely," she said, defending herself. "I have to find something to do."

"Remind me of the good times. There must be some good times."

She told me this:

Martín took her to the country, deep into the country, a long way south, to the valley of El Bolsón, to the end of a dirt road, to the house of some friends who were in away in Europe. A house surrounded by old willows and a tree she did not know, which had grey-blue flowers and yellow fruit at the same time. At the back of the house, an unruly vegetable garden and a massive, much-used barbecue. A verandah with a hammock. Hills rising up steeply behind the house, dense with poplars and pines.

The first evening, at the close of dusk, they saw an owl fly by on silent wings. Grey on grey. The owl of Minerva, Martín called it.

The air was intensely clear. It stood like a presence in the doorway, it shivered on the hills.

The Milky Way, the high road of Saint James, spun out above them in the dark. Old Santiago was the original easy rider, Martín said.

The large rooms of the house were untidy and comfortable, with peeling plaster, ancient armchairs, and an extensive, disorganized library in Spanish, English, French, and Italian. On the wall, the usual poster of Che and a picture of Ho Chi Minh as an old man. Uncle Ho was sitting in a wicker chair in a tropical garden, looking cool and relaxed, smiling wispily.

In the bedroom was a brass bed and a record player, LPs scattered about. Outside the bedroom windows, the willows held sway. Along the front wall, jasmine was in bloom.

"We played the records, two especially," she said. "'Lay, Lady, Lay' and the 'Flower Duet.' Those were *our* songs. We'd lie in bed and smell that watery smell willows have, and listen to the 'Flower Duet.'"

"At least it wasn't 'Tit Willow.'"

"It feels so far away and long ago."

"Things'll get better. Mark my words."

"You could also smell the jasmine. Martín was a bit allergic to it. Made him sneeze."

"It should be 'Lie, Lady, Lie,'" she added after awhile. "Unless you're a chook. It doesn't seem quite the same somehow, does it?"

"So you did a lot of lying across the big brass bed."

"Until all hours. Then we'd have coffee and sweet-potato jam with cheese on rolls. The jam was homemade. It was a sort of hippie town, selling homemade this and homemade that. Not that we went into town often."

"Earth mothers all barefoot in the kitchen."

"And Martín unwound. He let go. He said that this was the one place he'd been wanting to bring me ever since the beginning, ever since that day he'd come back from Hue. It was the still centre of his world, he said, and he wanted to stay there with me forever. "

"What did you say?"

"I wondered who he'd been there with before, of course."

She paused.

"And as for staying forever, out there in the bush — not that they call it that — I thought, Oh come on, Martín, what a pile, in three month's time you'd be chomping at the bit."

"Sounds all right to me. Staying out in the bush. I could go for it."

"There were a few times — we were both worn out — there were a few times when he'd just lie beside me. I felt — I felt he was totally present. Not pushing and seeking, not like when you're actually making love, but simply, completely there. We were doing nothing more than lying side by side on the bed.

"It was incredible Bernie. *This is it*, I told myself. *This is it*. I am clothed with the heavens and crowned with the stars."

On New Year's Eve we went to Disneyland. When we were getting ready to leave, we bumped into a parade to celebrate the beginning of the U.S. bicentennial. A happy little band was coming down one of the make-believe streets, Mickey leading the way, conducting. Goofy brought up the rear, passing out candy canes. In the middle, a float: a *papier-mâché* world tied up with a big red-white-and-blue bow.

"So cheerfully blatant," Deirdre said. "If you described this to someone, they'd accuse you of being some kind of crude ideologue."

"Take a picture," I urged. "Take it to show Martín. It'll give him a laugh."

That night, at a party up at Altadena, there was talk about football and the next day's parade, the Rose Bowl.

Deirdre drank martinis, one after the other. "It's my drink, wouldn't you say? Teeny Martíns. That's what I'm going to have when things get better, isn't it?"

Coming home she told me something of what was going on in Buenos Aires, things she hadn't included in letters.

Fear, she said, was something she had discovered.

Fear was a hollow, burning, lifting sensation deep inside the guts. An intense emptiness and a hunger, but a sick hunger, nauseating.

"That's what it feels like sometimes," she told me, "when Martín's out and he's late getting back. As if you're so hungry you're going to throw up until you pass out. Then —" (she paused, fumbling for the words) "this is the strangest thing, *this*: the feeling seeps upward until your head detaches itself, and it's as if you're floating away, and you're watching the hunger down there, happening to someone else."

When she was saying this I came to a stop at a red light. I remember thinking that it was right that the car had come to standstill because such things should not be said when you're just driving along, carrying on, keeping an eye on traffic.

"Why do you think they talk about bowls?" she asked, abruptly changing the subject.

"I'm not sure. I bet it has something to do with the shape of the field and the stands all around."

She told me some more, then. About what was happening to people Martín and Paco had grown up with, gone to university with, people who had been neighbours, colleagues, girlfriends. Now some of them were Montoneros on the run. Montos, she called them. Others were in groups she referred to only by their initials. (I thought of the day in London when she and Martín had sat at the breakfast table making jokes: the Impecunious Socialists.)

"I'm worried about them. About Martín. About Paco." In a rush, emphatic, she added: "I want to be of use."

"Your Spanish is ratshit," I pointed out. "You admit as much yourself."

She started talking about something she'd read in a magazine. The movie stars go into hospital and have their freckles taken off. Permanently erased.

"Maybe I should save up," she said, not meaning it.

"Why would they want to do a thing like that? Surely they'd look terribly washed out."

"I wonder what I'd look like?" She grabbed the rear-view mirror, inspected her face.

"Stop messing about with the mirror."

"I'm washed out as it is. I look like the Wreck of the Hesperus. My mother used to say that."

"Mine, too. And, I look like something the cat dragged in."

Trust Deirdre to have pitched up in yet another of the world's trouble spots. I didn't want her being of use, as she so solemnly put it. I wanted to be able to use the pat phrase, *trouble spot*, and leave it at that. She and Martín couldn't swan about being opposed to the

war in Vietnam, as they had in London. That war was over, lost
or won. There was a lot going on in B.A., I gathered, but she didn't
have a handle on it. What exactly Martín was up to, I couldn't tell.
It sounded to me as if he was keeping his head down. Being a
journalist. Paying attention — too much of it — to his mother and
brother. In a year or so, I told myself, Martín would get itchy feet
and they'd be on the move again.

"Do you think Martín will want to stay?" I asked. "Or will he
get a case of southern hemisphere syndrome?"

"I don't know." Her voice was uncertain but she tried to lift it.
"I don't see signs of early onset."

*She loves him. Keep your mouth shut. Don't start in.*

It was always my idea that she and Martín would move back to
London, or maybe Paris, where they could be ex-pats together and
avoid the imbalance of it being home for one of them but not the
other. London and Paris were full of such people, those who had
come adrift.

I had a clear image of being with Deirdre, sometime in the
future.

It wasn't like this. It wasn't like this at all.


We'd be walking along the Thames late at night. The signs would
flash and their reflections shine in the river. *Deep and dissolving
verticals of light.*

We're off to listen to jazz. Inside the nightclub — and we'll be
inside soon, we're almost there — it will be dark and intimate and
we will be able to talk quietly. I will lean back in my seat and look
at her.

She'll move her chair closer.

Deirdre and me. Out on the town together.

In the background, somebody will be playing a piano arrangement of "I'll Be Seeing You."

Martín often stayed in San Telmo with Paco and his mother, and now, Paco's wife.

Isabel had come back. Back to Paco.

"Martín didn't get home to Belgrano every night. At first I was afraid he was up to something, but it was just family. He feels the need to see them."

"You're family too," I replied quickly.

She made a back-and-forth gesture with her hand, meaning *maybe, maybe not.* "Give me twenty years. Give me fifty."

"So what's Paco's wife doing there?" I asked, pleased to move on.

"Paco's over the moon. He can't believe he's got her back."

"I thought you said they'd broken up for good. You wrote to me, a while back."

"They'd broken up. She'd dumped him."

"So what happened?"

"I'm not supposed to know any of this, you understand. The guy she was with had to scarper and he left her behind. I've heard Martín and Paco talking about it, in Spanish. As soon as I come into the room they clam up."

This was a change. Once she would have gone right ahead and demanded to be told.

"Paco was the port in the storm?"

"Looks that way. She showed up with her bags one Sunday morning and moved in, just like that. Stays in their room all the time, lying on the bed. I think she might be having a nervous breakdown. Martín's mother takes her food on trays. Custard flan bursting with sugar. And of course Paco fusses.

"I'm not sure if it's a nervous breakdown," she went on. "I'm not sure how you can tell."

I thought of Dorcas back in Kelly's Creek, jumping from the light into the shade. Was that a nervous breakdown? Trying to drown yourself in an empty dam was a nervous breakdown, everyone had agreed about that.

"Do you think she's gone into hiding?" I asked. It felt embarrassing, and in some way false, for me to be asking such a question.

"I'm not sure. Things are getting bad down there, you know."

Martín, Deirdre said, had a school friend who'd been murdered. He'd been in London, this friend, in the summer of 1973. He'd been at the wedding feast. He'd eaten that wildly English food Sandy had cooked up.

Deirdre said his name. I searched for a face, but couldn't be sure.

His body had turned up under some casuarinas in a picnic area near the road to the airport.

How could such a thing happen? To someone who knew Deirdre and Martín?

A mutilated body.

The Triple A squads were operating: *Alianza Anti-Comunista Argentina*.

Triple A, Deirdre explained, were death squads busy in the defence of God, tradition, family, property, and the sacred interests of the nation.

"Sounds like God pointing His finger and saying No!" I said.

"That's their God all right," Deirdre replied in a tired voice.

"Martín says Paco should get the fuck out while there's still time," she added.

On what I thought would be her last night with me in L.A., we heard a police helicopter overhead, saw its searchlight. Then the cars, the sirens, the harsh flashing of lights.

"It's the whole B movie out there," I said.

Deirdre crawled over me to look out the window and disapprove. I could feel the anxiety building up in her, so I started to sing a dopey jingle from childhood.

"*I like Aeroplane Jelly,*" I sang, hoping she'd join in. I wanted her to admit that this particular show of police power had nothing to do with her, she could afford to let it go.

"*I like it for dinner, I like it for tea / A little each day is a good recipe.*"

She frowned and quoted something from Orwell, his opening line about a bright cold day in April and the clocks all striking thirteen.

"I always loved him," she said, and it took me a few seconds to understand that she was speaking of George Orwell, Eric Blair.

The police-car lights were flashing into the room. Her cotton nightdress was across me, and her hair fell on my face.

Stuff George Orwell. What about *you*?

The powdery warmth of her made me want to put my arms around her and pull her down. Hold her close. (*It's me in here. Deirdre.*) I imagined grabbing her, pushing her — let us tumble off the bed onto the floor for all I care — refusing to let her go, insisting that she change the plane ticket, that she not go back.

I snivelled instead; I begged.

"Just a few more days. You've got to give me a few more days."

The flashing lights from the cop cars continued to fall across her face.

I wept and would not be comforted, not until I saw the beginning of assent.

By the end of the next day she'd permitted herself to extend her ticket, she'd telephoned Martín — delay upon delay: the finicky B.A. telephone exchange was mucking up as usual. (I didn't listen to what she told him.)

She'd called the airlines locally, been put on hold, had haggled and cajoled and demanded. I'd called my cat-sitter, lied extravagantly to the school principal, and decided to run my credit card up to the limit.

We were in a rented car on the freeway, heading north.

~

We would be travelling without maps, we'd agreed on that. The plan was to throw a pile of second-hand paperbacks in the back of the car and drive, just drive.

"We'll be living in the moment," I told her. "Going down the road, you must abandon all suffering, especially desire."

It was early-winter dusk by the time we drove out of the city in a sea of red tail-lights. She was excited by the freeway, by the way in which the city was caught up in its many skeins. She enjoyed in particular those places where one freeway flies over another: from the middle of your lane of traffic you look down and there is yet another bunch of tail-lights, all similarly sweeping along. Even as she took pleasure in these things she was busy condemning the seduction of abundance, its need to overstate in order to convince itself.

When she talked I was reminded of how she and Martín constantly tossed ideas and opinions back and forth, how companionably combative they were.

"You two were always pretty good at nervy generalizations," I told her.

As we reached the edge of the city, the hum of the motor and the dim light from the dashboard began to calm her. She curled up in the passenger seat and relaxed.

For a long time I drove while she dozed. She woke, and we murmured about this and that. We stopped for something to eat.

"Okay," she said, after we'd got back in the car and had settled in, on the road again. "Tell me something you haven't dared tell anyone before. Something you've always classified as top secret. Remember: guilt is out, big time; atonement has pretty much had the bun; but confession is still very much in."

"I can't think of anything," I said, prevaricating. (Christ, does she know about me and Martín?)

"Go on, Bern," she coaxed.

"No. You first."

"All right. Mine is actually pretty sordid. Are you ready for sordid?"

"Ready." (He wouldn't have told her, I'm pretty sure of that. Maybe she figured it out; one day she was sitting at her desk or lying on her bed when the image drifted up, fully formed. And she knew.)

"Go on," I urge.

"There's this man, an Englishman, who's in love with a woman. He's totally in love, he's staggered by the force of it. He's had heaps of sexual experiences, but nothing has prepared him for this. He feels as if all the air has been sucked out of the room just because she's walked in.

"She's not in love with him; she's engaged to someone else. She's about to be married.

"They're both invited to an anti-war conference in Paris. The man, the one I'm talking about, is billeted with a famous French film director, the husband of an even more famous Hollywood actress. The sparkling couple have opened their house to the conference participants; our man is given a couch to sleep on in a living room the size of small cathedral.

"After much conferencing, our man comes back to the director's place to crash. It's late. Off he goes to the couch in the living room and prepares to fall asleep. What's this? The door opens, and in comes — you guessed it — the director and a woman — not his actress wife, but the woman the man is in love with. They settle down on a sofa and appear not to see the sleeping figure on the couch, who isn't asleep at all, who has merely drawn the blanket over his head, to hide himself.

"The director and the woman start making love, having sex, and he's lying under his blanket, tormented, and of course tremendously upset. He feels guilty for being there, and angry at having been put so definitely in the wrong. And terribly turned on. He can't see what they're doing, thank goodness, but it sounds as if it's being a success.

"They're completely oblivious by now, so furtively he starts to jerk off, more or less keeping time.

"When that's over, he thinks, thank Christ, now they'll both fall into a stupor and he can get up and sneak out.

"It seems as if they may be going ahead with another round. It's hideously embarrassing — especially now that he's come himself. Just when he's thinking he can't take it any more, a telephone rings in the hallway. The ringing goes on and doesn't stop."

"Wouldn't there be servants or someone to answer it?"

"Don't interrupt," she says. "The director grumbles, gets up, pulls his pants on and hurries out. Is he going to come back? The man on the couch lies as still as possible. The murmuring of the director on the phone stops, but he doesn't return. An age goes by: no director.

"That's when he begins to hear the woman crying.

"She's still lying on the sofa, and he can hear her small chokes of tears. Does she miss the director, or has she suddenly sobered up?

"For him, her tears are worse than anything that's gone before. They are simply unbearable. With his heart burning, he crawls out of his hiding place, lies down beside her.

"She doesn't push him away; she lets him kiss and hold her until the sun comes up. They finally fall asleep, and when they awake late the next morning — a grey, headachy, hungover morning — she's aghast at herself, can barely remember the jumbled events of the night before, her double opportunism.

"He says to her, as if they've shared some sacred thing: 'Come what may, we can say we have had this one night.'"

"We'll always have Paris," I put in.

"He believes it then and he believes it later. In the space of a few hours, he's managed to blank out all the rough edges, you see. He's forgotten his humiliation, the gross, unflattering beginning, the incomplete seduction. She protests, of course. Reminds him that she's engaged."

"So what happened? After they got back to England?"

"When she was back in London, when she was feeling neglected by her fiancé, she'd go and see him; she'd sneak out, finding some excuse. She claimed to be 'going to a meeting.' She was surprised to find she could do this, that she was capable.

"They'd meet at his flat, a daggy little place in Earl's Court. Much of the time he's wildly happy, even though he knows the plans for the wedding are going ahead, and that as soon as she's married she'll be leaving the country."

"Surely he sulked sometimes? Gloom and despair, the tearing of hair?"

"Not much. Well, of course he did. But he pulled himself together when he was with her, he didn't want to ruin the time they had. He always made a point of tidying the flat, you could tell. He'd have books carefully lying around, to impress. She thought, that's funny, I thought only women did that. It was quite touching, really."

"What was the turn-on for her? The secrecy? The limits?"

"She was going to him to fill up the gaps. Isn't that terrible? And there's something about a person loving you hungrily like that; it has its own force-field."

"What did they talk about? In his flat, in the stolen time?"

"He read her a book about Julian Bell, about his travelling to China and having a mistress, then going to Spain and driving an ambulance and getting killed at the front. They got Bell to a field

210

hospital but the life was draining out of him, he was already grey as marble. He whispered to the doctor: 'I always wanted an affair and a war, and now I suppose I've had both.'"

"Good grief," I said. "Just as well she was leaving. I suspect it's precisely the kind of story she'd be most susceptible to."

"There's always more going on than we let on," she said. "Don't you think?"

We drove into a motel at that hour of the night when the earth, even in winter, begins to give back its essential smell. It was mixed with the chill coming off the ocean.

While Deirdre slept, I lay awake and wondered what we thought we were doing. Were we going to keep on driving, go right through to Canada? Have you anything to declare? She's the closest person to me in the entire world and one night when her back was turned I went to bed with the man she was about to marry.

What was I going to say when it was my turn to share top secrets? Was there any way I could tell about Martín and not have it be Martín? Christ, how low can you go.

Breakfast, with its endless refills of coffee, kept me on edge. We went pushing through the fog while some medieval music, with its tinny, predictable rhythms, drifted in and out on the radio.

Up the dangerous road we drove in steady coastal fog. On into the tawny canyons. It was a landscape for bold questions.

Head things off at the pass, I decided. Get back to Earl's Court.

"Did you want him? Being in love with Martín, did you find you could actually want someone else?"

"No, but he wanted me. He tried to pass it off as sex but it was desire, a huge longing. I used to feel like an actress in a play."

"Were you any good at it? Did you feel you were being a terrific actress?"

"God, yes. Poor boy, I could see the emotions surging over his face as he cast about, trying to find a suitable disguise. He didn't make a scene, didn't dare risk it."

I imagined him, this stranger, fierce with illusion. He must have persuaded her to speak the words he wanted. Bright, generous words that would put her forever in the wrong.

"So what was the thing with the director?" That was simpler, surely.

"Martín hadn't been in London for four months. And I was dead drunk."

"He came to the wedding," she added later.

"The director?"

"Of course not, silly. The other one."

"Jesus."

"Gatecrashed the party. Walked into the living room and out into the garden and began drinking with some people he knew, pretending to be much at ease. Naturally I was petrified. The mourner at the wedding feast."

"What did you do?"

"I went over and danced with him, shoved my arms around him, held him tight, showered him with attention."

"Until you got him safely out the door and nobody knew. Nobody knew a thing."

"Exactly."

Deirdre looked out at the canyons and the wild sea below. I tried to keep my eyes on the road.

She turned her head towards me.

"It's dreadful, isn't it? What we're capable of. You look back and you can't believe that the person who did those things was actually you."

A bit actor, in and out. The perfect candidate for revelations. But a husband is different. If I spoke the truth the mountains would fall upon me, the seas would rise up. From your best friend's husband, you come away empty-handed, with not even a story to tell.

At the end of the day we found a cabin on a weekly rental. The bedroom was a dark little place, with thin imitation cedar on the walls and ceiling. We dragged the mattress into the main room and set up camp in front of the fire.

"California white wine," she said. "Beans on toast. What more could you want?"

We finished the bottle. I got up and put another log on the fire.

"So what's your verdict, Bern? Does love create understanding or does it surpass it?"

Where did that come from?

"Surpasses," I said. "I'd go for surpasses, every time."

We did not discuss what we'd do when the week was up.

In the morning, we go with a blanket down to the hard black rocks, where we lie staring down at the rafts of kelp, searching for the small roundness of seals. Our eyes keep coming back to the clear water directly below. It moves like massive glass plates.

The fog has finally burned off. Behind us are the weighty flanks of the mountains. Above us, gobs of pale new sky, moving clouds. In front, the Pacific (Asia, and down to the left a bit, home). Below, the cliffs.

"I could be happy here," she says. "I think I could be happy here."

*Evening.*

*Lavender oil, clean and colourless, heated with a candle. Warm oil on warm skin.*

*The room, in candlelight, is warm. Your hands, too, are warm.*

*Your movements slide into one another, no gap between the ebb and flow.*

*Be silent.*

*Begin.*

We tramped through the village wishing for dope. She was complaining about men. "Why do they assume your life is going to fit in with theirs? Everything's still so patrilocal it's a bloody joke."

"We could go to the Legion," I suggested. "Find the Vietnam vets, score a few joints."

"Doesn't look like there's a Legion here. Anyway, I doubt if you'd have the nerve."

"It's a matter of patience, not nerve," I replied. "You listen to their life stories first. Then you acknowledge that you couldn't possibly know a single thing about it because you weren't fucking there, were you?"

"But I was," she pointed out. "I *was* there."

"So you were. Christ, we'd be forced to sit around drinking with them for hours while they got that sorted out. Forget it. I wouldn't have the stamina."

The coffee shop, soft in grey weather-beaten wood, didn't look too promising in the dope department. Date squares were all that was on offer, and they were drowning in wheat germ. Behind the counter, a dreamy-faced woman exclaimed that someone's infant was just too cute.

Out on the deck, a faded fish kite drifted in the returning fog.

"Has Martín ever been here?" I asked.

"I don't think so. Wouldn't be enough of a war zone for him."

*Start with swimming, in the middle of the body. Your hands are flat on either side of her abdomen. They slither across, slowly inching upwards towards her breasts.*

We went down to the beach to walk in the fog. When Deirdre was about ten feet in front of me, she disappeared completely.

We made a game of it. One of us ran away into the fog, the other searched.

*Press the flat of your hands across her breasts and down to the waist. Slowly slip your hands around her waist. Draw them up her back, and gently, gently, lift her.*

In a good mood, she urged me to climb down with her to the narrow shelf of beach. Once there, she took a stone and began to carve his name in the sand, humming, *On a day like today, we passed the time away.*

"Help me," she commanded.

While she worked on the M, I did the A, and working together like that, we inscribed a huge *Martín.*

Back on the rocks above, we watched as within the hour waves began to nibble at the top of the M.

"My poor pet," she said. "He's being washed away."

"That's funny. We did him facing inland. Mostly when you write on the sand the words face outwards."

"Lord, I miss him so. I miss him Bernie."

"You could try phoning."

"It would frighten him. He practically had a heart attack when I finally got through the other day. You know how bad the phones are down there."

*Stroke her hair up and away.*

*Press your hands into the depression at the back of the neck. All of her body's nerves pass through here; this is the junction. The place where thought turns into feeling.*

She couldn't sleep, so we went driving around in the night.

"Kerouac had a cabin down there under the bridge," I claimed. "Rented it from Ferlinghetti."

"What did he think he was up to? Kerouac."

"Overdosing on nature. Being a Buddhist. When he couldn't

215

stand it any more he'd scamper back up to San Francisco for bouts of booze and gossip."

"He grew up in a town, I suppose."

"They were urban kids from back east, him and his mates. This was the end of the world for them, the edge of everything."

"I can see why they'd be unnerved."

We read aloud to each other from Kerouac's novel, *Big Sur*. They did this and then they did that; beer for lunch. But we both liked the bit at the hot tubs where the boys from Catholic backgrounds have trouble taking off all their clothes.

*The soft purse of her earlobe. Just behind the ear, the edge of her skull.*

She sat at the table with a tightness in her face. She'd developed the habit of jiggling her right thigh up and down like a nervous adolescent male.

I offered San Francisco; how could she resist? She was the one who always sought out adventure, embraced it, who took the chances and urged me to do likewise. (*Are you experienced?* the man asked. Yes, she wanted to say, *yes*.)

"I don't think I can," she said in a defeated, guilty voice.

Jiggle, jiggle.

She was going to turn tail, go back to L.A. and take that plane.

"I don't have the time."

I got up then and stood at the door, leaning on one side of the door frame and stretching out my hand to brace it on the other, the way someone does when they're at home and a stranger is coming up the path. She was going to just pack her bags and go back.

I looked out at the cypresses, and beyond to the sea, to the dull flare of grey light at the line where the ocean meets the sky.

I turned and caught sight of myself in the glass door: I hadn't even brushed my hair.

"You could at least stop jiggling your leg like that," I said.

And she was wrong; there would have been time. We could have had that time.

After Deirdre catches her plane (Miami, Mexico City, Buenos Aires), I go back to the room we shared on our last night. There is an empty bottle of massage oil in the wastepaper basket. I retrieve it, smell it, put it in my purse.

At the end of the school year I take it back to Sydney with me.

# 7

The Dutch and English authorities worked smoothly together. It took them only one day to trace Sandy's address. When Sandy came home, he found the message waiting.

Sandy was the one who phoned me. London to Sydney, a call in the night.

There was a witness on the ferry. An Englishman, a lawyer. He was riding his motorbike overland to Turkey. His smallpox injection had swelled up hugely under his arm. He couldn't sleep, he'd gone out on deck.

He told himself he must have been taking too many painkillers: the skirt flying up, the slender white legs.

It was quick, so quick, he said.

At first he thought he'd been seeing things. After that, he didn't know what got into him. It was as if someone else took over, he said.

In London, Deirdre finds that Sandy isn't home. He's away on assignment, off in that perennial journo destination, the Middle East. A neighbour has to let her in.

Next morning a young friend of Sandy's comes by to water the garden. He arrives to find Deirdre in her dressing gown with her feet up on the sofa. What's she doing here, why wasn't he told?

He pouts.

It's early April 1977. In Sandy's garden, it's spring; in Buenos Aires, autumn.

Deirdre tries to listen to the radio, to watch TV. What they are saying is tremendously disjointed. What do they think they're talking about? What is that laughter supposed to mean?

"*O the moon shone bright on Mrs. Porter / And on her daughter / They wash their feet in soda water,*" she writes in her diary.

Mostly she sits in Sandy's living room, waiting. She knows that if she waits long enough, she will hear Martín's voice talking to her. If she opens the door in the night, if she lets the darkness in, he will speak to her.

She talks to Martín in her diary. She is waiting, she tells him, for his instructions about what she should do next.

She walks through the streets, pausing at the corner to see if he has opinions about which way to go, left or right.

"You must take the train," he says to her in his most comforting voice. It's the sweetness she hears; she has to strain to make out the actual words.

His voice grows stronger, she finds, at Liverpool Street.

In front of Liverpool Street station, she runs into Ong Ba, selling fruit and vegetables at a stall. Ong Ba! She hasn't seen him in years. On a low stool, he sits hunched against the bitter wind. She tries to get him to look at her, so she can say something, a few words of greeting. She gestures and he looks up. She sees into his eyes. There is not a trace of recognition.

She reaches out her hand and touches the apples. Their cold is intense. She takes one in her hand, buys it, carries it with her. It is a simple gift, complete. It expresses the rules of harmony, *concordia*.

Martín tells her what train she needs.

At last she knows that she will be able to do something.

The logic of it is absolutely plain.

She goes to Dunwich and walks on the crumbling cliffs, waiting to hear from Martín.

"The north sea is freezing," she tells him.

Sometimes, she knows, Martín just wants information. On the local bus she talks to the bus driver about the nuclear power plant that is being built. "How do people feel about it?" she asks. "They like it," the bus driver replies. "Around here," he explains, "they like to work for something big. They used to work at the long shop, making steamrollers. They supplied steamrollers to the entire world. But that's all over."

She records this for Martín, convinced of its relevance.

Maybe they are related, she speculates. The bus driver, Martín, and herself. Back before the Norman invaders came. *He's probably a distant relative of ours*, she writes.

But that's all over. You can pull the chain on that.

She walks down to the grey ocean.

*Where have you gone? The tide is over you.*

He doesn't speak.

It becomes clear to her that she must go back to London and wait for him to give her directions again.

One night in London she sees on TV the face of Ron Ryan, the soldier from the Royal Australian Regiment. He's in parade gear, crisply pressed. He barks at her as if she were some raw recruit. She is to follow Martín's instructions, he admonishes, follow them to the letter. At all times she must pay the most meticulous attention.

"But I *am* listening," she protests. "I *am* paying attention."

He is not appeased.

It's a relief when the television goes off and Ron Ryan disappears.

In the quiet of midnight, Martín speaks to her from Sandy's spring garden. He tells her to go farther north. "You must go to the end of line," Martín says.

She studies the map, then the train schedules, and takes the train to the end of the Sheringham line. When the train arrives it pulls into a station at the end of which is a concrete bulkhead. It's the end of the line, right enough, the terminus. She met someone once (where?) who claimed that "terminus" meant a place where you turn around and go back the way you came.

She's running out of money.

She walks down to the sea at the end of the town. You must never go down to the end of town, Martín has said, if you don't go down with me. There are fences on the stony beach. She draws a sketch, for Martín. The fences are to stop stone erosion, she tells him.

*Rive, cleave*, she writes. To split, tear apart, or rend asunder. Forsaking all others, I will cleave only unto thee.

She looks carefully at the Dutch houses. They're English houses, of course, but they are looking out to Holland and are built in the Dutch style. There is something to be learned from that, she decides. Something about affinities, about giving back what has been given to you. But how and where? And why is it so difficult to know?

A cart goes by loaded with sugar beets.

She walks along the stony seawall by the marshes. They seem to be a bird sanctuary, there are paths and hides — at first she mistook the hides for old bunkers.

A man is doing the rounds of the hides on a bicycle. He comes here every day, she decides. He knows what he's looking for, he knows what he must do.

She sits in one of the hides and peers out at the seawall.

You can't glimpse the sea from the marshes. You know it's there. Although hidden, it's the focal point of everything.

Small dark birds land in flocks and take off again, crying. Are they dark green or dark blue?

It's chilly inside the hide. After a while the cold becomes unbearable.

She asks Martín what he wants her to do next.

He doesn't answer.

She goes back to London, to wait.

Ron Ryan shows up on TV again, squinting angrily in the strong Vietnamese sun. "You're a total idiot," he shouts at her. "Making a complete balls-up of everything. You haven't been listening."

She must learn to pay better attention.

"How many times do I have to tell you?" he sneers. "I knew I couldn't rely on *you*."

The nights are getting shorter. She leaves the door open into the garden.

"Speak to me, Martín," she urges. "Martín, my darling. Tell me what to do. I know you will not fail me. You know what I should do, what's best."

While she waits for Martín to get in touch with her, she goes to Sainsbury's and buys food, which she forgets to eat.

She sits in the living room.

Finally he does speak; he hasn't forgotten her, he's been thinking about her all along. He's been figuring out what she should do, what they should do together.

She listens to his voice. So calm and clear. She is to take the ferry from Harwich to the Hook of Holland.

She goes to Liverpool Street and gets the boat train. Sits by the window, eating a cheese-and-pickle sandwich because that's Martín's choice.

*I will go boldly to the deepest abyss*, she promises Martín. *I will take you with me to see again the stars*. Today it's wonderful, he's with her all the time.

In the damp fields that slip by the train, black-faced sheep look up, startled. Flung out over the fields, finding its own reflection in the puddles, the low, frail sky of spring. *This is my mother's country*, she writes in her diary.

When she gets to Harwich the ferry is there, waiting for her.

The anxiety of the seabirds' voices seems far away. The birds shepherd the ferry out to sea, wheeling and banking and squabbling with fervour.

After dark, when the boat is well out into the channel, she will find that Martín's voice is at its most compelling.

‎ ‎ ‎ ‎ ‎ ‎ ‎ ‎ ‎ ‎ ‎ ‎ ‎ ‎ ‎ ‎ ‎ ‎ ‎ ‎ ‎ ‎ ‎ ‎ ‎ ‎ ‎ ‎ ‎ ‎ ‎ ‎ ‎ ‎ ‎ ‎ ‎ ‎ ‎ ‎ ‎ ‎ ‎ ‎ ‎ ‎ ‎ ‎ ‎ ‎ ‎ ‎ ‎ ‎ ‎ ‎ ‎ ‎ ‎ *⌣*

I cannot remember a time when I did not know her.

This is not a trumpet solo played at the edge of distant field: long sigh (get it all out, good for you) and now on to dinner.

This is a bell made of stone.

Stone lodges under the skin.

When you aren't thinking about anything much, certainly not about her, stone sits. Waits quietly.

Stone has become transparent. Bright and shifty; pretends it's blood or muscle. Or has gone away. Gone for good.

Bullshit.

Wherever you go, stone goes too.

Deirdre and Hogan, the bookends, Irish. Her full name: Deirdre Margaret Rose Hogan.

Margaret Rose was in honour of the little princess. The one who couldn't have her handsome flyer and who's looked pissed off ever since.

⤳

With Sandy's help I ferreted him out, the Englishman with the motorbike who'd seen Deirdre on the ferry.

He'd immigrated to Sydney, which shouldn't have surprised me — although it did, a little. People wander around the world all the time, nobody stays put any more, nobody ever has.

He agreed to meet me, suggested lunch at Doyle's, Watson's Bay. "Let's break bread rolls together," is what he actually said. A comedian, I told myself. Just what I needed.

He was courteous and formal, in his seventies. I knew immediately that I would have to sit through the whole meal before he'd broach what I'd come for.

First, lunch and chit-chat.

We take the small motorboat from the Quay to Watson's Bay. A summer squall is threatening, so we are forced to sit beneath the canvas awning, which has been pulled over the passenger seats. In this tight, enclosed space, the engine is loud and the small compartment fills with fumes.

It's a relief when the engines are cut and the motorboat edges into the dock.

He tries to help me out, because I'm a middle-aged woman and he's a gentleman. I try to help him, because he's almost an old man now and I'm a bit younger.

Leaning on one another, we walk up the steps.

I eat my salad and stare at the harbour. On a nearby buoy a shag is hanging out its wings to dry.

He'd given away his motorbike and taken up sailing. He asks if I sail, says Sydney is made for sailing. How original.

I tell him I don't sail.

"I was getting too old for the bike," he confides. "It had become ridiculous."

He's got one of those voices that carry. Not that it matters; let the whole world hear what he has to say. Deirdre has a voice that carries too. She got it from Dorcas.

I'm busy being a polite listener. A rewarding retirement, best years of his life, a frequent flyer.

It wouldn't be fitting to rush him, to tell him that the night she took the ferry, I felt the wet push its thumb-balls in, I heard my eardrums crack, saw my lips turn blue.

He is being generous, doing me a favour. Inappropriate to bawl her name.

Family in Strathfield, in Dunedin, in High Wycombe. When he speaks of his grandchildren, his eyes are full of them.

At last, he's ready.

He'd gone out on deck because of the swelling under his arm, he couldn't sleep, he was in pain from the smallpox injection, he had a fever. There was no one else around; it was the middle of the night, with snatches of rain.

"The wee small hours," he says. "Cold. The wind was really getting up."

Spare us the hideous clichés. Spare us the wee small hours.

At the other end of the deck he saw a young woman running about like a wild thing, looking for something. She ran fast, jerkily, here and there. Even from a distance, he could tell she was extremely agitated. "She was searching for a reel or one of those lifesaver things they keep stowed on deck."

For a lawyer, for a sailor, he is not particularly precise.

"She kept running back to one side and looking down. It seemed to me — and bear in mind, I was a fair way away at the time — it seemed to me she was shouting something."

"What? What was she shouting?"

"I couldn't make it out, it was like a silent film. I began walking down the deck towards her."

Get on with it. Dear God get on with it.

"I don't know how long it was before I realized that there must be a man overboard and that she was shouting down to him."

"Did you hear the words?"

"No, you couldn't. I couldn't. Not in that wind. I assumed somebody had fallen overboard.

"She took her coat off. Quick and deliberate, she threw it into the sea. I thought, she's throwing down her coat for him. I didn't think, you see. It was only a matter of seconds. I didn't think that a wet coat is of no use in the ocean. I thought, she's throwing him down her coat, good."

Across the table I am waiting for him.

"I started running then," he continues. "I ran down the deck towards her. She was leaning over, shouting."

I am silent.

"She must have heard my footsteps. I was wearing boots. She looked up at me, startled. I couldn't see her face, the deck wasn't well lit. But I could sense she was very much afraid."

"And then . . ." I prompt.

"She turned back to the ocean, she leaned even farther over the rails. I could see she was leaning over way too far. I was about to call out something, a warning.

"In front of my eyes," he says.

"I couldn't believe it. Her feet slipped, I think. It was slippery and she went. By that time I was right there, I was standing exactly where she'd been standing. I'm seeing her go down, her legs."

"Her legs," I repeat. He nods.

The rigid moment. The same, over and over. This one pale, terrible fluttering: her white legs.

He reaches out, he grabs her by her right ankle. He hangs on. Hangs on.

Hauls her up.

"There's not much more I can tell you," he says after a pause. "It all seemed completely unreal, as if I was there but wasn't. It didn't feel like me."

His face has become knotted with his own emotion; his words have summoned up the confused, feverish night. I suspect he's in those moments when he's reaching out and pulling her over the rails, throwing all his strength into it.

These are the few seconds when, acting on instinct, he becomes a hero. Unrecognizable to himself.

I'd like to say something to thank him, to acknowledge what he did. I should at least reach over and give him an appropriately reticent hug.

But I'm feeling sarcastic. *Tell me about it.* That's what I want to say.

I'm meant to be controlling myself.

It was not his story, he just bumped into it out there on the ferry deck. Yet there he was, taking it on.

He did his best for Deirdre, this stranger, the man on the ferry.

Deirdre — a sodden, rescued lump — lies exhausted on the deck.

Tomorrow there will be solicitous Dutch authorities, English authorities, phone calls to Sandy. Arrangements will be made.

People are leaning over Deirdre. They must be trying to tell her something. She turns her face away.

The man on the ferry didn't hear what Deirdre cried out.

It seems obvious to me what it would have been.

*Martín!*

His name in her mouth.

*Martín!*

Reaching across the water. Ringing out, like a bell.

## 8

*A* truck is driving over a frozen lake. A dark figure, bundled up against the killing cold, is holding a lantern to guide the way. The truck is coming with supplies. When it reaches the city, the siege will be broken. But the truck is falling through the ice, into a black hole. The figure runs towards the hole and she, too, is falling. She cannot see the lantern any more. She's falling through water.

That's the dream; it's just a dream. Deirdre does not place great faith in her dreams. Dreams, she claims, have very little to do with dreaming. Dreams are little; dreaming, big.

She rolls over and looks at the travel clock. Ten past three. He should be home by half past at the latest.

Deirdre is awake in the dark, waiting for Martín.

She'll tell Martín about the dream. He might smile and say,

Where did that one come from? Or nod because he has not really been listening.

It's a wet winter's night. She rehearses the sound of a car arriving outside, the reassuring hiss of tires.

Martín gets a lift home with Jorge, another one of the journalists. Jorge drops him off.

The car door slams.

Jorge does a U-turn, drives back to Libertador, and then turns north, off to his dormitory suburb.

Jorge works with Martín. They have adjoining desks. From time to time Jorge receives death threats on his telephone. One afternoon Martín picked up Jorge's phone and barked *¡Hola!* as a matter of course. The caller informed him that he was going to shoot him in front of his family, next Sunday morning as he was coming out of church. The caller named the church and the time of Mass.

Martín's heart beat so loudly it seemed as if it had split in two and gone into his ears. For hours, Martín could hear nothing.

Now, when he think of it — he tells Deirdre, the ritual of retelling, husband to wife — he can watch himself: his real self was standing behind that person who was answering the phone.

Not that it felt like that at the time, he adds; not at all.

Late at night, Martín leaves the press building and rides with Jorge, who is making plans to move with his family to Mexico City. At three in the morning, two is safer than one.

Deirdre is pleased with this new arrangement. It means Martín comes home to Belgrano every night, comes home to her.

Deirdre writes that she and Martín have two lives as a couple. In one life, they are distant and courteous. Martín will open the door for her and step back so that she does not bump into him. They make love in a grave, considerate way, as if handling fine porcelain.

They do not quarrel. They are too careful for that. Curled together in the dark, they tell each other stories.

"A poor thing," Martín offers, "but mine own."

"Go on," she urges.

"A ghost was exposed as a fraud. The last and late child of Doña Mercedes, she was born with not a drop of blood in her face, and thought her future was clear. As it happened, the only way she could get turned on was if her tiger lover agreed to smoke a cigar, a good cigar mind you, nothing tacky.

"Back home she would have got away with it, nobody would have thought twice about a ghost smelling of cigars (if anything it would have been an asset). But in Paris, in the *sixième*, it had begun to arouse suspicion. They were on to her even before she slipped up.

"So one afternoon she came as usual to the apartment of her lover."

"What did her lover look like?" Deirdre interrupts.

"Nothing special. A chunky tiger who'd misspent his youth sitting at his desk, filing stories. Short-sleeved sweater, yellow. A forehead that in a few years' time would crumple like tissue paper.

"That afternoon, as the rain fell on the skylight, her tiger lover kissed her as if she were honey, he caressed her as if he were smoke. And something happened. For the first time in her life, blood began to creep up into her cheeks. It was the cigar, her tiger lover assured her. The best Havana.

"Out into the evening streets she went, replete, humming a *jubilate*. Unaware that now she looked exactly like a living person, and was no longer a ghost in any passable sense."

But Deirdre has fallen briefly asleep.

"Have I told you" Martín was asking, "about Julio's bear who lived in the pipes?" Julio, who understood both cats and philosophy better than anyone, knew that time could be a quick and slippery customer.

231

"In the morning the bear comes out of the taps and licks the faces of people who are standing at their basins, washing themselves."

Martín demonstrates.

"That way," Martín continues, "the bear in the pipes feels somewhat sure of having done some good."

They take refuge in domestic life, which can be lived from hour to hour. To their surprise they are both learning to cook, at the high end. *Bif bourguignon,* their new specialty. They take all Sunday to make it, chopping the beef, washing mushrooms, simmering, consulting, sniffing. They eat it themselves; they do not entertain.

They go shopping on Avenida Santa Fe and debate about espresso cups.

"I like the ones with the red-and-green checks around the rim," she says.

"No, no. Cheap hotel stuff."

They consider, instead, octagonal ones that are black outside and red inside.

"Take a walk on the wild side," he urges.

"We can't afford them."

These days the money is going to Paco.

They leave without buying anything, but feeling happier, almost close. Martín takes her hand to guide her through the traffic, like a benign uncle.

*Martín's gone away from me again*: that's how she describes it to herself.

The last time this happened was when his friend disappeared. The one who was at the wedding, who was found mutilated in bushland near the airport at Ezeiza.

In a wood, as Martín puts it.

This time, she realizes, it's because Paco is making plans to get out. He's going soon, any day (perhaps tonight).

Immediately after the military coup, Paco went into hiding somewhere in the city. That arrangement has been getting more and more untenable all the time. The decision has been made: Paco must leave the country, get out.

Deirdre does not know where Paco is now. She knows that Martín occasionally meets Paco, or his contact, in some anonymous public place. She knows that leaving the country means false papers and that they cost money.

They do not discuss any of this in detail.

Martín has admitted to her that he does not know exactly where Paco will go. "It's better he doesn't tell me. Even if he did, what could I do? Besides giving him what money we have."

Martín, the elder son and family protector, has had to accept this.

He has begun to talk about moving his mother in with them, into the apartment. "We would all be together. It might be for the best."

Deirdre doesn't want his mother, of all people, moving in on them. Going on and on about her boy, her big little man.

If only she could get a job. She almost got the fashion job but it fell through. (That was a relief as well as a disappointment.) She must keep looking, she must find a job teaching English. If she had a job and his mother moved in, at least she could get out of the house some of the time.

What about Isabel? Jesus, if darling bloody Mamá moved in, where was Isabel supposed to go? Isabel would be looking down her nose at her in five minutes flat.

"I suppose you want to bring Isabel here too," she accused him one day. "Tell me it isn't so."

He looked guilty. Guilty and worn out.

"Who else do you have in mind? Who else are you planning on moving in with us? Everyone's more important to you than I am. I'm your wife, remember. Your wife."

"I do recall rumours to that effect."

"Anyway, there's not enough room," she said, defending herself. "We'd have to crawl off and sleep in the bath."

So far so good; no definite plans have been made. Maybe it's all just anxious talk. The only thing for real is that Paco's getting out.

If Paco leaves, it might be months before they hear from him, or know for certain they will not.

She looks at the travel clock again. A quarter past three.

When Martín comes in from work she'll pretend to have just woken up. Perhaps he'll be in a sweet mood, solicitous. Would she like some warm milk? Nutmeg? Vanilla?

Soon, he'll be home. Here, with her. Beside her in their warm bed.

She'll hug him. Put her ear on his chest and hear his heart, chugging away.

One day soon, she knows, he'll begin saying it would be best if she left, too.

Then there's the other life, the one in which they're not careful, in which they dig their fingers into each other's skin, seeking one another, insistent, demanding, until at last they're sliding, easy — so easy now, all barriers gone — as one, as nothing.

Afterwards, amazed at where they've been, they whisper together. This is when he becomes her man, the one who staggered back from Hue and found her waiting for him.

When Paco has gone, when they've heard one way or another that Paco is safe, everything will be better.

"I promise," he murmurs.

"I know," she says. "I know."

Soon she'll make love to him again. She'll turn him on his belly and nuzzle his neck, kiss the ridge of bones along his back. Her lips and tongue will move to the base of his spine, and he will moan and finally roll over.

And she won't go.

She won't go. She's decided.

⌒

Paco has told me what he learned after he came back.

In the second week of September 1976, Martín was sucked up, abducted.

At about 11:30 p.m. Martín was in a café having a Cinzano and coffee before going back to work at the paper, half a block away. He was on his lunch break, you could say.

It wasn't busy in the café — one of those old places with high ceilings and black marble tables. Once it had always been crowded, especially at that time of night. But in the months following the military takeover people scuttled home early. "Since the fucking *golpe*," Martín complained, "the place has turned into a morgue."

Martín had just left the café and was beginning to walk back to the newspaper office.

Five men, three armed with rifles and all in civilian clothing, approached him, full of noisy, swift aggression. They grabbed Martín, threw him to the ground. Two of them seized an arm each and hauled him up, kicking his legs out from under him as they did so. They pulled Martín like that into the waiting green Ford Falcon without licence plates.

As he was being dragged off, Martín called out his name and phone number, as people did at that time, in that terrible situation.

The number he shouted out was for the apartment in San Telmo.

By the time Martín was abducted, Paco had already left town. Eight days before, at great risk, he had taken the night ferry to Montevideo.

Although in extremely hostile country, Paco's luck would hold, Paco would be safe.

Martín's mother received a call. A woman's voice. The voice described the Falcon, the five men, the rifles. The woman happened to have left the café at the same time as Martín. He was a regular like herself. She described the Cinzano and coffee. He always had that.

A demitasse, black, she added.

Anything was enough, Paco says. It was enough to have once worked in the slums, to have known worker priests, to have been active in your union. Enough to have, for any reason, visited Allende's Chile. Enough to have a beard and long hair. It was enough to be in someone's address book. More than enough to have been opposed to the war in Vietnam.

More than enough to be Paco's brother, Paco's wife, Paco's mother, Paco's sister-in-law.

Somebody might have known. Somebody might have been there in the audience, in London, keeping an eye on Martín. They would have heard him describe the prison at Con Son. They would have heard Deirdre speak of Dien Bien Phu, of the defences named Claudine, Beatrice, and Elaine.

It is Martín's mother who approaches Deirdre at the bus stop, where she is waiting for the *colectivo*, the city bus.

Belgrano has by this time become a high-risk area. A lot of military people have apartments there. On Calle Arcos, in the heart of Belgrano, is the Mexican embassy where, in March, Cámpora himself took refuge. Now the district is brimming with military and police, there to prevent anyone on the run from reaching the asylum of that embassy.

Martín's mother does not know where Martín is being held. As they both stand at the bus stop, she urges Deirdre to leave the country as soon as possible.

"Go," Martín's mother advises. "Go back to London. It would be for the best."

"I can't go now," Deirdre replies. "I need to know that Martín is safe." In a few days, surely, they'll know what's going on.

"He is my husband," she says to Martín's mother. "I have come all this way."

They decide upon the lawyer to contact: he and Martín were altar boys together. Martín's mother will go to his office. The phone might not be a good idea.

Deirdre will take the train up to the suburb where Jorge lives, on the Tigre line. (He'd been all set to leave for Mexico when his father had fallen ill.) Jorge has contacts. He will know what to do next.

Two women embrace at a bus stop. They are trying to figure out what to do about their son, their husband.

In two weeks' time it will be his birthday. He'll be thirty-nine.

The term *desaparecidos* has not yet come into general use throughout the city.

The lawyer said it was likely he'd been taken to ESMA, *Escuela de Mecánica de la Armada*, the Navy Mechanics School on Avenida del Libertador.

The stupid thing was, you could practically see the Navy Mechanics School from Martín and Deirdre's high-rise apartment. From the bathroom window, if you stood on tiptoe, you could pick out the road that led directly there. You could imagine the spacious grounds, the smart white buildings with their freshly painted wooden shutters. You could picture the flower beds, the slate roofs of the officers' mess, and the Gillette factory next to the small café on the other side of the wide road.

If Martín was indeed at the Navy Mechanics School, he was not far away.

Martín's mother filed the writ of habeas corpus for Martín at the central court of Buenos Aires. The lawyer who helped her draw up the writ was himself abducted three months later. As for the writ, it was sent back, stamped "*Rechazado*": Refused. There was no warrant for Martín and he was not under arrest.

⤳

Neither Martín's mother nor Deirdre knew what was happening, in the Navy Mechanics School, to Martín.

"They had no way of knowing at the time," Paco says.

Twenty years on, the truth is available to everyone, is part of history. The slender facts have been documented in the scrupulous detail that the living owe the dead.

Still, it remains impossible, Paco admits. Impossible.

Impossible to understand Caroline. I have read about Caroline: a thick broom handle. Two long wires ran in one end and out the other. I have read that Caroline was invented and christened by an electrician at ESMA. This, in addition to other devices of persuasion: *picana*, the cattle prod; *submarino*, immersion.

"What happened at the Navy Mechanics School is far beyond any words of mine," I tell Paco.

"Aren't we the lucky ones."

"Besides, I was in another country."

"The dead speak for themselves," Paco murmurs. "To anyone who'll listen."

It is late at night in his city, a night full of rain. We are in Paco's office. A lamp shines on his desk. We sit inside the light it casts, drinking the high-class duty-free scotch I brought with me as a gift.

"Take up gardening," Paco says, surprising me. "Promise me, right now. Promise you'll take up gardening."

For a moment this seems trite. Then I remember that Paco, the most citified of men, got by as a gardener when he was in hiding in

Uruguay. Digging in the soil, putting in shrubs, fussing and feeding and watering.

"I've never grown a thing in my life."

"You were raised on a farm," he replies, as if that settles the matter.

"It was a gentleman's coup," he says. "The headline-writers were lovey-dovey about it. Down with unions, off with tariffs, up with salaries for the military. Night and fog? No prob! Let the market rule! You people who come to visit persist in having the wildest ideas about the dimensions of the militancy. Like that horse-shit about tons of people in France being in the resistance, when in fact they were home by the fire having sweet dreams of Vichy."

"Who are these 'you people'?" I demand. "You don't have them arriving by the busload, surely."

"They fly in and they talk about the Mothers. I see them on TV. Lovely liberal ladies like yourself. Unknown to me personally, I very much regret to say." He gives a wicked grin.

Come from afar, I am Paco's own particular, exclusive, international witness. I understand that this is why, from the second day of my visit, I have been having sex with him. It's not about chemistry, not because from the moment he saw me, Paco was overcome by my compelling charms, etcetera. Impossible to be here with him and be prudent, to stay in the lanes.

*What do you think you're playing at here? First one brother, then the other. Christ, it's bloody embarrassing. Step up for the living, seek him with your tongue, hold him in your mouth, drink him down, throw your legs around him and urge him, further, further. Mother T. — that's T for Trespasser, you understand — the worker priestess, very hands on and of course that's just for starters. Hold him fast against the unlived lives, hold him lest we all drown.*

*You're way out of your territory here, mate, way out.*

"The unspeakable," Paco says, "has all the wrong endings."

"In what way?"

"Gratuitous rather than inevitable. No harmony, no dignity, no purpose, no reason, no anything."

And we have been undermined, reduced. Numbed, Paco claims, numbed by the ceaseless flickering images in our living rooms, real but completely unbelievable. It has become necessary to return to the imagination.

"Call up that old fart, the corrupt narrator," Paco declares. "Make way for the fool's lucid intervals."

He's staying awfully late. What bullshit line is he going to string his wife when he gets home?

(Not that I've a right to talk. When I get home I'll have secrets of my own to keep.)

Paco reaches out, takes my left hand, the one that I write with. Presses his right hand into it. It is an exchange of skin, of the warmth pumping underneath.

With his hand against mine, Paco whispers. Like a penitent in a confessional, he whispers.

He tells me what he knows of his brother.


Walled up, isolated, disoriented into slow time by the constant darkness of the hood.

Prisoners were held in the officers' quarters, which had been converted for that purpose. In the basement were torture rooms, a photo lab, and an infirmary. Martín would have been on the third floor, called the *capucha*, the hood. (He was there before they built the *capuchita* in the attic.)

Paco gets up and opens his file cabinet. Rummages about, takes something out, shows me.

Drawings of this prison. The cells were separated from each other by concrete partitions topped with chipboard panels. The partitions were covered with wire mesh. Martín would probably have been hooded, shackled, and chained to one of the large crossbeams. Overhead, a naked bulb in the sloping roof. Martín, hooded, might not have had much opportunity to see the bulb.

They played Julio Iglesias, Paco tells me, to depress the prisoners.

I stare at the drawings, at the concrete, the chipboard, the wire mesh, the light bulb. These are quick sketches someone has done (from memory?). Paco has a stack of them; this is the one at the top of the pile.

I gather myself against what is coming.

"Can you begin to imagine," Paco asks, "what it is like to be hooded, unable to see?"

I shake my head.

"Imagine," Paco demands, "imagine how you'd listen."

Information, Paco tells me, information, however brief, became the most important currency of all. The flat statement of facts was hoarded and passed along, mouth to mouth.

On the *capucha*, the toilets were located between the cells and the storeroom. In the storeroom were piles of clothes that had been taken from the prisoners.

A man who had been sucked up and brought to the *capucha* the same night as Martín had the good fortune to be taken to the toilets. When he came out of the toilets he had the further good fortune to hear his guard gossiping with another one, talking about their children's school holidays. The prisoner was able to lift his hood partially and look about. He was even able to walk a few steps in the direction opposite to the cells. He stopped in front of the storeroom and he looked in. He recognized the blue shirt Martín had been wearing.

Paco has this information now. But he does not have the date, the place, the time, not precisely. He knows that Martín was "transferred."

*Transferred* is the word for murdered.

241

At the time Martín was at the Navy Mechanics School, they were throwing prisoners out of planes into the estuary of the Río de La Plata.

"Don't confuse me," Paco says, "with the big H harbinger scurrying to the post office, or with the corner newsboy, or even the chorus. I'm just the familiar figure jawing on, jarring, insistent: we all know one or two of those I bet, a bit gone in the head, a few centimes short, the nutbar who won't even pause for breath there he goes again telling it over and over, and if ever you figure out a way to shut him up, you tell me, be sure to tell me."

Nobody bothered to check on the currents, and the bodies washed up on the beautiful beaches of Uruguay. Later, they took them farther out to sea, where they would not wash up anywhere. To prevent identification, their arms were cut off or their jaws smashed, their faces disfigured. Bellies slit open, to make sure they'd sink.

Fish food.

The naval solution.

Usually the trucks arrived on a Wednesday, Paco says. Sometimes Thursdays. They listened for their number. If it was called they were taken to the basement. After that they were loaded into a truck, driven to the municipal airport or a military airport, and put on a plane or helicopter. (At first there was a rumour that they were being sent south, to Rawson.)

Someone must have seen the *verdes*, the guards, bringing Martín to the basement. Hooded, in shackles, his hands tied behind his back with wire.

"Doorless flights," they were called. I thought they got that name because once you took off, you never landed. Paco says no, it's because the doors were removed. All the better to throw you out, he adds.

There must have been occasions when the prisoners' hands were not effectively bound. A naval petty officer who made himself famous providing interviews about what went on at ESMA has described how he noticed, around the opening where the door had been removed, the marks of people's fingers.

Martín might or might not have been given sodium pentothal. He might or might not have been injected with curare.

All the seas of the world tumbled about his heart.

His hair, soft in the water, adrift.

↬

I think of Deirdre in the months following Martín's abduction.

She still has had no news about Martín. Where is he being held?

She is lying on the sofa in the living room of the Belgrano apartment, listening to the lazy *pock pock pock* of tennis balls on the court across the road. She hears the occasional bragging shout.

It is afternoon and the high summer sun shines. Behind the tennis court is a magnificent jacaranda. The dream tree: that's the name she learned for jacarandas back home.

In October — three weeks after Martín, three weeks after, three weeks — it blossomed into heavy purple flower. Now it's in thin green leaf, delicate, feathery, abundant.

She sees the jacaranda in her mind; she's not looking out the window.

On the tennis court a woman laughs again.

Sometime in the afternoon Deirdre goes to the fridge and takes out a piece of cheese. Surprising how long it takes to unwrap this cheese. Although her stomach feels hollow, she finds she can't put the cheese in her mouth. Strange how solid the wrapper looks, how slippery it feels to the touch; incredible that the cheese is still there, totally substantial inside its wrapper.

She leaves the food on the counter by the sink. The idea of eating has become absurd.

Taking slow, deliberate steps, she goes back to the couch and sits down. Everything is still, drugged with the heat.

You wouldn't see him. Even through binoculars he would be quite impossible to spot. That's because he's in the dense sheltering shade of the ombu tree, silent as a bird that knows it's being watched. He's moving right into the tree now, into its massive trunk. Nothing can hurt him; the tree doesn't so much as scratch his skin because he has a robe wrapped around him of soft, white, quilted cotton. There's heaps of room in the trunk, he's completely safe and comfortable, it's as big as a living room in there. He can stretch out like a tiger. If he ever needs to, if he hears someone coming, he can easily burrow into the roots that reach luxuriously down through the topsoil. Christ, the pampas has topsoil more than three feet deep and people here think nothing of it.

She gets up, walks into the bathroom, takes all her clothes off. Stands in the shower, puts her face against the cool tiles. She washes her hair with shampoo that smells unconvincingly of apples.

*I am a woman washing herself*, she thinks.

Steps out of the shower. Puts a towel round her head, a turban.

In the mirror she sees her shoulders lift, nudge the air, fall.

Naked on the bed, she sleeps.

She's out in the bush, definitely not the pampas this time. A long way away. Some place she's never been. Above her, tall trees go up and up to a sketch of leaves against the sky. These aren't any trees she knows, they're totally foreign. Martín's here with her, and apples are falling out of these strange trees onto her body, pummelling her all over, turning her on. Martín's still fully clothed, and he's talking. Talking and talking, driving her wild. "The way to proceed," Martín declares, "is with unbridled, dangerous, necessary romanticism." What the hell is he on about? What can be so important? She's lying down now, she's opening her legs and raising her hips, and the apples — that's what they look like — keep falling against her. Comfort me with apples, she cries out, in terrible exasperation and pleasure. Comfort me with apples for I am faint with love.

Her own cry wakes her up. The apartment takes shape, again. She's in the bedroom. Here is their room, with its familiar walls and ceiling, its emptiness.

This is what is real, she reminds herself. This is not a dream.

There's some movement in the hallway, on the landing; she can hear it. Someone's out there, standing in front of her door. Someone has come with news of Martín.

It's the lawyer, for sure.

*At last he has come*, she thinks. *Now I will know.*

In a hurry, she pulls on her robe. She opens the door.


It is not true that nobody knows exactly what happened. In every single case, Paco says, somebody knows what happened; they know because they did it.

One hot Saturday morning in February 1977, almost a year after the Process of National Reorganization had begun, Paco's wife was found at the bottom of a cliff in a green Citroën. Her body was badly burned because the petrol tank had burst into flames upon impact.

It was on the coast road between Mar del Plata and Miramar.

Nobody had seen it. Nobody who was coming forward to say so.

The local police were most correct. They were pleased to be able to inform the mother-in-law what had happened. Although with great regret.

The verdict: an accident.

The young lady must have fallen asleep at the wheel. The road does wind close to the cliff. It's the only place where it does.

No, there was no question of force. They were most anxious to reassure her.

(No signs of force in the San Telmo apartment either, when the mother-in-law came back from shopping. Isabel hadn't been with her, she'd been staying with friends on the outskirts of the city.)

Yes, they regretted to inform her that there were some bones broken. In the impact of the crash, without any doubt. A fall of over twenty metres, you understand. Head injuries would have been inevitable.

Also most regrettable, they were sorry to have to advise her, her daughter-in-law had been driving a stolen car. A young lady like that, someone might have taken advantage of her.

The investigation was thorough, the documents neatly filled out. The name and make and year of the car, all there on the forms.

Martín's mother went to the provincial headquarters in Buenos Aires, aware that as a mother of "subversives" she might not emerge from such a place.

One son abducted, the other in hiding. Despite this, she opened her wardrobe and selected her best suit. From its hiding place, she took her small string of real pearls. Went into the city, found the building, and walked up the steps.

They weren't interested in her, the mother-in-law. Instead, they were polite.

They would make inquiries.

They hadn't had time to look into the matter, but yes, as they had already assured her, they would be making inquiries. She could come back later if she wished.

She did wish.

Car thieves, most assuredly. Perhaps the young lady had bought the vehicle innocently enough, conned by a cheap deal. All too common these days. Unfortunately.

When the mother-in-law began to look unconvinced, when she planted her feet and drew up her shoulders and gave them the patient, fierce stare that said she was way past caring about consequences to her own body, when she began, in short, to act like one of the mothers of that country, they said:

They hadn't been going to mention this, it was a delicate matter, you understand, and they had not wanted to bring it up, a thousand pardons, but was it possible that the young lady had been ill, depressed? Was there, perhaps, a little difficulty, a misunderstanding, between the lady and her husband?

Martín's mother comes to Deirdre, to the apartment, and knocks on the door. Finds Deirdre in her robe, sleepy and confused.

Martín's mother wants to ask, needs to say:

What was Isabel doing on the road to Miramar?

At the wheel of a car?

Isabelita, who had never learned to drive.

Of Martín, neither Martín's mother nor Deirdre has had any news.

When Martín's mother leaves the Belgrano apartment, she goes back into the city, sells her small string of real pearls, and begins the arrangements for a one-way plane ticket for Deirdre.

To London.

⌒

I am able to invent for Deirdre a number of futures, all of them more plausible than what actually happened.

Like this one:

It is the late Eighties, at the time in Australia when there is a last-gasp interest in war crimes, the crimes of the Second World War.

Deirdre seeks these stories out.

She is on the train, going up to Woy Woy to interview two veterans of that war. Each of them has written to a Sydney newspaper. One has described how he shot some Italian prisoners, shot them in the back, needlessly. "If you're looking for war criminals," he wrote, "you'd better start with me." The other old man had been in what they used to call Batavia, had been part of an underground group during the occupation. "Of course we killed villagers. We didn't know if they were innocent or not. It was war. In heaven's name, *what on earth did you think we were doing?*"

She's going to talk to both of them.

I have the first line of her article written: "*Woy Woy* is an aboriginal word meaning deep waters."

The train is electric, fast, with soft green seats. She hears tinnies being popped open. *Bloody boozers at nine in the morning*, Deirdre thinks. *I bet that's not just Pepsi.*

The gums have their new spring growth. Shining red tips quiver in the wash created by the speeding train.

She crosses the Hawkesbury and the river is wide and quiet, a message from another time.


Or this one:

We're enjoying the luxury of the ordinary, the banal.

It's morning, and Martín has come in from his night at the paper. In the country in which they live, an elected government is bickering its way through another mediocre term.

Martín laments that nobody cares, nobody has any political ideals any more. All they can think about is getting away to the beach, having their barbecues.

They have a place at the beach themselves, Martín and Deirdre.

This morning, after sleeping for a few hours, they make love. They're sleepy, sated.

"My wife is beautiful," he says, stroking her neck.

"What your wife needs is her caffeine."

"I'm sure she does," he replies, not making a move.

"I can't think why I married you," she grumbles, pretending to push him out of bed. "Why ever did I marry such a lump of lard?"

She pads into the small kitchen, makes drip coffee, takes it back to bed.

"Want some?"

"Not this puppy. This old pupster's got serious sleeping to do."

She gets dressed while he watches, enjoying it. She puts on her green skirt and her beige sweater, over which — it's cold today — she throws her gold-and-green shawl, with the dark-green fringe.

"*Ciao*," he calls when she's at the door.

"Bye sweetie," she calls back.

She sits on the train as it rocks along. It's a pleasant railway carriage with leather and polished wood and old-fashioned lamps. She catches a glimpse of herself in the railway car window.

*I always feel good in green*, she thinks. *Maybe I was a tree in a former life.*

She's got her hair up because she's going to an interview in one of the posh northern suburbs.

Does she want to coach some snotty kids in English? Christ no, but you have to do something. You can't loaf around all day pretending to write fiction.

She gets off the train, and now she's coming up out of the underground, into the nineteenth-century railway station with its scalloped wood and intricate wrought-iron.

I follow behind her up the stairs.

Small strands of her hair are falling onto the back of her neck.

She almost at the top of stairs, she's almost outside.

⌣

Paco acknowledges my endless need to know. For years we have written irregular, rambling, jokey letters with bits of gossip, other people's conversation, personal commentary. He never bothers to edit. For his own entertainment, he takes care to use as many stupid English idioms as he can.

"That Salman is one smart cookie. If you want to keep a secret, if you don't want everyone in the world to know, tell *nobody*.

"The dead are quite shameless," Paco continues. "Martín doesn't care if you lived in another country, or if you never met him. He wants you to remember, demands nothing less. It really pisses him off that the Dirty War is becoming like 'Normans Win at Hastings.' Martín sees how it goes: when we have a sporting event or an international conference or a change of government, a network in your country will do a thirty-second clip on the doorless flights, then on to the next; or hey, big-time, sixty-minute special, in-depth, the entire enchilada plus a bit of adagio thrown in, you better believe it. It's not enough for Martín, no way. I tell you, Martín's become downright pushy in his middle age. Bends my ear, grabs my arm, shakes me awake. I'm afraid big brother Martín's turned into what one of your poets — how do you say it? — Martín's turned into the old mariner."

When I go to B.A. — just that one time, in the late 1980s — it is not a holiday, it's a pilgrimage, emphasis on the *grim*. I go to see Paco, to talk with him face to face, to hear, his own terrible burden of story.

He sees the fact that I don't eat meat as an amazing oddity. We go to a grill, and he orders kidneys, intestines, and udders. "Delicious," he says, putting on an act. "Crispy critters."

I tell him about James Joyce's enthusiasm for the taste of fresh urine in his breakfast kidneys. I teach him the childhood rhyme, "Yum, yum pig's bum makes good chewing gum." I recite all my

Lourdes jokes. A man who is crippled has a chair with broken wheels. They dunk him in the water and when he comes out his legs are still crippled but behold, the wheels of the chair are better than new.

Paco would much rather fool around like this than talk about what he calls ancient politics. Persiflage, camouflage.

"I've had a gutful," he says. "An eyeful, too." His good eye winks. With a conscious, stereotypical, gallant flourish he pours us both more wine.

"When we get back to your hotel," he offers, "I'll do my folkie routine for you, get you in the mood. Used to play acoustic guitar, you know. *Better start swimming or you'll sink like a stone.* I bet you know the words. I bet you know the words to that one, don't you?"

Paco would be happy to have me think of him as a cynical man. He claims he can keep the different parts of his life discrete, in sealed compartments. "Back in my political days," he says, "I developed the knack."

Paco struggles to get by as a social worker with a little legal work on the side. He's married to a woman in her thirties. She's a nurse, has two young children by a previous marriage. Paco tells her nothing of my letters or my visit. In this way, he explains, he seeks to protect his present from his past.

If he listens to somebody making a political speech, Paco says, if he hears the slightly hectoring, public tone, the stagy sincerity, he turns right off. Even if he agrees with every single word the speaker is saying, he simply cannot bear the rhetoric.

But before I've spent more than two days with him, Paco's talking about the current government, his fingers stabbing the air in blunt accusation.

"The murderers dwell amongst us. The *comandantes* are pardoned, the torturers promoted, given pensions. They live well: their children are beautiful; they go to church on Sundays; they will die in their beds."

"I thought you said you weren't interested."

His mood changes. "As it happens I'm not, not particularly."

He stares over my shoulder.

"What do you take me for? Some sententious prick in a secular pulpit?"

We're in my hotel room, in bed. Curtains closed, cushions propped up, TV on but turned down low.

He's supposed to be at work.

Paco's underwear is parked on top of the desk lamp. God only knows where mine is. We're stretched out across the bed, recovering.

When he makes love Paco becomes tender, boyish; all of his edginess evaporates. I warn myself not to take it too personally. When he leaves this room, he won't find it difficult to slough off the day. I won't complicate his evening; he won't be stealing off to the phone box to call me, desperate for the sound of my voice. I know it isn't possible, I don't even want it. But still.

He'll be relieved. When I've gone through the gate at the airport and he's turned away. Over and done with.

"Send me all the photos, not just the handsome ones," Paco says, surprising me. "I want the ones with my eyes shut and the ones where you cut off my feet."

"What will you do with them?"

"Keep them in a drawer at work. Look through them a few times. Hold them to my heart forever." He grins.

(Deirdre had the plane ticket in her hand: she was leaving, getting out. Who was with Deirdre that last day at the airport? Was Paco's mother there to say goodbye? Yes, surely she would have been.)

"Promise me," urges Paco. "I expect a full report on your gardening, you hear?"

Now he has to get up, take a shower, put his clothes on, act normal, join the evening rush hour.

I listen to him whistling in the bathroom. No reason for me to stir myself, I might as well stay in bed. When he goes, I'll get up and lock the door.

I draw my knees up under the sheets, one at a time, making shapes. Put one foot on top of another and get a snowy mountain going. Wriggle wriggle. Avalanche.

What will I do when he leaves? Watch television maybe. The evening news in a language you don't understand is a good guessing game, but you have to be up for it. Maybe later I'll feel hungry. Can't be bothered getting dressed and going downstairs, out into the street. I could order room service, stuff the cost. Trouble is, when the guy wheels it in and it's obvious I'm eating alone, I'll feel like a loser.

"We've put the past behind us," Paco announces, coming out of the shower. "And we're doing just fine, the little lady can see that for herself, should she care to take a look out the window. We're far from perfect, but hey, life is complex. The main thing is, business is back on its feet and I ask you, what could be more important than that?"

He pats at his cheeks, pretends to be putting on cologne. "All sweet and clean now. Wanna kiss?" He turns and strides back into the bathroom.

A few minutes later he emerges with a completely different demeanour. Now he's affable again, easy to talk to. He sits in the chair by the bed, companionably putting on his shoes and socks.

"I was convinced Deirdre would come back here," I confide. "I was sure she'd come back — if not to me, then to you."

Paco's face tightens. He stands up. "Listen, my friend," he says. "Martín's been saying it's high time I had a few words with you about Mr. Grief."

"Martín's been saying what?"

"We quite like your old geezer, Mr. Grief. A good friend of the family, as a matter of fact. Sunday afternoon poet, though, you've got to admit, with an embarrassing taste for the obvious. His blood pressure's shot all to hell and his breath isn't anything to write home about either.

"Just between me and you, strictly *entre nous* you understand, the fucker's infatuated with himself. All he ever thinks about. Grief goes out walking and the only thing he can see is himself, reflected in the shop windows. Sooner or later you'll discover that what he has on offer is no more than an endless supply of warm baths. Granted, at the time they feel so *sincere*, so *right*."

"What's that supposed to mean? Do tell."

Paco sits down beside me on the bed. Smooths the quilt with his hands. Sighs. "You mustn't mind me, Bernie. I'm full of crap; it simply pours out of my mouth."

"No, tell me. What was that little homily all about?" I've been found wanting. Weighed in the balance and found wanting. Well, what did I expect, coming here?

Paco splays his fingers out across the quilt. "Like the man said, old folks live on memory, young folks live on hope. That should make me just about half-and-half by now."

Let it go, I tell myself. Don't go scrambling for solace. That's the last thing you should be doing. Think about Paco, instead.

I run one of my own fingers around his, tracing their shapes, pausing at the points where his fingers join his hand.

I hear his breathing.

In a low, detached voice, as if the thought belonged to someone else, he says, "It was pretty amazing being young, wasn't it?"

A soft semicircle. A harbour. The safe harbour of his skin.

"However, I've had to face facts," he adds, withdrawing his

hand. He gets up, puts on his jacket. "I'm not a spring chick any more, am I?"

"Spring chicken," I say. "Not exactly a spring chicken."

Paco suggests I go with him to see the unmarked *nihil nomen* graves: the no-name graves, the graves of just a few of the disappeared.

"They were caught between a rock and a hard place," Paco says. "Between the sword and the wall. Didn't have a snowball's."

With a false suddenness he says: "What could I be I thinking of? You haven't seen my mother's grave."

He leads me to another part of the cemetery.

In late 1978, Paco's mother, Martín's mother, died of a heart attack. Paco was in Uruguay in hiding. Martín was gone, disappeared, *muerto*.

Briefly, Paco puts his hand around my waist and we lean upon each other. We're the same height, exactly.

We do not speak.

We stand side by side in what I take to be a moment of closeness.

Abruptly he says, "Let's split."

With that, he moves away from me and walks fast down the path between the graves, his shoes clicking on the tiles.

I definitely feel I have been keeping him too long.

We're sitting in a café in the affluent Barrio Norte. Across the plaza, La Recoleta. "I suppose you'll *have* to go *there*," he says, grumpily.

In the early Seventies, he tells me, this café was a target for bombs.

"Sex, food, and cemeteries," Paco announces, sitting down and waving his hand for a waiter. "Give the tourists what they want."

(Birth, food, sex, sex, food, *kaput*. What else is there? Martín had asked, the summer morning sun pouring in the kitchen window.)

255

Now Paco's reading the paper. I'm watching the woman at the table opposite. In her cream wool suit and dove-grey boots, she's waiting for someone.

It's cool today, autumn is finally here.

She's probably younger than I am, I'm thinking, but elegant women always seem twenty, thirty years older than me. Why is that?

Paco looks over the paper, sees me eyeing her boots.

"Ferragamo," he pronounces. "Salvatore, as I'm sure you know."

She would have had her wardrobe reorganized for the new season. At the back of the closet, the fur coat from her husband. Inside, on the satin lining, embroidered in silk thread, her initials.

Paco has been eyeing the woman too. Folding the paper, he begins to carry on about the enticing scratchiness of lace, how it contrasts with the smoothness beneath. He sniffs as if inhaling deeply, and we both begin to giggle.

I ask him what Martín was up to in Paris, in Mexico.

"Nothing much. Martín was a journalist, he knew people, he had contacts. People on the surface, most likely. Not underground. Maybe Martín would have introduced them to someone sympathetic."

And back home, when things got bad? What did Martín do then?

"A bit more of the same, probably. The same as in Mexico City."

"Was he small potatoes, then?"

"Wasn't even in the spud business. He was parsley, that's what he was." *Parsley* was the slang term the military gave to the small fry who weren't involved in anything political but who were sucked in, caught up.

"But I thought they let the parsleys go . . . they let them go," I repeat.

Paco shakes his head. "They had blunt instruments for measuring these kinds of things."

He touches my knee with what feels like gentle contempt.

It's almost a week before Paco refers to Isabel.

"You met her in London," he says.

He already knows this, I've told him in letters, but now that I'm here with him, it's not the same.

I look at him when he speaks her name.

His voice climbs, then falters. His lower lip drops. (Towards some particular of breast or throat — she is lifting her arms to adjust her hat — nobody can know that, no one but him. Then I tell myself, don't be such a sentimental idiot, it could just as easily be a betrayal. Also exclusively his.)

I do not mention my jokes with Deirdre. Or the sandals of buttercup leather.

"Why would they go to that trouble with her?" I ask. "Why bother to do things differently?"

"I don't know. Maybe they took her for someone else and got cold feet. Thought they'd get in shit."

He passes his hand over the dome of his head.

"Sometimes," he says, "I believe she might have passed herself off as the other wife."

By "the other wife" he means Deirdre.

I remember Isabel's upper-class Home Counties accent. Who on earth would have thought for one moment that Deirdre would speak like that?

Someone from another culture, that's who. In that leap you are forced into the crudest of assumptions, as I have learned from my own daily unknowing, here with Paco.

"Then I think perhaps they didn't have any clue at all as to who she was," he goes on. "When she was abducted she wasn't with my mother, you see. She was staying outside the city."

I'm wondering, who was Isabel with, outside the city? Why did she go there? Were they abducted too, and what happened to them? And at the same time I'm thinking, who has the right to ask such

questions without the anguished heart of love? I didn't even like
Isabel; nor did Deirdre.

All this goes spinning through my mind, and Paco sees me sitting
opposite, my mouth open, looking to him.

He draws himself up, as if facing down accusations, and makes
a short speech.

"We know the *that*," he says, deliberately. "That it happened, that
we know. We know the *what*; we're unfortunately able to fill in a lot
of the blanks. But please don't come to me for the *why*; if you're
going to ask me about the *why*, we should just go to the movies."

He sounds so much like his elder brother. That's exactly what
Martín would have said.

Paco enjoys trashy Hollywood pictures, the kind with Charles
Bronson in them.

"But on the road to Miramar?"

"Give it a rest," Paco says. He lifts his shoulders. Martín's gesture.
"Who likes having questions asked about their work? Besides,
it was a weekend, wasn't it? In February. The hottest month of
the year."

He pauses.

"They were probably going to the beach anyway."

After a minute Paco starts to sing, "*Oh I do like to be beside the
seaside. I do like to be beside the sea.*"

"Paco!"

He kisses my neck, puts his tongue in my ear, still humming.
*Beside the seaside, beside the sea.*

"You're too much," I say.

"What's the matter with you? Don't you like a good singsong?
Does you the world of good."

He takes me about the city. We go to Belgrano, and Paco suggests
something that surprises me, something that I wouldn't have the

nerve to do, not even in Sydney. He encourages me to go up to the wrought-iron gate at the front of an apartment building and press the buzzer. To the woman who answers the door Paco explains that his brother and his wife used to live there, and his brother's wife was a dear friend of the lady.

The young woman lets us in and shows us around. She has an infant riding on her hip. During the Military Process she would have been no more than twelve, thirteen.

I can hear the tennis players on the court across the road. I look in the bedroom, in the living room, in the small kitchen. I go into the bathroom and look out the window on tiptoe.

Paco takes me over to San Telmo, to the old apartment. The street, which was more shabby than genteel in his youth, has now become fashionable again, with art galleries, restaurants. The courtyard in which Paco once played among washing lines and dustbins is the outdoor plaza of a café busy with the important two-hour midday meal. We stand in the entrance and Paco points out the three big windows of the old apartment. It's now an architects' office; I can see people up there in one of the windows. They appear to be bending over a desk, looking into what might be a light-table. You can make out the light shining on their faces, an unnatural brightness.

I think of Deirdre looking out that window, down into the courtyard, trying to understand where she was.

"There should be a law," I blurt out, "a law that stops someone from falling in love and marrying someone from another culture, another place. You just don't know what it will cost. You have no idea."

I didn't mean to say this out loud. I try to make a joke out of it: "We should keep them down on the farm, don't let them see Paree."

Paco says, "Let's sit down for a while, shall we?"

Here in the sheltered courtyard the air is mild and sweet. I make

Paco let me buy a bottle of red wine, a top quality local Malbec, and we drink it in the sunny warmth.

He looks around. "A million years ago. It was a million years ago."

I am conscious of the three big windows; my eyes keep going back to them.

In the first year of the democracy, Paco returned. He didn't have any money — the peso was worthless, anyway. Everyone was gone. His brother. His wife. The friends of his youth, *compañeros*.

"She should have come back," I say. "To see you, she should have come back."

"You're raving, my friend. Raving."

I can't bear to think about it. I decide to break down and order some steak instead.

The grass-fed beef is amazingly good; the vegetables are real. The wine, the wine is fabulous, over the top. They know how to live, I say to myself. How to eat and drink, I mean. "This is terrific," I say to Paco. "I haven't had meat like this since I was a kid at home and my father killed a steer."

Flushed, I refill my glass and raise it: "To Paco, in the courtyard of his childhood. To my good friend Paco, who has lived so many lives."

He barely raises his own glass. "To my nine lives," he says, "the majority of them superfluous."

By the time we've finished the bottle of wine, shadows are beginning to reach across the courtyard. It's still an absolutely lovely day. I'm stretched out in my chair.

Paco's looking at me in an impatient, irritated way.

Gawd, he's a moody bugger. Today the wine didn't agree with him. Usually it makes him more enthusiastic, ebullient. That was the word Deirdre used to describe him, ebullient.

"You're somewhat less than ebullient today," I say easily.

Paco stares at me.

"Mistake." I giggle. (Maybe I did have too much to drink. No worries, it'll wear off.) "Let's go back to my hotel. I could do with a lie-down."

"I'm going to tell you something."

I know from his tone how he's seeing me: the foreigner, the ignorant drop-in, not quite a Yanqui but just as infuriating. Keen to bleat in sympathy — and step on a plane in a week's time.

It isn't fair, I tell myself. He shouldn't be turning on me like this. "But Paco."

He cuts me off.

"Let me tell you something," he insists. "During the *Proceso*, several months after Deirdre left, my mother was detained. For seven nights."

He mentions a suburb in the north of the city not far from Belgrano, an affluent district famous for its fine parks. During the Dirty War, *la guerra sucia*, the army ran a torture centre there. Why would they have taken the mother all the way up to Palermo?

Paco has never told me this about his mother before, not a single word.

"Sometime during her detention the apartment changed hands, became the property of a mid-level military functionary who, in those years, appears to have acquired a great deal of property. Did quite well when gentrification set in, quite well."

Paco's speaking rapidly; I don't have time to think.

"From that time on she was affected with *incontinencia* and her urine, her urine flowed constantly because there was a hole, you understand, a hole in the wall. *Fístula* is I believe the term."

The brutal comfort of anger energizes Paco. At this moment he looks younger than Martín did the summer I knew him. There was something solid and comfortable about Martín. In middle-age he would have complained about his little pot.

I thought they'd left the mother alone.

If I concentrate, if I focus, I swear I can hear Martín, hear him grumbling about his tummy while he pats it, in complacent display.

I'm not thinking about the mother.

Not at all.

The following morning we drive down to Mar del Plata, then on to Miramar. At a headland on the coastal route, we get out of the car and look over the cliffs.

"There is the sea; who will drain it?" Paco asks. "Get your bucket out, Bern."

He darts about the headland, full of quick, empty movements designed to suggest purpose and panache.

"You look like a surveyor on speed," I call out to him. To my relief, the wind carries the silly words away.

*Jesus Christ, it's pathetic what comes out of your mouth on a jaunt down the coast with a friend*

*to see where his wife*

*and there, look! Out to sea, that's where his brother . . .*

Paco's brought a picnic.

*Fresh bread, wine, and weeping cheese, and him with a condom in his pocket, patting at it the way men do as he got into the car this morning, the blood in his face before he looked away. Delicate animation or flush of guilt? Whatever. Some things are said only with the body's soft grip, the rubble of facts dissolving, tongue on tongue.*

"A dead body is heavier than water," Paco says. "The head is the heaviest of all. You sink headfirst to the bottom. You float like that, upside down, while gas builds in your tissues. For several days, maybe weeks."

I wish he wouldn't speak of such things; I don't want to hear them, ever.

"Depends on the water temperature." Paco's letting himself

go into a relentless, brittle mood. Like sunlight, glinting on the rocks below.

The waves push and push.

I turn away from the cliff, gather my jacket around me. I think of how Deirdre, at Tet, listened to Sandy playing *Tu se' morta*, how she listened to the voice decending on *profondi abissi*: I shall go boldly to the deepest abyss.

"Do you know that drowning in saltwater is practically the reverse process to drowning in fresh water?" asks Paco, with fake ambiability. "Fresh water goes into the circulation system from the lungs. Dilutes the blood, destroying the red blood cells. The red blood cells release huge amounts of potassium into the circulation, poisoning the heart — fibrillation sets in, the heart collapses. But in seawater, the water gets into the lungs from the circulation system, causing pulmonary edema."

There's no stopping him. Beneath the deceptive, conversational tone, he's running on cold euphoria.

"You can also have pulmonary edema in a swimming pool. Because of the chlorine."

I can't follow much of this.

"You can have dry drowning, too. Vagus nerve seizes up. Usually caused by a drop in body temperature. Out of a nice warm sky into the ocean." *Vagus nerve*: the clinical, technical words are a raft to hang onto.

"What I want to know," says Paco, "is what happens if someone drowns at precisely that line where the fresh water meets the salt. Is there a specific word for that place in English?"

"I'm not sure. It's probably just *confluence*."

"*Si si, confluencia*, the same. What happens at the confluence," says Paco, taking it up again, "of a great river meeting the ocean? Río de La Plata, let's say, joining the Atlantic. That's what I'd like to know."

I have seen that line from planes — not of the Río de La Plata, but of other big rivers. The muddy water meets the dark, clear colour of the ocean, green or grey, in a long and surprisingly definite border.

"It's all the same in the end, of course. Sooner or later you puff up and float to the surface. Provided you've not had your stomach slit."

I recognize him, this Paco who looks up such things in medical books, reading them with his one good eye, greedy for the torment of details.

Fibrillation versus edema. I bet Paco's made himself a lay expert.

But right now I'm impatient with him, I'm not in the mood for any of it. I'm exhausted. I don't want to be here with Paco, not when he's feeling like this. There's only so much you can take.

Then Paco shouts out the long, full name of his brother. The name of his wife.

Shouts them out into the ocean, into the sky.

Comes to his mother's name.


He turns and walks back to the car.

## 9

*D*eirdre wakes to find he has not come home. She climbs out of bed and stands in the dark. She begins to rub her body with her hands.

⸙

When Sandy visited, she sat up in her bed and listened with pained concentration, like a child ordered to memorize directions.

It was an old city hospital with the air of one for whom the necessary daily chores have grown too burdensome. There'd be a full-scale fuss one day, Sandy decided, he'd put money on it: patients parked in cupboards, in defunct hallways. Community outcry, full inquiry, faces on the telly, heads to roll.

Deirdre's bed was in a large public ward. Nurses swept by and pinned back her curtains. Socializing with the other patients was mandatory. "Join in!" the nurses declared. "You could do with some cheering up! You the husband, love?"

"Yep," Sandy said, "I'm the hubby."

*Deirdre, Deirdre,* he did not say, *only in drama does it end with the tragedy; in life it grinds right on. Moanday, tearsday, happy days, right through to shatterday. And again.*

The woman in the next bed talked — in a steady normal voice, without ceasing — about a limbo baby that had taken shelter in the corner of her living room. She'd vacuumed it up and God could not forgive her.

Deirdre asked Sandy to search through her bags and bring in Martín's little sharkskin globe. It was the only thing she requested.

The figure curled in upon herself, feigning sleep, was not the Deirdre whose sharp eyes had seen much in Saigon. What was he supposed to do? The hospital was demanding to discharge her. But he'd a holiday lined up, a boating trip, one glorious fortnight all to himself.

He couldn't leave her at the flat.

"I guess you'd better come along with me," he told her.

A floating world, a slow boat on rural waterways that wander through fen and pasture.

Sandy, in the wheelhouse, brushes up on his locksmanship, the correct procedure for meeting barges or passing a ferry.

"Where did you learn all this?" Deirdre asks. "I didn't know you messed about with boats."

"Kiwis are born messing about with boats," he replies, studying his book. "The privilege of an island birth. And I've had a little help from my friends."

As the boat meanders along, Sandy stands at the wheel. Deirdre sits behind him. He talks; she listens. He tells her why he loves canals. It's a diversion.

When Sandy was a student at Oxford, an older man, an engineer, courted him in the privacy of a narrowboat on an aqueduct that ran above a dual-track railway line. (Edstone Aqueduct, Stratford-on-Avon canal, lunch beforehand at the Rose and Castle: the details, indelible.) While passengers chugged by on the train below, Sandy and his engineer, amid the gleaming brightwork, had a prolonged and glorious time.

Enough to make you believe in Heaven, Sandy claims. Gave him a predilection for everything beginning with the word *aqua*: aqueduct, acquifer, aqueous, Aqua Velva, aquelibrium.

"What might that be?" asks Deirdre, her interest finally engaged.

"The ability to walk on water."

"The ability to walk on water while on downers," Deirdre elaborates.

"Correct," he says, pleased with her.

Encouraged, he begins to hold forth about the trip he mapped out for himself. "We'll be going through some pretty big guillotine locks; they operate as you'd expect. The rest will be broad locks: two pairs of mitred gates, with the mitre pointing against the water pressure. The heavy wooden gates are held in place with a balance beam. The beam is typically painted black, with white ends. The gates are anchored with a collar and turn on a cast-iron pin in a pot. All terribly elegant in a butch kind of way, you understand."

"I thought a mitre was something a bishop wore."

Ah ha. So she has been listening.

"Something with a point to it. In your case, his lordship's pointy little hat."

"It was quite big. With jewels in it, green and red. I wonder if they were junk or semi-precious."

"What can a Protestant boy say? Best keep his big mouth shut."

"The altar boy would carry the mitre on a stole so his hands wouldn't touch it. The monsignor would take the mitre off the stole and place it on the bishop's head. Then the bishop himself would reach up and adjust it. I can't remember what the stole was called."

"Is it possible it could have been called a stole? Or do I hope for too much?"

"Martín was an altar boy."

Of course, this is where this conversation has been headed. From the mechanics of locks to Martín in a few easy sentences.

"When he was at high school, Martín was an altar boy." Deirdre's voice, as she repeats this, becomes closed off, private. A door shutting in an inner room.

*The greater grief*, Sandy thinks.

At his back, silence grows. Trespassers will be prosecuted.


They are beginning a journey across the Frisian countryside along waterways Sandy selected because the guidebook described them as "desolate," which he took to mean not a hundred boats per square inch. Besides, there are some odd left-handed locks he's planning to check out. This canal system was once used by the Kaiser, taking coal to his war. Hasn't been used much since, except by the locals and anti-social tourists like themselves.

This is early summer and the light stays in the marsh, although by evening a chilly wind has fetched up, bringing with it the peculiar, utterly ancient smell of wetlands.

Sandy makes fast the moorings, checks his bank anchors.

He points out the tall, ripening reed mace. As it's tossed by the wind, the light moves with it.

With their boat settled for the night, Sandy hums while he prepares a meal in the impossible galley. Deirdre helps, setting the table, polishing the already shining glasses.

At dinner Sandy waves his hands around, shows Deirdre the guidebooks. "All of this is well below sea level; these fields belong to the water. Pliny had something to say about it, if I could only find it, it was here this morning. Something like, the land drifts at its edge, the wind has to push the water out of it. Not quite the sea, nor quite the land."

They pull out bunks in the alcove where they have been sitting at dinner. He lies awake, stares up at the sky through the pigeon box on the cabin roof. The smell of water is strongest in the dark; it dominates completely. Moisture rises up and reclaims the fields.

He turns and watches Deirdre, beside him. She has the quilt pulled up over her shoulders and is lying flat on her back. Completely still.

The cabin moves and flickers.

Even at night, water gathers up the half-light. It swims into the boat, to seep into dreaming.


Over the last few months, in London, Sandy has become a regular at the Amnesty International office. If there is any news of Martín, AI will know where to get hold of him. He left the name of the boat with them. Letters can be delivered at any of the locks. He hasn't told Deirdre about these arrangements. It might be best if she believes herself to be away from all possibility of news.

I write to Sandy regularly. To my relief he writes back, often and at length. Nothing from Deirdre, not even a postcard.

At the locks Sandy does his best to get into conversations with the lock-keepers, sturdy men of few words. Having extracted a few observations about the weather, lock conditions, and supplies, he turns to Deirdre to marvel at the pleasure of hearing Frisian. All the two of them need concern themselves with, he assures her, is their daily *bred in butter*, the marvel of a language that sounds English but isn't.

Speaking of these two languages, English and Frisian, Sandy puts the thumbs and fingers of his two hands together, holds them straight, tenses them against each other until he feels the thin glassy pane between them. "Like that," he says. "As close as that."

On the other side of the world, I believed that I knew what would be good for Deirdre, what would be best.

Sandy would take her boating and then she would come home to me. She would live here until she heard that Martín was okay.

(Did I really believe that? I think perhaps I did.)

I was teaching at a girls' school, aware that I'd come to the end, that if I kept it up I would do myself some kind of damage. I had lost sympathy with schoolgirls, grown irritated with the intense giggling that erupted out of them as they discovered the enormity of the world. But I was hanging on at the school because I wanted to have a job when Deirdre arrived. For the first time in my life I was working not for myself, not because I liked it, but because I needed to support someone I loved.

I was also doing my master's, at Macquarie Uni. Not on Middle English this time, but on Virginia Woolf. In the afternoons after school I struggled with what happened to Rachel Vinrace. In *The Voyage Out*, Rachel, a tall, dark girl who just missed out on being handsome, falls in love with Terence. His name, she says, is like the cry of an owl. Rachel finds she wants not only him but also — the sea, the sky.

Why, I demanded of my thesis supervisor, why does Woolf go to all the trouble of letting you get to know Rachel when she's just going to kill her off? The kind of question that from my own students I would have dismissed as callow.

I visit Kelly's Creek and drive up to the cemetery, to take the news to Dorcas and Jack. I imagine them as I last saw them: Dorcas, finally bright and determined, a mover in the Country Women's

Association; Jack taking care of the cricket pitch, dragging the roller up and down until he attained perfection. I stand by their joint grave and pretend we are in the lounge room behind the general store. I tell them that soon Deirdre will be coming home.

That night I dream of the lounge room, smoky moonlight making shadows on the floor. Only it isn't the Hogans' lounge room: there are modern glass sliding doors, open wide to the smell of bushfires. Unperturbed, Deirdre moves with the light, familiar step of a woman in her own home. She's picking up a few empty glasses, tidying up, not a real task, just the round before bedtime.

(Whenever I go home to Kelly's Creek I dream intensely and wake exhausted, scrambling for the pieces.)

Back in Sydney, I was spending the weekends decorating my rented house near Bondi Junction, a worker's cottage from the 1890s. It had a hallway right down one side, three rooms off: front room, her room, my room. Kitchen and bath at the back. I was painting her room a pale lavender, so pale it looked cream in most lights. White picture rail, white ornate ceiling.

In the tiny passage outside, blue hydrangeas bloomed, encouraged by the shade.

On the weekends I crouched on a ladder and did the ceiling myself. As I painted the baskets of ornamental apples, I listened to the radio and rehearsed conversations we were going to have. About Martín. How word would surely come.

I needed her in Bondi Junction, needed her because I had such news. It was to be my story, and it was completely fresh and new.

I'd met someone, you see. We were going to be together, we knew we had to be. But he lived on the other side of the world; he had a wife, he had an infant child, he needed to extricate himself, it was *dire*.

(He'd deserted from the U.S. army and was living in Sweden, where he'd married. He was studying biology *in Swedish*. They'd come to Italy on a holiday, their first ever as a couple — on the journey south he'd been daydreaming about cicadas in resinous pines, vipers slithering behind warm boulders — but the child, the child had fallen ill on the train, so they'd stopped in a town along the way and the mother had stayed behind that day to be with the child. He'd been on his own there in the square, the great grey-white square, waiting for the cathedral — no, the *duomo* — to reopen after lunch, and I looked up because his shadow fell over me.)

I was longing to let the details come pouring out.

Morning, and Sandy is up early, making coffee, heating rolls. The wind has dropped, the white sky is turning blue. Mist sits inches thick on top of the water.

As soon as breakfast is over, Sandy noses the boat downstream. He explains that the early hours of the morning are the best for travelling. They're not quite out of the marshes, but today there are fields with crops. "The blue-green fields are sugar beet," Sandy tells Deirdre "Green ones are the spuds."

"Think I haven't seen spuds before?"

"And the cream ones, barley."

"Long fields of barley and of rye."

"You're getting the big picture. Watch for when the mist lifts, how the water looks thinner."

The flat fields disappear from view, and they're in the waterway between high embankments, moving along in a grass tunnel.

"This afternoon, when it's warmer, you'll see the bloom on the water, a thickness in the air. And listen up, here's your local lark."

"Ascending."

"Right on the money. Rushing skywards in a tangle of song. Totally drab up close, you wouldn't think of giving a frump like her the part — until she opens her extraordinary mouth. Like big Joanie, *la Stupenda*.

272

"There used to be storks around here too. Black-and-white storks to go with the cows, colour-coordinated. You'd be lucky to see a stork these days."

"No more babies then?"

"On the contrary. Too many babies; too few storks. There's still a heron or two, though. We'll look for them this evening. And maybe we'll see a snipe showing off in the sky."

She doesn't answer. Can't be bothered.

She'll rally for a while, enter into small bouts of conversation; they'll be doing quite well, fairly batting along. Then without warning, like this, she'll close down, fold into silence. For whole chunks of time she'll have about her a maddening air of passivity, of the desire to yield.

It makes him want to shake her.

By eleven o'clock they've found their moorings for the day.

"And now," Sandy announces, getting into the dinghy, "You will allow the *schipper* to introduce you to the waterworld."

"You're acting more like Ratty every minute. Am I supposed to be Mole?"

"I'm not sure you qualify. Ratty and Mole were, as I'm sure you realize, a closet item."

"They didn't seem to have much sex though, did they?"

"Mole stayed one night with Ratty and for months quite forgot about going home. Never mind that for now. Think of my bright-eyed little friend down there in the bank. Slithering out for a mid-morning swim, watching our dinghy breaking the light. He's heard us coming, has *waterrat*."

Together, Sandy and Deirdre watch the dinghy's small wake widen, then swish against the bank. "Right onto his living-room carpet," says Sandy. "Not that he minds a bit of glittering mud."

Deirdre gives him a bleached look.

"On the river," he says, "you will find that the river is everything."

They continue to *slip-slip* along, keeping close to the bank. From beneath his sunhat (the old cricket hat, his standard) Sandy watches Deirdre. She's wearing a flowery head scarf — a recycled Provençal serviette from the looks of it. Short shorts, blue shirt. She sits hunched in the dinghy.

"See this stuff? See the rough leaves? The white tubular bells? That's comfrey, Deir. And the pink spiky stuff is water betony."

"You're quite sure about all this?"

"Here, of all places, you should be paying attention to the details. The guy who invented the microscope came from these parts, more or less. He'd go after anything: blood, teeth scrapings, pond scum. Stick them under his *microscopia*. A drop of clear water turned out to be a veritable Peyton Place."

She's wrapped her arms around her legs; her head's tucked on her knees. All she can hear is the throb of absence.

As in a silent film, his mouth keeps on moving.

"Anton, his name was. Anton the haberdasher, he's our man. In between selling ribbons and buttons to the good burghers' wives, Anton was the first to cop a look at spermatozoa. In the male seed, little wrigglers!"

Deirdre sends him a dutiful, disconsolate smile.

"Listen to the cows on the other side of the bank, cropping the grass," he burbles on, unable to stop. And he genuinely likes this sound; he more than likes it, he believes in its magnificent simplicity. "You'll find it's always those city boys," he asserts, "who write of rural dystopia."

Surely she'll take the bait at that. A skeptical nibble at least.

In this way the temper of the holiday is set: Sandy enthusing and Deirdre lethargic, letting herself be taken along the waterways. Sandy naming many things but avoiding others.

They slip around a bend in the high bank.

"Hush," Sandy says, "*waterhoen*."

A fine evening has arrived and is everything Sandy promised. "Look at that sunset," he commands, "the colour of poppies."

Two heron are fishing, one under the willows, the other on the far bank. Like clay statues of themselves, the herons wait.

Sandy says, "From Great Yarmouth to the Hook, there is practically no vertical movement of water. Rotterdam has one of the smallest tide exchanges in the world. Good for biz, the docks are in full swing twenty-four hours a day."

This time Deirdre is half listening.

"If you drew a line straight from this canal across the Channel," she asks, "wouldn't it bisect the Wash and come out in the Fens?"

"It certainly would," Sandy replies. *Listen to yourself,* he thinks. *Auntie Sandy encouraging the little one.*

"It will all come out in the Wash," Deirdre goes on. One of her mother's paltry store of jokes.

"Tell me some of your mother's stories," Sandy prompts.

Deirdre's mother, Dorcas, had eaten during Depression winters because her younger brother won skating competitions back up in the Fens. Bread-and-meat races, they were called. The lean skaters bent their bodies into the wind, hungry for the prize.

Dorcas's family came from up there, from the black fens of Huntingdonshire. When someone died, the church bell, muffled, would toll three times for a man, five times for a woman, then once for each year of the person's life. Dorcas's grandmother died at the age of ninety-seven. One foggy winter afternoon the bell tolled until the day had grown dark. The ceaseless tolling spooked the rooks, who did not return to their rookery but huddled in the copse behind the churchyard.

The next morning the child, Dorcas's mother, found them frozen in puddles of thin ice.

There was whispering that the child had taken those birds into herself. From them, it was said, she had learned the power of flight.

A strange girl, with inky violet eyes. Touched by the rooks. Caught the next summer trying to soar out from a tree over rows of cut barley, cawing.

After her fiancé was killed at Ypres, it surprised nobody that she climbed the church bell tower, intending to fly up to join him. Pulled back by firm hands, she was made to continue, to cope, to carry on.

Several years later she married Dorcas's father, who had come back more or less intact, and who in time got himself a steady job down in Leiston, in Suffolk.

There was another war, and the boy, Bert, brought home the Australian soldier, his mate Jack Hogan . . .

"Tell me more," urges Sandy. "You're just getting to the best part."

But Deirdre pushes her plate away, gets up and stares out at the water.

In the deepening evening, the herons are waiting. Their legs listen. Only their eyes move.

Another morning. In the wheelhouse Sandy feels his way through the locks. Their journey has become busier. Working barges, lighters, all sorts of boats. Sandy is forced to recall how to dodge and weave, to judge space. He's done this before, but only in England, where there is much less serious traffic about.

Outside their alcove, mountains of cyclamen drift by, going to market.

Sandy tells Deirdre the story of a boat laden with flowers which, during the Second World War, slipped down the *Nieuwe Waterweg* to the Hook and under a clear sky chugged right across to the English coast. A totally uneventful crossing, almost boring. "The grace of flowers," Sandy claims, "saw them through."

"Does every water-town have a story like this? The flower boat that escaped the enemy?"

"It's true, it really did happen. But I bet there are tons of apoc-
ryphal stories about the Spanish oppressors. Centuries conflated,
the hyacinth stuck in the barrel of the gun. It can't be all boiling tar
and lime pits; we have to have our magic, too."

A mob of sheep float by the window, guarded by intense sheep-
dogs. They are followed by a load of orange-red bricks.

Sometimes when one working barge passes another, the women
on each barge will run to the bow. Then walk back to the stern,
calling out news to one another until the two barges have moved
apart and the women's voices can carry no farther.


Dear Bern:
The wheelhouse is the only place I can stretch out my legs.
Last night Deirdre rabbited on about her ancestors in the
Fens. Hers and Martín's. But I always saw Martín as his
mother's child, striding along some wharf in Genoa, grumbling about how difficult it was to finagle the financing to sail
over the rim of the world. Never doubting for one moment
that he was going to get there.

It's only half-past three and already I can make out a bunch
of houses on the bank. Steep-pitched gables crouched like
chooks on the roost. When I point out things like that to
Deirdre she gives me the bum's rush. (Look, the watery Dutch
sky! Brass pump-handles in the head! I never know when to
shut up.) Yesterday, though, I did manage to get her thinking
out loud about how the artist painted an ordinary raised
bridge, and now strangers like us, seeing such a bridge, think
of it as essentially a painterly thing. Arse over tit, she agreed
it was. Had he known that at the time, she said, it would have
made his hand tremble. I'm always so relieved when she takes
a bit of interest. She's fragile, mate, easily dismayed.

Deirdre, egged on by Sandy, decides to take a bike ride along the towpath. (The boat came with a ladies' bicycle, a heavy, old-fashioned black thing.) Sandy, watching her go, is glad to see the back of her.

Yesterday they were lying on the bank in the sun. He was talking about the principle of maximum movement of water for minimum turbulence. An amazing achievement, he claimed. And it was; it is. They were smart buggers, the builders of locks. More than that, these things had a beauty to them, an economy of brick and stone and iron and wood. If he were an artist he'd draw them: the chambers swelling open, the rush of contained energy. Strong, definite lines of charcoal.

He rambled on, hoping Deirdre would get into it, say that this was a prime case of man over nature, patriarchs on the loose.

She blinked and sighed and looked profoundly tolerant.

At least today she is doing something, getting out on the bike. As for himself, he's going to roll a few joints and stretch out, stare up at the sky. Help himself to a few choice fantasies.

He watches her get smaller as she rides away.

Sandy is dozing when the beeping starts. Summoned to the gang-plank by the noise, he can see, down at the end of the moorings, a taxi, its driver banging urgently away on the horn. The fool thinks he's escaped into the movies, he decides.

The back door of the taxi opens. A young man gets out and runs around to open the other side. After much bobbing about by the young man, Deirdre emerges, on crutches.

The two of them stand beside the taxi — Deirdre swaying on her crutches — and look down at the mooring site.

The young man speaks to the taxi driver, who opens his door and gets out of the cab. The young man scoops Deirdre up while the taxi driver grabs at the crutches.

The taxi doors are still open; the young man, carrying Deirdre, promptly bumps into one of them. He staggers, has to be steadied by the taxi driver.

With Deirdre providing directions, the young man begins to walk along the moorings to the gangplank. He is clasping Deirdre in such an amateur way that Sandy has a swift image of her turning to liquid and falling down through those arms, eluding him.

Finally the young man climbs aboard, and, with much inept manoeuvering, deposits Deirdre in the dining alcove.

Their bicycles collided, he explains, and Deirdre was thrown to the ground. He took her to the hospital, and insisted on bringing her home, at his own expense.

Now the young man stands in the alcove, certain of his right to a welcome but unsure whether he is about to be given one.

*Who does he think I am*, Sandy wonders, *the lover?*

Sandy catches Deirdre's eye — he insists on making her look at him. Bicycles colliding? On the flat towpath? She juts out her chin and closes her eyes.

Along comes the taxi driver, holding aloft the brand-new crutches. He scrambles down the companionway, enjoying all the fuss. His eyes dart from Sandy to the young man and back again.

There is small chatter about the smashed-up bicycle. The taxi driver, who has stuck it in the boot, volunteers to bring it aboard too.

Deirdre smells of the hospital. She has a silly plastic tag on her wrist. As for the young man, he reeks of drama and sexual arousal.

Disgusted, Sandy puts the kettle on.

The three adventurers settle in to tell the story. The young man is on holiday. Has just finished his post-doc in chemistry at Trinity. At the end of the summer he is going to Boston: his post-post-doc.

"Fascinating," says Sandy.

The taxi driver adds his bit: one of his kids broke an ankle skating last winter. Winter before last.

Deirdre, high on some painkiller, drinks her tea and smiles far too vaguely. She has begun to carry her sexuality in front of her as if it were a burden she cannot dispose of. She looks like that now, her hair awry, her blouse crumpled.

The young man can't get enough of it. Doesn't know enough to smell trouble, that's clear. He's been doing that post-doc for too long, Sandy decides. Sexual savvy zero. Work work work, then Friday night down at the pub, watching other people being foolish, taking risks, speaking their hearts and making something happen.

The young man's chest rises, he shivers. Hands twist. He ventures: Could he come to visit her?

She supposes he could if he wanted.

As soon as they've gone, the taxi driver and the young man — who lingered, turned and looked back, completely cornball — Deirdre immediately gets into the bunk Sandy has arranged for her.

"What do you think you're up to?" Sandy demands. "Showering that lad with the aphrodisiac of inattention."

At their next moorings, there he is, the young man, standing triumphantly beside a rented Deux Chevaux, having plundered his small pile of holiday cash. He is inexperienced, smitten, and ready to be rash.

Deirdre, in an unironed tomato-coloured skirt Sandy has dug out for her from the bottom of her pack, can't stop herself from yawning.

The one-dimensional young man, the post-doc (Sandy insists upon never using his name), went from mooring site to mooring site until he found them.

"How does the bugger do it?" Sandy asks. "Do you suppose he's wearing one of those radio-collars?"

She gives a brief, cat-like shrug.

To foil him, Sandy takes to stopping the boat at out-of-the-way parts of the towpath, mooring it by driving a few stakes into the ground in the messy English fashion.

Deirdre, carried by Sandy up to the fo'c'sle, lies back on cushions in the first real blast of hot weather. The water below them is unnaturally still, subdued by the heat.

There is the young twerp again, sweating and keen in the midday sun. Clambering aboard.

"The barge she sat in . . ." Sandy says. Deirdre almost laughs, and fans herself with her book. Pleased and puzzled, the post-doc looks around for a possible joke, as if it might be hiding in the nearest flat field.

Dear Bern:
We're lurching downward into melodrama here. I've a small speaking role as the superannuated nanny. She hasn't told him how coupled she is and he's too clueless to figure it out. Poor bloke probably believes that what he has here is a beginning.

One of these days she'll come round, she'll have to. It can't be stopped; it simply cannot be stopped. When she does, she'll reach out with such need that the bloke in question will mistake it for a torrent of sexual passion. It's fucked, it truly is. But for now, she's got the baby bunny by the throat. Even as I write she's letting him carry her off along the towpath. (What films did that boy see in his adolescence, I wonder?) As soon as he's parked her in the precious Deux Chevaux, he'll be back for the crutches. That's my chance, I reckon. What do you reckon I should do with the little gnat? Ding him one with the boat hook?

At night, when Sandy gets the beds down, they lie side by side in the alcove just as they did before the post-doc's appearance.

Deirdre, in her sleep, continues to spoon herself against his back. Sandy looks at the water-light, shifting on the cabin ceiling. Feels his own watery self answer (for what is blood but water?). For days after he's gone ashore, whenever he closes his eyes, he'll be rocking slightly, back and forth, held in the lingering sway.

Once he gets Deirdre onto the plane for London (she's not taking the ferry, he won't let that happen), he'll have a few days to himself in Rotterdam.

The light fades, the water moves, the cabin moves, and their bodies move with it, accepting. It makes you want to stay afloat forever.

Still, Rotterdam lies ahead. Down by the docks in Rotterdam there are bars, working-class bars, that smell wonderfully of the Fifties. Sandy's going to sit in one of those bars, drinking Amstel and watching the young men. In their scrubbed anxiety you can sense the interminable Sunday Bible reading, the text from Leviticus stern on the living-room wall. None of it enough to prevent the sons of the house from making this journey. They have taken the first enormous, dangerous step and reached the bar, with its unnerving splashes of laughter. They huddle in the smoky yellow light, unable as yet to bring themselves to plunge into the shadows beyond. They drum their fingers and toss back the beer to calm themselves. They go to the toilet *to comb their hair*, for crying out loud.

Maybe he'll get lucky, maybe not. Then back to the place where he always stays, an eighteenth-century house on a leafy canal, with a long-case clock in the hallway and thin panes of glass that distort the world quite nicely, thank you very much.

A long lie-in. Coffee. Rolls. An afternoon walk. A good dinner. Later, well, you never know.

After he gets home to London, he'll put Deirdre on the plane for Sydney. Home to Bernie.

Passengers on Qantas Flight 723 to Rome, Cairo, Bahrain, Bangkok, Singapore, Perth, and Sydney. Please board now at gate number eight.

Over and out.

⌒

I have been calling in sick, not going in to my teaching job.

I sleep late, and in the early afternoon I walk down to the Junction to get fresh library books.

The library smells strongly of the gas heaters and the plastic covers they put on the books. In the far corner by the local collection, it's warm and almost deserted. The collection's librarian, on the phone, is answering a caller's question about when the Bondi trams started running (*She shot through like a Bondi tram*). The caller probably has a bet on at the pub. The librarian, who has an oddly dented chin, is checking several texts. I'm well disposed towards her because I once heard her say, "There's no such thing as an irrelevant reference question."

Nothing is lost. That's how it's supposed to be.

(What if he didn't have a wife and child? What if things weren't so difficult? Would I want him as much then?)

Opposite me an old man is reading the newspaper and a woman is leafing through a magazine with large, full-colour plates. The magazine's cover has pictures of Russian cosmonauts. From my side of the table the cosmonauts are upside down. No big deal in space. Their suits are updated versions of ancient diving suits, I decide. Arthur Mee's Encyclopedias had lovely sepia pictures of divers. We had a set of Arthur Mee's in our lounge room on Ardara, the entire top shelf dominated by the confidence of gold and maroon. Each volume was examined closely by me and Deirdre. The divers' heads stuck out of huge collars while workers began to lift their helmets into place. Being locked in and screwed down like that. How could they stand it?

I've selected an expensive music mag from England. I'm reading about a singer. In the world of bel canto, she says, singers create a whole different voice. It is not their normal speaking voice, but it is, nonetheless, their own.

There is nothing physically wrong with me, I shouldn't be skiving off work like this. No sore throat, no fever. No excuse.

(Of course I would want him. Take my word for it, Deir. I would want him.)

The old man who has been reading the newspaper begins to rock in his chair. Gathering momentum, he prepares to make his move. A few determined tries, and he's standing up. He grasps his cane, shaking his head. He cannot believe that this is happening, that his heart is kicking up a ruckus at such a simple task.

(You should see him, Deir. Sitting at his desk, absorbed. The back of his head is almost too much for me, I get a case of violent crumble legs.)

I can't sit here all day. But why not? It would be pleasant enough, at least until the schoolchildren arrived to use it as their indoor playground.

I take my books and leave the library. On the way home I buy a carton of milk.

The winter sun falls on the old terraces, rewired, re-plumbed, fashionable once more; whoever would have foreseen such a future? At the pinnacle of the roof's plaster work, a large ornate urn is painted part navy, part yellow, to match two separate homes below. In the calm of mid-afternoon, before the surge of people returning, cats lie about on windowsills, oblivious to anything but the present. They put their heads down on the warm bricks; they drape themselves like luxurious socks.

I lock my front door and walk down the hallway to the kitchen.

I have an easy chair next to the heater: my lair, in the coziest part of the house. There I can put my feet up, read my library books, drink beer with whisky chasers. In Kelly's Creek the men drank whisky and beer; the women, sherry or shandies.

When I'm good and ready, I go down the hallway to the room I painted when I thought Deirdre was coming home.

I look in at the empty shelves, the bed.

I did receive one letter, written before she left London with the post-doc, bound for Boston.

"*The fact that I barely know him,*" she added, "*is what makes it possible.*"

I have not had a letter since. I no longer expect one.

(Why won't you let me talk to you?)

I walk into the room, sit on the floor with my back to the wall. I shut my eyes and carefully position my head. I summon up an image. Two lovers meet in an enclosed garden, an arcadian refuge in the centre of a huge city. Unknown to them, they are being watched by a photographer. He is cocky, thin and innocent, no more than a blue-eyed boy. The most important thing is that this image is completely silent. All you can hear are the leaves as the wind moves through the trees.

I have made myself ready.

I can understand that being with me or Sandy had become unbearable.

But then not to make contact, not to tell us anything, to send no word. Not to let me talk to you.

*That's what I don't — get —*

*That's what I can't — accept —*

*Why don't you write, you —*

I open my eyes and my neighbour is looking in at the window. She stands in the shady passage, framed by the hydrangeas, exposed and humiliated.

Deliberately, I continue:
*Why are you hiding —*
*from —*
*me —?*
Drummy plaster; it falls away in small pieces.
The landlord's problem, not mine.


I'm fed up. Sick of everything.

I go back home to Ardara, where my father and brother work the land, pushing the woollies around. I hike over to the river, rig up a bit of a lean-to. My brother helps; he knows I'm barmy.

Can opener, frying pan, socks, toothpaste, sweater — we want so much.

The grey roos make their day camp on the other side of the river, just behind the feathery she-oaks, where the gums begin. The scout takes note of my arrival, decides I won't amount to anything; then the mob lies back and watches. Lots of fastidious scratching. Left paw to left side, right paw, right side; no wasteful crossover.

When it gets dark I zip up my sleeping bag and listen to the river breathing.

Bush time begins. Sun bowls over, sinks to night, waits to be sung up again. Bush time knows about silence, knows people can be taken away.

I make myself cups of tea. Keep an eye out for snakes (black with red stripey bellies, no huge deal; brown — watch out). Listen to mobs of currawongs getting a game going, hurling cries from gum to gum.

As for the roos, they've begun to ignore me, to not even watch.

Smoke sneaks in from the eastern gorges, up my nose, making straight for the heart. At boarding school, we'd wake one morning in third term and there it would be, the first slender scent of bush-fires. Soon, we would be going home.

In Sydney I went to the march last Anzac Day, knowing I shouldn't be there. All that Queen and Country crap.

I was there because of the fathers. Jack Hogan and his other mates on the hill above the sports grounds in Kelly's Creek. My own father. Sandy's father, a hungry POW. Deirdre's uncles, the unkempt shearers. Maybe even Martín's father.

I watch for my father's battalion but there are just a few men — they were mainly from Victoria so those who are left might be marching in Melbourne. Jack Hogan's battalion had lots of Sydney boys so their contingent is large. Warm autumn sun in the city. No commuter crowds on the trains and buses. Groups of older men, some ancient; one man falling, painfully, to the hard cement footpath. The city is strangely quiet. Inside this quietness, the sound of medals. *Chinker-chink, chinker-chink*. There are few women. Particular applause, though, for the Second World War nurses who were prisoners. (Said Matron as they were driven into the surf to be shot, *Chin up girls, I love the lot of you*.) A few cadet bands, the inevitable bagpipes. But mainly the march is silent, a long river of men, walking, some trying to remember how to march in time. *Chinker-chink . . .*

The dead are out in force today. Behind every banner, more of them each year. (They lead to too much grog, later, at the RSL club.) And from your possie on the footpath along the route, you notice that each little group around you is waiting for someone. When he finally shows up, they point and wave wildly, *There's he is, there's Granddad!* They wait until he gets close enough, then hurry out into the march to greet him, walk a short way with him. In front of you, men are bending to catch up children, being kissed by their adult daughters. A few people — women, children — march with medals on the right-hand side of their jackets. They are there for the dead.

At the tail end of the long march comes the Vietnam contingent, an insignificant, dispirited bunch. Many of the groups on the footpath have already gone to collect Granddad. Not much applause. (In years to come this will change, but for now, nobody wants to know.) I look for Ron Ryan's regiment and find it. Marching in this group is a girl. She'd be about fifteen, in a green Santa Sabina uniform. Marching alone with the men. Her face is carefully rigid. I know the look; I teach girls that age. She glances over, and it is one of those unplanned moments when your eyes meet a stranger's and you are both embarrassed. I find I cannot clap. My gaze slides away.

Next day her picture's on the front page of the *Herald*. Probably the press photographer got to the march late. Or maybe he saw what I did. For the camera, she has been encouraged to look confident, but the smile doesn't work. (From the cutline, you will know exactly whose daughter she was. I made a clipping for you but had nowhere to send it.)

After a fortnight out here on Ardara, I know why I put down the paper and scissors and wept buckets. It has to do with home and Ron Ryan and you. With the colour and flavour of your letters from Vietnam. With how your letters got briefer, more opaque, then ceased.

Give me one adult story that isn't about the search for the enormous paddocks of home.

Here's the deal. You need to come home. That's all. Someday, somehow, you have to come home. It's the only life you'll ever be truly fluent in.

If you need to stay lost, it is possible even now. Particularly if you are a woman and in a foreign country.

But sociable Sandy maintains a network of informants — lovers past and present, sexual partners, colleagues, contacts, friends — flung out across the world in an invisible grid.

After he finished his post-post-doc in the States, he of the Deux Chevaux came back to London. By the time Sandy located him, he was a tentatively successful academic and a safely married man. Not pleased, not pleased at all, to have his past dredged up. All he could give Sandy, in order to send him away, was the news that Deirdre had "gone off, before the year was out, with a violin instructor."

"Violin instructor," Sandy mocked. "As in ski instructor."

"Even that would have been an improvement," I said.

"Violinists fall in love more quickly than anyone else in the world, I'm told. It's an occupational hazard."

I didn't like the sound of that. "What are we going to do now?"

"I'm not sure. I fear the trail may have grown cold."

The violinist was as far as we got.

Until the mid-Nineties, that is.

One of Sandy's spies saw her.

She was walking down the street in Cannon Beach, Oregon. It was a summer afternoon, and Sandy's spy was doing a photo shoot of the puffins at Haystack Rock. Turned out the little buggers were all out at sea. Sandy's spy was having to wait around.

As a slim youth he had on several occasions stayed overnight at Sandy's flat in London and come down to breakfast. Deirdre had been there, and Martín.

When he spotted Deirdre in Cannon Beach, the photographer couldn't place her at first but sensed there was something familiar about her.

He was too good a photographer not to follow a possible lead.

Down the street they went, into a upscale bookstore, where she bought two paperbacks. Into a wine shop, with its large selection of local wines on trendy wooden shelves. There was something about the way she inspected the labels, reading the little boasts about soil and micro-climate, that suggested she wasn't local, she wasn't just down from Portland for the day.

As she left the wine shop she was met by two teenage boys. In their high-top sneakers and baggy pants, they were looking around for anything the least bit interesting. The reluctant way they fell in behind her convinced the photographer that these were her children, stuck with their distinctly unawesome mother, cut off from the necessities of life.

"Like young lions," the photographer said. "They dawdled behind her like bored young lions."

It was the face of the younger one that told him who she was.

How did she look?

Comfortable. Relaxed, sort of.

Happy?

Hard to tell, isn't it?

His first reaction was to reach for his camera. Damn! In the trunk of his rented car. (A stupid place to keep it, but was the motel any safer?) He saw a drug store, dashed in, bought one of those deplorable disposables.

When he came out, they'd gone.

Vanished.

Swearing, incredulous, upset at himself, he patrolled the streets, the beach.

# 10

*I*n Sydney, Sandy prepares for his annual bash.

His Christmas rages are famous throughout the suburb and beyond. Each year they come, all the neighbours, and they drink and dance and shout and carry on.

I've driven over to help Sandy prepare. (This is not my story, but I married him, my American Swedish biologist, and I would say that we have been happy.)

"I've been having the dream again," I tell Sandy.

"Not again. Don't tell me."

Like Deirdre, Sandy thinks dreams are overrated, never to be confused with dreaming. Dreaming is one's life entire, what we know we are born for. Dreams, on the other hand, are shallow, skewed narratives, second-rate reruns of waking anxiety. He'd be pretty worried if he ever met the man of his dreams, Sandy says.

This particular dream, appropriated and modified from a documentary on the ABC, is about two women, identical twins. When they left school, one studied art, the other cello. There was a time in their early twenties when if one would wear blue, the other would insist on white. But they have long since abandoned their half-hearted efforts to establish separate lives. They share the same lover, and have done so for over twenty-five years. When one of them answers the phone, she does not give her own name. She says simply, "It is us."

At the beginning of the dream I'm only mildly interested. Sometimes these two women are walking along a street; more often they are in a house absorbed in some domestic task: folding laundry, or making the king-size bed.

As these flat images unfold I realize that I have to step into the picture, I have to get in there, because they are the living, and they are very close.

"So what were those two up to this time?" Sandy asks. "Wash or walkies?"

⌒

Sandy rolls back the carpet and we string up a forest of shining Christmas balls across the ornate ceiling of his living room. Sandy doesn't believe in Christmas trees. Australian trees in midsummer, he says, are all for staying in the ground.

A few years ago I happened to drop by when he was taking down the Christmas decorations. I offered to help and was puzzled by his response: a found-out look, a mixture of resentment and mild defiance. Reluctantly he climbed the ladder and handed the Christmas balls down to me. I began to pack them away in their boxes, little globes of iridescent red, blue, green, silver, and gold.

At first I noticed nothing.

Then I saw it. Hidden on the top of one of the balls, completely obscured from normal view, was Tran's name. Printed carefully, inexpertly, in nail polish.

I began to check the others.

Martín. Martín's mother. Isabel, who was estranged from her family.

The names of friends and lovers, men I'd never known.

Interspersed throughout, balls with no names.

Sandy was on the ladder, his ankles at eye-level. The ladder smelled of seasons of Sydney humidity and chalky old paint. Someone who owned this ladder had once painted something — kitchen or bathroom cabinet? — a mustard yellow.

Sandy continued to hand the balls down to me.

I took out the hooks, and separated balls and hooks into two piles. I placed the hooks in a plastic baggie. I wrapped the balls in tissue and packed them away in their boxes. He passed down strands of satin ribbon, which I began to roll into rounds, held in place with silver sewing pins.

The room had gone quiet. Just the yielding shuffle of tissue and satin. Background urban hum.

I spoke to his legs. "Amazing," I said, "what people get up to when they think nobody's looking."

At the end of the street, a bus trundled up, stopped. Started.

"They liked parties. Well, most of them did." Sandy's defensive voice came from the height of the ladder. "Anyway, I bet they all enjoy chilled champagne on the hottest nights of the year."

Today we string the Christmas balls out again, across the ceiling. There they sparkle, each one of them. The nameless and the named.

⌒

Before the guests arrive, Sandy puts on a CD and we dance. We discuss the letter that has arrived, the letter that has been preoccupying our thoughts, making this Christmas unlike any other.

"Soon," he says. "Not long to go now."

Sandy's parties run on champagne and song. Music, homemade and stereophonic: Sixties' rock 'n' roll, Motown, a bit of hip hop, world music. At one point in the evening, there is much singing in the languages of Sandy's street: Spanish, Vietnamese, Turkish, Laotian. Old-timers throw themselves into "On the Banks of the Condamine" and "The Wild Colonial Boy" while the Chilean guy from next door picks out the melodies on his flute, by ear.

We eat hugely, dance again. Children fall asleep on the stairs, the toilet begins to act up, the fridge door is left hanging open. Buoyed and feeling momentous, people begin to fall into one another's arms.

Passionate words are exchanged about the republic.

The front door and window have been thrown open wide and drunks wandering home from the pub on the corner stumble in, confused and hopeful.

In the kitchen an impromptu jam session starts up, heavy on the percussion. From two doors down Bluey jumps the fences to join us, barking. Towards the end of "Song of the Volga Boatmen" the cops come knocking and have to be bribed with Johnnie Walker, Black Label.

Early in the evening, before the rot sets in, I stand in the doorway to file the scene clearly in my mind: men and women dance, children ride on their parents' heads, candles shiver in the hot northerly, and the champagne is renewed again and yet again.

Hundreds of fragile Christmas balls, on satin ribbons across the ceiling, take up the light, then give it back. They lift us up again, to the stars.

⌒

I want to lie on the couch and look at old movies with you. Watch Dr. Strangelove having trouble with that hand of his. And the President telling George C. Scott, "You can't fight in here, this is the

War Room!" At the reruns in the Student Union on Saturday night, we sang along as the huge cloud mushroomed. *But I know we'll meet again some sunny day.* Ironic and ever so grown-up.

Were those your children walking behind you?

All you ever needed to do was what you finally did: mail an envelope to Bernadette Behan, Ardara, Kelly's Creek. My brother runs the property, and everyone over forty remembers Jack Hogan's girl, the one who went away. Message in a bottle: Ardara, Kelly's Creek, New South Wales, Australia, the World.

I was up at the cemetery putting my mother's ashes in with my father's bones and the currawongs gathered round for a stickybeak. You should have been there with me on that day, Deirdre. You should have been there.

You were the one who went away and neglected to come back.

Oh, did I miss something?

Just a quarter of a century, don't mention it.

Are you still living with the violinist? Do you have a cat tippeting up the stairs to join you on the bed? In one of those great big suburban homes with a three-car garage? On average, middle-class North Americans our age have as much square footage in their garages as they had in the houses they grew up in. I claim that we didn't grow up in houses, you and I, we grew up on the land, with earth, sky, and air. Children think they're immortal, say the specialists, who must have all been city kids.

Have I told you that Sandy and I finally took ourselves off to a grief group? They thought we were husband and wife. "In this particular story," Sandy said, "I'm afraid we are."

There was only one other guy at the grief group so of course Sandy got pally with him right away. Don, his name was. His wife, Edna, had died of MS. For the last six years he'd been devoting himself entirely to Edna, he'd hardly ever left the house.

"Edna, where have you gone?" Don would call out, at group.

Sandy and I would hug him. We would cry for Don and Edna.

But almost as soon as we got away from group, within a few hours, we'd be yukking it up about Gone and Deadna. It felt just as authentic doing that as being at group and weeping.

"Maybe we're just born hypocrites," Sandy said, "or victims of an uptight upbringing."

Did the grief group make us feel any better? I don't think so; perhaps we didn't do enough of it.

And of course Sandy couldn't behave himself. Told the group that once, years ago, he'd been responsible for the death of a man at a crossroads.

Have you been to groups like that? Deirdre of the Sorrows, I bet they call you behind your back. Maybe in your part of the world they don't joke about such things; it would be an offence against decorum.

Perhaps you lead such groups yourself. From coast to coast, share with Deirdre "How to Put the Past Where It Belongs." Book now for her acclaimed twenty-five-step series.

Were they your children, walking behind you? Those two bored young lions. They'd be well into their twenties by now. I want to meet them. When they leave the room I want to fall about the sofa with you, exclaiming: Their silky skin! Their long bones. Their confidence; their innocence. Such shining eyes. Such hair. Such indifference. Christ!

I suspect you became absorbed in the demands of those two, swept up in their exhausting modern schedules, awed by your own feeling for them, its height and depth.

But you've dropped them off. They're gone, and all their noisy energy has departed with them; they're absorbed offstage some-where and you're not needed any more, at least not for that.

I make it a day of mild rain. You're in a residential tree-lined street, early afternoon. The tree trunks are saturated with colour, moisture sits heavy in the branches. You're in the car alone, the engine isn't running.

Silence has spread, quiet as water.

That's what I'll ask you about.

⌇

You left that silver lipstick case behind in London; I was so hurt you didn't take it with you. I wonder if you still have Martín's sharkskin globe with the stars of the heavens. Sandy said you asked for it in the hospital.

Did you ever go back to working as a journo? Last week, the *Herald* reported that the opening bat for New South Wales saw an angel come down from the members' stand and hover three feet above the bowler. "How did you *feel*?" the journalist asked the opening bat (their only question these days). "I told him to bugger off," the man replied.

What happens when we are young happens forever. You were the one who said it.

I've got booze still running around in my veins; I need my sleep.

*What can I say?* your letter asked.

Then it gave the date and time of the flight.

*I'm coming home.*

Tomorrow at this ungodly hour of the morning we'll both be at the airport, Sandy and me. We'll go up to the roof to watch your plane come down out of the blue. I'll feel the old anxiety in my gut.

*Do you want to see me?*

We'll buy flowers in the arrivals lounge, our eyes on the gate.

⌇

After the dregs have departed, Sandy and I clean up his house and we drive down to the beach for a dawn Bondi-Bronte walk. Nobody around.

Sandy stands on the edge of the cliff, opens his arm to the coming day.

It's too early for sunblock or chips; I can smell the tough old scent that sandstone and scrub give off. The sea itself.

"No pussyfooting round here," declares Sandy. "The waves, the undulating waves, the uneven waves, the emulous waves — life, not art, I'd say, the gathering, the thump, the fizzle."

Must be that green powder he sticks in his juice for breakfast.

"On they come, rolling in to crash against the cliffs and then break up in a hefty postscript of foam. All the way across the Pacific and see how we finish. Ha!"

When the door opens you'll walk out and you'll see Sandy and me and you'll think how much older we are and how much the same. *The pair of you*, you'll say, *look at the pair of you*. And before the long day has ended, while you still can smell the staleness of the plane on your clothes, we will speak of Martín.

By the time I first wrote about Martín he was already sailing above the chaotic city of Saigon. The pressure of flight had elongated his body, even though he was pretty chunky on the ground.

He took his details with him.

That's why it was so important to me to know whether the embassy, at Tet, had its front door broken in, or whether it was just the reception desk that was smashed.

And tomorrow I shall see you face to face.

"So what's your verdict?" Sandy says, turning to me. "Choliformes below, huge ozone hole above."

"It's gorgeous," I say. "Absolutely gorgeous."

*I'm lying in the hammock in the living room.*

*Martín is at Hue and Sandy has gone down to the Delta. I'm nearly asleep, but I'm listening to the news.*

"Rimming the edge of the courtyard, someone noticed small holes, camouflaged. In almost every one there's an enemy soldier, a few dead from the day's shooting, but some still alive. Others are not so lucky. Marines fire into the holes. Another one is lucky; he stuck his arms out of the hole in surrender as a Marine approved and he's pulled out alive and uninjured.

"Sometimes these prisoners can be very useful, giving valuable intelligence information. But in this battle of Hue, it's been going on so long now and there are so many prisoners, there's really nothing left to be learned."

As I listen to this I think of how Martín, the day before he left, got up from the de Gaulle couch. He'd been sitting at the end, close to where he'd stashed his stuff in a tidy pile. The two of us were listening to the news.

Martín was barefoot.

He got up and walked in front of me to look at something. Nothing remarkable. He stood at the French windows with the light behind him. Reached his arms out in a lazy stretch. He was wearing crumpled beige shorts with a ratty T-shirt.

It had been raining. There was a city smell of earth and fumes.

I'm listening to the radio and I recall how he got up. In replay I note the sound of his bare feet on the tiles, I consider his back.

I was in the hammock then and I'm in the hammock now. The point of view is the same.

Same time, late afternoon. Same newscast.

No rain today. At the French windows, cloudless bright.

The room fills with his absence.

Several weeks later, when I hear him turn the key in the lock, I don't go over; I wait.

I already know what is about to happen.

# Acknowledgments

For help in placing fictional characters into real settings, the debts are deep and many.

In imagining Argentina, the core document was *Nunca Mas: The Report of the Argentina National Commission on the Disappeared (CONADEP)*. I am also indebted to the extraordinary works of Andrew Graham-Yooll, in particular *A State of Fear* (London: Eland, 1983).

In imagining Vietnam, my debts include one to Stuart Rintoul's *Ashes of Vietnam* (Melbourne: Heinemann, 1987) and one to the works of Terry Burstall, in particular *A Soldier Returns: A Long Tan Veteran Discovers the Other Side of Vietnam* (Brisbane: University of Queensland Press, 1990).

Kenneth Slessor's poem "Five Bells" tolls at the back of this text. His short poem "Country Towns" gave me the name of my central character.

The incidental references to Orwell owe a debt to David Caute's *Dr. Orwell and Mr. Blair: A Novel* (London: Weidenfeld & Nicolson, 1994).

## Acknowledgments

The lines on page 2 are from "I'm Explaining a Few Things," by Pablo Neruda, *Selected Poems*, edited by Nathaniel Tarn. Reprinted by permission of The Random House Group Ltd.

The lyrics on page 38 are from "You Can't Hurry Love," written by Brian Holland, Lamont Dozier, and Edward Holland, Jr., recorded by Diana Ross and The Supremes, Motown, 1966.

The lyrics on page 42 are from the Fifties hits "Cool Water," by Bob Nolan, and "How Much Is That Doggie in the Window?" by Bob Merrill.

The line on page 44, "I want to die out of sight of the sea," is from "The Return," by Federico Garcia Lorca, quoted from *Selected Verse*, edited by Christopher Maurer, translated by Francisco Aragón et al. (New York: Farrar, Straus and Giroux, 1995).

The lyrics on page 62 are from "The Wild Mountain Thyme," a traditional Scottish song.

The lines on page 134 are from Allen Ginsberg's *Howl, Collected Poems 1947–1980* (copyright 1955 by Allen Ginsberg), and are used by permission of HarperCollins Publishers, Inc.

The references on page 144 are to Julio Cortázar's novel *Hopscotch*, translated by Gregory Rabassa (New York: Pantheon Books, Random House, 1966). The reference to Julio on page 231 is to "Discourse of the Bear," in *Cronopios and Famas* by Julio Cortázar, translated by Paul Blackburn (New York: Pantheon Books, Random House, 1969).

The anachronistic lines "Almost me / almost you / almost blue" on page 160 are from "Almost Blue," by Elvis Costello, performed by Chet Baker on *Chet Baker Sings and Plays from the Film "Let's Get Lost"* (Novus 83054).

The line on page 162, "We're terribly *House & Garden* at number 7B," is from Michael Flanders and Donald Swann, *At the Drop of a Hat* (Parlophone PCS 3001).

## Acknowledgments

The lines on page 203, "Deep and dissolving verticals of light," and page 220, "Where have you gone? The tide is over you," are from Kenneth Slessor's "Five Bells," quoted from *A Map of Australian Verse*, edited by James McAuley (Oxford: Oxford University Press, 1975). Additional quotations from "Five Bells" are the description of the dead lying "in quiet astonishment" (page 73), of Deirdre "groaning to God from Darlinghurst" (page 133), and of death by drowning, where the wet pushes its "thumb-balls in" (page 225). Used with permission of the Slessor estate.

The Aeroplane Jelly jingle on page 206 is familiar to all Australians over the age of forty. It was allegedly written in 1927 by the jelly company's founder, Bert Appleroth.

The lines on page 219 are from "The Waste Land," by T. S. Eliot, *Collected Poems 1909–1935* (London: Faber and Faber, 1958).

The lyrics on page 287 are from "We'll Meet Again," composed by Ross Parker and Hughie Charles and sung by Vera Lynn, 1942. The song concludes the Stanley Kubrick film *Dr. Strangelove, or How I Learned to Stop Worrying and Love the Bomb*, 1964.

The "enormous paddocks" on page 288 belong to Les Murray's poem "The Dream of Wearing Shorts Forever." ("To go home and wear shorts forever / in the enormous paddocks, in that warm climate, / adding a sweater when winter soaks the grass.") Quoted from *The Quality of Sprawl: Thoughts About Australia*, by Les Murray (Sydney: Duffy & Snellgrove, 1999).

The "radio report" on page 299 is taken from the CBS evening news commentary on Hue by Don Webster, February 7, 1968.